ISBN: 978-1-66783-019-3

eBook ISBN: 978-1-66783-020-9

AL
KRAMER

COMPETING HARMS

A NOVEL

Acknowledgments

My thanks to many who have made contributions to this novel. I am particularly indebted for the inspiration I received from my enthusiasts who painstakingly lived with me through multiple drafts of the book as it progressed: Dr. Margaret Ackerman (a talented writer and voracious reader for giving me the benefit of her observations and a confidence I was in the game); Andrew Klein, Ph.D. (for his critical perspective of the developing plot having served both in government and the courts); Darren Moss (for his unvarnished review telling me what I needed to take out rather than just put in) Russel Pergament (a Publisher of newspapers whose keen eye for details throughout the book helped lend coherence to the plot); Linda Simpson (for burning the midnight oil to let me know if I nailed something I just wrote), David Stein (a wordsmith in his own right with the kind of invaluable line editing to my novel that should encourage him to write one of his own) and Orman Beckles (who is the most tech-savvy person I know for utilizing his skills to help design the book cover.)

With appreciation to my formal editors: Bill Thompson, editor of Stephen King's and John Grisham's breakout novels, for his encouragement that I was writing something important. It inspired me to settle for nothing less. Sandra Haven, for helping me pump life into the plot earlier in the book, and Tom Delgiacco and Andrea Thompson for the meticulous copyright editing.

To my wife, Ruth, and my close family: Lee, Kerry, Joanne and Ella, thanks for all your help and encouragement- this one's for you.

Come you masters of war

You that build the big guns

You that build the death planes

You that build all the bombs

You that hide behind walls

You that hide behind desks

I just want you to know

I can see through your masks

Let me ask you one question

Is your money that good?

Will it buy you forgiveness

Do you think that it could?

I think you will find

When your death takes its toll

All the money you made

Will never buy back your soul

Bob Dylan

(Excerpts from his song Masters of War)

CHAPTER 1

THE SUN BEGAN to rise slowly from under its nocturnal blanket, dimly lighting up Alan's room. He lay across the couch motionless, with his feet extending over its arm…awake throughout most of the night, deep in thought. The room was small, the furniture sparse: a bed, couch, chair and a table doubling as a desk and shelves that were filled with law school books and various literary works varying from Norman Mailer and Hemingway to Plato and Thoreau, and Thorp's *Beat the Dealer,* a newly-published card-counting method of playing blackjack. The pages of the books were crumpled somewhat with notes written on many of them.

Record albums were scrambled near the stereo player, some on the floor. Tonight's selections were folk songs by Bob Dylan and Pete Seeger, especially Dylan's "A Hard Rain's A-Gonna Fall," replayed many times in the room and in his head as he dozed:

I'm a-goin' back out 'fore the rain starts a-fallin'

I'll walk to the depths of the deepest dark forest

Where the people are many and their hands are all empty

Where the pellets of poison are flooding their waters

The sun's rays began to pierce the window with increasing light, slowly lifting the shadow covering his face, revealing his good looks and smooth complexion. It was dawn, and the shadows clouding his thoughts were also lifted. He had come to a decision. Strange, he had felt anxious and exhausted throughout the night, but with the decision, relaxed and energized.

By now, the rising sun had brightly lit the entire room. The heat magnified by the window glass focused on Alan's face. He could feel the warmth.

It was a wake-up call, morning had arrived. He got up and turned off the music. He was late, but quickly showered and changed his jeans and T-shirt to another pair of jeans and T-shirt, all in less than 20 minutes. He combed back his curly black hair that should have been cut weeks ago. He went out the door hurrying to make his scheduled appointment with the Dean at the Law School. It was a 20-minute walk, but somehow this morning, it seemed shorter. It would be a warm May day. He liked the warmth, and it was most inviting on this day that he had been envisioning for some time.

The clock on the building covered with ivy chimed ten strokes as Alan opened the heavy door and walked up the stairs turning to the right until he reached the door that read "Dean William Lauder, Boston University School of Law." While he had been to the Dean's office a couple of times before, this time he paused for more than a moment before opening the door.

"Good morning, Mr. Roberts," the Dean's secretary cheerfully greeted his entrance.

"Good morning, Evelyn." Most law students called her "Miss Anderson." Alan was always more informal. She never allowed her facial expressions to give it away, but she enjoyed being addressed by her first name by Alan. He had a certain casual but unassuming charm that came across as both friendly and respectful. "If only I were 20 years younger," she thought.

"The Dean is waiting for you, Alan. I will buzz him, but go right in."

Alan entered and stood at the door waiting for almost a minute before the Dean, sitting behind his desk looking down at papers, finally looked up and acknowledged his presence.

"Good Morning, Mr. Roberts," formally greeted the Dean. "Come have a seat," pointing to the chair across from his desk.

"Good morning, Sir." Alan approached but chose to remain standing.

Though he had met Alan only a few times, the Dean knew him well. Why wouldn't he? Alan was at the top of his class, though a surprise to faculty given his repeated unpreparedness in classes each time he was called upon. "Alan, what is the overriding principle in this case?" asked the criminal law professor. "Sorry, sir," replied Alan, "I did not get to read that assignment yesterday."

He was a crammer, using Dexedrine pills he got clandestinely from a friend who worked at a pharmacy to keep awake and pull all-nighters to study for the exams. Waiting until the last moment, he squeezed in a year's homework for five courses during the two weeks' exam period, reading entire books of the assigned cases that he had not read during the year, and going over class notes he took copiously, but never reviewed until the exams.

Alan reconciled himself to the fact that he was simply unable to let the homework interfere with his daily visit to the upstairs pool room to socialize with his friends or late afternoon pickup games of basketball at the park. A dangerous habit, especially in law school where there is only one exam at the end of the year for each of the five subjects - no others. Scores on these exams defined your academic rating for the year. Cramming all of it at the end of the year was living on the edge. Yet, Alan nailed each of his courses. Only one of the other 154 students had slightly better marks. But it was Alan, not the other student, who in his very first year made Law Review, a scholarly journal to which only the highest-ranking students with writing skills, normally in their second year, were selected.

Alan was from a working-class family of little means. Using whatever he could save from summer jobs, and with the benefit of earned scholarships, he just about scraped up tuition to pay for his Liberal Arts undergraduate degree and the two years he was now completing at law school. The university had a shorter six-year program for a combined BA and law degree. Alan, having pursued the program, was the youngest student in his class.

The Dean was not informed of the reason for the meeting, but guessed, knowing of Alan's financial struggles. So he was a bit taken back by Alan's very informal attire: jeans, T-shirt, and sneakers. It was not unusual attire even for law students during warm weather, but not when you are coming to see the Dean looking for a full scholarship. He would grant it, but would make Alan squirm a bit. Law students, no matter their accomplishments, were just that, students. As was the tradition, they were to be treated in that lowly state until they passed the Bar and became part of the "Brotherhood".

"Alan, my watch says that you are now five minutes late. Let's not burn up any more time. My next appointment is 10 minutes from now. So, what can we do for you?"

Alan found the Dean's remarks, reminding him who was the low man on the totem pole, somewhat liberating, "Sir, I can accommodate your request to make it brief. I made this appointment to seek greater financial aid, but instead decided to quit law school."

"*What?*" shouted the Dean.

"I just decided today," repeated Alan calmly.

"You have to be kidding," gasped the Dean. "There is, but what, a few weeks left to the semester. With your marks, all the big firms chasing you, and a judicial clerkship, perhaps even a Supreme Court Clerkship, all at your beck and call when you graduate, tell me I did not hear you correctly!"

"Sorry, but you did hear me correctly, and I thought it best to inform you in person."

"When did you decide this?" the Dean asked, a little more calmly, adjusting to Alan's tone.

"A few hours ago, but was thinking about it for some time now."

The Dean regained his composure. He was concerned. Losing his star pupil under unexplained circumstances could reflect poorly on the school…on him.

The Dean got up from his chair and walked toward Alan, who was still standing. Placing his hand on his shoulder, he lowered his voice to a more sympathetic tone. "This is a serious life decision, Alan. We need to take a breath and step back and think about the ramifications. You are a model student, perhaps our best in many years, with an illustrious legal career ahead of you. I am saying this for your own good. You need to rethink this. What can we do to help change your mind? We can offer you a full scholarship next year and more."

Alan sensed that the Dean's attempt to persuade him to reconsider was not entirely altruistic, but still felt it deserved a frank reply. He took a step closer to the Dean so they were now literally and figuratively on equal footing,

"Dean, I appreciate your concern and offer. As you say, there are just a few minutes left before your next appointment, so let me sum it up as briefly as I can. It was not an easy decision, but I decided that I don't want to wake up four years from now as associate counsel behind a desk in a law firm welcoming the seventies, having just watched one of the most unique revolutionary decades in history, with all its volcanic changes, pass me by while I stood on the sidelines. The 'illustrious legal career' will always be there to pursue in the future."

With that, Alan did not wait for a retort, but proceeded directly out the door of the Dean's inner office, leaving a puzzled Dean, who was still alert enough to hear Alan's voice as he was leaving the outer waiting room. "Adios, Evelyn. If you don't mind some friendly advice, you do not have to be 20 years younger to realize there is an interesting world out there. Don't waste too many more moments before exploring it."

CHAPTER 2

AT 10:20 AM, Alan stepped out of the law school building as words of a spiritual hymn dominated his thoughts: *Free at last -free at last.* He, along with a roaring crowd, heard those inspiring words of Martin Luther King's "I Have a Dream" speech, having driven over 500 miles to support the March on Washington civil rights protest several summers before.

But Alan's new-found freedom felt freaky. Yes, "free at last." There would be no more rushing to classes, no more cramming for exams, no worries about tuition, but that also meant nothing on the agenda, nothing to do, nowhere to go and no one to see. He was feeling like the Dylan lyrics: *To be on your own. With no direction home, Like a complete unknown, Like a rolling stone.*

He was dying for that first cup of coffee and needed to walk less than a few hundred yards to the BU large cafeteria called The Commons where the students gathered between classes for snacks and meals. It was bustling with the usual noisy morning undergrad students sitting with their books and note pads flopped down beside them on the table and some gym bags on the floor. The chatter was mostly about sports, movies and plans for the weekend, little if any discussion about what they were learning. The place was packed. He spotted two empty seats, one at a table next to a few guys laughing and the other next to a rather attractive girl alone intensely reading a book. The choice was never in doubt.

"Hi, mind if I sit here?" he asked.

Having already begun to pull the chair out a bit, it was a rhetorical question, so she simply looked up for a moment and resumed her reading with neither approval nor protest.

Alan pulled out a pair of sunglasses from his pocket and placed it on the table to claim ownership to the chair and started to walk toward the coffee display and cashier. Looking back at her, he asked, "Getting a cup of coffee, would you like one?"

Without looking up she responded, "As payment for renting the chair?"

"No," he replied as he continued to walk toward the coffee display, "as payment for the privilege of sitting next to you."

"You don't look the type that needs to pay for a girl's company." She had to shout a bit to reach him as he continued to walk away.

Alan returned in a few moments balancing a paper tray of two coffees. "Wasn't sure how you took it, so there is cream, milk and sugar all on the side."

"Thanks," she said, reaching only for the cup of black coffee. "To be clear, I consider the coffee as payment for the seat, not my company, so no obligation here," she added with the beginning of a smile.

He smiled back and started to sip his coffee as she continued to read. More than five minutes passed without a word spoken when she finally lifted her head from the book and said, "May I ask you a personal question?"

"Sure, feel free."

"You must know you appear somewhat different than almost anyone here… did you notice?"

"How so?" he was flattered to get that attention.

"Well, look around you, everyone without exception has a book, a notebook, pen and paper, a briefcase or a gym bag, and you…nothing."

"I gather sunglasses don't count," he replied jokingly." Then, in what appeared to be a deliberate avoidance of her question, he asked, "Would you please lend me your pen and paper for just a moment?" She gently pushed them over to him.

"OK, now that I have a pen and paper like all the other students and that distinction is no longer in play, curious to know if you have any other first impressions of me that stand out from the others?"

She clearly understood it for what it was – a clever invitation to determine her initial interest.

She was not about to give him that.

"What else is different?" she mused. "For one thing, you are not as clean-shaven as the rest."

"Good observation," Alan responded, feeling his rough unshaven chin and covering up his mild disappointment in the response.

Another five minutes went by in silence as she resumed reading. "And me?" she asked as if there were no break in the continuity.

"What about you?"

"Notice anything different about me?"

Big pause as Alan gazed at her with squinted eyes as if making a serious assessment, and then responded with a similarly neutral observation, "You're a person who never takes her eyes off what she is reading."

"Touché," she thought.

After another moment of silence, he asked, "By the way, what is it that you're reading?" She lifted the book showing its cover.

"Ah, Dante's Divine Comedy, a class assignment no doubt," he remarked.

"Yes, did you read it?"

"Yes."

"What did you think?" she asked, expecting him, like so many others, to show off some erudition by quoting or saying something about its most famous passage about purgatory: "Ye Who Enter, Abandon All Hope."

He didn't follow suit. "What interested me most is Dante's affirmation of the moral theme that God unforgivingly inflicts eternal punishment on those who pursue their natural passions in violation of moral and religious dictates, no matter their purity or innocence," he responded, not looking up while sipping his coffee.

She was impressed with the casual manner and ease in which he spontaneously and so articulately threw out a one-sentence critical review of one of the most discussed philosophical treatises of sin and the afterlife.

"What do you mean 'no matter the purity of their innocence', we are condemned? I am not sure that was the meaning Dante intended to convey," she asked, curious as to what his follow-up would be.

Alan put down his coffee and looked up at her. "Well, Dante's views reflect societal norms. Love that is forbidden by religion, morality, or even law, such as infidelity, is considered as lust no matter the purity of heart of the lovers, or the circumstances that compelled them to succumb. So, with Dante, if you dare go there, hell awaits you."

She realized that they were not semi-flirting anymore. They were evolving into a more profound exchange about fundamental beliefs, and to her, that was as intimate as it gets, though they had not even introduced themselves to each other. No matter, she was being lured into it by interest and his intellect. She wanted more of him. "I'm curious, what specifically in the book led you to that conclusion? I thought only sinners were to be punished in Dante's world, not those who are pure at heart."

With that, Alan moved the Dante book toward him and began to flip through the pages with a speed and familiarity as if he had written it, stopping and going a few times and finally stopping and pointing, "There, Canto 5, these are the passages." An odd sense came over her, that he would have been just as familiar with almost any book she studied or mentioned. "Who is this guy anyway?" she pondered.

She looked at the passages that he pointed to, where Francesca, forced to marry her husband for political reasons, falls deeply in love with her husband's sweet younger brother, Paola. She relates how their tender love led to their being killed by her husband and forever consigned to the winds of Hell, along with the other sinners in Dante's Inferno who died for their forbidden love, such as Cleopatra and Mark Antony, Helen of Troy, and Paris, and Lancelot and Guinevere.

"So, what's the answer, avoid society's forbidden fruit or partake of it even at the risk of damnation?" Sevena half grinned as if she were the forbidden fruit.

"Well, there are many in this world paying the price of hell on earth for embracing love or a desire for a forbidden someone. And forbidden fruit is usually the most alluring temptation even if you know the consequences – just ask Adam and Eve."

"Interesting, I admit, but I am not sure you quite answered my question," she pressed. "I was asking about *you.*" She posed the question in a tone as if the conversation was no longer about a hypothetical philosophical exchange or even a romantic one. "Are you a risk-taker when your passions drive you to a path where only fools jump in …?"

"And angels fear to tread?" Alan finished her sentence. He thought for a moment. Was she for some reason testing him in some way as to what risks he would chance for something that moved him deeply? And if so, why? He could tell her about his having just quit law school, throwing away a predictable path of comfort to go down Robert Frost's "road less traveled," but decided not to let a stranger be privy to his most intimate decisions. He found a safer way of answering.

"Let me put it this way, I bought a book called 'Beat the Dealer.' It is a way to count cards in blackjack to try to beat the odds at the casino. Ordinarily, the chances of beating a casino are even worse than beating the Devil or God himself. Yet, in a week or two, I will take what's left of my small savings and will be off to Vegas trying to do just that. It should tell you a little about my risk-taking and a willingness even to confront the Satan of Chance – the casinos."

The answer intrigued her for more reasons than he could guess. Though now thoroughly engaged, she happened to look down at her watch. "Shit," she whispered to herself.

"Look, gotta run, late for class. Maybe it should be me paying your rent for the privilege," she said as she got up to leave.

He got up as well. "Thanks for the temporary loan of the pen and paper. I'm getting a second cup of coffee, and hopefully, when I come back, you will have used them to leave me a note of some kind. Here, I will start it for you." He scribbled 'Alan…' on the paper and handed her back the pen. "Maybe you will finish it for me. If not, all I can say is I hope you find whatever you are looking for."

"You would totally freak out if you knew what that was," she said under her breath.

When Alan returned to the table, she was gone, but there was the folded piece of paper on his chair. He unfolded it quickly, and indeed there was a note:

Alan,

Ye who dares enter MY world, Abandon all hope.

617-544- 2211

Sevena

———

SEVENA GOT TO her class a little after the professor started his lecture in her Philosophy of Religion course. She found herself struggling to pay attention as she kept thinking of her stimulating exchanges with Alan. Then she became all ears; the professor struck a chord.

"The best-known description of the afterlife is in Dante's *Divine Comedy*. The first part of his book is *The Inferno*. which I am sure all of you read without struggle," a remark that elicited some laughter given that the language is considered more challenging to understand than Shakespeare's Elizabethan verse.

He continued, "What is interesting is that Dante's exploration of Hell is heavily derived from Virgil's *The Aeneid*. There, we see the contrast. Virgil confronts the demons of Hell, while in the Inferno, Dante hides in fear."

"Virgil confronts the demons and doesn't hide in fear," Sevena repeats the thought in her mind and is quickly drawn back to thinking of Alan's blackjack metaphor in which he is willing to confront the casinos-the Satan of Chance as he put it-without fear of going against its impossible odds and losing his life's savings. "Jesus, I am envisioning him as having the courage of Virgil and I don't even know the guy. And it's only a card game. This is foolish," she chastised herself. "We had a cup of coffee and some verbal play for, what, a few moments," she thought." Yet there was that feeling of antici-pation and excitement that her world had suddenly become more alive and interesting because Alan was in it. "Wonder if he will call?"

CHAPTER 3

ALAN WAS RIGHT. In a casino, the Devil rules exclusively without interference. The God of Luck is present but neutered , allowing the game of chance to be rigged by the House employing its own set of favorable rules based on unalterable laws of statistics. The breathtaking architecture, neon lights and the sign towering over the building enticing one into the heavenly world of "Caesars Palace" would more honestly reveal what was in store for those who entered, if the sign painter were Dante with the warning, "Ye Who Enter, Abandon All Hope."

No one walking through a casino door seeing lines of unending tables of chance welcoming them to make a fortune, hearing the deafening musical sounds announcing winning spins coming from all different types of slot machines, or the joyful screams of a crowd around a red- hot crap table with piles of winning chips, or watching the payoff of a large bet at the blackjack table when the ace draws a jack, goes in without hope and a dream. But that is accompanied by an underlying respect for who rules there. Down deep, no one enters this world without some fear in his heart that he could be tempted to lose control and lose more than he can afford… perhaps his life savings.

For serious gamblers, it is a Faustian tale. You make a pact with the Devil by selling your soul for free booze, luxury and entertainment at every turn, and most importantly, the rush at a chance to win a fortune. But like Daniel Webster's battle with the Devil, the question is, are you good enough, or is it lucky enough, to come out of it saving what you sold?

That evening, Alan checked into the Flamingo Las Vegas Hotel and Casino directly across from Caesars Palace, which was built, but not due to open for another month or so. He was armed only with the untested playing strategy from Thorp's book and the $2,000 he had saved for living expenses during his last year at law school. Without succumbing to that inner fear, Alan was ready to risk all and confront the odds at the blackjack tables.

But first, he would walk around, survey the room and watch the play to get the feel of the place. It was like in high school when he bribed a janitor at the famed Boston Gardens where the Celtics played, with his last $5 to let him and another player go in for just 15 minutes. It was to get a feel of the basketball court the night before the big game he and his team were to play for the Class A State Championship. They lost the game by a point, but it was hard-fought, with Alan, the team's leading scorer, showing no hesitation in taking the last shot from 20 feet out. It fell just short, hitting the rim as the buzzer ended the game. He was to replay that shot in his head repeatedly for a long time to come. If only he had flipped it a little bit harder to give it a height of just two more inches, a kind of unending Dante-like punishment for daring to reach for the stars and failing.

Food was plentiful with a great variety at the dinner buffet, but like most Vegas buffets, it looked a bit better than it tasted. As Alan finished his meal and got up to go for a second cup of coffee, it reminded him of the exchange with Sevena at The Commons. It brought a smile to his face. She had been on his mind off and on since then, but for some reason he hesitated to call- though he memorized her telephone number. He had also bothered to look up the telephone exchange, and it was a Brighton number. He calculated that his apartment near Fenway Park was not more than a 10 or 15-minute drive from where she lived, an exercise he realized made no sense until he called, but somehow made him feel closer.

However, Alan did have another call to make. House phones were available in the casino to make free long-distance calls as a courtesy, especially for those calling home to someone who could wire some money in a hurry. He pulled out a piece of paper and dialed the number on it and got a "hello".

"Hi, Evelyn, how are you?" Without waiting for an answer, he continued, "Look, I'm calling from Vegas. I got your letter before leaving Boston asking me to call you at home at this number. Sorry for the delay, but things have been a bit hectic of late. What's up? Is the Dean looking for me to return this year's scholarship money?" he asked jokingly.

"If that were the case, you would not have gotten that note to call me. The Dean would have already attached your bank account." Having to deal with pesky students for over 12 years, Evelyn could hold her own in sarcastic exchanges. She continued in a more serious tone. "Alan, I asked you to call me at home because the Dean would be most unhappy with me if he knew I was talking to you, but I think you ought to know about it." The Dean had told her explicitly not to discuss it with anyone, especially Alan, but she was doing it precisely because it was Alan.

"That serious, huh?" remarked Alan, not having a clue where this was going.

"When you saw the Dean, he asked me to bring him the Report to review before you came to see him, and I distinctly remember putting it right back into your file immediately after you left. Three days ago, when I went to update your file to record your withdrawal, the Report was no longer in the file. It was gone."

"Wait, Evelyn, whoa, whoa, slow down; I am not following you. What Report was gone? What are you talking about?"

"The Investigator's Report."

"What Investigator's Report?" Alan asked, still puzzled. "It's why the Dean did not want me to talk about it."

"About *what*, Evelyn?" Alan raised his voice considerably higher, as he was beginning to lose his patience.

"As soon as the first-year student grades are out, the Dean retains a private investigator to investigate the top five students. He gets an extensive report about them, their family, their friends, their girlfriends, their court records, politics, jobs-you name it. Some reports run 40 pages, yours even longer."

"You got to be fucking kidding me. Is that legal?" Alan shouted the question even louder.

"You asking *me*? You should know better than me. You're the fucking star law student?"

Wow, that was the first time he ever heard Evelyn swear. He had always liked her, but now she had his respect.

"I can't believe this. What was in it about me?"

"I never read it. It was marked for the Dean's eyes only. It was in a large, thick plastic, sealed envelope, with a wired string around it running from top to bottom with a tiny combination lock. You can't open it without the combination."

"Why would he do such a thing, and what was so secretive?"

"Not sure. When I discovered he was doing the investigations and wanted to know why, he said he would tell me if I held it in confidence. He said that in his second year as Dean, he got burned. He said he once recommended a top student to a prestigious law firm who turned out to be a member of a radical political group that turned out to be embarrassing. He said that could have been avoided, had someone bothered to check that student's background."

"Do you believe it?"

"I don't know, but I always had my doubts."

"Why is that?" he asked.

"Because every year at the time he asks me to retrieve these reports from the file, he makes calls to his old law firm. He was the managing partner there before becoming Dean. Of course, both he and I get lots of calls from former students who became partners at various law firms wanting to get an edge in the competition to recruit the best and the brightest. I suspect, but have no proof, that he is using the reports to give that edge to his old firm."

"Knowing the Dean, I would not put it past him. You lock the doors to your office when you close up, right?"

"Of course, we have all kinds of private correspondence and school records there."

"Any signs of a break-in?" Alan asked, sounding like a lawyer.

"No, none whatever," she answered like a witness.

"How could someone get into the office?" he asked her and himself, wondering if by chance someone pulled the nighttime-bribe janitor shtick he pulled off at the Boston Garden. "Does the janitor or any cleaning people have keys?" he probed further.

"That is the mystery. The Dean and I have the only keys, and for security sake, we require that the janitorial services be completed before we leave."

"Well, the real mystery is why in the hell is the Dean *and* someone *else* who stole the report so interested in me, and how could that someone else know they could find what they were looking for in your office and get it without a key or breaking in. And that, Evelyn, is the $64,000 frightening question."

"Sorry, Alan, I can't help you there."

"I know and I appreciate the risk you are taking in telling me about this. Let me know if the police find out anything."

"Won't be able to help you there either. Not only am I sworn to confidence, but the Dean would never report it. If it were to be made known that he was secretly investigating his top students, there would be an uproar that would send him back to his old firm in a hurry."

"Over and out" came to Alan's mind for some reason. "Thanks, Evelyn, not sure where we can go from here, but I owe you a drink."

"I will take you up on that one day. Goodbye Alan."

Puzzled, Alan started to head for the elevator to go up to his room when he heard a page over the casino loudspeaker. Funny, pages go on all day and night in casinos calling out players and their family's names. Given the competing loud noises of the music and the gambling activities, no one notices or hears them, except when your name is called. Then, for some reason, noise and all, the brain is conditioned to catch it.

"Alan Roberts… Alan Roberts, telephone call. Please pick up on any phone on the floor." Clearly, he misheard the name. "Can't be."

No one, but no one knew he was there. However, as he picked up the phone, an unsettling feeling came over him, given the conversation with Evelyn.

"Connecting you to your call, sir," said the casino operator. "Hello, this is Alan," he said, deliberately leaving out his last name.

"Yes, am I speaking to Alan *Roberts*?" responded the voice on the other end.

CHAPTER 4

DEAN LAUDER GOT off the elevator on the 21st floor. He walked toward the two heavy glass doors with a large intimidating font painted on them enshrining the law firm's name: Latham, Hogan & McLeish. As he entered, immediately facing him was a wall-to-wall glass window from floor to ceiling across the entire room, with a 180-degree breathtaking view of Boston harbor and the Boston skyline below.

The receptionist greeted him, "Good afternoon, Dean."

"Good afternoon, Rose," the Dean acknowledged, walking by, without ever looking at her, going in the direction of the office furthest down a long corridor lined with a row of plush offices. He knew that office well, for he had occupied it as a senior partner for 15 years before accepting the Dean's position at the law school. His associate, Walter Myers, had moved in right after the Dean's retirement party.

"Hi, Bill," said Walter, getting up from his desk to shake the Dean's hand.

"Hello, Walter," responded the Dean. "How's business?"

"Can't complain, Bill," a huge understatement of which the Dean was well-aware. Latham, Hogan & McLeish was an international, global law firm with its corporate office in Boston and offices in New York, California, Washington, London, Amsterdam, Zurich, and 46 satellite offices in six continents, employing over 1,955 attorneys. It was the second leading law firm in the nation, perhaps the world, in generating revenue. The firm represented the country's major industries and established one of the top lobbying groups, including former high-ranking government officials, military officers and members of Congress- a significant contingent of influential people who occupied its Washington, New York and Wall Street offices.

"Bill, as you requested, here is a copy of that Investigator's Report you gave us last year. You say someone stole the original from your office."

"Yes, my secretary noticed it was gone yesterday."

"Why would someone want what's his name's report?"

"Alan Roberts"

"Why would someone want Roberts' report and even stranger, how would they know you had one?" queried Walter mystified.

"Good questions. I can't think how anyone would know, or for that matter, anyone who would want to know about him to the degree that they would steal it. My only concern is that it references our P-7 project."

"Been a while since I saw the report, so I don't remember what it said about our project," Walter commented, inviting an answer.

"Nothing specific, thank God, but it did say Roberts was not a good candidate for the project.

My concern is that might get whoever stole it, very curious."

"Well, if so, nothing we can do about it right now. Just need to keep our eyes open. Suggest you keep this copy at home since your office appears to be like Grand Central Station," said Walter, rubbing it in.

"Sometimes I wonder if I made a mistake recommending you as my replacement," retaliated the Dean jokingly, or maybe not.

"So, how *is* our P-7 project going?"

"Good," responded the Dean. "Given the help of our donors, the seven college Presidents we recruited are now in place and ready for my directives. I am setting things in motion to carry out our plans."

"Glad to hear, I would not delay it any longer. I have some inside information for you. Our Washington people have learned from President Johnson's advisors that they are going to expand Operation Rolling Thunder by increasing the bombing of North Korea's transportation corridors to prevent their furnishing arms to North Vietnam. That also means a further increase of our troops in Vietnam to wage the war more aggressively. When this is announced, we can expect the now scattered rumblings about the war and its increasing casualties could get some traction on college campuses. This is what we have been preparing for during the last two years, so let's get it all in place."

"We are ready," boasted the Dean.

CHAPTER 5

ALAN ORDERED A scotch at the nearest bar in that part of the casino where he took the mysterious call. He was completely puzzled. No one could possibly know he was in Vegas and certainly not at this hotel that he chose at the last moment, yet he was just paged there. Why would someone call him and then hang up after he identified his presence? What was the real reason why the Dean was investigating him, and why did someone else go to the trouble of stealing his report? Was this call connected in some way with the investigation, and the stolen report?

Was there something going on now or something in his past that might give him a clue?

Thinking back, he was drawn into reminiscing about his life, his family, growing up in Chelsea, a city adjoining Boston, and like so many other towns, densely populated by immigrants who had fled to America during the early 1900s to avoid religious oppression in their native lands.

Chelsea had a sizeable Jewish population, many of whom had escaped from the rampant anti- Semitism in Russia and Poland.

Alan's mother, orphaned at 16, fled with her older sister from a farm in a Polish village to a Warsaw Jewish orphanage. The day before, her uncle had hidden her by holding her and himself underwater for almost a full 30 seconds beneath a bridge being crossed over by Cossack army troops during one of its pogroms. The Jews lived in constant fear of pogroms, where Russian troops periodically went on a spree without cause or warning to massacre defenseless Jews, looting and burning their homes and shops, raping their women and teenage daughters and murdering them indiscriminately. Alan's mother, Sarah, and her sister worked at the Warsaw orphanage, scrubbing floors and taking on any work they could find for two years to save up enough to gain passage to America.

Alan's father, birth name, Samuel Robertson, emigrated from Russia at age 22. He was one of the few Jews who had graduated from a Russian high school or gymnasium as they called it. Jews were educated at synagogues, not generally permitted to attend Russian schools on any level, but Sam had displayed such a desire and aptitude for learning that his father bribed the headmaster of the gymnasium with the few rubles he had. A Russian high school education at that time included subjects now taught on a college level in the USA. Alan was later to have many thoughtful discussions with his dad about books written by the great Russian novelists that his dad read in school at that time.

Sam was the last of his siblings to leave for America, but not because he was waiting for his turn, based on age. His older brother, Jake, age 25, had to leave quickly under the cover of darkness and find a way to get to America by way of a boat to Argentina where they needed laborers and paid for their passage. He then made it to the states five years later. He had left Russia in a hurry because he had assaulted a Cossack soldier in the act of burning down a neighbor's barn. Sam's younger sister, Lillie, age 17, left 6 months earlier than Jake in similar haste, having been reported for organizing a group of Jewish kids to hand out flyers condemning the pogroms. She met her husband-to-be in Florida a year after arriving in America and refused to tie the knot unless and until he paid the passage to bring Sam over. Because Jake and Lillie were wanted for crimes, Sam was advised to change his name on the shipping documents from Robertson to Roberts.

Sam was worried when he landed at Ellis Island. He could make his way around, but had very poor eyesight. He could read with thick glasses, but was close to being legally blind. Doctors stationed on the second floor of the registration building observed immigrants coming in on the first floor. They were looking for weaknesses and telltale signs of disease or unfitness. They specifically searched for an eye disease called trachoma, which could cause blindness and lead to death. Half of those examined a second time before registration were suspected of this eye disease. If the doctors diagnosed trachoma, the immigrant was sent back home. Because of his poor eyesight, Sam was examined a second time, but not having that disease, in a close call, was finally welcomed as one of the "poor and huddled masses yearning to be free." If not by his eyes, he was blinded by the glittering lights of New York City and the glow of his new-found land.

While Sam had poor eyesight, he was very independent and moved around by himself, without the need of assistance. He was like many immigrants who would have been eminently qualified to become lawyers, doctors, engineers and the like under normal circumstances, but in a new country, unfamiliar with its culture, without initial fluency in its language, and not a cent to their names, these immigrants found work as electricians, tailors, shoemakers and other laboring jobs to support their families. The professions they would have been qualified for would have to await their children.

Sam made his living by owning two newspaper corners in downtown Boston. Owning a newspaper corner did not result from purchasing or leasing a piece of real estate. You had to establish your presence over time since the four Boston newspapers-the *Boston Post, Boston Globe, Boston Herald,* and *Record-American-* would only distribute their papers to you to sell in that area and you had to be ready to defend your territory by chasing away the strays that periodically sneaked into your domain to compete. Sam sold papers during the late night and early morning.

As soon as Alan was 12 years old in the eighth grade and throughout his high school years, he helped his father selling newspapers on Saturday nights, the busiest night of the week when people were out on the town to have a good time. Starting from 7:30 pm until 10:30 pm, with the help of his dad, he first set up bundles of the four early editions of the Sunday morning papers in front of the Metropolitan Movie Theatre on Tremont

Street in the heart of the entertainment district of Boston. He sold them to the moviegoers mostly when the show let out, and then he went across the street to the Shubert Theatre when the play was over. After covering the shows, he received later editions and went around selling to customers and the help in restaurants, nightclubs and hotels until 2 am.

Alan wasn't on the job for more than a few weeks when he learned something about the struggle of the working man to earn a living wage. The truck drivers that delivered newspapers went on strike for better wages and work conditions. They picketed the four newspapers who hired scabs to take their place to break the strike. The truckers asked the newspaper sellers to support their strike by refusing the papers being delivered to them by the scabs. All four papers warned the newspaper sellers that if they refused the papers, they would be cut off from further deliveries even when the strike ended, literally putting them out of business for good. As a result, only 10% of the newspaper sellers refused the deliveries.

That Saturday when the scab truck drivers dropped off bundle after bundle of the *Globe, Post, Herald,* and *American,* Alan's father pushed each of the bundles off the sidewalk onto the curb, indicating non-acceptance. One angry scab driver threatened him with force if he did not accept delivery. Alan's father still refused and was then punched, kicked and thrown down onto the sidewalk. Alan rushed to pick him up. Noticing he was bleeding, he screamed, "Dad, dad, you alright?"

"Yes, I'm OK," he answered, getting up and pulling out a handkerchief to wipe off some of the blood from his forehead.

"Dad, I'm scared. That guy said that they didn't want to see me or you here next time when they come, that they have other newsboys to take our place. I like Tony and the other truck drivers, but we can't keep doing this for them."

"Alan, yes, we are doing it for them," Sam said, looking directly into his eyes. "But I am also doing it for you."

Alan was only to understand what his father meant much later when he was to join in the Martin Luther King protest marches for Negro civil rights and realized that he was not just fighting for their rights, but everyone's rights, including his own.

Despite the threats, Sam showed up at the corner every evening, never allowing delivery of the papers or letting anyone else come on his corners to accept delivery for five days until the strike was settled. After the strike, he was still there receiving and selling the four papers with the affection of the truck drivers who would do anything for him for many years to come, and a son who couldn't be prouder of his courageous father and role model setting examples for him to follow.

Perhaps the teachings of one of the greatest Jewish religious leaders, Hillel, would have explained Sam's act and courage best:

If I am not for myself, who will be? If I am only for myself, what am I? And if not now, when?

If you are on the streets weekend nights in Boston at the center of activity, you are experiencing a microcosm of the world around you. Alan was to learn more on the streets than in school.

He learned that generosity did not always correlate with a person's financial means.

Customers to whom he sold newspapers, who ate at the most expensive gourmet restaurants and fancy nightclubs, tended to be the ones that tipped the least, and when they did, in the least amount. The help, however, the cooks in the kitchen, the waiters and waitresses, coat-check girls, even dishwashers were the ones that tipped most often. The Sunday papers were 15 cents, and a good number of the help would give Alan a quarter and let him keep the dime change.

There was also a difference in other forms of treatment. Alan was generally dressed in dungarees and a flannel shirt, and in winter, a warm, mostly worn coat with a hood. When high- end restaurant and nightclub customers exchanged money for their papers, Alan felt, he was just as invisible to them as a person, as were Black help he saw in the movies tending to the needs of houseguests in a southern mansion before the Civil War.

Conversely, when selling a waitress, a cook, or a barmaid, there was always a conversation. "How is it going?" or "Is it cold out there?" And if it were cold out there at 1 am with snow blowing all around, they would always ask him to put his papers aside and sit down in the kitchen, warm up and have a bowl of free hot soup and sometimes even a sandwich.

No, Alan was not enamored by the well-to-do, and he was not about to let any one of them show off at his expense. Steubens was the hottest restaurant in town, providing unmatched food and dinner shows. The manager liked Alan and let him come in to sell to customers just before closing. One evening, as Alan was going around the tables, a grey-haired gentleman in a bow tie and expensive suit was sitting with a pretty blonde looking like half his age. He asked for a *Boston Herald*. Alan gave him the paper and placed a dime and a quarter on the table next to him as change for his half a dollar. As Alan began to leave, the girl said, "Jason, give the kid the dime for a tip."

Jason picked up the dime and said, "Here, kid," and moved his hand toward Alan. As Alan reached for the money, Jason pulled his hand back completely embarrassing Alan, and said, "I have a better tip for you, young man, that is of more value than money and will guide you well the rest of your life."

Sober, though having had some drinks and thinking he was in some way impressing his date, Jason went on to quote loudly and proudly, "As the Bible says, 'To thine own self be true and thou cannot be... ". Alan quickly joined in to finish the quote in harmony with him, "false to any man."

The man was stunned by this paperboy. "Apparently, you know it," he said almost stuttering.

Alan put the papers he was carrying under his arm down on the floor. People at several tables nearby had their attention drawn to the discussion. "I do know it," Alan began. "First, it is not the Bible, it's Shakespeare. It's actually from Hamlet when Polonius gives advice to his son Laertes. And by the way, your quote was way off. To be accurate, Polonius' words were: 'This above all, to thine own self be true, and it must follow as the night the day, thou canst not then be false to any man.'"

Then without hesitation, Alan picked up his bundle of papers, took back the quarter and the paper on the table, pulled the dime back right out of Jason's hand, flipped Jason's half-dollar he paid for the paper to the lady and began to walk away to the admiration and the open applause of the customers at the tables nearby. He turned and gave a modest bow to them in return and winked at the manager who was smiling, having observed all this as he passed him on the way out.

Another time he was offered a tip other than cash, but under totally different circumstances. Alan circled the bars and small entertainment joints at closing time selling papers to the managers, cashiers, bartenders, entertainers and chorus girls who became steady customers. They were the best tippers. The chorus girls in their skimpy show outfits hung around the bars between acts to help the bar business. They also had steady customers who kept them company and bought them drinks at the bar. For a 15-year old kid like Alan, the atmosphere was stimulating. Over time, Alan not only got to know the papers each chorus girl wanted, but learned that one was in college, another was a single mom, but all were by nature of their work flirtatious and fun. As he moved around selling papers in the place, he tried to hide the fact that he would be sneaking glances at the ones with big boobs that were purposely exposed above the nipples by the design of the low-cut blouses they were wearing. Jean, the youngest and prettiest one, and to Alan the most heavily endowed, was the one he looked forward to seeing when he came into the place.

That year, July 3rd fell on a Saturday. There was a big July 4th eve party advertised to attract customers. When Alan came in near closing time, the joint was still jumping, and the girls were partying more than working. When he went backstage into a small dressing room behind the stage, to give Jean and the others their papers, Susan, one of the chorus girls, shouted, "Hey gang, tomorrow is Alan's birthday."

Jean asked, "Alan, were you a 4th of July baby?" Alan responded in a soft voice, "Yes."

"Well, it's past midnight, so happy birthday! You deserve bigger tips today," Jean shouted, slurring her words a bit. With that, Jean undid her top completely, grabbed his head, and moved it around her naked large breasts for five seconds or more, laughingly saying, "I meant bigger tits today."

"Oh, leave him alone," Susan said, "you don't want to ruin his pants." With that, Jean released Alan as they all sang happy birthday to him. He was unable to get that image and the feeling of that moment out of his head for a long time to come and made use of the memory when alone by himself when his libido would act up.

That evening in the casino in Vegas, Alan had surprised himself by spending all this time reminiscing about his dad and his newspaper days. He realized he missed Sam and his mother, who both passed away within a year of each other after he entered law school-his mother from a stroke, his father from a heart attack. Perhaps still missing them was the reason he found himself reliving those happy days.

He wondered how much of this background was in the Dean's investigator's report. How far back did it go? Alan made the honor roll in high school, but was not at the top of his class. He was not one to do homework, except for the assigned Shakespeare plays taught by a teacher who inspired him. However, he did find time to read a lot of other books that appealed to him, which he squeezed in between playing basketball on concrete playgrounds, or baseball on empty lots, shooting pool with his friends in Dave's upstairs pool room, or taking Hebrew lessons for his Bar Mitzvah, which he skipped more than he went. These were books that were not on the top ten lists for high school students. They ranged from biographies of Thomas Jefferson and Mark Twain, J.D. Salinger's *The Catcher in the Rye, How to Play Winning Poker, 30 Days to a More Powerful Vocabulary* to Freud's *28 Introductory Lectures on Psychoanalysis.*

In Hebrew school, Alan was introduced to the Torah and Talmud and other hallowed books containing Jewish biblical history, its religious laws and sacred traditions. He was fascinated by the scholarly discussions and dialogue between eminent rabbis throughout the ages interpreting, and arguing, how Jewish life should be conducted, ranging from moral and ethical commandments to everyday issues of daily living.

While Alan found these discourses intellectually stimulating, there were theologists from other religions and philosophers that he read that opened-up a world of thought he wanted to explore. He had made up his mind; he would major in philosophy in college.

Like many Jews, Alan held on to its cultural traditions but gave up most of its religious observance. What he did not give up, however, was both an idealism and radicalism deeply rooted in him by his heritage and the values instilled in him by his parents, and equally as important, the smarts he gained from his life on the streets.

Alan had just finished his second drink at the Casino bar and began to head for his room. If he were not so engrossed going down memory lane even as he walked to the elevator, he would have noticed a man at the other end of the bar who had been there almost as long as he was, who got up the exact same time he did and was now about 20 feet behind him walking at his same pace in the same direction.

CHAPTER 6

FBI SPECIAL AGENTS Andrews and Backman were summoned to the Director's office at 9 am, one morning in April shortly before Alan informed the Dean he was quitting school. They were escorted into the office and seated facing their boss, J. Edgar Hoover, who was on the phone at the other side of the desk leaning back on his swivel chair. Hoover raised the palm of his left hand and extended it toward both the agents while holding the phone with his right hand, indicating that they should remain mute while he was finishing his conversation, and then swiveled his chair around so his back was to the agents, unconcerned if his voice could be heard by them.

"But Carl, the House Appropriations Committee just cut Lyndon's $45.7 million funding request for our new building." Hoover was talking to Carl Hayden, Senate President Pro Tempore, who moved up to take that position when Hubert Humphrey vacated it when he became Vice President. "Look, the building went into planning over four years ago. The land is completely excavated for the structure to be built and without the money, I and my agents will be looking at an empty lot from this outgrown, outdated facility. I need the House-Senate Budget Conference Committee to put all or most of it back." Hoover was aware that it was said of Hayden, "No man in Senate history has wielded more influence with less oratory." He never spoke on the Senate floor.

"Edgar, leave it to Lyndon and me. You'll have your building."

"OK, but promise me that it will be in my lifetime." Hoover hung up the phone and swiveled back facing the agents. Both men instinctively rose and stood up straight as if they were in the army and a five-star general suddenly appeared.

Hoover motioned them to sit down again and picked up a few bound pages that had just been placed on his desk by the lady who escorted the agents into his office. He glanced at them quickly, turning each page as if he were a speed reader. He was reading the headlines.

"Which one is Andrews?"

"I am, sir." Andrews rose again and was politely motioned to sit again.

"They say that you and Fred Backman here entered the COINTELPRO Project three years ago around the same time and have worked as a team. Your evaluations state 'Performance exemplary.' Congratulations."

"Thank you, sir," they responded appreciatively, but knew that being complimented for their work would not be a reason for taking up 1/10th of a second of this Director's time. Being summoned by the Big Guy at the Bureau for an assignment was as good as it gets. Big Guy indeed-the only Guy! Hoover was the first and only Director of the FBI since it was established in 1935 and before that was the Director of The Bureau of Investigation since 1924, the group from which the FBI evolved. He had headed the US investigatory agencies for over 40 years, respected by some, predominantly in the Bureau, and feared by most, including sitting presidents, congressmen and senators, for he knew where all the bodies were buried or helped create some of them himself to intimidate or threaten those he needed. Senator Hayden was not one of them, but he knew J. Edgar was not one to fool with.

COINTELPRO was an acronym for the Counter-Intelligence Program. Hoover gathered a group of special agents like Andrews and Backman and created his own secret police to conduct covert and illegal operations that surveyed, infiltrated, harassed and defamed political organizations, dissenting groups and activists such as the Civil Rights organization and political leaders like Martin Luther King, whom he termed either anarchists, communists, communist sympathizers, terrorists, spies or subversives. Hoover had King's bedroom bugged and then anonymously sent him a copy of the sex recordings to harass and intimidate him, and when he wouldn't cave and resign from the movement, anonymously circulated it around the Capitol trying to derail his receiving a Nobel Peace Prize.

Hoover considered those in the Civil Rights movement, and, since the outbreak of the Vietnam War, anyone voicing an opinion against it, enemies of the state. Files were kept on people who even wrote letters to the editor supporting civil rights or anti-war views. It was later discovered that he developed a "Secret Enemies List," containing his version of high profile "subversives" like King. To protect the nation's security, prevent violent outbreaks and maintain law and order and stability, they were to be under surveillance by any means legal or illegal and prevented in any way possible from conducting their "subversive" activities.

Hoover then picked up a couple of other packets that were delivered to him along with the bound papers he had glanced at, and got up and handed them to Andrews and Backman. "This will tell you the purpose of the meeting you will be attending this morning, the list of attendees, their backgrounds, and what your role will be in furthering the Bureau's and their objectives. It is a COINTELPRO mission, so all the confidentiality applies. You two have been singled out because of your record of accomplishment on similar type missions. However, I wanted to give you the assignment myself to emphasize the importance of this project. It must not fail!" Raising his voice somewhat, then asked, "What did I say?"

"It must not fail," both repeated loudly.

"Good. Your Bureau leader and contacts are in the packet. They set up some 'coffee and' for you in the small conference room on the second floor where you will have some privacy to study the contents of the packets. Make no copies. No notes, except for your Bureau contacts, then come back up and leave the packets with my secretary before you leave. She is the one who brought you in here. If they ever get off their asses to finally construct our new building, next time we can set up your coffee in a small private dining room.

Hoover no sooner opened the door to let them out when he called out to his secretary, "Get Hubert's scheduler on the phone and see if the Vice President has time to see me today or we will never get out of this run-down building."

Andrews and Backman knew what "coffee and" on the 2nd-floor small conference room was like. It meant coffee and two types of donuts: jelly and crullers. The room was one of several set aside for agents needing privacy to talk or review sensitive documents on a first come first serve basis unless reserved for exceptionally important assignments. In this instance, it did have a sign "Reserved 9:15 -10:00 per order of the Director." Reviewing new assignments for COINTELPRO was not new to them. The written assignment they were about to read was to be read without the taking of any notes and memorized.

Operation: Loyalty <u>The Purpose</u> – To discourage, degrade, and when necessary prevent the subversive activities, protests, demonstrations, and acts of civil disobedience by students at colleges and universities to protest the Vietnam War waged by our Government to defend its people.

<u>Bureau Contacts</u> – You will have priority and unlimited access to Bureau personnel and equipment for bugging, surveillance, and other such needs as is reasonably necessary to carry out the purposes of this Operation. The code to access these resources is "COINTELPRO Loyalty." Any financial support to carry out this assignment shall require the usual requests and approvals per COINTELPRO protocol.

<u>Non-Bureau Contacts</u> – Dean William Lauder, recently appointed President of Boston University. You are to meet with the Dean at the time and place of his calling and support his efforts and his plan to accomplish the purposes of this Operation.

They finished reading the rest of the packet material containing the names of the people that would be attending the meeting with the Dean and other details.

"Freddie!" Andrews sought his partner's attention, sounding amazed and accenting a particular word. "Did you read that: 'UNLIMITED access to Bureau personnel and equipment? Man, I never saw this before. This is a priority and what did he say?"

"It must not fail!" they both repeated at the same time.

"Freddie, this is an opportunity. I sense there is a promotion here if we get it right."

"Yeah, and a career-ender if we get it wrong," Andrews answered, dampening the mood a little.

CHAPTER 7

WITH THE LIGHTS unceasingly flickering through the windows of the cab passing the dazzling casino signs on the strip, the words "La Ville-Lumière," meaning "The City of Lights," came to her mind. "This famous nickname for Paris was better suited for Vegas," she thought.

Sevena came there hoping to locate Alan. The two had not communicated since they met for those few exchanges that morning 10 days ago. And if she got to see him, how was she going to explain all the bizarre events that took place since they met that would cause her to travel some 2700 miles away from home searching for him, having known nothing about him except his first name?

As the cab was traveling at a crawl through the heavy traffic, she hardly noticed, for she was deep in thought. Throughout the ride, those unusual events during the previous 10 days would play over in her head like scenes from a melodrama.

Three days after their meeting, she still had Alan on her mind, trying to analyze every word, every gesture, every look of his. Was she misinterpreting his answer to her calculated question, that he would pursue something he was passionate about regardless of the risk? There was something about him that made her wonder, "Could he be the One?"

For sure, Sevena was attracted to him, but the question she was asking back then had nothing to do with any romantic interest. It was far more important. She needed to call Judd. She could remember the excitement when she called him.

"Hi, Judd, it's Sevena, really glad I caught you at home."

"Sounds serious, trouble?"

"No-troubling."

Normally a distinction without a difference, he thought, but knowing Sevena as a master of nuance, he knew there was meaning to it. "Tomorrow soon enough? I got a lot on my plate today."

"Sure," she answered.

"How about 9:15 in front of the Chapel? I teach a class at 10."

The BU Marsh Chapel is at the heart of the campus, situated somewhat back from the sidewalk on Commonwealth Ave, a main thoroughfare in Boston. The Chapel was built around 1850, a beautiful edifice right next to the Divinity School where lots of students tended to congregate, but at 9:15 in the morning, they tended to be mostly Divinity students-all men.

"Yes, good, 9:15 works for me, thanks," Sevena replied, and lightening up a bit she added in a less harried tone "...and Judd, you won't have a hard time recognizing me among the crowd of Divinity students there, I will be the one with tits."

SHE WOULD REMEMBER it was one of those beautiful New England spring mornings with a cool enough breeze when she arrived 10 minutes late, catching her breath. She first dropped by The Commons as she had been doing off and on now for three days, hoping that she might catch Alan there again. Judd, who arrived well before the appointed time, was sitting on the Chapel stairs drinking a cup of coffee and penning in some notes on a small pad of paper when Sevena approached him.

Judd adored Sevena. He first laid eyes on her during the attendance call of his Modern History class. "Sevena Citro?" he called out, taking the first day's attendance. "That's me," she replied. She had signed up as an undergraduate student. Judd had been teaching the Modern History class for nine years. Like most, he was captivated by both her appealing looks and intriguing personality. Besides being easy on the eyes with her light brown hair breezily flowing over her shoulders, and a sensual shapely figure that failed to be disguised by her non-suggestive clothing, she was smart, witty and as Judd was to later learn, loyal and trustworthy to the hilt. She was one of the brightest students not only in his class but on campus, with her 3.9 average.

Sevena signed up for Judd's class because it was one of the highest-rated courses in the Liberal Arts School, otherwise an odd elective for one of the only women at the school bold enough to major in physics. In addition to all her rare qualities, it was her freewheeling nature and playfulness that endeared her to Judd. No romantic interest. Though not noticeable, Judd was gay. Like most, he was not out of the closet.

"Slow down, take it easy, have a seat," Judd welcomed her, pointing to the stairs where he was sitting like it was a chair in an office. "Here, got an extra coffee for you- black." She appreciated the coffee not having had one yet, but more so the thoughtfulness and kindness that Judd had always shown her. He was like an older brother steadying her whenever she was about to go overboard.

Judd waited for Sevena to take just a couple of sips of the coffee and enjoy her physical presence. "Well, I am here, all ears, but I will need to head for class in 30 minutes," Judd reminded her.

"This won't take long because what I am about to relate didn't take long either." She then went on in every detail to relate her brief exchanges with Alan, without skipping a word and then added, "I think he can be the *One*."

"Hey, Sevena, I wasn't there, but I can tell by your verve, there was a spark of electricity or something that got you so enchanted. But whatever the magic of the moment, it was just that, a moment. You got to be fucking kidding me," he said, not in a harsh tone. "You met him for what, no more than 15 minutes, where the silences outlasted the talking, exchanged a handful of words and got a book review from him in a couple of sentences. You don't even know his full name, where he lives, what he does, who his friends are, never mind his politics, and you are seriously thinking at long last, we found our guy?"

"I know, it's fucking crazy, but something just won't let go in my thinking that he's the One we have been looking for."

"Even if your mystical hunch were correct, how would we find him? All we got to go on is his first name. It would be like finding a needle in a haystack." He cringed at his own worn-out but apropos clichés.

"We got more than that to go on," she said. "He goes to BU."

"We don't know that either," Judd contested.

"What, he went to seek out the BU Commons early in the morning because they are famous for their gourmet coffee?"

"Yeah, you got a point there, but how do you explain that he was without a book, a notepad, or even a pen in his hand?" he continued to argue.

"Yes, puzzling, can't explain that yet," she said.

"Yet," he repeated her word, "that means you are about to pursue finding out who he is, I take it."

At this point, she had stopped trying to convince him and was already on to how to find out who he was and what he was about. "Cindy," she said. "*Cindy*, isn't that the gal you helped get into Business School a few years ago and is now the Assistant Registrar?"

"Yes," he conceded, knowing where she was going and knowing it was now useless to try to persuade her otherwise.

"Can you tell her you need a favor and get her to talk to me?"

"I know better than try to argue you out of this one. Sure, I will call her right after my class."

"You're a doll. Are you off to your class now?"

"No, not yet, there are still five more minutes, and I am waiting for a girl to show up with tits," he jested. An insult if Sevena were flat-chested, but no worry there.

"Go run along and teach your class in Modern History," she said playfully, "and see if you can turn out a few more de Tocqueville's revolutionaries running around."

———————

SEVENA HEARD HER alarm go off early the next morning, but it was not her trusty clock, it was the phone. Fumbling to get at it, she finally got out a feeble "Hello."

"Sounds like I am disturbing your sleep," Judd said without announcing himself as he heard her struggling voice.

"That's OK, Judd, I had to get up to answer the phone anyway," using an overused joke to let him know he did.

"Good news. Cindy can meet you this evening. She will call you later this morning for details."

"Great, thanks, what did you tell her?"

"I told her you were a dear friend and that a student sat down next to you in the Commons, and when he left, your wallet with valuables and some sentimental stuff were gone. You were hoping to find out who he is to recover it."

"You did *what*?" If Sevena were not fully awake before, she certainly was now.

"Hey, had to come up with something, and that is as close to the truth as I could manufacture."

"Actually, that was clever," she thought. "I owe you one."

"One? I count it to be about one hundred and one. Got to go. Good luck in finding that needle."

Cindy was once a student in Judd's Modern History class. He was also her advisor until she switched from being a history major at the Liberal Arts School to the Business School. She got the transfer with full credits because of Judd's recommendation. She would do anything for Judd. She picked up and dialed her phone:

"Hi, Sevena, this is Cindy Harris. How can I help?

CHAPTER 8

"SORRY ABOUT THE traffic," said the cab driver.

"What?" Sevena responded, awakened from her thoughts for the moment. "Oh, it's OK, no problem.

Sevena was then back in thought about that next day when she went to the BU Registrar's Office to meet Cindy. The office was smaller than you would think, given that it maintained all the University's student academic records. The volume of records that needed to be kept could intimidate a librarian. It certainly did Sevena when Cindy escorted her into the area.

There were two ladders to reach the higher shelves and a small desk with a couple of chairs where they both sat. "We have a coffee maker in the reception area. Would you like a cup?" Cindy asked. They were alone having purposely arranged to meet at 6 pm when no one would be around.

"I appreciate it, but no thanks," Sevena responded, anxious to get on with it.

"Judd tells me that all you know about this guy is that he said his name was Alan and nothing more and you want to track him down. Is that right?"

"Yes, hoping you can help," responded Sevena.

"Well, not a lot to go on even if he is a student here. Look around; we have 30,000 students enrolled in our various undergraduate and graduate schools. Time-consuming, but I can get you copies of the names of every student enrolled at the different schools during this year. However, while they are arranged alphabetically, it's by last names, not first names. So, you can imagine the work it would take to identify all the ones whose first name is Alan. Also, a further problem, even if we could identify all the Alan's in the University, Security, not our Registers Office, keeps the students' admission photos. I would have to make a formal written request to get pictures of all those identified as Alan for you to try and identify your guy. I can make a reasonable request, but not hundreds. And Alan seems like a very popular name."

"The guy who stole my wallet is 22, maybe 23 or 24-years-old at most, so I went back 24 years to 1942 and looked up the most popular names of those born that year in the USA and out of the 100 very most popular, Alan is smack in the middle of them."

"So, you agree, we sort of have a hopeless task here," Cindy responded in a voice conveying disappointment and therefore beginning to ready herself to lock up and leave.

"Well, tough, but not hopeless. We are not talking about finding hundreds of Alans," Sevena explained as she pulled out a piece of paper from her pocket with some figures written on it. "As I said, I feel comfortable with placing his age between 22 and 24, so we can reasonably calculate that Alan was born around 1942 plus or minus a year or two. That year, the statistical records I researched showed there were 3,138 babies born in the USA that were named Alan. Recorded live births for that same year in the USA were approximately three million, give or take 100,000. When you do the math dividing the 3 million by 3,138, it comes out to exactly 1/10th of a percent of all those born in the US that year were named Alan, meaning that that for every thousand students enrolled, we can expect on average to find only one with that first name. From what you say, BU's entire student enrollment this year is around 30,000, so if we reviewed the University's entire enrollment list for this year, the probability is that we would find plus or minus 30 of them having Alan as their first name."

Cindy was amazed by both the logic and the math. It was like when some professional entertainer at a birthday party she had attended recently asked the group how many people do you need at a party to have a 50% chance that two of them would have the same birthday? Given 365 possible birthdays in a year, some answers were as high as 180 people. Most were shocked, including Cindy, that the answer was only 23. Something to do with 23 people in the room creates all kinds of combinations for a possible match. Just like that birthday riddle, Cindy was just as surprised as to the small number of Alan's per thousand, but willing to accept Sevena's conclusion, though still expressed her concern.

"So, even if we were to find only 30 names or even a few less, we would have to go through the 30,000 student names pull out all those with Alan as a first name, quite a task."

"I understand, but I am not suggesting that we seek out the Alans from the entire University's student body. We can make some reasonable assumptions. For instance, age-wise, he looks in his early 20s, and given the maturity of his manner and conversations, he seems much too sophisticated to be a freshman, a sophomore, or even a junior for that matter, so let's limit the search for Alans only among seniors in undergrad schools and grad students. From the conversation I had with him, if I had to bet, it would be that he is not in Medical or Dental School or the School of Public Health, so I would cut those grad schools out of the search."

Sevena had Cindy's attention, if not her fascination, as she continued. "We may miss the boat, but I would also rule out Divinity School. I do not see him as a priest touting dogma. I would also rule out the School of Education. He did not seem to be the sort of guy that was interested in teaching elementary or high school students. The Business School as well, he did not impress me at all as being a money-hungry guy seeking a Wall Street career."

"The School of Management," Cindy stated a bit harshly.

"What?" asked Sevena, somewhat confused by the non-sequitur.

"The school, it's called the School of Management."

"Oh, of course." Sevena now remembering that Cindy graduated from that school and feeling somewhat embarrassed by her "money-hungry" expression, tried to make a recovery. "Yes, I would rule out the School of Management as well. I think he would lack the dedication for such a high-powered career. So, Cindy," Sevena trying to move on by drawing Cindy back into the conversation as a partner "if we eliminate those schools, what other school enrollments are left?"

"Let's see: Liberal Arts School seniors, our graduate schools awarding Masters and Doctorate Degrees, excluding the fields you mentioned, and the Law School, give me a few moments," responded Cindy as she got up to go to her office to retrieve some actual enrollment figures. She was back in less than 20 minutes. "If we cut out all the schools we talked about and looked at only the seniors and graduate students, we would be down to an enrollment of a little more than 11,000."

"And hopefully, we will find plus or minus 11 Alans in them."

"OK, if we are to have a chance at making a winning play, I need to get started copying the enrollment lists of the schools we discussed. I know you are in a hurry, so I will have the lists delivered to your house by the courier before 10 tomorrow morning." While she would not question it out of loyalty to Judd, she could guess from the effort undertaken, that a lot more was at stake here than finding the mysterious Alan just to retrieve a wallet.

As PROMISED, THE courier was at Sevena's apartment the next morning at 9:45, asking her to sign for a package with a note from Cindy.

Dear Sevena,

The lists are copies of the original pages on file containing all the students enrolled in the various schools we discussed. There are 11,210 students on these nearly 300 pages. I think it should take you less than two hours to scan and mark them to find the Alans.

Never thought I would say this to anyone, but hope you find less than what you are looking for.

Good luck,

Cindy

Sevena wasted no time getting at it. She started with the pile containing lists of Liberal Arts seniors, flipping page after page after page moving her finger down the second column looking for an Alan. When she found one, she underlined it and set the page aside. Things were going as predicted. It took 1,878 enrollees to produce the two Alans – on average one per 939 names. In less than 90 minutes, she had finished Liberal Arts and all the graduate schools with just the Law School left. She counted the pages she set aside containing an Alan; there were 13 of them.

Sevena then went on to count the ten pages of the Law School enrollees that were left to review. Hoping to find no Alans out of the 402 students, surprisingly and disappointingly she found two: Alan Lacy, a third-year law student from South Boston, and Alan Roberts, a second-year law student from Boston. So, the number was in; there were a total of fifteen of them. Her predictions were close enough.

She immediately called Cindy with the fifteen names. "How fast can we get the photos?"

"I will walk the names over. Security is in our building. I should be able to get them while there. Want me to courier the photos over to you?"

"No. I am on my way."

As soon as Sevena arrived, Cindy began to hand her the fifteen photos she obtained-one at a time. The first twelve Sevena looked at were smiling, were not him. Cindy then gave her the next one, Alan Roberts.

"Bingo," Sevena shouted as if she were claiming the prize at the church hall. There he was. Unlike the others in a suit, he wore a sweater, had curly black hair, a few of the curls falling lightly over his forehead, soft features with a slight dimple, instead of a smile, an expression of strength and just as she remembered he was noticeably handsome by any standards. Sevena then re-examined his file and read it aloud. "He is a junior at the law school. Lives at 205 Park Drive, not far from the school, born on the 4th of July would you believe. He will be 23 in July."

"What's next?" asked Cindy.

"Well, I need to find him." What Sevena really meant but did not share with Cindy was, "I need to **find out** about him."

CHAPTER 9

SEVENA HAD ALAN'S photo, his address and the city he grew up in. She knew his Liberal Arts major, the courses he took both there and at the Law School. He would probably still be in town since it was only a week from the time they met, and he said he was going to Vegas in one or two weeks.

She dialed the phone. "Hi, Judd. Look, I need to talk to you about next steps. We may need to engage an investigator to get the personal info we need to see if he is our guy. I am thinking..."

"Hey, put the brakes on," Judd interrupted. "I know you are feeling the rush from having found your needle in a haystack, but for Christ's sake, Sevena, all you did was find out the guy's full name. You usually get that when you meet and say hello to someone. The fact that you now know his address, the schools he attended and had a 10-minute chat, doesn't even win him a tryout for what we need."

"Judd, as I was saying, I need to find a way..." Sevena continued as if Judd never spoke.

"OK, all right, I know when there is no stopping you, but we need more info through normal means and see if that gets him over the low bar before we start the Dick Tracy stuff to get what we need. Maybe Cindy can get to see his file at the law school. As a start, we look at his application, who recommended him and whatever else we find. Cindy can say they are updating the Registrar's records if she thinks that won't raise anyone's eyebrows. Call her and tell her to drop by my office tomorrow. I will talk to her. I will need to make up some other kind of excuse as to why we need it. OK?"

Sevena knew he was right. "OK, I will call Cindy and tell her to see you as soon as we hang up."

Judd always was there like an older brother to Sevena, steadying her and keeping her feet to the ground when she was willing to take off without putting together a well-reasoned flight plan.

Actually, Sevena did have an older brother who played a similar role when she would go off the rails while at Saint Mary Catholic Elementary School, located in Revere that bordered East Boston. There, especially during her last year in the 9th grade, she was always getting in trouble with the sisters by constantly challenging the validity of their lessons in religious classes. She had the dual distinction of recording the highest marks in the school and the highest number of trips down to the principal's office.

Her father, Angelo Citro, at age 25, emigrated from Sicily, fell in love and married the first Italian woman he dated and moved to Revere among a large Italian population of immigrants. He sold fruit for a time and later became a member of the local mason's union.

Sevena's mother died at her birth. So, with her father working long hours as a mason, building roads wherever in the country he could find good-paying jobs, it fell to her brother, Matty, just seven years older than she, to smooth things out with the principal when the call went to the family concerning each of her violations.

Matty had also gone to St. Mary's. He was well-liked by the principal, priests and nuns, which gave him a little leverage when dealing with Sevena's "violations." Matthew, as he was called at St. Mary's, perhaps because it was the blessed name of one of Christ's apostles, served as an altar boy, sang in the choir and unlike Sevena, was right at home in the parochial environment. For a while, everyone thought he would become a priest. But instead, right after high school, he went to work in the trades as an electrician on local projects to help support the family, but still hoping (perhaps dreaming) someday to get back to school and become an engineer.

"Come on, Seven," Matty would say to Sevena each time they walked out of the principal's office. "You promised how many times before? Please. Hand to God now, no more screwing around, OK?"

"Seven" was the sound that came out of his mouth by mistake when he called her one time chewing something. They both liked the sound of it, and so he called her that ever since.

"I promise I won't do it again," she would say with her hand raised, "and cross my heart," she would add, as her finger sketched two imaginary lines traversed on her chest, but with a big smile that seemed more like asking his forgiveness in advance of the next transgression.

"Yeah, let's go, you little shit," he said with his arm around her. "What am I gonna do with you?" and they both continued walking, breaking out into a chuckle.

Sevena learned and memorized the Golden Rule the very first time it was taught to her at parochial school:

"Do unto others as you would have them do unto you."

She was taken by its very simplicity and yet it was the most profound moral commandment she had ever heard. Many similar teachings of Christ resonated with her.

His love and humanity: "*Thou shall love thy neighbor as thyself.*"

His love and concern for the poor, the sick, the hungry, the outcasts, and the homeless: "*Whatever you do to the least of these my brethren, you do unto me.*"

However, while finding these spiritual teachings moving and the scriptures (both New and Old testaments) instructive, she was bothered and unable to reconcile them with the strict and literal interpretation given by her Church to events she considered metaphoric, such as Genesis' explanation of creation, the concept of the Trinity, the crucifixion and resurrection of Jesus so man's sins could be forgiven and the magic of the Eucharist-that by sipping wine and eating a piece of bread, one could receive the blood and body of Christ and thereby be sanctified. To Sevena, they indeed had meaning symbolically, but she was turned off by the literal, unyielding, dogmatic form in which they were being instilled in them and the harsh, unloving, un-Christlike (she thought) way they were being taught by some of the sisters. To put it mildly, she could not contain these feelings as occasions arose. And of course, they often did, as what happened in her class on Bible Studies one morning.

"Sorry, Sister Rita," apologized Christina, a pupil rushing to sit down after the bell had rung just three minutes before. She spoke in English, but with a Spanish accent that made what she said hard to understand unless you listened carefully. Speaking out of breath did not help either. Her single mom, two-year-old brother and Christina had newly moved into the area but lived more than two miles from the school, which was all they could afford, making her walk the longest distance of any pupil in the class.

"What did I tell you last time you came in late and interrupted my class like this," shouted the sister walking briskly toward Christina with a leather strap in her hand. "Tardiness is not a virtue."

Stand up and show me both your hands," she commanded. Strapping was a method of punishment not forbidden at the school to discipline unruly students.

"I am so sorry, Sister. I had to wait for my aunt to come over to care for my little brother Joseph before I could leave. Next time, I will run harder, I promise…I promise," she pleaded and repeated the plea as Sister Rita approached with the strap.

"You promised me you would never be late again last time. Lying and deceitfulness are sins that cannot go unpunished if you are to be made into a God-fearing woman. Turn up your hands." And with that, the sister started to strike both the child's hands with the strap, once, twice….

"*Whatever you do to the least of these my brethren, you do unto me,*" came a loud voice from the back of the room.

The sister, stunned by it as if it were a command from above, interrupted the strapping and after looking up to the ceiling as if the voice came from above, turned toward the back of the room, "Who said that?" she shouted.

"*Whatever you do to the least of these my brethren, you do unto me,*" repeated the voice even louder. It was Sevena standing up looking straight at Sister Rita.

"Sevena, come here!" the sister demanded.

Sevena walked up to her without flinching and turned her hands over without being asked to receive her expected punishment. Sister Rita did not continue striking Christina, but added Christina's remaining strikes to Sevena's more severe punishment and sent her down to the principal's office.

Sevena was not shy in contesting the material being taught as well. She raised her hand in another class just one week later. "Yes, Sevena, you have a question about salvation?" the sister asked having just given a lecture on it.

"Yes, Sister Mary, I know you say that the only way to be saved is to accept our Lord, Jesus, into our hearts. But some of my neighbors are Jewish, decent God-fearing people who don't believe in Christ. Are they to be damned while some of our people who go to church on Sunday confess to get a pass on their sins and then go out and do it again?"

"Blasphemous, blasphemous," shrieked Sister Mary. "We need to tie your tongue to your cheek. Right down to the principal's office, young lady," she added, literally pulling Sevena by the collar of her shirt and dragging her out of the room down to his office.

Sevena did not only spar with her teachers. She had tried out and was selected to the five-girl cheering squad. There were just a few extracurricular or sporting activities for girls at the school. So, while being on the cheering squad was not particularly appealing to her, this was one of the few ways to test one's competitiveness. The squad was to give its first cheer of the season at the school's opening basketball game. Sevena saw the team being led in a quick prayer by Coach Father Moran on the sidelines as they were about to take the court. She went over where they were bending into the circle with their hands bunched one on top of the other. Just as they ended the prayer with the group saying Amen, she said a little above a whisper, "Hey, won't they consider it cheating to ask God to help us win?"

Just three minutes into the game, when the star player made a cross on his chest when about to shoot a foul shot, she shouted. "Come on, Bill, it's not fair to ask him to help you make the shot."

Bill looked over to her angrily. He made another cross on his chest, but this time as he drew the final line upward with his middle finger, he turned and raised it so it stood pointing up with the other fingers' knuckled down and let it remain for a moment. He turned toward the basket, aimed confidently but missed the shot. It didn't even touch the rim.

Sevena and her brother were called to the principal's office first thing the very next morning. This time, unlike the other violations, she was suspended for a week and thrown off the cheering squad. With that punishment, she told her brother that she had learned a lot.

"I finally hope so, Seven," he said. "What in particular?"

"Fucking around with God is one thing, but fucking with sports, hey that's a no-no!"

The suspension week was not without its benefits. She had time to walk along the streets of the North End of Boston that bustles with shops and small restaurants run by Italian shopkeepers. It was a place that excited her. In August, her dad would sure to be home for the St. Anthony's Feast. The Feast gave Italian immigrants an opportunity to rejoice with their families and friends in the traditions of their ancestral villages in Southern Italy and Sicily, where the Citros had come from. An array of home-cooked Italian food was sold at sidewalk stands, with fireworks and general merriment going well into the late evening. Sevena loved the bliss, and religious spirit emanating from this type of celebration in contrast to the more solemn atmosphere at school.

What became a dilemma for the school was what to do at graduation. There were more than three meetings attended by the principal and some of the teaching staff, and finally all the teachers discussed a most sensitive issue. Sevena by far had the highest grades. Despite her disciplinary issues, she got straight A's in all her courses. By both rule and tradition, given that Sevena obtained the highest academic ratings, the school was required to select her as the class valedictorian and for her to deliver the Valedictory Address at graduation. However, given her unpredictable behavior, or perhaps more fearful "predictable" behavior, the teachers did not trust what she might say. It could prove embarrassing to the school, to all the graduate students and their families, as well as dignitaries, including the Cardinal himself, who had accepted the invitation to give the Commencement Address.

After much consideration, it was finally decided they would not break precedent. They would select Sevena as valedictorian to give the Valedictory Address. However, she was to be called in before the principal and the Commencement Committee to be both advised and warned that diplomas are awarded at the very end of the ceremony and one's graduation was not official until then. If she were to give a speech considered by the Committee to question the teachings of the Church in any way, they had the right and would exercise that right to expel her from the school as of that moment and prevent her graduation.

———————

THE SMALL CHURCH where graduation was held each year could accommodate as many as 500 people. So, that sunny Sunday morning when 300 people came to attend, they were comfortably seated not too distant from the altar where speakers were seated and the diplomas awarded. Most were already there, including the graduates who had just paraded together into the front rows exclusively reserved for them when the Cardinal arrived.

The program went smoothly, running the usual 30 minutes behind schedule. It began with the opening prayer; then the principal welcoming the Cardinal and the families and friends of the graduates; a few academic awards, of which Sevena was one of the recipients; the singing of a couple of hymns, ending with the class song. What remained was the Valedictory Address by Sevena, to be followed by the Cardinal's Commencement Address and the presenting of the diplomas at the altar.

Sevena was introduced and called upon to give her speech. She approached the altar confidently in even steps, with just a small piece of paper with notes hidden in her pocket under her graduation gown if needed. She was going to deliver her remarks totally by heart. No valedictorian or any commencement speaker had ever done that before.

"Your Eminence," she began, looking directly at the Cardinal while offering a small, respectful bow. "Principal O'Connell, whom I have had the privilege to get to know and had the benefit of his advice more than most," which drew some giggles and laughter from her classmates. The principal did not laugh so much. "Our distinguished teachers to whom we owe so much for all the knowledge you have imparted to us, members of the school staff, my fellow classmates and our proud families, invited guests and Mr. Casey O'Brien and Mr. Eugene Olivero." She had just included the two school janitors who were sitting way in the back of the hall waiting to clean up, but came in their suits out of respect. The Cardinal was seen asking the principal next to him who they were.

"Today, we leave the hallowed halls of St. Mary's, but rest assured we do not leave behind the knowledge we learned from our teachers and wisdom we gained from studying the sacred books of the Bible, the teachings of Christ, and the moral principles that they command. From here, we will go forth to acquire more knowledge from the treasures found in existing scrolls and books of philosophy, science and the humanities, that not only exist today but are yet to be written, to further educate us to know and do God's will.

"I believe as we have been taught, that God's will can be found in the teachings of Christ, in the love and compassion for one another that he preached so that we may live righteously and in harmony with all our neighbors. In my view, there is a single teaching of his that rises above all the rest and can by itself guide us to a moral path. It is Jesus' most simple but profound commandment-the Golden Rule: 'Do unto others as you would have them do unto you.'

"But I see it not as a commandment that must be strictly obeyed, but as a tenet for moral guidance to be lovingly embraced.

"It is not just a Catholic rule or even a rule exclusively preached by Jesus. One hundred years before the birth of Christ, Hillel, a great Jewish religious sage, also preached the Golden Rule: 'That which is hateful to you, do not do to your fellow.'

"Although treasuring all the great teachings in the bible, their Torah, and all their many scholarly books of religious teaching of Hillel, he said of the Golden Rule, 'This one rule IS our Bible, the rest of the Scriptures and all our studies are just commentary and explanation.'"

"And so, I believe that salvation is not reserved for Christians alone who accept Christ into their hearts, but is there for everyone, for every Catholic, Jew, Protestant, Muslim, Buddhist, Believer or Non-believer, that lives by that Rule."

With that, Sevena ended. The room was strangely quiet and remained in dead silence except for the noise of Sevena's steps as she left the altar back to her seat. There was no applause from the students or anyone else. They all were looking to see how the priests and nuns would react and they saw tightened and stern faces.

The Cardinal got up and went to the microphone without awaiting an introduction. He began without any salutations. "Blasphemous!" he shouted in a loud voice.

He waited another few seconds and repeated the word, "Blasphemous."

One of the Commencement Committee members started to get in position to move to the table to remove Sevena's diploma and strike her name from the list to be called up to receive diplomas.

"Blasphemous," repeated the Cardinal a third time, but this time completing the thought, "was the word many of the orthodox Jewish rabbis then in power and their followers cried out against our Savior in giving his Sermon on the Mount and fearlessly speaking the words of God as he knew them."

"Our Valedictorian reminded me of what our Lord Jesus encountered and was willing to suffer in daring to teach new ways from those being practiced. Her speaking the words of God from her heart as she knows it, aware that she could be figuratively crucified for speaking them, for imploring us to embrace the words of our Lord to truly *love our neighbors as ourselves*, our neighbors of any religion or belief, or even non-belief, who have lived righteous lives, not only warms the heart of this old prelate but is a testament and a tribute to the fine teaching that goes on in this school. However, I will ask her to listen as I preach otherwise about the salvation of those who do not give themselves to Christ in my commencement address."

Her brother Matty, sitting next to their father in the audience, smiled and said to himself, "Seven, you little shit, you did it again."

Sevena, however, was to refuse many scholarships she was offered to Catholic prep schools and instead opted for Revere public high school. She later accepted a full scholarship to Boston University, looking to become a physicist and search for answers about creation, but through a different lens.

But now her focus was on something more important. She picked up the phone. "Hi, Cindy, Judd asked me to call you and ask if you would be kind enough to drop by his office tomorrow morning."

CHAPTER 10

"I'M SORRY ABOUT the traffic, but there are a lot of conventions in Vegas this week", said the cab driver, "but won't be long now."

Sevena was still too deep in thought to respond, thinking about the evens that Judd told her about in recruiting Cindy's help to find out more about Alan. As each detail crossed her mind, she wondered if it was something they could ever admit doing.

Cindy had opened the familiar door that read "Professor Judd Lampert" the next day in response to Sevena's request. It was 8:45 am and there were already four students waiting to see Judd.

Everyone who took his course considered switching their major to history and wanted him to be their advisor. She could not blame them. His knowledge, passion for the subject, spellbinding teaching style and sense of humor mesmerized those lucky enough to avoid a long waiting list to get into his class. She had been one of them. "And where did he find the time to give them all so much personal attention?" she wondered.

"Oh, hi, Cindy," Judd greeted her as he came out of his inner office with a student. "Hey, grab some more coffee, I will be with you all in 15 minutes," he said to the waiting students, pointing to the coffee maker in the corner. He was the only professor to set up a small table with coffee in his waiting area.

"Come on in, Cindy. Much thanks for coming by on such short notice." Judd shut the door as soon as they entered the inner office. "I'll be brief, I need a favor," he said candidly.

"Of course, anything, you know that," she answered. "Whatever it is, I would need to do 50 of them just to get even with the help you gave me."

"Well, I wouldn't say 'yes' so quickly. I need to see Alan Roberts' file in the Law School Dean's office without anyone knowing it, and I need you to help get it."

"Why?" she asked.

"That's exactly it. I can't share that with you." He decided to be honest since he could not think of any believable excuse. Even so, he was asking her to cross a line on this one, so did not want to lie to her.

"Whatever it is, you know I will help in any way I can." She was sure that whatever it was, Judd would be on the right side. "Besides, you must have guessed, I had my suspicions about the 'stolen wallet' bit. What do you want me to do?"

"Can you ask the Dean to see student files to update the Registrar's file or something like that?" he queried.

"That won't work, Judd. We get the student marks to record them in the University's registry. But to request to see the contents of their files would make no sense given our responsibilities and would be certain to raise eyebrows."

"There goes the non-covert way of getting it," Judd thought. However, he trusted Sevena's instinct about people, about Alan, more than he admitted to her, so he was willing to explore covert ways to learn more about him.

"Can we possibly gain entrance to the Law School Dean's office when no one is around?" he asked. "Does the Registrar have a key?"

"This must be important," thought Cindy and so was not offended by the question. "No, as I understand it only the Deans have the keys to their offices. There is no need for us to have one."

"That ends that," Judd thought.

"Of course, Security has a key to each office in case of an emergency, a fire, etc.," Cindy added as an afterthought. "But there is no plausible reason for me to ask for the key."

"And where are they kept? Do you know?" Judd asked with revived interest.

"I do. Inside the Security Office, down the hall from me, there is a big wooden-framed open box attached to the office wall, with hooks in it holding the keys to each of the Deans' offices. It is in open sight, which is going to be a problem if you are thinking of borrowing it without permission," she put it politely. "It's only about 10 feet away from where Jerry sits."

"Who's Jerry?"

"He is the security officer. I go there from time to time and just saw him the other day to request the pictures of the various Alans for Sevena."

They talked a bit more, Judd stressing the importance of obtaining the key without revealing the reason and discussed a possible plan to get it. They would meet at noon at the Security Office.

"HI, JERRY," CINDY greeted him in a cheerful voice. "This is Professor Lampert. He is planning to have a colleague from Yale give a lecture next month and will be reserving a hall for it. It will be a controversial subject and could fuel a protest demonstration and he wanted to discuss security with you."

"Sure thing. Sit down, Professor. Do you have an exact date in mind?" Jerry asked, pointing to the chair beside his desk.

As they talked, Cindy began to edge toward the wall where the keys were hanging, pretending to look at nearby pictures of the university landscape, but she was and would always be within Jerry's peripheral view. Judd noticed that as well.

Judd also noticed the map of the school grounds on Jerry's desk. He got up, picked up the map and brought it over to Jerry. When he got beside him, he held the map in front of Jerry's face blocking his view of the part of the room where Cindy was standing.

Pointing to the map, Judd said, "Jerry, this is the area where I might hold the lecture, and I was thinking that if we...."

Cindy saw Jerry looking at the map that blocked his vision of her and quickly went in front of the framed box holding the keys. Above the hooks were the names of the schools: Divinity, Liberal Arts, Education, Law School-Law School, there it was. She unhooked it and put it in her pocket and slowly continued to look at pictures around the room as Judd and Jerry continued to talk.

"That really won't help us, Professor," Jerry said. "You need to first settle on the exact hall you are going to reserve and estimate how many people will attend and then we can figure out how to help."

"Makes sense," Judd said. "Thanks, I appreciate it. I think I can make that decision and get that info back to you in a couple of hours."

As they were walking out the door, Cindy said in a loud voice, "See you later, Professor," and shook Judd's hand as if to say goodbye, dropping in it a small metal object as she let go.

Judd wasted no time getting to his car and on the way to the hardware store he had checked out before going to Security.

"I will need three duplicates," he said handing the key to the storekeeper.

"Here they are, Sir. That will be $2.60," said the storekeeper, who was back in just a few moments.

Two hours later, Judd and Cindy were back in the Security Office with Judd again holding up the map of the grounds soliciting Jerry's advice as to the best of several halls to conduct the lecture, blocking his view as Cindy was busy getting the key back in place. This time they both left shaking hands goodbye, with nothing passing between them except smiles of self- congratulations.

AT 6 PM that night, Judd tried the door that said, "Dean William Lauder, Boston University School of Law." As expected, it was locked. He knocked several times expecting no answer and there was none. He took out the key, inserted it in the door lock and turned it, but it only turned a little. He tried again and even a third time without success. Either it was the wrong key they obtained or a badly made duplicate. He reached for a second duplicate. It turned with a little difficulty-and there was the click. He opened the door gratefully, remembering why he decided to order three duplicates of the keys.

It was getting dark, but Judd decided to work without any lights. He had brought a flashlight if needed. He had no trouble finding the cabinet holding the student files. They were arranged alphabetically and he quickly came to "Olsen," "Price," "Raymond," and yes, "Roberts." He pulled out the file. He had already noticed where the copy machine was located. He would take out each sheet, copy it and carefully put it back in the same condition he found it. So far, the file contained what was expected: copies of his application, grades in each course, the files that Sevena had already seen, Alan's selection to Law Review, reports on his summer intern job at a law firm, etc., etc. Nothing unusual, and so of no great interest.

Judd then found something strange. There was a large, very thick plastic envelope sealed by strong adhesive and more strangely by a wire with a small combination lock on it wrapped around the envelope, binding it from opening without knowing the combination. It was marked "For Dean's Eyes Only." Judd would have to leave it without reading it or taking it, knowing they would eventually discover it had been stolen. There was no choice. Judd would take it with him and be in that hardware store again when it opened in the morning to purchase a wire cutter.

CHAPTER 11

"HERE, YOU CAN have the honor," said Judd handing the wire cutter over to Sevena, who hurriedly cut the wire. The thickly glued envelope was now free to open.

"Got scissors anywhere?" she asked, looking around Judd's office. Before Judd could take a step, Sevena uttered, "Never mind."

Taking the wire cutter instead, she cut along the top edge of the glued envelope allowing her to remove a large, multi-page stapled report marked "Confidential Report on Alan Roberts." The Report's cover page also bore the name of the investigating agency, "Martin Confidential Investigations," and the date: August 10, 1965. It had been done the year before.

The second page had a short table of contents:

- Background on Subject and His Family
- Subject's Education
- Subject's Political Views and Activities
- Recommendation

Below the table of contents was a single paragraph:

The Report's information was gathered by 35 hours of interviews with a selective number of the subject's friends, acquaintances, neighbors, teachers, coaches, and the subject himself, as well as obtaining and reviewing subject's Year Books and various government, school, travel, and court records. The interviews were obtained and conducted by one of our young investigators posing as a college newspaper reporter gathering background information for a story on

*the subject's academic achievement and successful selection
to BU Law Review. As a cover, we were then able, with a
pair of Boston Red Sox/Yankee tickets to induce the editor
of the BU student newspaper to publish our six-paragraph
story containing the subject's picture and a couple of quotes
from our interview with him. Our investigator mailed three
copies of the newspaper article to the subject to ward off any
suspicion that there was a purpose other than the story.*

"Fucking brilliant," Sevena thought, and began to read and flip
through the pages rapidly with Judd looking over her shoulder.

"My God, Judd, look what they got. Not only the date his father
emigrated here but the name of the boat, where he went right after landing
and when he got his citizenship as well. There is a whole page about the
experiences Alan had as a kid selling newspapers in Boston, his junior high
school marks and awards, and what the teachers and his basketball coach
thought of him, even the name of his 9th-grade girlfriend, for Christ's sake."

As they read more and more of such personal and extensive information, Judd could not help spitting out, "Un-fucking believable. Next, we
are going to find out how often he takes a piss each day."

"And look here," Sevena continued as she turned to another page,
"they even elicited what his Hebrew school and high school teachers and
college professors thought of him. They interviewed a number of them."

"And all of them, without exception, describe him as super smart,
very popular, extremely well- spoken, quick on his feet and a natural leader,"
noted Judd.

More and more personal details unfolded on the pages that followed
confirming those qualities, as related by the debating coach while he was
being interviewed by the investigator/student reporter. The debating coach
stated that during Alan's senior year in high school, the captain of the high

school debating team got into a serious auto accident on his way over to the state-wide championship finals, and his absence would have resulted in an automatic forfeit. The debate was on whether capital punishment should be abolished. Alan, not on the team, but having come to watch the debate, stepped from the audience and told the coach that rather than forfeit, he would volunteer to take his place, to give him the anchor position so he could listen to all the debaters to learn about the subject and would then do his best to be the closer playing it by ear.

The coach said that after the presentations by two debaters on each side and a closing debater for the opposition, Alan walked up to the mike to close for his team. Without a note or piece of paper, Alan delivered the most impassioned argument the coach had ever heard by any high school debater in his 20 years of coaching. The coach went on to say, "First, he took apart the opponents' arguments piece by piece. Then he delivered such a compelling factual and profoundly emotional argument, he left the audience spellbound. He then intentionally started to leave the mike with still 15 seconds of unused time remaining. After taking two steps away from the mike, he turned back and gripped it, and bending down and tipping the mike in the direction of the opponents, he finished his remarks in a gentle voice as if from the scriptures: "And who among you is without sin feel purified enough to throw the first switch."

The coach said it took 15 raps of the gavel by the moderator asking for quiet before the thunderous applause ceased, making the subsequent announcement by the judges as to the winning team a foregone conclusion. More such anecdotal incidents were to follow, one page after the next.

"*Wow*, here is another interesting section," Sevena said, looking up at Judd. "Read this."

"*Attached is a list of books, magazines, and record albums owned by Subject.*"

"They fucking broke into his apartment," Sevena said.

"Hey, saved us the trouble," joked Judd with a smile, as if to say don't get holier-than-thou.

They were both thinking the same thing. They had struck gold. Someone else had done their job for them, and an exhaustive one at that, even a health report.

"He was hospitalized twice. The first time was for an injury to his knee while playing on the freshman basketball squad at BU that ended his college play. The hospital report diagnosed it as an Anterior Cruciate Ligament injury. The examination indicated that the knee's range of motion had a flexibility of less than 90 degrees, which means that after his 2S deferment as a law school student ends, he will be ineligible for the draft and available to take a position at a law firm immediately upon graduation."

Sevena was first to speak. "As far as his personal qualities, he is a perfect 10 for what we need. He is smart, quick-witted, strategic, exceedingly well-spoken, cool under pressure, people like him and follow him, he is a leader in every sense of the word. I feel like we just hit the lottery."

Judd readily agreed. "But we don't know enough to know if he will buy into our plan." Both knew that if the next section, *Subject's Political Views and Activities,* was half as thorough as the report of his background, it would give them some indication.

The report commented on Alan, his father and aunts and uncles as having liberal to socialistic leanings. It reported on books, record albums and unpublished letters to the editor of the New York Times that they found in Alan's apartment. They confirmed his leanings and sympathy for civil rights and anti-war sentiments going on at the time. The report indicated that Alan had attended the March on Washington on August 28, 1963. Court and police records showed Alan was arrested in Selma, Alabama, on March 7, 1965, and treated for lacerations to the head and possible concussion at the Good Samaritan, one of two black hospitals in Selma. He was injured while joining 600 demonstrators on an intended 54-mile march from Selma to Montgomery to protest the killing of a civil rights leader and demand voting rights for blacks who were denied registration. Out of 15,000 blacks old enough to vote, only 130 were registered. On what was called Bloody Sunday, troopers, some on horseback, fired tear gas into the marching crowd and began to knock demonstrators down to the ground and beat them with nightsticks. Alan was one of the few whites on the March and having refused to retreat, suffered injuries that required stitches that kept him in the hospital overnight. The charges against him for trespassing and disorderly conduct were later dismissed.

"He took time off from law school to go down to Selma into what everyone knew was a very dangerous march and stood firm knowing that he was about to be beaten for doing so. We can now add 'courage' and an unshakable commitment to social justice to those qualities," said Sevena.

The jury is no longer out," admitted Judd, going over to Sevena to give her a big celebratory hug. "You were right all along; we've got our man!!"

With that out of the way, the other question immediately arose to both of them. "Why was the Dean interested in Alan, and why was he looking and hoping to find the same qualities we were?"

They turned to the Recommendation Section and soon found that they weren't looking for the same things. The Report concluded:

> *The Subject has more leadership qualities than any other students we have investigated, but his radical views would not only eliminate our recruiting him, but to the contrary, he would pose a danger to the P-7 project. Given his street sense and exceptional intelligence, although unlikely, he could figure out that he was investigated, he could also pose a danger to the project. We therefore recommend that his activities be monitored from time to time throughout the length of the project.*

CHAPTER 12

SEVENA RECALLED THAT Judd and she decided it was time to meet with Alan after reading the Investigators Report. Sevena had thought of calling him to arrange a meeting, but she would have to explain how she got his number. It was agreed that she should see him in person. She decided to wait until dinnertime, thinking it would be the best time to catch him at home.

She had felt a bit nervous when she opened the outside door into the hallway of his building two days earlier. There were three mail slots on either side with the names of the occupants and a button to ring each bell. There it was: Alan Roberts, Apartment 3. She rang the bell and waited to be buzzed in through the locked inside doorway. As she waited, she was practicing the first words she would say to him. There was no immediate buzz. She waited a few more seconds and rang again; still no answer. Right after the third try, a young guy about Alan's age, opened the outside entrance door to enter the hallway.

Seeing Sevena still facing the mail slots, he asked, "Can I help you?"

"No, thanks, I am waiting for Mr. Roberts to answer the bell," she responded.

"Oh, you are here to see Alan. I am afraid it will be a long wait," he said. "He isn't home."

"Do you know when he will be back?"

"You a friend of his?" he asked.

"In a way. We are both classmates at the same school," she replied, trying to stay close to the truth but willing to stretch it to gain whatever information she could.

"Me too. I mean friends, not classmates. Look, Alan won't be back.

We were going to the Y to play a pickup basketball game yesterday, but Alan told me he was leaving probably to see his cousin in New York and then off to Vegas, so no game that night or again for that matter."

"What do mean, not again?" she asked.

"As he may have told you, he quit law school. He settled up with our landlord, packed up his books, clothes and stuff and moved out of the furnished apartment."

Sevena was stunned. "Quit law school, moved out?" she uttered to herself, but recovered enough to ask, "Did he say where he was staying in Vegas."

"No."

"Do you know where his cousin lives in New York? I need to reach him."

"No idea who she is. Look, we've been neighbors a real short time and share milk and sugar once in a while and play a little basketball together, but I don't know much more, sorry."

"That's OK. Thanks anyway," she said and hurriedly left the building and drove around until she spotted a phone booth.

"Judd, after all this, we may have lost him."

"Hey, catch your breath and slowly tell me what you mean," responded Judd.

"You won't fucking believe it. He quit school, moved out of his apartment yesterday and supposedly off to Vegas after visiting a cousin in New York. But we don't know if he will be in Vegas in two days, two weeks, or never if he changes his mind, and off to who knows fucking where."

"Hey, don't sound so hopeless. We got a window here," Judd said, expressing his usual adeptness at not dwelling long on setbacks, but rather on steps to be taken to recover from them. "Let's give it another day for him to hopefully finish the New York visit and both fly to Vegas tomorrow."

"What, and the two of us station ourselves at a couple of entrances or exits at McCarran Airport day and night for who knows how long hoping to catch him coming or going? Don't much like those odds."

"Have something better in mind," Judd replied. "I'll get the plane tickets and make the hotel reservations and let you know what time Friday I will be by with a cab."

The next day, Judd came with a cab right on the appointed time and they both were soon winging their way to Las Vegas. As the plane widely circled McCarran airport on its final descent, Sevena looked down and saw the Potosi Mountain, one of several high points southwest of Vegas. It was into that mountain, in January 1942, that a TWA flight crashed, killing 22 passengers, among them one of her favorite actors, Carole Lombard, wife of Clark Gable.

Lombard was the love of his life and he never got over her loss. Sevena wondered why that thought occurred to her.

In the cab from the airport on the way to the Sands Hotel on the Strip where they were to stay, Judd detailed his plan with Sevena. He had a list of casino hotels and their phone numbers he felt were likely places Alan might stay. Two of them were the Golden Nugget and the Silver Slipper, both located in downtown Las Vegas, known as Glitter Gulch. It got its name from the blinding neon lights on the casinos and other signs that literally lit up the entire area as if it were day rather than night. All the other casinos were on the Strip, a stretch along South Las Vegas Boulevard, where the newest and largest glitzy hotels and casinos were concentrated. He felt that if Alan were going to Vegas to test his skills at beating the casino with his card-counting shtick, he would want to do it in the staple hotels at Glitter Gulch or on the Strip.

One of them on the Strip was the Sands where Judd had booked their rooms. That was the hotel where the Rat Pack performed: Sinatra, Dean Martin, Sammy Davis Jr., Peter Lawford and Joey Bishop. A few years earlier, it was the first hotel that had allowed a black entertainer-Nat King Cole to live and gamble in it– probably why Judd booked it. When they registered, they enquired whether an Alan Roberts had checked into the hotel and they were told no one by that name had.

Judd had already divided the list of casino hotels into two pages and gave one to Sevena. "OK, let the games begin," he said as they both headed for separate phones in the room.

"The Sahara Hotel, how can I help you?"

"Yes, would you ring Mr. Alan Roberts' room, please?" asked Sevena.

"There is no one checked in or expected by that name," answered the operator. "Would you try paging him in the casino, please?"

After a few moments, "Sorry, no one has answered the page."

"The Stardust Hotel, how can I help you?"

"Yes, would you ring Mr. Alan Roberts' room, please?" asked Judd

"There is no one registered by that name," answered the operator. "Any reservations in his name?"

"Wait a moment...don't see any."

"Would you try paging him in the casino, please?"

After a few moments, "Sorry, no one has picked up."

Both continued with their calls: the Frontier Hotel, the Landmark the Riviera, Golden Nugget and Silver Slipper Hotels. Same response.

Finally: "The Flamingo Hotel, how can I help you?"

"Yes, would you ring Mr. Alan Roberts' room, please?" asked Judd

"He has not checked in yet. Can I leave a message when he does?" answered the operator. "No, and *thank you very much*." Judd hung up the phone and shouted, "*Yes!*" Sevena heard the shout and knew the home team had scored.

Judd had some coffee sent up to their room. "Don't know why you don't like to lighten it with some cream or milk?" Judd asked while handing her a cup of fresh black coffee.

"I guess I don't like to dilute any of my pleasures," she answered suggestively. She lifted the cup for a sip, tilting it at Judd as if to salute. "So now you're the genius, congratulations. What's next?"

"I don't think you should be hanging around the Flamingo and catch him in some public place.

You have some explaining to do and it is best to do it in private. Give me his picture. I will go there and when I spot him going to his room, I'll call you with the room number and you can take a cab over to see him. I'll then hang out in the casino or at one of its bars. As soon as you reengage, page me and I will join you in presenting our proposition."

Judd arrived at the Flamingo at 9 pm and went right to one of the phones in the lobby. He asked the operator to page Alan Roberts and got no response. He tried again in half an hour.

"Let me connect you," said the operator. "Hello, this is Alan."

"Alan Roberts?" Judd asked, wanting to make sure. "Yes, who is this?"

Judd hung up without responding. With his picture in hand, he then began to walk around the casino trying to spot Alan, starting at the blackjack tables. The casino blackjack area was not very big, and he did not have to spend more than 20 minutes to determine that Alan was not there. He started to look in one of the lounges and there he was at the piano bar by himself having a drink. Judd went in and sat at the end of the bar across from Alan and ordered himself a drink. Alan seemed deep in thought and after a half-hour when he finished his second drink, got up and headed toward the reception desk area where the elevators were located. Judd got up and followed him and entered the elevator right after Alan did. When Alan got off on the 10th floor, Judd was right behind and walked past him toward the rooms further down the hall while Alan was reaching for his key to unlock the door to 1006.

"Sevena, it's Room 1006," Judd said, giving her the message from the nearest house phone in the lobby. "Take a cab over. I am going back to the bar where I first spotted him and will wait for your page after you reacquaint yourselves."

———————

"OK, FLAMINGO LOBBY." the cab driver repeated it twice pulling Sevena into the present from the marathon of thoughts leading up to the present.

Alan unlocked the door and called down to room service for some coffee as soon as he entered the room. Twenty-five minutes later, while still dressed and resting on the bed in the dark, he heard a knock on the door.

"Come on in. The door is unlocked," he shouted without getting up. "You can put the coffee on the table next to the TV in the living room. I will take care of you later."

He heard the door open, but the sound of footsteps came all the way through the living room and into his darkened bedroom, causing him to suddenly rise and look up. He saw the silhouette of a woman as sensual as a Gauguin painting coming toward him. It was then he heard her soft-toned voice, "How about taking care of me now?"

CHAPTER 13

ALAN LIFTED HIMSELF to a sitting position on the bed looking in the direction of the voice he had just heard. He recognized who it was as soon as the shapely figure came out of the shadows. It was Sevena, now a few feet in front of him. She continued to stand there without moving for what almost seemed to be a full minute, looking into his wondering-what-was-next eyes. He did not move or speak.

Sevena had rehearsed the words she would first use to re-engage with Alan and explain the search for him and the reasons behind it. They were not the ones she had just spoken. The rehearsed words completely vanished from her consciousness. When she saw him, she was suddenly transfixed by feelings over which she had no control and found herself in uncharted emotional territory.

Though immediately recognizing her, Alan could not speak either. It was all too surreal-her being on his mind since their meeting, wondering when to call and what their next meeting would be like, and suddenly she appears like an apparition in his very hotel bedroom in Las Vegas. All she knew was his first name. How did she get here? What was happening? Was he imagining this? It was Kafkaesque. They were two complete strangers magically transformed from a crowded table at BU to very intimate surroundings in his hotel bedroom, all alone by themselves. Words that served them well in their initial exchange now were without the power of communication. The mystique of the moment would be lost if it fell into questions and heavy explanations to explain the unexplainable.

They both preferred to ride the moment without explanations and give themselves solely to their physical movements and visual expressions as a means of communicating. He was good- looking, and his eyes! "Oh, those seductive eyes," she thought, "they alone could undress me." When they first met, Alan had glanced more than once at her erotic body sculptured into a pair of white shorts and a black cropped top that housed a curvaceous pair of prizes. This time Sevena was wearing a loose olive and oak striped button-down blouse tucked into fitted black pants with a thin red belt around the waistline. She was still standing directly in front of him and he was sitting on the bed facing her.

As they continued to look at each other without a word spoken, Sevena was overtaken with thoughts about being next to him in his bed in that dark room. She had come for another purpose, but she couldn't deny the desire coming over her. She sensed that Alan might have the same thoughts, but she would have to be cautious in testing that impression. So, she very slowly began to fiddle with the top button of her blouse just short of undoing it, while looking at him as if to say, "Shall I?"

She studied his eyes. She thought she had seen that exciting look of anticipation before when she was about to remove her bra in front of a partner with whom she was to have sex for the first time in their relationship. It had given her the feeling of power that a stripper has over paid patrons, knowing she has a body that they are longing to see and that she had total control as to whether or how it would unfold.

Sevena stepped even closer to Alan so her knees were now touching his that were hanging over the side of the bed. She was close enough so Alan could feel her breath and the tightening and intensity of her face that appeared to reveal a growing sexual excitement, though she had not moved to reveal any part of her body. Not knowing what came next excited him even more.

As Sevena unfastened the top button of her blouse, there was a loud knock on the door that she had left slightly open and a man shouting, "Room Service, sorry we're late."

Both thinking, "Not late enough." Almost in harmony, they yelled back from the bedroom, "You can put it on the table next to the TV. We will take care of you later." Hearing their almost similar answers in unison, they both began to smile.

"OK, but be careful, the coffee is steaming hot," said the waiter. "I suggest you let everything cool down." With that, they looked at each other and burst into roaring laughter. The mood was not only broken, but they looked at each other equally perplexed as if they had suddenly come out of a trance, wondering what actually happened.

Alan was the first to speak. He was curious beyond belief. So, he would get right to it but in a non-accusatory, playful way. "I apologize for that very untimely interruption, but no harm done I gather, for you couldn't have gone to all this trouble to find me and travel all this way simply looking for-how shall I put it, *some physical stimulus.*"

"You're right, maybe next time." She continued to flirt while refastening the button on her blouse. "But to explain how and why I came here, we will have to make this a ménage à trois," she said, continuing with her sexual playfulness. "May I use the phone?"

CHAPTER 14

"ANOTHER ONE?" ASKED the bartender.

"No, thanks," replied Judd.

It was now closing in on half an hour since he had called Sevena giving her Alan's room number. He had just finished his second drink, refusing another when asked by the bartender, and was growing a bit impatient wondering how Sevena was making out.

"Hey," Judd called back to the bartender, "maybe I will. This time just some plain seltzer water with a twist of lemon."

Judd was still looking at a very attractive young blonde guy across the bar wearing a white silk, expensive shirt with a large V opening in the front revealing a gold necklace hanging down part of his bare chest. He was having a drink with two show gals before they left to perform. Judd could tell from overhearing their conversation that he was an entertainer of sorts. The guy seemed to glance at Judd from time to time. It is funny, Judd thought, like members of a tribe, we somehow know if someone is one of us, but he had too much on his mind to explore that possibility other than to observe.

Judd thought of being at a similar bar in Washington, DC, two years earlier during the late summer of 1964 when he took a sabbatical leave to work in US Senator Wayne Morse's office. He wanted to help advance both the civil rights legislation President Johnson proposed as well as legislation he wanted to have introduced to grant equal rights for women. The year before, Betty Friedan, a women's rights leader and activist, published her book *The Feminine Mystique*, which was to spark the beginning of the second wave of feminism in the United States. Judd had met her during her book tour in Boston and succeeded in convincing her to have breakfast with him the following morning to continue their discussion. They had talked about the need for legislation. It was then that Judd decided to take his sabbatical the following year and had convinced Senator Morse, a Republican turned liberal Democrat, to allow him to come on the staff with a one-year fellowship that Judd secured to specifically work on the legislation.

"Here's your soda water with a lemon twist," said the bartender interrupting his thoughts.

"Thanks," responded Judd, going back to thinking of those events that were to become a seminal moment in his life.

At that bar in Washington was a New York Times reporter. He told him that he was filing a story that North Vietnamese torpedo boats launched an unprovoked attack against the U.S. destroyer, USS Maddox, on routine patrol in the Tonkin Gulf on August 2, and as it turned out, launched another attack on the Maddox and another US ship two days later.

The night of the second alleged attack, President Johnson appeared on national TV announcing he was ordering retaliatory air strikes against North Vietnam. Because of the unprovoked incidents, Johnson was asking Congress to pass the Gulf of Tonkin Resolution providing him with the legal justification for the commencement of open warfare against North Vietnam.

Judd had his doubts about these politically convenient incidents. For good reason. He had been dating a guy, Mike Bennet, since arriving in Washington who was high up in the CIA. One evening over a few drinks, Mike told Judd that while he could not disclose specific information that was classified, it was well known even beyond the intelligence community that there were US covert operations already going on against North Vietnam. It was called *Operation Plan 34-Alpha.*

Judd liked Mike. He was completely dedicated to his work in protecting the nation, but not blind to governmental wrongdoing when it occurred. Mike was unhappy with the Administration's recent transfer of the Alpha Operation from the CIA to the Defense Department. He was concerned that the Administration was now looking for an excuse to enhance their covert supportive efforts with more direct open attacks.

"They now had their excuse," Judd thought when he heard Johnson's speech.

The next day Judd called Mike, but not to renew the social relationship. He asked Mike if he would meet him outside of the Smithsonian Castle on the National Mall at noon. Mike agreed.

"Hey, Judd," Mike, carrying a newspaper under his arm, hollered as he approached Judd at the Castle steps. "Am I in for a free lecture from my favorite history professor?" Mike asked reaching out to shake Judd's hand.

"Not quite. This time I need *you* to teach me how government operates," Judd responded. "Let me set the stage. I wanted to meet you here because I would think this is the last place your colleagues at the CIA would set up any bugging device to listen to our talks."

"That serious," Mike replied. "Let's walk then. You will be surprised. Our boys have ears everywhere."

They hadn't taken more than ten steps when Judd asked, "Did you hear that Johnson was asking for a declaration of war on North Vietnam by seeking passage of the Gulf of Tonkin Resolution?"

"Of course, and it will pass without a dissenting vote. Every newspaper and TV station is covering this double unprovoked attack on our ships like it is another Pearl Harbor," Mike responded.

"Do you believe that is what happened?" Judd asked.

"Who knows, but I have my suspicions. But ours is not to reason why, ours is but to…"

"Cut the shit," Judd interrupted. "You are in the CIA, not the Light Brigade. You are paid to reason."

"From what I think I am about to hear, I suspect I am not paid enough," Mike sensing his work at the CIA might be related somehow.

"Now you're thinking," Judd replied smiling. "Whatever happened on those two days of the so-called attacks had to be communicated from the ship to someone, who then communicates it up the line. What do you know about the makeup of that chain of command on such an event?"

"I gather that cables from the Maddox would go to the Admiralty, then to the Joint Chiefs, the Secretary of Defense, and maybe the Secretary of State, and one or several of them would brief the President."

"Who are the people who hold those positions?"

"Well, let's see. Roy Lee Johnson is the Navy Admiral who oversees that area. The President appointed General Earle Wheeler as Chairman of the Joint Chiefs of Staff to succeed General Maxwell Taylor just last month. As you know, Robert McNamara is Secretary of Defense and Dean Rusk is Secretary of State."

"And the CIA?" asked Judd. "What about the CIA?"

"Would they be involved?" asked Judd, lining up his next question.

"Not officially."

"What do you mean 'not officially'?"

"We would not be copied on these."

"Come on, Mike, that is half the answer." Judd pressed for the unofficial part.

"Look, what can I say? We have our ways of learning about this stuff. We need to know what is going on if we are to do our job in protecting guys like you."

"So, you think the CIA was able to get copies of these cables or radio messages?"

"Would be surprised if they didn't," Mike responded, directly and proudly.

Judd hesitated. He and Mike had been intimate. They both liked and respected each other, but they never became a couple. He was about to make a request that went way beyond the limits of their relationship. But he felt it was important to do so.

"Mike, do you think…"

"Judd, don't," Mike interrupted, anticipating the question.

Judd knew it was inappropriate. He would be asking Mike to obtain and share highly classified material. He would love to know the content of the exchanges about the alleged attacks on the Maddox, but as he thought of it in a calmer moment, he was asking him to commit an unlawful act. He would not go further.

"Mike, let me repeat. Do you think…it is going to rain tomorrow?" finishing up the last uncompleted question to change the subject.

Mike appreciated that Judd had backed off in such a way that they could honestly say they never discussed the intended request.

"Sorry. Judd, can't help you there. CIA intelligence on the predictions of rain is classified."

JUDD TOOK A cab back to his office. There he learned that the Gulf of Tonkin Resolution was up for a vote in two days. He sat down and wrote a two-sentence memo to his boss, Senator Morse.

"If *we adopt the Resolution, we will be in for an unnecessary, long, very costly war and I fear with an untold number of casualties. I also have my suspicions – but unfortunately no proof – that the two incidents of unprovoked attacks on the Maddox did not actually occur exactly as reported.*"

He ended without a recommendation, knowing that he had offered nothing of substance that would allow him to ask the senator to vote against it. Judd was too distraught to go on to other work and left the building early that day, going directly to the package store a block away on his way to his apartment. He bought an 18-year-old Glenlivet Scotch. When he arrived at his apartment, he turned on the TV. He consumed almost half the bottle, putting himself to sleep while watching the news with interviews of one American after another hysterically calling for a retaliatory military response.

The alarm rang at the time set for each morning. Judd had slept through the entire night but without much rest. Fully shaved and dressed, he left his apartment. When he unlocked the door to his car to drive to the office, a sealed envelope fell from the inside doorknob to the floor. There was nothing written on the envelope. Judd went back into the apartment and opened the envelope. There were three typewritten pages without a name or signature. The first sentence read, "Our prediction is that it will rain today." It was as good as a signature.

Judd proceeded to read the report from a CIA agent.

Agent (Name Redacted) Report on August 4, 1964, 9:00 PM.
We intercepted a cable from Vice Admiral James Stockdale who led aerial attacks on the North Vietnamese boats from the carrier USS Ticonderoga in response to the Gulf of Tonkin Incidents. Stockdale is one of the most highly decorated officers in the history of the U.S. Navy.

Cable: *"Contrary to confusing messages coming from the Maddox, our destroyers were just shooting at phantom targets—there were no North Vietnamese PT boats in the area. There was nothing there but black water and American firepower. There were no provoked attacks by the North Vietnamese." —Stockdale.*

Forty minutes later there was a response cable to Stockdale from Admiral Roy Lee Johnson. Cable: *"You are ordered not to discuss the details of that night to anyone." —Roy Johnson*

It appears that Admiral Johnson ordered US bombers to 'retaliate' for a North Vietnamese torpedo attack that never happened and they are silencing Stockdale by disregarding his observations that our ships were not fired upon. I will continue to monitor. **This communication is classified and may be reviewed by Top Secret Clearance only."**

Judd went on to read the report from a second CIA agent made later the same evening.

Agent (Name Redacted) Report on August 4, 1964, at 11 pm.

"We intercepted cables sent from Captain John J. Herrick, the US Task Force Commander in the Tonkin Gulf, He referred to 'freak weather effects' mistaken for enemy fire:

'It was almost total darkness and an overeager sonar-man was hearing the ship's own propeller beat mistaken for the firing of torpedoes from North Vietnamese PT Boats.'

We also learned that the Maddox was not on routine maneuvers, but rather engaged in aggressive intelligence-gathering maneuvers to help attacks on North Vietnam by the South Vietnamese navy and the Laotian air force. This is consistent with our knowledge of the Administration's plans for gradually increasing its overt military pressure against the North. **This communication is classified and may be reviewed by Top Secret Clearance only."**

A last sentence was added below the two CIA reports, written in a short rhyme:

"Judd, you can show it, but you cannot publicly quote or reveal you know it."

Judd understood what Mike meant. He could use it to advise the senator on his vote on the Resolution, but neither he nor the senator could reveal that they knew its contents. Even if Judd were inclined to disobey the directive, which he would never do, there would be no way to show it came from a creditable source, since Mike would deny that it came from the CIA and the validity of its contents. The senator would have to find an independent means to obtain the information if he wished to make its contents public someday.

Judd gasped at what he had in his hand. He immediately resealed the envelope and headed back out the door toward the office. He interrupted his brisk walk to stop only for a moment at a newsstand to read the headlines and a column or two of several newspapers. The *Los Angeles Times* editorial was indicative of an unquestioning media that took what they were fed by the Administration: *"Americans must face the fact that the Communists, by their unprovoked attack on American vessels in international waters, have themselves escalated the hostilities."*

Judd was frustrated. America was about to go to war and engage in heavy combat based on false information. He had just been handed a smoking gun to stop it, but his hands were tied. He stepped up his brisk walk to a run, bursting into the senatorial outer office.

"Is the senator busy?" Judd asked out of breath, heading for Morse's office without waiting for a reply.

"Looks like he will be," Gladys, the senator's secretary answered, seeing Judd already entering the senator's inner office.

"Hi, Judd," the senator greeted him with a surprised voice. "I'd invite you in except you're already here."

"Sorry, sir, but what I have to tell you can't wait. One question, though. Any chance your office is bugged?"

"You're apparently as paranoid as I am. We're OK. I have the office swept clean periodically.

Your stuff that good?"

"That bad to be more accurate, sir." Except for the source, Judd shared all the information with the senator. The senator reread the three-page document several times.

"Incredible, fucking incredible, but without my being able to prove it is from a creditable source, I can't do anything with it."

"I know, sir, but at least it can serve the purpose of saving you from joining your colleagues in voting for a totally fabricated reason to go to war."

"Yes, but it more likely will serve the purpose of my *not* joining my colleagues in getting reelected. By standing up against the Resolution with the hysteria calling for its quick and unanimous passage, I could well end up being the only senator to vote against it and bye-bye reelection. Can you possibly get your source to come out of the closet?"

"Out of the closet?" Judd allowed his thoughts to divert for a moment, thinking of how well Mike had protected his being gay. "No, sir, not a chance. He would lose everything. Besides, he feels his job at the CIA is like a photographer monitoring and recording the activity of animals in the wild. When one animal is about to strike and kill a defenseless young prey, he may want to save the little creature, but his job is not to interfere, only capture the event and record it."

The analogy did not resonate with the senator; he had a better one. "Thanks, Judd, you just handed me a grenade and I will be walking around holding it with the pin down unable to release it."

CHAPTER 15

THE SENATE CHAMBERS were packed. There was no need for the Senate President to call for a quorum and gather up the senators from their various committee meetings or from a local bar having an afternoon drink, as was the usual case. Everyone was there and the international media had gathered in full force having waited for hours.

At last, the Senate President banged his gavel. "Debate being concluded, the question now comes on Joint Resolution 384 PUBLIC LAW 88-408. The clerk will now read the Joint Resolution and call the Roll."

JOINT RESOLUTION 384 PUBLIC LAW 88-408:

Whereas naval units of the Communist regime in Vietnam, in violation of the principles of the Charter of the United Nations and of international law, have deliberately and repeatedly attacked United States naval vessels lawfully present in international waters, and have thereby created a serious threat to international peace....

Now therefore, be it resolved by the Senate and House of Representatives of the United States of America in Congress assembled that the Congress approves and supports the determination of the President, as Commander in Chief, to take all necessary measures (including the use of armed force) to repel any armed attack against the forces of the United States and to prevent further aggression.

THE ROLL CALL of the House was taken and passed 416 in favor — 0 against. The roll call of the Senate was taken 88 in favor — 2 against. A formal declaration of war had been enacted by Congress for the use of US military force in Southeast Asia. The *Vietnam War* had formally begun! Two senators, Wayne Morse of Oregon and Ernest Gruening of Alaska, were the only ones of the 506 Congressional votes cast to vote "no." Theirs were courageous votes that were to cost them both their reelections.

Senator Morse had argued vehemently against the Resolution's passage during the Senate debate without success and strongly suggested, but without any supportive facts, that the provocation may not have been as reported. When it was passed, he stated, "I believe that within the next century, future generations will look with dismay and great disappointment upon a Congress which is now about to make such a historic mistake." He would prove to be a prophet, but soon no longer a US senator.

Judd would complete the obligations of the fellowship working on the civil rights and women's equal rights legislation, but his heart was no longer in it. He was furious at the lies and the consequences that would ensue from such deceit. A new, more passionate cause had taken over his entire being. He was determined to dedicate every bit of energy to bring an end to what he knew to be a completely fraudulent and unnecessary war with predictably devastating results.

———————————

NOT HALFWAY THROUGH his seltzer and lemon soft drink, Judd's ruminating thoughts of his Washington experience were interrupted by a page calling him to pick up a casino phone.

"Sevena?"

CHAPTER 16

JUDD RUSHED FROM the elevator to get to Rm. 1006, but then suddenly hesitated to catch his breath. Like a baseball player going through a ritual of straightening his cap and adjusting his batting gloves to get ready for the next pitch, Judd tightened the knot on his tie, ran his hands through his hair and thought, "Well, here goes," and knocked with three hard raps on the door.

"Come on in," a loud male voice responded.

Alan was pouring coffee into a cup that Sevena was holding.

"Care for some coffee…" Alan looked at Judd waiting for him to complete the sentence. "It's Judd-Judd Lampert. Yes, thanks."

All three sipped their coffees for an awkward moment, when Alan put his cup down and looked at them both, as if to say, "So?"

Judd spoke first. "Alan, I am sure you are wondering why we are here," clearly an understatement, but a beginning.

"Yes, but more than wondering *why* you are here, I am utterly mystified *how* you are here, how you found out where 'here' even *is*, when I, myself, didn't know I would be *here* until I reserved this room just yesterday."

"I certainly can see why you are startled," Judd responded.

"No, not startled, only mystified. Startled, is how I felt earlier when suddenly someone I just met in Boston and with whom I exchanged but a few words-and who only knew my first name –appears like a ghost out of thin air in my very bedroom in Las Vegas at the Flamingo Casino Hotel."

"I am sure nothing could be more puzzling," Judd replied, trying to be empathetic.

"You would think so, but welcome to my world lately. Besides this, I just learned that I have become a center of attention not just to both of you, but to a detective agency who did a thorough investigation of me - and to some others who were so desperate to find out more about me, they committed a crime of breaking and entering to steal that agency's report. Perhaps you can understand why I am not just startled and mystified, but totally freaked out."

"I can only begin to imagine." Judd looked at Sevena to continue and she immediately did.

"Well, Alan, with all that occurred, you probably wish you had chosen to sit at a different table the morning we met," Sevena said, searching for some remark to confirm their ongoing mutual attraction, and somewhat got it.

"You may still be worth it, but, that depends on what I hear. Besides, I had little choice since all the other tables were full," Alan responded with a smile that brought out the dimple in his right cheek that reminded Sevena of his law school picture.

"Well, Alan, here goes…" Sevena began from the very beginning to explain step by step how she was able to go through the student enrollment of persons with their first name being Alan, her deductive reasoning to locate his picture, the detailed way they gained entrance to the Law School Dean's Office and their pilfering of the Investigator's Report. She also explained how she went to his apartment, talking to his neighbor and tracing his whereabouts in Vegas.

Alan listened incredulously and simultaneously in admiration of the methodical and risky undertaking just to locate him. "So, you both were willing to go to all this trouble to get my school records and *you* are the ones who stole the Investigative Report. *Wow*, I am impressed and perhaps a bit flattered, but just as puzzled as to why all this just to talk to me."

It was Judd's turn. He reached down to the floor to retrieve one of the two large envelopes he had brought in the room. "Let's start with this. I have the original and a copy we made of the Investigators Report. Here is the original. It's extensive. For all the trouble we caused you, at least you can now know what's in that report. We would like you to read it carefully and then let's meet tomorrow for breakfast, away from casino ears, and we will reveal why all this fuss in finding you. Important you read the report first before our discussion. I will call you in the morning with the time and the restaurant."

As the Investigator's Report was being handed to him, Alan said, "I'd rather have the copy if you don't mind."

"Sure, here it is," Judd substituting his copy for the original. "But, why a copy? It's about you. I thought you might like to have the original."

"Well, I will be here a couple of days playing blackjack, and better if you safeguard it," Alan explained. That was not the real reason. Alan was thinking about his criminal law course. The original Investigator's Report was stolen property. Anyone who receives and keeps it knowing it was stolen is committing the crime of "Receiving Stolen Property," which in Massachusetts carries a maximum penalty of 2½ years in the House of Correction. Receiving a copy would not be a crime.

As Judd and Sevena said their polite goodbyes and walked toward the door, Alan uttered, "Sevena, just wanted to let you know I was going to give you a call after my Vegas adventure."

"So, you still have my note then?" she asked. "No."

"'No?"

"Don't need it…617-544-2211."

CHAPTER 17

"EVELYN, CALL BAXTER University and get President Wilson on the line for me," he shouted so she could hear him through the door.

"Hi, this is Evelyn Anderson calling for Dean Lauder. Is President Wilson available?"

"One moment please, I will get him on the line."

"Dean, how are you? I was intending to call you. The second of the 5-year mega donations to our university came through. Much obliged."

"Part of the reason for my call, I wanted to make sure it did," the Dean said, though it was not at all the reason for the call. "I hope the donations will help."

"I'll say. They will certainly help get our new science building equipped."

"Good to hear. Listen, I was wondering if as Chairman of the P-7 Project, you could schedule a confidential luncheon meeting of the members in Boston the week after next at a day convenient to all of you."

"Glad to. I will get right on it."

"Thanks. As soon as I hear back from you, I'll make reservations for a private dining room at the Harvard Club right down the street from my school."

Everything was coming into place, but the Dean was worried about his own president at BU, one of the P-7 Project members. He felt some of his liberal statements lately suggested he could become a problem.

"Evelyn, get me Walter at my old firm."

"Dean?"

"Walter, I have arranged to have my P-7 Project meeting in 2 weeks. Can we get Milton out of the picture by then?" The Dean was referring to Milton Swartz, the BU president who by nature of his position was selected to be a member of the P-7 Project. "He could be a wild card at my next meeting. I am not sure I can count on him as things heat up".

"It's under control," responded Walter. "Our Washington people put the pressure on and informed me that the Administration had vetted our distinguished BU president and he will be appointed Assistant Secretary of Labor any day now. Your Board of Trustees has been informed of his impending appointment and the votes are there to appoint you as his replacement the very day after. So, he will soon be out of the way, congratulations, Mr. President! And as President, congratulations on replacing him as a P-7 member."

The Dean hung up the phone clutching both his hands behind his head while leaning back in his expensive swivel chair, taking a deep satisfying breath and thinking: "President of one of the major universities in the country, still a senior partner in one of the most distinguished international law firms and a lot of political power to go with it. Not bad for a guy who clawed his way up the ladder."

But, "hook and by crook" would have been a more accurate description of his climb to the top than "clawing his way up." Bill Lauder came from a privileged environment. His father made his money (as the Dean would put it) by "steeling" it. Henry Lauder, who mentored and aided his son all along the way, worked his way up from the purchasing agent to the CEO of a major steel company in Gary, Indiana, acquiring a substantial interest in it. He was to earn his reputation as a staunch fighter against the formation of steel employee unions and was to instill in his son his passionate feelings that employee strikes and public protests were communist-inspired acts of disobedience contrived to undo the free enterprise system that so justly rewarded him for his well-earned success.

The Dean attended a grade school in Gary. He then attended and graduated from Park School, an exclusive private boarding school in Indianapolis. Over some drinks, the Dean would boast at law school dinners that he had been a star quarterback and captain of the Park School football team, but with others on different occasions, that he was a tight end who caught a Hail-Mary pass to win the regional championship game. In fact, he did try out for the team but didn't make it.

Instead, he finessed himself into being its student manager. He did co-edit the school newspaper.

Although the Dean probably would have made it on his own, it was never in doubt that he would be admitted to Notre Dame and Notre Dame Law School, where his dad served on the Board of Trustees. The Dean was to graduate both college and law school with respectable but not outstanding academic achievements, though he was popular with his classmates. He had been elected Vice President of the Student Council while an undergraduate student. Not long after the election, he moved up to President of the Council when the elected President suddenly resigned for personal reasons. Rumors began to float around as to his resignation when this 21-year-old kid, working his way through college, was now seen driving a brand new, open-top Bentley sports car around campus.

After passing the Indiana Bar, the Dean was "fortunate" to obtain one of the Assistant AG's positions in the newly elected Attorney General's Office. Bill's father had made substantial donations to both candidates for that office. After one year mainly handling real estate matters, the Dean left the AG's office to enter private law practice as an Associate Counsel at the Indianapolis office of the prestigious law firm of Latham, Hogan & McLeish. It just so happened that the law firm handled the legal work of Henry Lauder's steel company and the lobbying for the Regional Steel Owners Industry's Consortium of which Henry Lauder was its prominent President.

Bill Lauder was a welcome addition to the firm. "Hope this office is to your liking, Bill," Abel Peabody, the firm's managing partner, welcomed the Dean on his first day. Of course, no other new associate received such a hospitable greeting and shown such a large office on the high floors of the building with a striking view of the city. With that, every other Associate knew what the pecking order among them was to be, and the Dean was not shy in exploiting that inherited role. Regardless of their differing stature in the firm, Abel and the Dean were to bond over the years as if equals and the two shared many luncheons and dinners at Henry Lauder's private club, joined by Henry himself on many occasions. Their families became close. The Dean had married his high school sweetheart, Alice Boswell, within a year of taking the job at the firm and they had a boy and a girl just one year apart.

During the 10 years that followed, the Dean received various expected promotions. In a shorter time than most, he made Partner and then Equity Partner. As an Equity Partner, he gained ownership interest in the firm and shared in its annual profits. He spent most of his early years heading a division that specialized in helping companies defend against the formation of employee unions. However, with the breakout of World War 2 and his dad's influence, he took on a new role of traveling back and forth to Washington, lobbying for favorable munitions contracts for steel companies that the firm represented.

On February 5, 1943, the Dean received a call from Abel's secretary to come to his office on the double. February 5th was the Dean's birthday, one reason he'd remember the day that brought major changes to his life.

"Bill, you are going to have to sit down for this one," Abel greeted his entrance as soon as the door opened. "I just got an offer to transfer to the Boston Corporate Office. Would you believe it? They want *me*, to take over the Managing Partner's position there."

Many expected Abel to be promoted to manage one of the firm's major offices. He had earned a reputation of having turned a failing operation at the Indiana office into a very profitable one. Courting the steel industry and the Dean's father was no small reason for the turnaround Nevertheless, this offer came as a huge surprise – it was an offer to manage *the* corporate office central to the firm's entire worldwide operations.

"Wow, unbelievable. What an opportunity. Congratulations! Out of the blue comes Nirvana," the Dean said, expressing shock. "What happened to Jenkins in Boston? Did he resign as Managing Partner for some reason?"

"Roosevelt is appointing him to the opening on the Circuit Court. Bill, I know Alice just went back to her teaching job at the high school and you just enrolled the kids in private elementary schools, but how would you like to come to Boston with me?"

The Dean was heading to be a very big fish in this small Indiana pond, and with Abel's departure, still a bigger fish. But was there suddenly an opportunity to swim with the sharks in a bigger pond? he wondered. The Boston Corporate Office of the worldwide law firm of Latham, Hogan & McLeish: this was not just a very big pond, this was the five great oceans combined into one.

Bill was not shy in telling Abel what would make him happy: a lateral transfer into the Boston Office as a Senior Equity Partner with all its added bonuses, a substantial salary increase, continuing to receive bonuses for revenue generated by his clients in Indiana, full moving expenses, including the firm's immediate purchase of his Indiana home at its replacement value so he could buy a new one in Boston and some other substantial perks. The Dean was sitting in the first-class seat next to Abel on their way to Boston the following week.

Now, still sitting back in his first-class swivel chair, the Dean thought about the wise choice he had made back then and the years that followed at the firm. He would continue to specialize in representing the steel companies and an expanded number of arms and munitions companies.

With World War 2 still going on at that time, and the significant military build-up that followed to arm America and its allies in both the Korean and Vietnam wars (including the cold war with Russia), the Dean knew where the money was. The money was with the suppliers of those military weapons: guns, machine guns, planes, helicopters, tanks, trucks, clothing, specially packaged food and a host of other supplies to aid the pilots, sailors and the troops fighting to protect democracy.

The armaments industry was where a fortune could be made and Lauder, and the lobbyists he hired, led the firm in exploiting that opportunity. The growing unchecked economic and political influence of these suppliers of war so concerned President and former General Dwight Eisenhower that upon leaving office, he warned America about the danger posed by this "Military Industrial Complex", whose fiscal livelihood relied on the waging of war.

No one understood this better than the Dean. He knew, like Dracula, this munitions industry would always be nourished and re-nourished by the blood spilled on the battlefield to protect democracy and would pay handsomely for effective lobbying efforts to gain lucrative contracts. Yes, that was where the money was, "and it would never dry up," thought the Dean, remembering Plato's quote about the inevitability of conflict: "Only the dead have seen the end of war."

The Dean was to spend his next 19 years building a lobbying group within the firm consisting of former congressmen, executive cabinet officers, generals and admirals who helped the firm gain a virtual monopoly in representing the major companies that made up the Military-Industrial Complex.

At the end of a very late night of too many drinks, the Dean was once asked by Abel whether he felt any moral compunctions about the firm getting super-rich representing the industry that benefited from wars and the blood spilled on account of them. The Dean answered, without any hesitation or any apparent feeling of the slightest remorse, "I think it was Einstein who was asked in an interview after World War 2, 'Given modern technology in the advancement of lethal weapons, what weapons do you think would be used in a Third World War?' Einstein said, 'I don't know but, I can tell you what they will use in the Fourth-sticks and rocks.' Let's face it, Abel, we both know that if that happened, you and I would be the first ones out there hustling to represent the companies manufacturing the sticks and rocks." Abel was never to broach that subject again.

CHAPTER 18

JUDD HAD FOUND a convenient restaurant that would give them some privacy a short block from the Sands Hotel and chosen an isolated booth. He ordered a pot of coffee, reached within his briefcase for some papers and began to re-read the copies of the CIA cables he received from Mike that he intended to share with Alan. It regenerated some of the anger he felt when he had first viewed them.

Sevena came through the door and headed to the corner booth sitting on Judd's side. Alan arrived by cab shortly after, and they all exchanged their "good mornings."

The waitress came over to hand each of them a menu. Judd suggested the eggs benedict, but Alan waved off his menu and the suggestion, ordering an egg white omelet with an English muffin. The other two nodded for the same with minor exceptions, echoing that they, too, felt anxious to get on with their meeting.

Judd began without delay. "Alan, did you have a chance to look over the Investigator's Report?"

"Read it all twice as a matter of fact. It was like reading a novel about yourself. I went through it a second time very carefully trying to find clues about what this investigation was all about. I can't believe that they were able to get at all my records since being a kid, even those of my family, seduce my teachers, coaches even my closest friends to talk about me so freely and extensively and then go so far as to violate my privacy by apparently breaking into my apartment. As infuriating as that is, what troubles me more is *why*? Why such detailed scrutiny about me? Why would they go to all that trouble, even break the law, to get my life's history?"

"Something is going on with your Dean that must be pretty big," noted Judd. "They spent a lot of money to get this information. Whoever they are attempting to recruit and for whatever reasons, they are not looking to conscript run-of-the-mill type people. They are going after the crème de la crème. You probably noted from the report, they ranked you as first among the very best. But what turned them off were your views and political activities. It does tell you that whatever they are up to, it is totally inconsistent with your values."

"And what about my not qualifying for the P-7 project? What the hell was that about?"

"I think the words were that they would not 'recruit you' and that you would actually 'pose a danger' to the P-7 Project," Judd added. "I took note of those words for they are the key to what puzzles you and puzzles us."

"Puzzles you, too? You say you both **know nothing** more about this than what's in the report? You must know something more. You broke into the Dean's office to steal it?" Alan sounded surprised and disappointed, but still hoped to get some explanation.

"Yes, I am afraid to say that's right," Judd answered, sounding apologetic. "That is all we know. We have no independent information as to why they investigated you in the first place or what this P-7 project is all about. The report came to our attention by total accident."

"Who was it that wanted the omelet with the regular cheese?" interrupted the waitress carrying two trays.

"That's me," answered Sevena. "And you can put the other one with the orange juice there," pointing to Judd.

Alan, clearly disappointed that they knew nothing that would explain why he was being investigated, did not respond to Judd immediately. Instead, he reached for the jam and took his time spreading it on his English muffin, so he could calmly express his disappointment.

"Well, I am sure you must have figured that I would be concerned about why I seem to be the center of everyone's attention – including yours. Coming here to meet you, I will admit I was hoping-expecting-that you could clear up some of the mysteries."

"Look, Alan," it was time for Sevena to join in. "We're sorry we don't have the answers you're seeking. But the fact is that we are here for a different reason unrelated to the report, except by stumbling on to it, we got the benefit of learning a lot about you. We know it is a worrisome document. That is why we wanted to deliver it to you in person as fast as we could. But, to be clear, that investigation, the report and the Dean's project, whatever that is all about, is not why we went to all this trouble to vet you and fly down here to talk to you."

"OK, then, why this Odyssey in tracking me down across the country?"

Judd was back on stage. "For our own purposes, we too have been looking at the crème de la crème for over a year now. Having the benefit of the report, our own investigation and Sevena's mostly infallible intuition, we also agree with the report's s assessment of your leadership attributes. One difference, however. The Dean's project would not recruit you because of your views, but it is precisely because of your views and activities that we have gone to all this trouble to try-Judd intentionally paused for a moment-to recruit you."

"Recruit me? Recruit me… for what?" Alan, slightly raising his voice, expressed his anxiety over yet another secretive plot about to unfold that he was not in the mood to entertain. "Look, try to understand. Just about two weeks ago, I made the difficult decision to quit law school. I did so to untangle myself from every commitment and unburden myself of all daily pressures. Like a kind of Thoreau move, I wanted to travel light and feel completely free to explore the happenings of the world around me spontaneously. The very uncertainty of it excited me. Well, as a poet put it 'the best-laid plans of mice and men often go astray.'"

Alan paused for a moment and then continued. "So, what's happened to my plans to go under the radar screen and clothe myself in anonymity? In less than two weeks, the Dean's secretary informs me that I was being investigated by the Dean without an explanation as to why. She also tells me another party broke into their office and stole the Investigator's Report and no one knows why. So now I learn that there are two separate parties interested in me for whatever unholy reasons. Then I get paged while in my Vegas hotel-casino when no one could possibly know I was there, and the party hangs up when I answer the phone and identify myself. Then I thought someone followed me to my room but wasn't sure and dismissed it as paranoia given all that was happening, only now to learn that it was you (looking at Judd) that was following me.

And if that isn't enough intrigue, you (looking at Sevena), a person I met but for moments and knew only by first name-and who knew nothing about me except *my* first name-suddenly appears out of nowhere one night inside my bedroom at my Vegas hotel. By the way, that is the one thing I am not complaining about," Alan said with a smile.

"Citro," Sevena interrupted.

"What?" responded Alan.

"Citro, now you know my last name."

"Italian, I would not have guessed. Then, Ms. Citro and you, Judd, supply me with a copy of the Investigator's Report that lays bare every part of my life to you, the Dean and who knows how many other people. And now the scary part. Look at this section of the report that I marked.

"Given his street sense and exceptional intelligence, although unlikely, he could figure out that he was investigated and that could also pose a danger to the project. We, therefore, recommend that his activities be monitored from time to time throughout the length of the project."

"They, whoever they are, could be following me right now, and who knows what they are capable of doing, believing that I may pose a danger to whatever they are planning to do, of which I do not have a freaking clue. Lastly, with all due respect, I am now about to be recruited by you to take on something that I assume may be as clandestine and dangerous as the P-7 Project-*and* my joining you would be of no help in my finding out if I am some sort of target of the Dean or his P-7 mysterious people. Kafka would feel he went overboard to dare write such a script. I don't mean to be sarcastic, but with all this, you must have guessed by now what my answer would be in getting involved in a Walter Mitty adventure."

Alan then paused, looking at Sevena and pointing to the ketchup. "Would you please reach next to you and pass me the ketchup." Alan's deliberate request was intended to end the discussion entirely. "Wait, never mind, I can reach it myself."

"Alan, it's OK. I'll get it," Sevena grasped his hand very gently before it got to the ketchup bottle. She then picked up the bottle and turned it upside down to flow better and handed it to him. "Here, sometimes things that seem upside down turn out to be the way to go." There was something about the gentle physical touch and her deference to his request that was to soften the tone of the ensuing discussion.

"Alan," Sevena continued in a level voice, "I understand your frustration and, of course, why you are so mystified. Indeed, this whole thing is surreal. These past few days you have been living a mystery within a riddle with many more questions than answers. I know the Report must both infuriate and concern you. And, as you say, you know little about us, not even my last name until now. And you are right, despite all the unsettling things happening to you, of which we are of little help in explaining, here we are, strangers coming out of nowhere chasing you down to ask you to consider some shadowy thing that you must sense is no minor undertaking."

Her empathetic summary resonated with Alan enough to earn his continued attention.

"Look, I am going to try to clear up some of the still unanswered questions about Judd and me and why we are here. However, I am going to need to take you into my world of intuition and ask you to rely on some of yours in determining whether to trust us, even without our resumes."

"Fair enough," Alan's answer was intentionally short. He was intrigued and wanted to hear more.

"You and I had a cup of coffee and a very brief discussion when we met at the Commons. It lasted how long, less than 15 minutes with no more than half a dozen exchanges? Here is where it gets somewhat mystical. From that short magical encounter–at least for me- and without a ton of knowledge I would ordinarily need to confirm it, somehow I knew right then and there that you were the person that Judd and I had been searching for without success for over a year, that you had the skills we needed for our vital undertaking when we were beginning to believe we would never find such a person. With the Investigators Report, we now know we have found the person we were looking for. So, whether we continue talking now depends on what your intuition told you about me during our encounter."

She had touched Alan, not so much by the flattering remarks, but because he could relate to that magic moment since he intuitively had had a similar feeling about her extraordinary qualities. But he had a question of a more personal nature. "So as long as we are being completely open, was the only reason you left me your phone number so you could explore recruiting me?"

Sevena hesitated and then answered, "I think that question should be for another time."

Alan did not press the point further. "Well, we are here and it would be a shame to end the discussion letting our untouched food go to waste, particularly given the difficulty and the distance you traveled just to find me. So, without raising your expectations even a twitter, let's hear about the 'just cause' you want to recruit me for."

That was Judd's cue. He handed Alan the CIA cables and asked him to read them. Alan read and studied them carefully and understood their indictment. "Where did you get these?"

"As you will note from those documents, I can't tell you," Judd answered.

"How creditable are they?"

"On a scale of 1-10, 10 being extremely creditable, it's a 15."

Without revealing the source, Judd explained the reason that he could do nothing with the cables except help Senator Morse do the right thing, and as they would soon find out, lose his upcoming election because of it.

Judd, with the ease and manner of a seasoned professor, continued to explain the facts in a clear didactic manner. "Alan, as you may know, the Vietnam war has both broadened and intensified since the Gulf of Tonkin Resolution was enacted on falsified grounds. It has gotten much worse than what I even feared. In a little over a year since I left Washington, the 100,000 US combat troops then on the ground in Vietnam have increased to 200,000 and now we hear are going to double again to 400,000. Over six thousand Americans have been killed since then and the number is growing at an alarming rate, not counting the untold North Vietnam civilian deaths."

"I am aware of some of it from news reports, but didn't know it was getting that bad." Alan reacted.

"No reason why you should," Judd responded. "The truth is that the war is spreading to Cambodia as well. There are rumors that millions of gallons of a chemical herbicide, called Agent Orange, are being used as a chemical weapon by spraying parts of Vietnam, Cambodia and even eastern Laos to defoliate rural/forested land, to deprive the Vietcong of food and cover. If these rumors prove to be true, who knows the long-term effects of these chemicals not just on Vietnam innocent civilians, but on our own troops who have no idea that they are being subjected to such toxic chemicals."

"I read somewhere in the press that Johnson was looking to negotiate some kind of peaceful settlement," Alan stated as if asking a question.

"True, but don't hold your breath," responded Judd. "With these escalating military actions on all sides, there is little hope of a cease-fire and a diplomatic solution anytime soon." Judd stopped and leaned toward Alan. In almost a whisper, indicating the seriousness of what he was about to say and not wanting to be overheard., he added, "Alan, as this goes on, and right now I see nothing but an escalation, we could be talking about deaths to our soldiers, *not* in the thousands, but the tens of thousands, and casualties in the hundreds of thousands, and you can double that death toll and the number of casualties for North and South Vietnamese soldiers and their civilian populations."

Sevena delivered the request: "Our 'just cause,' Alan, as you put it, is to help bring this unjust war to an end, to prevent this unholy and unnecessary devastation based on a fraudulent narrative, and we are here simply to ask you to join us in doing so."

"Judd, what do you do for a living?" Alan asked, impressed with his knowledge and idealism.

"He is Professor of Modern History at your alma mater," said Sevena, beating Judd's reply.

Alan hesitated for a moment and then connected the dots. "Judd… Judd Lampert," he exclaimed. "It gets more surreal with each minute. I wanted to attend your class as an undergraduate, but the wait list was too long."

Sevena was heartened, hoping that remark meant they had gained some creditability that could help win Alan over.

"Professor, having read these CIA reports, I am, as anybody would be, infuriated as to how this war started. However, as an historian, you know more than anyone, it won't be the first time, nor I am afraid the last time, that the government lied to go to war or promote its interests. But, I am not sure what you, Sevena, and I could possibly do about it. You can't really believe that you have a viable plan that the three of us sitting here can implement to bring this war to an end?"

"Yes, I believe we have a plan that can possibly help shorten the war, certainly a better chance than if we don't act and do nothing."

Judd began to lay out the underpinning of the plan with still more passion and in the kind of didactic lecture that made his courses so popular. "I am sure you have seen some scattered, locally unorganized student protests spring up at a couple of universities. There are even some protest folk songs that are taking hold. It is clear to me that the students and the country's youth, many worried about being enlisted into the war, have an appetite to make their voices heard in protest. Perhaps it is somewhat conditioned by the civil rights movement, but I believe it is more than that. I can tell you with some scholarship in modern history, there is something unique about this 60s decade. Among the youth, there is an emerging and growing anti-establishment counter-culture. They are not bound by traditional values; they desire a freer lifestyle that I think is more idealistic. They are prone to rally for causes they believe in. Their very music, the Beatles, Dylan, and I believe more songs to come that are revolutionary and provocative. If mobilized and organized and given a belief in the justice of a cause, and with the right training and tools to register their protest, I believe they have the youthful energy, spirit and endurance to take on something as big as ending a war."

"Be candid with me. You really believe that teenagers and college students walking around with peace symbols and often high on pot, can be organized to mount a resistance powerful enough to stop this war?"

"Maybe not, but if it can be done, I profoundly believe they are the only ones that can awaken America and arouse a national protest big enough to do it. Peace is going to have to be won by a non-violent concerted effort by students raising political hell on campuses, at governmental buildings, and on the streets and not by politicians in the sanctity of the congressional chambers. But it will need a charismatic leader to take charge-and frankly, Sevena and I believe that's *you*."

Alan noticeably swallowed hard the bite-sized piece of English muffin he was chewing when he heard the words "and frankly Sevena and I believe that's *you*." The unintended gesture did not escape Judd and Sevena.

"You may want to sip some coffee to help digest *it*."

Alan recovered quickly. "Look, I am deeply flattered, but frankly you have a perverted sense of my capabilities and I think of the enormity of the task. Your plan is to mobilize students from campuses across the country to be political soldiers to be led by me in a battle to stop the war . You need to be kidding, Professor... Judd. Unless you have access to the US Mint to print unlimited money day and night, and by the way, they do, how in the world are the two of you going to finance this? And how in the world and with what credentials would I be able to organize an entire country of students and gain their trust of leadership?"

"I am not saying it will be easy," responded Judd. "You are probably right. The makeup of students and student organizations in existence are probably too diverse and independent to accept God himself as a single leader over them. Even if we could recruit *him*, the atheistic organizations would of course question *his* credentials as well." The remark brought a slight smile from Alan.

Judd did not leave it there. "But to quote John Kennedy when he explained why he was taking on a seemingly impossible task, 'We choose to go to the Moon in this decade and do other things, not because it is easy, because it is hard.'"

Judd then bent down and pulled out a thick notebook. "Not for now, but please take this back to your hotel with you. It contains our detailed plan to mobilize the students. It also has both Sevena's and my Curriculum Vitae."

Sevena lifted the coffeepot to freshen both Alan's and her own as she took on the task of bringing the discussion to a head. "Alan, along with the Investigators Report and its emotional content that you reviewed last night, you have had to process an enormous amount of other heavy-duty stuff that we hit you with this morning. So now you know what we are committed to do, the righteousness of our cause as we see it, and our intent to motivate students across the country to accomplish our ends. I want you to know that we have doubts, too. Even with our strong commitment and our well-thought-out plan, we know it will be far from a walk in the park and there is no guarantee of success. I want to be clear. If you were to decide to take the leadership role as we envision it, you will have to dedicate the next year of your life, maybe two or more, solely and totally to this endeavor, and it still may not work. We owe you that honesty. So, take a few days to review our plan and think it all over. That's all we can ask."

"Thanks for being candid. Given all you went through to deliver this to me, I will review the plan. At least, I owe you that, but please don't get your hopes up, OK?"

"My intuition, it tells me otherwise," Sevena said, injecting a note of optimism. "I get the feeling you quit law school, not as you say to free yourself up from *everything*, but rather to free yourself up for *something* – something more important than completing law school – something that would put you smack in the middle of the happenings of this unique, exciting decade of change and counter-revolutions."

Alan picked up the notebook that Judd gave him. "Well, *precedence* for me also means keeping myself safe and alive. I need to find out what this P-7 Project is all about and whether those involved pose a danger to me. Right now, I find myself peeking out that window behind you from time to time to see if someone is following me…other than you Judd." Judd smiled and Alan continued. "Here is the deal. I will review your plan and over the

next few days, I will think over everything that has been said, and by chance
– and I mean by the remote chance – if I were to decide to do it, it must be
reciprocal. You two must commit to helping me untangle this P-7 thing and
have my back regarding it at all times."

Judd was encouraged. "It's a deal, where do I sign?"

"On your Diner's Club credit card slip to pick up this check will do."
They all laughed.

Judd was no sooner off to the cashier, when Alan, took advantage of
the opportunity. "I am truly flattered to find out you got such positive vibes
from our limited exchange at the BU."

Sevena, as usual, got in the last words. "I don't think 'flattered' is the
right word to use. 'Flattered' might have been proper if it were my libido
and not my intuition about recruiting you that stirred those vibes. And, by
the way, I would not tell anyone about your illusion that seductive women
drop into your bedroom out of nowhere at night, or they will lock you up.
Good luck at the blackjack tables."

CHAPTER 19

THE HARVARD CLUB is one of the oldest and most prestigious private clubs in Boston. It was founded by a group of Harvard alumni in 1908. Like all private clubs, its access is restricted to its members and their guests. Members are faculty, alumni and students of Harvard University, or members of other private clubs given reciprocal visiting privileges. Many famous people have spoken at the Club at planned events, such as Eleanor Roosevelt, the poet, Robert Frost, and others of that ilk.

The Club was perfectly suited for the meeting of the P-7 members who were all college or university presidents. Centered in Boston's Back Bay, one of Boston's historic and most fashionable neighborhoods, the building's late 1800s/early 1900s architecture welcomes you into the quiet elegance of a different era. You step out of a bustling street and turn a page into another century as you feel rightfully privileged, or intimidated depending on your background, and pass through rooms and halls of natural, heavy dark oak wooden panels, silver chandeliers, large older leather couches, oversized fireplaces and as an impatient patron described it, a single elevator that takes forever. Large picture portraits of famous Americans of the Revolutionary period hang proudly in halls and all the rooms. In addition to its impressive ballroom of similar decor, the Club has several dining rooms, a lounge, function rooms that can accommodate privately catered luncheon and dinner meetings, and guest rooms, which the Dean now had arranged to accommodate five of the presidents traveling from greater distances who arrived the night before.

President Jack "Speedy" Wilson was one of them. Speedy was a nickname he earned as an all- American halfback in his university's winning football team and the name stuck with him throughout his academic career. Many of his colleagues and friends who called him that would have to think hard to remember his first name.

It was a little past noon just before the luncheon, which was scheduled for 1 pm when Speedy's phone rang.

"Speedy, it's Dean Lauder. How are you?"

"Good, Dean, yourself?"

"Great, how are the accommodations?"

"If the place had some ivy growing down the outside walls, I would think I was still in the hallowed halls of my university. It's very comfortable. I had a drink at the lounge last evening with a couple of the boys. I'll say one thing, they sure know how to mix a drink here, or should I say drinks. Everyone is anxious to hear what you want to discuss."

"Good. Evelyn has confirmed that the others have been picked up by limo at the airport and have arrived at the Club or will be there soon. I arranged for cocktails before lunch so some may already be there getting a head start. The room is on the second floor. You can't miss it. They have my name on the door. Tell the group I will be just a few minutes late. I want to make sure the menu options are as ordered. Listen, do you have a few minutes now to discuss something between us?"

"Sure, I am all ears."

A grandfather clock chimed 13 times and a waiter was still busy carrying a tray of ordered drinks at the Lauder gathering. Every one of the invited was there, including Speedy, all chatting away awaiting the Dean's arrival. "Quiet, I hear him coming up the hall," Speedy called out with a voice just above a whisper. The group went immediately silent. As soon as the Dean entered, they all broke out with applause, shouting in unison, "Congratulations, Mr. President."

"How the hell did you hear so soon?" asked the Dean at the door trying to sound surprised.

"News travels fast through the grapevine," responded a loud voice from the group with a drink in his hand.

"Well, thanks. I appreciate all your support. It's true, the Trustees voted for my appointment just yesterday to take effect on Monday. Can't think of a better group to help me celebrate-and I think you are going to find the food here is up for the occasion. So, let's dig in. We can talk business during the dessert."

With that, all took their seats along a round table specially placed in the room at the Dean's request to provide greater intimacy. The Dean positioned himself next to Speedy. If a meal could help soften up a group to a host's point of view during a subsequent discussion, the Dean had outdone himself. He combined the Club's gourmet food with some specially catered dishes prepared by an outside chef. Starters were the Club's signature Lobster Bisque and a Caesar Salad prepared at the table by two waiters, one to assemble the salad and one to serve it. New England baked stuffed Maine lobsters, or an upper-trimmed, aged filet mignon wrapped in double-smoked hickory bacon were the choices of entrée. They were accompanied by a selection of appropriate wines to match the elegance of the dishes, all to be followed by table-prepared crepes Suzette and/or banana fritters as dessert. Everyone except the Dean and one other who was from the east coast chose the lobster dish.

When the waiters finished serving coffee and dessert, the Dean requested that they leave behind the pots of coffee next to the tray of brandy and the array of cordials, a sign they would be there for quite a while. The Dean then informed the group they could help themselves to the Cuban Montecristo cigars in the humidifier on the side table. He told them-some thought they saw him wink as he did-that he had purchased the cigars a few years ago, before the Kennedy-imposed trade embargo of Cuban goods.

Speedy Wilson, as Chairman of the P-7 group, waited until most were halfway through dessert when he picked up his empty water glass and used it as a gavel, gently banging on the table a few times to get everyone's attention. After the usual lingering chatter died out, the group gave him their undivided attention.

"I don't know about you gentlemen, but given this treatment, I am thinking we should ask President Bill here"-as Speedy put his hand on the Dean's shoulder-"to put us up at the Club for three or four months."

"Not a bad idea," one man jokingly agreed while lighting up one of the Cuban cigars.

Whether it was the relaxed atmosphere or the free-flowing sauce, as Abel Peabody and his Yankee friends often referred to liquor, it was clear that these distinguished college and university presidents were relaxing and letting their hair down somewhat, a mood that the Dean had hoped to create with his luxurious spread before standing to start the discussion.

"I owe it to you to share some of the background that led to my seeking each of you out to join this important effort," the Dean said, about to offer some patriotic verse to ready them for what he was about to propose. "As you know, like many of you, I come from a family that benefited from the unique opportunity to realize the American dream if you are willing to work hard – something that only a democracy can offer. I got many advantages because of my father's hard work and success. They were given to me with his constant reminder that with those advantages comes a responsibility to protect, and if necessary, to fight to protect, the economic freedoms that allow us to succeed. He educated me to the fact that to protect those freedoms, you had to know their enemies, however disguised- and those enemies were those seeking to replace our way of life with the totalitarianism of socialism and communism."

"Hear, hear," shouted one of the presidents in the group, hitting his open palm on the table twice as he said it.

The Dean was not surprised at the approval. He knew that the university presidents he recruited shared these conservative views.

The Dean continued, "Many people at my firm wondered why I took time from my position as a senior partner to accept the position of Dean of the law school and why I approached each of you to form this select P-7 group. Well, it was to protect those very freedoms.

Just about four years ago, in May 1962, I learned from my sources that President Kennedy was rightfully concerned about a communist takeover of South Vietnam and the dangerous spread of communism throughout the entire region. For like dominos, if one country went communist, surely other countries in the region would follow. It was becoming evident that this cold war battle against communism was now spreading to East Asia and the only nation in the world committed to freedom and democracy having the power to stop it was the USA. Even before the unprovoked attack by the North Vietnamese on our ships two years later at the Gulf of Tonkin requiring us to go to war, the handwriting was on the wall back then."

The Dean paused for a moment to pour some more water into an almost full glass and took a couple of sips, giving the group time to fully absorb what he had said, before going on with his version of the history lesson. It was worth the risk of being somewhat preachy to get his point across.

"As you know, no war, no matter how necessary, especially one that would require US combat troops to fight and die in a foreign land, can be fought without some resistance at home. That is especially true as the ultimate sacrifice of our boys begins to mount, even though our very way of life may be at stake. It took several years and a sneak attack at Pearl Harbor for Roosevelt to finally overcome that resistance to join the fight against Hitler and Nazism, an evil even more menacing than Communism. So, as this Vietnam War continues and escalates, as it must for us to gain a victory over the spread of communism, we can anticipate some resistance will begin to foment in the form of demonstrations."

The Dean looked around. It was now time to draw them in directly.

"So, where do I and all of you as presidents of universities come in? These types of anti-establishment demonstrations are naturally appealing to students on our campuses. Given their youthful idealistic stage in life, they are easily manipulated to grasp at any radical cause to give them relevance. I am sure this is something you as presidents know better than I or anyone else."

As the Dean was about to continue, he got some unexpected help from one of the presidents sitting across from him. "It's already happening, Dean. Some of that misguided fervor was seen popping up just a few weeks ago in New York City, where we saw a student demonstration against the Vietnam War by denigrating the flag and the sacrifices being made by our brave soldiers over there."

"Yes, we monitored it. The number at the gathering is nowhere near enough to worry about at this time. But make no mistake, there are now six million students in our public and private colleges in the US. This is a restless generation looking for causes," the Dean said with a passion as if he almost wished he were a part of their excitement, "They can bring your campuses down if this anti-war thing were to catch fire. We've got to be ready to ensure that it won't, just in case some false Moses comes along who they think can walk on water and who can excite and inspire them to engage in civil disobedience and unruly demonstrations."

Oddly, Judd, Sevena and the Dean had come to the same conclusion, though with different ends in mind. If the war were going to be stopped against the will and might of the richest and strongest nation on earth, astonishingly enough it would come from young, penniless and powerless college students. Based on that same belief, Judd and Sevena had developed a well- thought-out plan to spark a student anti-war movement, while the Dean had developed a well- thought-out, and well-resourced, counter-plan to ensure that any such attempt would not succeed.

"Dean, how does our P-7 Project come into play here?" asked one of the presidents.

"Good question. We have determined that your colleges and universities are among the likely targets, and if we quash the initial demonstrations there, we can demoralize any further protests."

Though somewhat inspired by the Dean's rallying effort, the mood of the group had changed from one of frivolity to the seriousness of what was to be their undertaking. Some were thinking of how they were first innocently approached by the Dean almost two years earlier. They were told that his old law firm had created a foundation with significant funds on behalf of anonymous, patriotic donors with a mission of making large multi-year donations to colleges and universities that best represented the values of the nation and committed to the protection of freedom and the Constitution. They were told that they were among the seven fortunate colleges selected.

One of the presidents pulled out his executed contract he brought with him to the meeting and glanced through it to see if there was a hint of what was being discussed today.

There was no mention, but it did have several clauses that he had taken for granted. One called for meetings from time to time of the P-7 group to discuss ways in which the members could contribute to the nation and the *cause of freedom*. Another, a confidentiality clause preventing the unauthorized disclosure by anyone of the existence and activities of the P-7 group. Upon any violation, the offending college would forfeit all future contracted donations and be required to reimburse the foundation for all prior ones. Lastly, there was a cancellation clause providing that the multiyear donations could immediately cease at the sole discretion of the trustee of the foundation, if the trustee were to determine that any of the presidents or their colleges or universities acted "contrary to the nation's interest." The Dean was the trustee of the foundation and had just defined what was in the nation's interest.

What they were now going to be told, but not quite all of it, was why the Dean left his firm to become Dean of the law school and how that was relevant to the group.

"I was asked by the foundation donors that provide the funds for your grants to take the job as Dean of the Law School, which was one of the likely targeted universities for student demonstrations. I was also asked to be the trustee of the foundation to develop a plan that would effectively counter any attempt to organize a national student movement against the war that would conduct unruly and disruptive demonstrations on our college campuses."

"What is the nature of the plan?" asked one of the presidents.

"It's called 'Operation Foolproof.' I am going to pass out a confidential notebook to each of you outlining it. It contains every conceivable tactic and type of demonstration that could be used and the countermeasures that you can employ to legally stop them and keep peace on campuses."

The Dean went to the back of the room and retrieved his large brief-case and began to distribute "The Bible" as he called it. "This was two years in the making with the consultation of former CIA operatives and law enforcement riot squad experts," he said proudly. "But the really good news and the reason I took the position of Dean, is so we could identify and recruit the top law school students that shared our political views to join my old law firm as associates upon graduation. At the law firm, we have been training them to become experts in the First Amendment and the right-to-public-assembly laws, as well as the handling of demonstrations.

They were not only the brightest but had a background of achievement demonstrating outstanding leadership qualities." The Dean told them that one of these P-7 trained lawyers would be loaned by the firm to each president to become his full-time special counsel and advisor on student relations at the Foundation's expense.

So, there it was. The meeting was to put everything on the line and determine if the Dean and his so-called donors had succeeded through financial support in establishing a united front at the college and university level.

Not surprisingly to the Dean, Speedy was again the first to react.

He gave his unconditional endorsement to the plan and thanked the Dean for his sacrifice not only in the "national interest" – that term again – but in trying to help them keep order at their universities where there could be disruptive riots if not handled properly.

"Dean, let me assure you we welcome any guidance to keep order in our schools while permitting lawful, and I repeat, lawful free speech, and we should remember what the Supreme Court said – you are entitled to free speech but 'you can't shout fire in a crowded theatre.'" This was a popular metaphor which any of the P-7 trained lawyers could tell them was being paraphrased from the opinion of Justice Oliver Wendell Holmes in the United States Supreme Court in the case *Schenck v. United States* in 1919, which held that the defendant's speech – distributing leaflets to draft-age men, urging resistance to induction in opposition to the draft during World War I – posed a clear and present danger and was not protected free speech under the First Amendment of the United States Constitution.

Speedy would not be seen driving a new car on campus when he got back, but if one were to examine the school's accounting, they might find that there was an increased non-alumni donation to his new Science Building of a very substantial amount not long after the meeting.

Speedy's remarks set the tone for a series of "amens" and when the meeting ended, the Dean had accomplished what he came for: an unwritten pact among them to implement the Operation Foolproof plan under his leadership. The presidents left duty-bound, and by pledging so, had the comfort of knowing that their multiyear donations from the foundation were intact.

However, what the presidents did not know and were never told was that in just two days the Dean would be flying to Washington for another secret meeting with so-called "donors" who controlled all the money and

pulled all the strings There, he would report on this dinner and the importance of obtaining more donations to quash student protests, and after that
meeting, the Dean and his partner, Walter Myers, were to meet with two
high-level agents of the FBI.

CHAPTER 20

ALAN TOOK A cab directly back to the hotel after breakfast with Sevena and Judd and went immediately up to his room. He was in no mood to try his skill and luck at the blackjack tables that afternoon. Too many thoughts and emotions were swirling around in his head. He had gotten over being spooked by their mystifying incidents and the unorthodox manner by which Judd and Sevena went about tracking him down. Now that the mystery was explained, he was impressed with both their ingenuity and perseverance, not to mention their flattery. His attraction to Sevena aside, he genuinely liked them and trusted their integrity and idealism.

He had already become skeptical about the Vietnam War before meeting Judd and Sevena and now was more so, learning that the reported Gulf of Tonkin attack was a ploy to provide an excuse to enter the war. It would be just like the Korean War back in the 50s, he thought.

The Korean War was fought for the same reason as the Vietnam War. It was a civil war. It was between North and South Korea and the USA again engaged in the so-called Cold War to stop the spread of communism. Russia and China helped the North Koreans, America fought for the South. After three years, it ended in a stalemate, but only after tens of thousands of soldiers and innocent civilians died. Alan thought, "If you asked anyone today, I doubt if they could tell you why that war was fought in the first place." He was right. The Korean War got termed, and one could say in the form of an oxymoron "remembered," as the "Forgotten War."

Alan could not help thinking that the Vietnam War was headed for the same fate. He wondered if they would ever learn and realized he had gotten the thought from the lyrics of the song written by Pete Seeger during the middle of the Korean War:

Where have all the soldiers gone?

Gone to graveyards, everyone.

Oh, when will they ever learn?

Alan did not have to be convinced of the need to end the war. That was not the question. The question was, why should he make that fight his fight? After all, there will always be a war, he reasoned, if not this one, then another, and another one after that. "It's been that way since the evolvement of the higher species called man," he thought sarcastically. Also, had he not just made one of the most difficult decisions in his life to quit school, release himself from all commitments and pressures, and, to misquote Thoreau slightly, "live a life of quiet inspiration," at least for a while? Didn't Sevena inform him if he were to take it on, this would be a day-and-night commitment for a year or two out of his life or maybe more? "Am I really to take seriously their contention that I could be that superman they sought to take on this herculean leadership role and, even more importantly, was it at all imaginable that such an insurmountable fight could be won?" The thoughts kept turning in his head.

He looked at the thick notebook he had just laid on the table containing the plan that Judd had given him. He was even in less of a mood to tackle that than gambling, though he thought of both as being somewhat the same. To beat the most powerful government in the world at its war game would be like trying to beat the casino at its games of chance. Both games were rigged to favor the House by the very nature of their own rules and commanding resources. The casino, a/k/a The House, never runs out of chips and the White House that controls the Mint never runs out of money.

Yet, Alan's reason for coming to Vegas was to do just that- to try to beat the House at its own game, knowing that at face value, it was a fool's errand. However, right next to Judd and Sevena's "playbook" was the "playbook" he brought, *Beat the Dealer,* a professed winning strategy at blackjack, written by Edward Thorp, an MIT professor who said you can.

Alan thought the analogy still held. To beat the government or the casino, you would need to devise a winning plan like Thorp's card-counting strategy that could neutralize the unfavorable odds or tilt it to your favor. But, as important, you would also need to possess the skill, discipline and guts to execute that strategy flawlessly, and even then, as the song goes, you would still need *luck to be a lady* that night. In other words, with all the thoughtful planning, there was no room for error or for Lady Luck to abandon you.

The more he thought of the similarities of the two challenges, the more Alan saw that the effort at winning at blackjack against the casino was a metaphor for successfully taking on the government. Perhaps if you could beat the insurmountable odds of winning against the casino, you could beat the insurmountable odds of winning against the government. He now began to regain his enthusiasm to test his will against the giant casinos, as if the outcome of his playing at the tables might well determine his decision regarding Judd's and Sevena's proposal.

Below the surface of these thoughts were the more disturbing ones that still spooked him. Again, why was he being investigated? What was the P-7 project about? Why did they find him to be a danger to its operations? Who were the people behind the investigation and why did they want to keep an eye on him? And he was bewildered by the coincidence that Dean, Judd and Sevena, for unrelated reasons, all went to extraordinary lengths to find out everything about him-or then again was it indeed merely a coincidence? Could they somehow turn out to be related? He felt like the two were linked somehow, but there was no earthly reason to think so.

Going over this, again and again, made no sense. He needed additional facts. So, for now, he would hit the blackjack tables for his long-planned encounter with the casino. Unlike David, he would not rely on a slingshot to slay this Goliath, but rather, a series of tables and charts developed by Professor Thorp with MIT's new IBM computer.

First, Alan needed to get away from the noises and glitz of the Las

Vegas Strip, develop calmness and confidence for the evening. He picked up the phone.

"Hi, this Alan Roberts, Room106. Would you please put me through to the concierge desk? I would like to book a tour to Hoover Dam this afternoon."

THE HOOVER DAM was built by a massive effort of thousands of then-unemployed workers during the Great Depression between 1931 and 1936. No one thought it could be done. Yet this man- made wonder was built two years ahead of schedule and is cited as one of the greatest engineering achievements in human history. This triumph over what some said at the time were insurmountable environmental and engineering difficulties, is now one of the world's largest producers of hydroelectric power and is still thought of as a miracle.

Alan got there within 90 minutes and spent two hours viewing and contemplating the breathtaking vistas of the 72-story-high structure that required over four million cubic feet of concrete to construct. He went inside the power plants and marveled over the machinery of the massive generators at work converting the flow of water from a controlled Lake Mead into power for use of the people of Arizona, Nevada and California.

Like so many visitors, he was struck by the motifs of the beautiful art décor and colors modeled after the Native American sand paintings that covered the walkways and interior halls of the dam. He observed the sculptures paying tribute to those who contributed to the construction, including a plaque to memorialize the daring workers killed working high up on the elevator towers. These High Scalers, as they called them, suspended themselves on ropes from the top of the canyon and while scaling down its walls high above the ground, removed the loose rocks with jackhammers and dynamite. It was extremely dangerous work.

One High Scaler saved the life of a government inspector who fell loose from his safety line. As the man was tumbling down a slope to his death, the High Scaler came swinging by and grabbed him, pulling him back up into the air and to safety. If not for many such courageous rescues, the large death toll of 112 during the construction would have been much higher.

Alan left with an encouraging feeling that there was nothing, no matter how tough the challenge, that man could not achieve if he had the will and courage to achieve it. He was now better poised to take on the casino.

IT'S FUNNY, GAMBLERS like to feel that the stars are aligned in the right order when they go to play. That means feeling fresh, nicely groomed and wearing the right clothes, so they feel neatly attired and comfortable when walking into the casino for some serious play. For that reason, Alan had gone to Filene's Basement before he left Boston where he found an attractive, solid-white cotton dress shirt that he wore open with black dress pants. He also found some conservative but attractive cuff links, for they would be the most noticeable during play. That evening all else would be put aside. He was to be a gambler.

Alan had just finished a well-planned dinner before gambling, just like someone picking a well-thought-out menu before running a marathon-in this case, a medium-rare filet mignon without a salad or any side veggies, delivered by Room Service. Two cups of coffee would be the only beverage for this dinner. He had done a last review of Thorp's charts and tables. In Boston, Alan had studied and memorized the strategy of card counting that Thorp theorized would overcome the House's advantage. He had practiced by dealing hundreds of hands to himself, using Thorp's computerized algorisms in determining when to draw a card, or stand, split a pair, double down, take out insurance, and how much to bet at any given time - terms defining all the decisions a player must make during the game. He was as ready as he could be. However, Alan knew that a successful execution would not depend solely on a strategy, but also on one's disposition, confidence and guts to make the play with a big bet riding when what the strategy calls for appears to be counterintuitive.

It was 7 pm. Time to get the show on the road. Alan went down to his safety deposit box at the front desk and took out the twenty $100 bills he had set aside for the game. He folded two of them and put them in his right front pocket and the rest into his left, next to his wallet. He was a bit nervous, like before a championship basketball game back in high school when all that you prepared for was on the line with this one game. It made him wonder what troops felt like going into battle when what was at stake was not the risk of simply losing a game or money, but your very life, and where, as in his case, luck as much as skill, could be the determining factor.

Getting off the elevator, one has to go only a few steps and there it is-the Casino, a world all to its own, heavily air-conditioned, artificial lighting throughout, without any windows or clocks so there is no day or night or time, with only one door by which to enter or leave. There are people busy pulling levers at rows of slot machines with their deafening sounds, or figuring out plays at crowded roulette and crap tables, and others sitting at various blackjack and other card tables, all making hundreds of bets every minute with one purpose in mind-to win some of the Casino's cash. For most, in fact, for more than most, they say, "the first bet is to win, and all the others are to try to get even." Alan was there to prove that adage wrong, with a system, if it worked, that was too new for the casinos to have made adjustments.

Alan walked by the slots, the roulette and crap tables and into a quieter area where there were rows of semicircular, felt-covered tables with people occupying some or all of the six seats around the perimeter, placing chips in a betting circle in front of them, and a dealer standing across from them waiting for a signal to deal a card to a particular player. Each of these tables had a small plaque at the end corner to the dealer's right indicating the minimum bet for that table – some $5, some $10, some $25, and for the high rollers $100 with a maximum bet of $500 for all of them. Alan had arrived where he wanted to be-at the blackjack tables, a game also known as twenty-one and cited as the most widely played casino banking game throughout the world, with few, if any, proven claims of anyone having a system able to beat the dealer.

Alan had been to Vegas for weekends twice before. He played blackjack off the Strip where smaller casinos allowed minimum bets of a dollar. He lost a hundred or two both times playing mostly by instinct and conventional wisdom, but loved the action and got to feel comfortable with the protocol and how the game operated. That was why he became fascinated with Thorp's strategy and was perhaps looking for revenge.

He began a walk by each of the tables looking at the dealers' faces and the action going on. He stopped and watched the play at several tables and finally settled for one that had several open seats with a woman dealer, who, unlike most dealers with their somewhat hardened and worn faces, seemed friendly. He would begin conservatively to test his play at a $5 minimum table. He reached into his pocket and took out the two $100 bills and after the conclusion of an existing round of play, placed them on the table. "Changing two hundred," the dealer called out to the Pit Boss behind her who managed several tables. She lifted a lever at her side that covered a small open slot on the table and slid the bills into it. She then exchanged the money for a stack of four green chips and two stacks of 10 red chips each, and placed them in front of Alan. Greens were $25 chips and the reds $5.

Most players see the game in its simplest form. They know the rules. The dealer deals the players and himself two cards, with one of the dealer's cards up and showing, the other down, an unforeseen "hole" card. The player signals the dealer to either draw cards or stand with the cards he has, trying to end up with a score closest to 21. Players need to avoid "busting," which means drawing a card that makes them exceed 21, because then they automatically lose regardless of what the dealer does. Picture cards count as 10 and an Ace can count as 1 or 11. What one hopes for is to get a blackjack on the first two cards – an Ace with a 10, or a picture card that counts as a ten, making 21 - that pays one and a half times the bet unless the dealer also gets a blackjack.

Players can also double-down, meaning double their bet after getting their two cards, thinking it gives them an edge on the dealer. Players can also split their two cards. For example, if they get two eights for a score of 16-not a good hand-they can place an equivalent bet and treat each 8 as a separate play as if two separate hands.

Alan knew the rules well. But knowing the rules and trying to make intelligent decisions on drawing a card or standing, doubling down, or splitting, based on the conventionally accepted notions, still gives the house up to a 4% advantage. With those heavy odds in favor of the house, no amount of good luck in the short run could withstand the inevitable statistical result of losing over any significant length of time. That is why casinos spend a fortune building and maintaining these Alice in Wonderland gambling and entertainment-centers and give you free drinks to keep you playing.

With the advent of computer digital technology even in its infant stage, Professor Thorp could run these plays thousands upon thousands of times through the new very large MIT IBM computer and come up with a strategy for these decisions based on game theory and statistical percentages that would give a player the best possible outcomes. If just his basic strategy were mastered, it would even the odds of winning against the house.

But here was the kicker that attracted Alan to Thorp's play. Unlike craps or roulette where the same numbers on the dice or the roulette wheel are in play at every role and so the odds of winning or losing are the same with every play, blackjack has a number of hands being dealt, and as played in the 1960s, dealt until the entire 52-card deck was finished. Therefore, like no other game, one can determine the likelihood or unlikelihood of certain cards being dealt next after seeing one hand played. If fewer pictures or aces were dealt in the first hand, there is a certainty that more will be dealt in subsequent hands. What Thorp determined was that the more the next hand was likely to be richer, meaning more 10s, pictures and aces, the greater chance the player would win. The more the next hand would likely be poorer, that is with low cards and fewer aces, the greater chance the house would win.

Thorp's betting strategy was to keep track of the cards that had been played, betting the minimum until the remaining deck became rich with high cards and aces. When that happens, raise your bet, doubling or even tripling it, depending on how rich the remaining deck. That way, even if the Casino wins more games than you, you will win more of the bigger bets and most of the games you lose will be for the minimum bets. According to Thorp, altering the bets in that manner would reverse the odds of the house having a 4% advantage – to the player having that 4% advantage. That was the theory, but it still required great concentration to track the cards accurately while they were being dealt rather quickly.

The dealer shuffled the deck and was about to begin dealing the first hand for Alan to play.

Alan placed his minimum bet not just in front of him, but also in the two betting circles to his left in front of those seats unoccupied by any players. As permitted by the casino, Alan would be playing all three hands at the same time. One of the reasons Alan chose this table was because of the three unoccupied seats. For if a deck got rich, he wanted to have three hands going at the same time in which take advantage of doubling or tripling his bets.

No more than two hands had been dealt when the Pit Boss signaled a well-endowed waitress in a skimpy outfit holding a tray to come to the table. Bending over, she asked Alan, "Would you like a drink, sir?" Casino drinks were complimentary. The house wanted guests to enjoy themselves and play longer. For they knew the more people drank, the more foolish their plays, and they would bet a lot more than they intended trying to win back their losses.

"Yes, but a coffee, no sugar please." He was at work - no alcohol for him. The player next to him joined in, "Make mine a double Chivas." When the waitress came back with his drink, Alan dropped a couple of dollars on her tray as a tip. The guy next to him simply grabbed his drink and said, "I'll catch ya next time, dearie."

The first couple of deals of the deck had the usually expected split in wins and losses but began to favor the house as time went on during the first hour. Alan was keeping up with the card tracking and playing the system without any deviation, raising and lowering bets based on the favorability of the undealt cards. What he noticed after the hour of play was that while the house won more hands than he overall, he had won more hands with his larger bets when the deck was rich as predicted. So, despite losing slightly more hands, he still found himself ahead by $300.

During the second hour, luck began to change in Alan's favor. Or was it luck? Sevena, the scientist, may have put it differently. "Outlier events catch up eventually to conform to statistical probabilities." And so here, as expected, the greater number of wins for the casino during hour one began to rebalance in favor of Alan during hour two, and with his perfect play by the end of that second hour, Alan was now $1,500 to the good.

While Alan's chips were growing, a couple of players at the table went broke and left, and were replaced by others. The guy who ordered the double Chivas making $50 bets was sustaining heavy losses. He was cashing more hundred-dollar bills to replace the chips he kept losing almost as fast as the drinks he kept re-ordering

Alan's unorthodox play did not go unnoticed, especially by the Chivas guy sitting next to him, angry over Alan's winnings while he was losing his small fortune. Alan was dealt a hand with two 6s and the dealer's open card a 7. Following Thorp's strategy, Alan split the 6s even though the dealer had a 7 showing. As required, he put another betting chip on the table and spread them apart side by side to play them separately. Everyone could hear the Chivas guy trying to whisper to the player next to him, but in a slurred voice that carried well beyond a whisper, "What an asshole. Now he has made one bad hand into two bad hands. Even if the jerk gets a 10 or a picture card on both hands, all he has is 16 on both and if the Dealer has a 10 hole- card, making 17, he's a goner."

Alan drew a 5 to the hand with the first 6. He now had 11 with the dealer having a 7. So, he put another chip on the table, doubling down his bet, and drew a ten for 21. Playing his second hand with the 6 card, he drew a 4 and now had a 10. He doubled down his bet with another chip and drew an 8 for a value of 18. The dealer then turned over his hole card. It was a Jack, making his value 17. Alan had taken one bad hand and by splitting them and doubling down on both won the equivalent of 4 hands. The loser next to him, in more of a shout than a whisper, reacted. "What a lucky prick. In this freaking game like anything else, you need more luck than brains." Alan looked at him, smiled, and then went about gathering a pile of his winning chips.

Now with both his winnings and increased confidence, Alan began to raise his minimum bet from $5 to $25. "It was OK," he thought, "for I am now playing with the house's money." After another hour or so of further play at the $25 minimum level, Alan decided it was time to take a break and asked the dealer to "count them up." The then male dealer placed both his hands around all of Alan's chips, pulled them toward him and began to separate them in stacks: the blacks, which were the $100 chips, a ton of green $25 chips. "I make it at $3,750", he said. Alan picked up the 37 black $100 chips and threw the 2 green chips back on the table, saying, "Thanks, it's for the dealers." Although winners sometime after a good win leave something for the dealers when they quit, $50 was a generous tip. Minus this tip and the $200 of his own money he started with, Alan had won $3,500.

Alan headed directly to the cashiers' cage located at the end of the casino. It is not by chance that there is only one such cage located far away from the one exit door. This way, a player looking to cash in any winnings or remaining chips must pass and resist stopping and resuming play at-a host of other games along the way to the cage. Then, after cashing in, he must resist being tempted to play some more as he again passes all the action taking place along the length of the casino to reach the one door that lets him leave.

Without diversion, Alan then went to his safety deposit box located in a room behind the lobby desk and re-deposited the $2,000 of the money he started with. He kept the $3,500 in winnings in his pockets. It was now 11:15 pm. He sat down in the lobby for a moment and said to himself, "Thank you, Professor Thorp!" But the real test was about to come. The match was not over yet. He would now pick another casino and play like the big boys at a $50 Minimum Table. This was it; the equivalent to his Championship Game.

Alan wanted to switch casinos because by now his type of play and the pattern of altering the size of his bets could at some point gain attention from the staff. Just to be sure there would be no unexpected counter-measures, he would resume play for the big dough at a different casino.

Not far down the strip from the Flamingo was the Stardust Hotel and Casino. "It was as good as any," he thought. Alan grabbed a cab and was there within minutes. It would be hard to miss. In front of the casino was the famous Stardust sign, an illuminating galaxy of lighting displaying a solar system of acrylic glass planets and neon starbursts that spun around a replica of the earth in its midst. It contained 11,000 lamps and 7,100 feet of neon tubing of which 975 of them were used just to light up the letter "S" of the STARDUST name, a name that was spelled within the 216-foot-long and 37-foot-high largest electric sign in the world. Whether true or not, it is said that the lit sign at night could be seen by motorists approaching the city from the desert some 60 miles away. That could be more intimidating than welcoming to someone coming to prove he could beat the house. But Alan was looking to take on the giants on the strip.

The sudden cold blast of air-conditioning that he encountered entering the lobby was welcoming even though he had been exposed to the outside heat for only moments. The Stardust lined up its games like the Flamingo and most other casinos. It was no different, except that it was now more crowded because the dinner show had emptied into it a little over an hour earlier. The blackjack tables were crowded but not surprisingly, less so at the $50 minimum ones. Alan watched the play at those tables for about 20 minutes before a couple of players left, leaving two empty seats for Alan to occupy and play two hands at the same time. He put down his thirty-five

$100 bills, all his winnings. "Money in," said the dealer, banking the cash in a similar slot to those at the Flamingo tables, and lined up stacks of $25 green and $100 black chips and pushed them over to Alan. The game was on.

Alan played his two hands at the $50 minimum table without interruption for close to three hours. It was now almost 3:00 am. He was the only one left at the table and with chips going back and forth in streaks going both ways, Alan had managed through concentrated accurate card counting and disciplined adherence to Thorp's strategy to squeeze out another $1,200 in winnings

He then became aware of something extraordinarily interesting. It was the last hand before the end of the deck. If his count were accurate, it meant that all the remaining five cards to be dealt, were all 10s, pictures, and an ace.

Alan quickly went through the variables in his mind. Since he was playing two hands, compared to the dealer, he would get 4 of the remaining 5 rich cards and so had the best chance of getting the ace and a blackjack. Since all the other cards were pictures or tens, he would also end up with a

20 hand and the dealer would be left with a ten-hand awaiting a new shuffle, with only a slim chance of getting an ace to avoid the blackjack payoff. This end-play presented as good an opportunity as a player could possibly wish for against the casino.

The deal would begin as soon as Alan laid down his bet. He was about to make an unusual move. He first asked the dealer to count his chips on the table for him. The dealer gathered them up and placed them in equal stacks and counted them up. "You got $4,700 even," he said.

"Look, these are my winnings for tonight both here and at other casinos. It's late so this hand, no matter what, will be my last. Your maximum is $500. I would like you to raise the limit for my last hand, so I can bet it all." The dealer called out to the Pit Boss, an older grey-haired guy in a black suit, who heard the request and was already on his way over.

"How much does he have on the table?" the Pit Boss asked the dealer. "I just counted it: $4,700 even," the dealer answered.

"How much of that is our money?"

"About $1,200." Players don't realize it, but casinos keep an ongoing count on all players' winnings.

"How much of it do you want to bet?" the Pit Boss asked Alan.

"As much as you let me. I either break even or make the time I spent worth it," Alan tried to sound like he was tired, that winnings of this amount were no big thing for him, and he was willing to take a fling no matter what the outcome.

"OK, whatever you want. That's why we are here. We will cover any amount you put in those betting circles."

"All of it," Alan responded.

"You got it, my man." The Pit Boss is always happy to get a chance of recovering losses and in this case, end his shift with better numbers.

Alan took $2,500 of the chips and stacked them up in the betting circle of his first-hand and

$2,000 in the other, so the total bet was the entire $4,500 in winnings. He also placed one black chip each in front of both betting circles as bets for the dealer – these bets and any winnings from them being the dealer's tip if Alan won any one or both bets.

"Thanks, appreciate it, and good luck," said the dealer.

"Yes, to both of us," Alan replied pointing to the dealer's bets. "And please deal all my cards facing up if you would."

The dealer dealt the first card to Alan's first hand – it was the Jack; then to his second hand – it was a 10, and then to himself– it was also a 10.

"So far my count is accurate, but no ace," Alan thought with mixed feelings.

There were now two more cards to deal to Alan's hands before finishing that deal. The dealer lifted the first card off the deck and turned it around in his hand so everyone could see. It was a king. He then put it next to the jack. Alan had a 20 on his first-hand. The dealer lifted the last card off the deck and again turned it around in his hand so everyone could see. It was the ace. "Blackjack," the dealer called out as he flipped it next to the 10. Alan hit his fist on the table twice with a controlled shout "Yes – Yes."

Alan had tracked everything perfectly. Yet, the game was not over. The dealer had a 10. The deck would be shuffled and the dealer would deal himself his next card. If the dealer did not draw an ace or a 10 or a picture card, Alan would win both bets, with one of them a blackjack, winning him an additional $5,500 for a total winning of the night of $10,000. If the dealer drew a 10 or a picture card, Alan would still win $3,000 on the blackjack for a total winnings of $7,500 for the night. But if the dealer drew an ace, giving him a draw on the blackjack and beating Alan's other hand, Alan's total winnings would be reduced to $2,000. A lot of money was at stake.

Alan could walk away with winnings of $10,000 or just $2,000, with the odds heavily in Alan's favor.

Alan waited for the new shuffle and the card to be dealt to the dealer when suddenly the dealer clapped his hands in an upward motion and looking at Alan said, "Good luck to you, sir." began to leave, allowing another younger dealer, who appeared to be in his early 40s and had a slight scar above his left eye, to replace him. The new dealer picked up the deck and began to shuffle it in several ways with dexterity and the flare of a confident and experienced card professional. Alan asked the Pit Boss why the change.

"Our labor agreement is that they work 40 minutes of each hour, so we rotate shifts to accommodate this schedule."

Alan was aware of the rotations, but he thought this one was premature. He worried about it because Thorp devoted a special chapter on cheating. He mentioned that during his tour at various casinos testing his strategy, he took card sharks with him to spot cheating that ordinary players could never detect, and they found cheating was not infrequent. The casino could only retain a few such dealers to keep it from being detected. They were called "mechanics" in the trade. One of the ways to defend against it suggested by Thorp was to be leery if you are winning a good amount and they prematurely change shifts so a mechanic can come in and clear the decks so to speak. Alan had no way of determining whether 40 minutes had elapsed.

Those who thought that casinos were on the up and up and would never engage in cheating might well have a different opinion if they knew that The Aladdin Casino, nearby, was controlled by the Detroit and St. Louis families of the mafia; the Desert Inn by the Mayfield Road Gang; the Dunes Casino by a Chicago Outfit, with Raymond Patriarca of the New England mafia also a part-owner; the Sands Casino by Doc Stacher, a New York mobster; the Tropicana Casino managed by Frank Costello, the frontman for Lou Lederer, who represented Chicago mobsters; the Flamingo where

Alan was staying was built and operated by the notorious Bugsy Siegel, Lucky Luciano's trusted affiliate until he was killed by his fellow mobsters, after which the Casino remained under mob control… and here at the Stardust, where Alan was awaiting his fate relying on an honest deal, its Credit Manager, Hyman Goldman, was a well- known criminal with seven known aliases, fourteen criminal convictions and served a three-year prison sentence for income tax evasion. The Stardust manager and part-owner, Johnny Drew, was a former Al Capone lieutenant and was convicted for running a crooked dice game at an Elks convention; Morris Kleinman, it's General Manager, also served three years for tax evasion.

Alan had not done the research. He did not have to for it was common knowledge that the mob ran the casinos in Vegas, and he was aware of it. Knowing this, he tried to reverse things.

"I am somewhat superstitious. Can we get our boy back to finish the deal?"

"Sorry, can't help you there. I don't want to start some labor dispute." The Pit Boss was not going to relent and Alan knew there was nothing more he could do.

"Thanks, no problem. Louis here looks like he knows how to behave." Alan got the dealer's first name "Louis" off the name tag pinned to his shirt.

"Not sure my wife would agree," added Louis as he handed the shuffled cards to Alan to cut. Alan cut the cards and did not notice any marriage or other rings on his fingers, though he had a very expensive watch and gold bracelet.

The dealer buried the first card, moved his hand over to Alan's betting circles to straighten the stacks of chips, and brushed the felt tabletop with the palms of his hands a couple of times near his own dealt card. Alan stood up, heart beating fast, as the dealer began to deal by turning over the next card.

"8 – 18," the dealer called out the card and the total of his hand. It was not an ace or a 10.

"*Yes!*" Alan gave a less controlled celebratory shout. The dealer having to stand on the 18 began to make the payoffs to cover Alan's two significant bets, including a 3 to 2 payoff for the blackjack. Alan, who had spent almost nine hours of play starting with $5 bets and working up to $50 bets, had taken two casinos for a total of $10,000.

The Pit Boss confirmed that the total amount of his chips was $10,000. He then came out of the area behind the tables to where Alan was now standing. "My name is Nick – Nick Manning," and handed him his card with all kinds of phone numbers. "Nice play. Let me have one of our boys take your chips to the cashier at the cage and get you your cash."

"Thanks, much appreciated. I would like it in hundreds, and could you have them break down one of them for me," Alan replied in a manner like it was an everyday occurrence for him, though his heart was still pounding

"Sure thing, we can do that." The Pitt Boss then went to a phone. In moments, a tall husky uniformed security guard came and picked up Alan's chips now in a tray and soon returned with five packets of hundred-dollar bills, with thin brown colored paper ringed around them to secure them like an elastic.

"I think you will find 20 big ones in each of the 5 packets, except for the one with one of the hundreds broken down. Feel free to sit there and count them." The Pit Boss pointed to the blackjack table where Alan was sitting.

"Thanks," Alan said, and counted each one, re-securing them back with the paper rings. "All there – thanks again.

"$10,000! $10,000! I beat the house for $10,000," he was thinking over and over again.

"Look," said Manning. "I would like to make VIP reservations for you and your guests for tomorrow night's spectacular Lido of Paris dinner show, all on the house. We like to take care of our players at these tables." What he really meant was, "We don't want to say goodbye to our money."

"Thanks, Nick, but I am leaving in the morning."

"OK," said Nick, "you got my card with all my numbers so you can reach me day or night, on or off duty. Anytime you and a guest want to come out and have fun for a couple of days, we will arrange flight tickets and a VIP suite on the house and comp all your shows, meals, and drinks. There is a code on that card, just mention it when you call."

"I'm sure I'll take you up on that," replied Alan, putting the card in his pocket.

Money in hand, Alan walked out of the casino casually though remaining keenly attuned to anything around him. He had the doorman signal him a cab and drew a sigh of relief as he headed back safely to the Flamingo. At the Flamingo, he immediately deposited the winnings in the safe deposit box and then went directly to the bar, ordered the scotch he had longed for all evening and carried it up to his room. He sat up on his bed and took a few gulps. As excited as he was, he was overtaken by the exhaustion of his nine hours of concentrated play. He pulled the sheet over him, cloths and all, and fell into a deep, comforting sleep. It was 9 am before he was awakened having heard his door starting to open. He jumped up.

"Oh, sorry, it's the maid. There was no sign on the door. I will be back later to clean the room."

Alan felt completely nourished with an elation similarly felt by one who cleanly got away pulling off a robbery at an impenetrable bank. "And it is all legal," he thought. He was hungry and found himself going back to the same restaurant where he had breakfast with Sevena and Judd. The waitress recognized him. "Hi, omelet with egg whites again?"

"No, I am in the mood to try your eggs benedict this time and a pot of your nice strong coffee." He remembered Judd having suggested it.

"You got it," she said taking back the menu on the table.

Alan had Judd's plan with him and began to read it with intensity as if studying for one of his exams. If it made sense, he was ready to consider it. All self-doubts he may have had about his leadership abilities and being able to successfully take on so-called insurmountable challenges dissipated when he beat the casinos at their game. As he continued to read the plan, he underlined and crossed out certain paragraphs and wrote some notes on various pages. It seemed as if he took a sip of his coffee in concert with each turn of the page. He was halfway through it when the eggs benedict arrived. He took a bite. It was delicious. He asked for some extra hollandaise sauce. He would finish reading the plan when he got back to his room.

It was almost 1 pm when he finally finished reading the entire plan in his room and decided to call Sevena. He dialed the number she had originally given him. There was no answer. Alan made flight reservations to Boston for late afternoon and began to pack. After packing, he tried Sevena once again. It rang several times without an answer, and finally: "Hello."

"Hi, it's Alan. You sound a bit out of breath."

"Yeah, a bit. I just got in and heard the rings as I was fumbling for my key. Hope my rushing to the phone was worth it."

"Depends on how you look at it. You can count me in. I decided to do it."

"That's *great*, simply great, Alan." Sevena was not hiding her emotions in her response. "When are you flying back?"

"This afternoon."

"Nice. So, can Judd and I meet with you tomorrow?"

"Not tomorrow. It will have to be the day after. Tomorrow, I have a lot to do. If I am going to lead a student revolution of sorts, then I'd better be a student and not a dropout, or there goes my credibility. I will need to go see Evelyn tomorrow and tell her to inform the Dean that I carefully considered what he said and decided to take his advice and not quit and would be taking the exams. They begin a week from tomorrow. Next, I got to get someone's notes from the last two weeks of lectures and make a call to my pharmacist friend for some Dexedrine pills. There will be a lot of sleepless nights ahead if I am to get by the finals. I also need to see Mrs. Fallon, my former landlord, and hope that she did not re-let my furnished apartment yet, or else I will need to find another to rent near the school."

"I understand. What did you think of our plan?"

"Very thorough and well-thought-out. However, I do have some suggestions to discuss with you."

"Good, look forward to it. Judd is still working on how to raise funds to finance it."

Alan took his wallet out of his pocket and pulled out Nick the Pitt Boss's card. "I may be able to help you there," he said smiling.

"OK, when you get a chance call me with a time to meet when you're ready - and Alan regarding your question that I didn't answer at the coffee shop, the thought of recruiting you was not the only reason I left you my phone number. Can't wait to see you again. Anything you want to add to that?"

"Yes, actually I do." After a pause, "Tell Judd when he gets to Vegas again, go back to that cafeteria and try their eggs benedict he had suggested. I think he will like it."

Both were smiling as she delicately hung up the phone.

CHAPTER 21

THE EXECUTIVE CONFERENCE Room at the Washington office of Latham, Hogan & McLeish was like the ones at the corporate headquarters of Fortune 100 companies. A mile-long, oblong mahogany conference table with one leather chair after another evenly spaced all around it, in a room with more glass than wall, to provide picture-perfect views of the seat of power, the Capitol Building – in short, the home of money and power. Projecting that feeling was important. For the four people to be welcomed by the Dean and Walter for the meeting that morning would find anything less disappointing. After all, these gentlemen were some of the most powerful industrial executives in the country, if not in the world, and the firm's biggest clients.

Collectively, they were what writer C. Wright Mills called the "Power Elite," wealthy individuals who hold prominent positions in corporate America that control the very process of determining a society's economic and political policies. It was important that when they arrived, all their senses told them that by retaining Latham, Hogan & McLeish, they had purchased the most influence that money could buy.

The Dean knew each one of them intimately. They were the CEOs of the biggest companies in the arms industry. He had recruited their business and personally handled their accounts over the years until he turned them over to Walter to formally manage them when he became Dean. However, he made sure to stay in the loop and meet with each several times a year. The Dean, as an equity partner on leave from the firm, still received his share of the partners' distributions based on the business from these and other companies he brought to the firm.

The Dean welcomed them by first extending his hand to J.C.

Jennings, the CEO of North American Dynamics, the biggest and most successful company in the armaments industry-a supplier of rifles, guns, machine guns and all types of military equipment and logistical support. Their proudest: the M25, a gas-operated, magazine-fed rifle, that could fire bullets accurately over several hundred yards at 850 rounds per minute on its automatic setting.

"Good to see you again, JC."

"Me too, Bill," responded JC, shaking the Dean's hand.

The Dean always wondered why it was that only important people seemed to be addressed by their first and middle initials. Was Jennings addressed as JC after he became successful, or was he called that as a kid when kids earned nicknames? He would not ask to find out.

He also would not ask JC how the last shareholders meeting went, although North American Dynamics reported substantial earnings above what the market anticipated. It seems that JC got carried away in his remarks to his annual board meeting when he promised that the next year the company would do even better in obtaining their share of defense contracts, assuring them that "his loyalty would continue to be to shareholders first, and the country second." When taken to task by the media for that remark, leaked to the public, he was forced to issue a seven-word statement that "the remarks were taken out of context."

The Dean began working the others in the room like a politician greeting donors at a fundraiser, with a warm, loud hello, a strong handshake, and adding a personal remark. "How is Barbara's school lunch program going?" he asked Carl Leonard, the CEO of Global Aircraft, referring to his wife's pet project at their local elementary school. Global was one of the largest producers of military aircraft, fighter jets, bombers and helicopters.

Carl was one of the Dean's oldest clients. The Dean got BU to award him an honorary doctorate degree at the university's graduation a year earlier. During the dinner for doctorate honorees the evening before, Carl was asked to give some remarks. He talked about the contributions of the arms industry to the nation's defense and in furthering peace. "A strong, capable and well-armed technically advanced military that intimidates those who would even consider attacking us is the best way to ensure a lasting peace and preserve our democratic way of life."

When he finished, he picked up his third glass of bourbon that he had laid aside for the moment and while he was enjoying applause from the crowd whispered to the Dean, "I just helped you do your job, old boy. So, go get those contracts. Maybe you haven't heard, private yachts and vacation homes in Paris and Italy are getting much more expensive to maintain these days."

The Dean had looked around at the crowd to assure himself that Carl's remarks were not overheard. He thought that in mentioning his expensive lifestyle, Carl at least was discreet not to have included the extravagancies of his not-so-secretive mistress.

Now Brian Nowinski reached for the Dean's hand before the Dean extended it. "You're looking good, Mr. President," he remarked.

"News travels fast," the Dean responded.

Nowinski, a Yale business school graduate and a former six-term congressman, headed Military Armaments and Systems Limited, a major supplier of tanks, military combat vehicles, artillery systems, naval guns and missile launchers. Like the mafia, the armaments industry tried to do its business without publicity. As a result, many in the industry were leery when Nowinski had agreed to address a class at West Point that was to be covered live by TV. Nowinski, consistent with his reputation, did not hold back when he was introduced to the cadets.

"As the nation's future warriors, I come here to tell you to wear that title 'Warriors' proudly, for war is not a bad thing. It is a good thing. It settles ongoing disputes when they cannot be resolved by diplomacy. It is, indeed, costly to our national treasury, and sadly, it is costly in terms of human lives. But without it, this nation would not have been born. The Revolutionary War created the world's most steadfast democracy. The Civil War freed the slaves. The Mexican/American War gave us the territory this nation needed. The two World Wars defeated nations that were intent on destroying us and economically pulled us out of the Great Depression into the most productive period in this nation's history. The Korean War was necessary to avoid conceding territory to the enemy during the Cold War, and the Vietnam War that we are engaged in today, like the Korean War, is being fought to defend us and other nations from being enslaved by the evils of communism."

He did not stop there. "I am not unmindful of the deaths and casualties that result from war," he continued. "Seven hundred and fifty thousand Americans died in the Civil War alone, but that was the necessary price to rid ourselves of the evil of slavery. I will not hide from the chilling horrors of war, so I will lay it on the line in its naked form without apology. I am proud to be in an industry that provides you with the tools that help you succeed in your honorable missions.

Because we do, some wish to blame us for wars and the killings that take place as a result. While it is true our industry provides the most destructive weapons we can develop to kill people, we provide these weapons at our nation's request and for our nation's defense. It is not you, nor our company, nor the weapons industry that is to blame for wars and the killings. It is our enemies and their evil that cause these wars to be fought who are to blame."

In the Latham, Megan & McLeish conference room, the Dean finished his hellos with Max Schmitt, founding director of Majestic Chemical, the largest producer of explosives, bombs, weaponized chemicals and biological materials such as Agent Orange and then motioned them to take their seats at the corner of the conference table. They occupied just six of the 40 seats circling the table causing JC to remark sarcastically, but in a playful tone, "Hey, Bill, couldn't you find a bigger room?"

"None that would meet your expectations, JC," the Dean quipped back politely. "Sorry for not meeting in a more intimate setting, but we will be talking about some very delicate matters and would not want any uninvited eavesdroppers listening in. This is where the partners hold their confidential meetings and so as a precautionary measure, we have this room swept clean every week to detect any possible surveillance equipment that could have been planted without our knowledge."

However, what the Dean did not tell them was that the partners had their own hidden cameras and microphones in the room recording all meetings for their own records. It had been installed by a company that used similar technology to record the audio portion of events for the President at the White House. The films were filed and guarded closely.

"Gentlemen, thanks for coming," the Dean officially began the meeting. "I know how busy you all are and I will try to have you back on your private jets before lunch, though our chef stands ready to prepare anything you would like at any time during or after our meeting. In about an hour, Walter and I and some of our firm's specially trained attorneys will be meeting with a couple of Hoover's special agents that he assigned to help us in the matter we are about to discuss, so I want to get our end of the business completed before their arrival."

The Dean then pressed a button on the table that pulled down a large screen. The first slide was entitled "Percentage of US Expenditures for Defense." It contained a line graph with years 1960 -1980 going up the vertical line, and the amounts and percentages of federal expenditures for defense during those years across the horizontal one.

"You pay good money to us to do two things," continued the Dean. "To use our lobbying influence and skills to increase the percentage of the national expenditures for defense, and secondly, to secure military contracts so your companies receive as large a share of that spending as possible. The former generals, Pentagon and Cabinet officials and legislators that we recruit to our firm's Strategic Division have delivered on both. As you will see from this graph, we have steadily grown the percentage of defense spending these last few years."

The Dean pointed to the year 1966. "This current year alone $301 billion of the $698 billion of the federal budget – that's 43.2% of all federal expenditures –have been allocated to be spent on defense. The contracts we secured for your four companies have averaged 13% of the entire defense spending. Do the math – 13% of $301 billion means that this year you collectively will be awarded over $39 billion in military contracts."

The Dean then pointed to the years 1967 and 68 and continued interpreting the figures. "And in the next two years, if we continue to do our work successfully, we project that the $301 billion in defense expenditures will grow to $400 billion with your end growing from $39 billion to over $50 billion. I don't know what your real margins are in determining profit for each of your companies, but published reports list all your businesses among the highest of the Fortune 100 companies."

Nowinski interrupted. "Dean, we of course applaud the firm's work. It is why we pay you the big bucks without blinking an eye. You must admit an annual retainer to your firm of $500 million from our four companies that grows when we grow is nothing to sneeze at. Did you call this special meeting looking to renegotiate our fee arrangement?"

"No, Brian, I called you here not to increase our fee, but to protect it and protect your revenue flow as well." The Dean went on to explain. "If you look at the graph beyond 1968 well into the 70s, you will see from our projections that if this war goes on until then, the profits to each of your companies during those years will be staggering – and of course, our firm's fees as well." The Dean was talking about continuing a war like a high roller hoping that his red-hot roll at a crap table doesn't stop.

"Dean, your graph shows the revenue flow all the way to 1978. Do you really think this war can go on for another 12 years?" asked JC, looking at the significant revenue that would be generated if it did.

"Good question. What we can say here is in the strictest confidence. We have reliable information coming from our friends at the White House that Johnson will escalate the fighting in a couple of months by resuming Operation Rolling Thunder's bombing of North Korea, hoping to cut supply lines from the Koreans to the Vietcong. The plan also calls for a steady increase of troop levels and the expansion of the battle into Laos and Cambodia, hoping to end it with overwhelming firepower. That means a major increase in defense spending to purchase the armaments as reflected in the graph. We are advised by some of our best military strategists, and this is highly Confidential, that despite this effort, the war can't be won against the Vietcong guerrilla-type warfare by simply increasing air and firepower. They forecast that the war is likely to go on with no end in sight unless they can come up with a diplomatic solution, or we withdraw without victory."

"What are the chances of a diplomatic solution?" JC asked.

"The Vietcong have no interest in negotiating and everything we hear is that Lyndon does not want to be the first American president to lose a war, so he is not going to back off. Also, McNamara is calling the shots and he is committed to a military victory. Given that both sides have dug in and given that there is no real dissent out there, we believe that unless some growing national grassroots antiwar movement takes root, this war will escalate and can predictably go on indefinitely."

"That's too bad," commented Carl Leonard of Global with political correctness, though that feeling was not exactly shared by the others and perhaps not even by Carl himself.

"Yes, for sure, none of us want to see our boys dying," the Dean was giving what he was about to say some moral cover. "But, as we know, the reality is that with each event there are winners and losers."

The Dean bent forward and lowered his voice and continued. "Let's be candid, guys. We are all grownups here. From a business standpoint, we have a significant amount to gain if the war does not, shall we say, end prematurely. Dissent will build as deaths and casualties of our soldiers mount and are flashed on news reports each evening, but unless some critical mass of protest grows from the grassroots against the president and our government, we believe this will be one of our country's longest wars."

The Dean stopped to drink some water. "So why are we here today? If we add your resources to well-designed countermeasures to prevent the evolvement of a grassroots movement to end the war prematurely, the benefit is enormous. But, if we don't," the Dean moved to slide two, entitled "Peacetime" which depicted the percentage of defense spending over the coming years if the war were to end. "If we don't," the Dean repeated, "the percentage of defense spending as you can see drops in half and your companies would lose multiples of billions of dollars each year during the ensuing peacetime. To be brutally frank, from a business standpoint, we all benefit greatly from a protracted war."

Talk of their getting richer in proportion to the rise in deaths and casualties was not shocking to a hardened group of armament industrialists who understood its corporate mission-a mission, a mission to generate as much revenue as possible from the sale of modern weapons designed to destroy lives as easily as hunting a deer with a guided missile. So, the next question merely got down to business.

"OK, Bill, so what's your plan and how much is it going to cost us?" JC asked the Dean, now wearing his CEO hat.

"At our request, you all made charitable donations to a foundation that we controlled to make substantial grants to universities. I told you at the right time I would reveal what it was all about."

"Not an insignificant amount, Dean, and by the way, I was questioned about it by our CFO and gave him very little information, as you requested," added Max Schmidt.

"And I appreciate that, Max, and the trust and confidence you all have shown in that regard. It's called the P-7 Project." The Dean then went on for the next 30 minutes explaining what the project was about and why he saw a possible student uprising as the biggest antiwar threat. "We have a well-thought-out plan," the Dean summed up, "and with your well-financed resources to implement it, we will isolate and degrade any student demonstrations, so their protests do not get off the ground. We have the cooperation of an administration that wants to prosecute the war without political fallout, the support of J. Edgar who rightfully sees these types of protests as unpatriotic, many friends in congress and the media, and our P-7 Project presidents of key universities who for patriotic reasons - want to act in support of the national interest. So, I am confident of a successful outcome."

"And the cost…?" JC pressed his earlier question.

"Not inexpensive, JC, but the financial rewards make those costs shrink by comparison. This endeavor may go on for several years. I and our firm will manage the project and employ the operatives and lawyers we trained to be at it 24/7. Besides needing more contributions to the foundation so it can fulfill its donations to the universities, we will need an operating budget of $5 million a year to implement the project, and a success bonus of another 2% of the increased contract revenue our firm secures for your companies."

"That's it?" JC asked. "That's it," replied the Dean.

"I suggest you submit your proposal to our lawyers, and we consider it," JC responded.

The Dean quickly reacted. "There is a need for strict confidentiality that warrants not taking this discussion or your decision out of this room. We will need to draft the agreement in language that in no way specifically spells out the nature and purpose of our mission. For many could argue that we and our friends in government and the universities are conspiring to prevent the people from exercising their first amendment rights to protest the war. If you sign on, I suggest that you get together and choose only one attorney to represent all four of your companies and that attorney will be under attorney-client privilege so he must keep it completely confidential. We cannot afford any leakage of our secret pact here today."

The four CEOs excused themselves to huddle in a distant corner and were back in just five minutes. JC, who had become their official spokesman, announced the consensus, "Bill, Walter, OK. The plan, the expenditures, and the firm's fees are all agreed to as proposed. Break out the bubbly and let's seal it with a toast."

Within 15 minutes of his call to the firm's chef, the Dean was pouring from a bottle of chilled (exactly at 45 degrees) 1928 Krug Brut Champagne into six fine fluted glasses. The firm contracted with collectors to buy their expensive wines at auctions. This bottle was purchased for $15,000.

"I hope you enjoy this," said the Dean as he poured, "for I am told that you are tasting a very rare champagne valued at $500 a sip."

"How can I enjoy it," quipped Nowinski, "when I know who is really paying for it? Kidding aside, Dean, do us the honors of an appropriate toast."

The Dean thought for just a moment and complied. "Hold up your glasses, gentleman." They all knew to lift by the stem. The Dean then raised his glass with a smile. "*Long* live the battle for freedom!"

CHAPTER 22

ALAN RANG UP Sevena bright and early on the third day he was back.

"Alan, how are you? How did it go yesterday?" Sevena asked in a cheerful tone.

"Good, but it was exhausting."

"Did you get your furnished apartment back?"

"Calling from it right now. Moved back my personal stuff, but had to sign a one-year lease this time, with two months' rent in advance. But no worries, had more than enough cash – will tell you about that as well when we get a spare moment."

"What about law school?" Sevena followed up like going down a punch list.

"Evelyn treated me like a long-lost child, actually greeted me with a hug as soon as I walked through the door. She said that no paperwork was necessary to reinstate me since my intent to withdraw was just that. It was not going to be officially recorded until the end of the semester, but she would have to talk with the Dean."

"What did he have to say?"

"She told me he was away in Washington on business, but she would reach him by phone. She called me a few hours later to tell me that she reached him, and he said he was delighted that I had come to my senses-so I am a student again."

"Great," reacted Sevena.

"Yeah 'great' you say, if you call great having to find someone who will let me copy their past two weeks of notes for all four courses, review my own for the whole year, cram tons of books into my head that I have not read and be ready to take exams just two or three days apart, starting next Monday. If you came here, you would think I was running a drug trafficking ring with the bags of stay-awake Dexedrine pills laying around that my pharmacy friend gave me without a prescription."

"A lot of work indeed – things people will do just to get high," Sevena was confident of Alan's ability to handle it and so joked showing no apparent concern. "By the way, you can get started preparing for those exams today because we need to push back our meeting until tomorrow. Your Dean is not the only one who had business in Washington. Judd was called away for a meeting there today and asked that I set up our meeting for 10 tomorrow in his office if that works for you."

"10 am in his office. Got it. See you both then." After a slight pause, "And Sevena," Alan said in a softer voice just catching her before she hung up.

"Yeah?"

"Remember the room service guy back at the Vegas hotel that evening knocking at the door to bring me the coffee?"

"Hard to forget."

"Just wanted to let you know that I have been thinking about it often."

"Him? Really, how so?"

"I keep thinking I should never have ordered that coffee."

"Me too," Sevena muttered to herself as she gently hung up the phone.

———————————

SEVENA WAS NOT as precise as she could have been concerning Judd's meeting. He had not been called away for a meeting in Washington. It was Judd who set up the meeting and as usual, arrived 15 minutes early at the pre-arranged local restaurant miles away from the Capitol Building. He sat at a two-person booth off in the corner observing the entrance. He looked at his watch for a third time. It was five minutes to 12. Noon, the time he had asked Mike to meet him. Judd then spotted him entering the restaurant with a couple of minutes to spare.

"How is my favorite professor?" Mike asked, wrapping his hands around Judd as he gave him a respectful hug.

"And how is my favorite meteorologist?" They both laughed.

After getting in their orders for salads, Judd ordered a beer and Mike a Coke. Mike was first to get down to business. "I loved getting your call to meet, but given the urgency to meet right away, I suspect you might be looking for another weather forecast. So, what's the climate been like since we last saw each other?"

"OK until now, but I suspect it is going to get stormy," Judd continued the metaphor.

Over the next 45 minutes, except for the few moments of interruption for the salads to be served, Judd went into detail explaining what he had been up to during the last two years.

He explained how Sevena and he were trying to recruit Alan as the new-found leader for the national antiwar movement he hoped to encourage. He told Mike about finding the highly unusual Investigator's Report on Alan, the fact that these investigators were going to continue monitoring his activities, and the report's strange reference to a P-7 Project. He emphasized that the Dean, recently appointed president of the university, and whom he had never met and knew little about, was involved with the Project, but he hadn't a clue in what way.

"There is a lot more detail in the Investigator's Report," Judd continued while bending down to reach into his briefcase to pull out a copy of the Report to hand to Mike.

"Judd, don't hand it to me or put it on the table," Mike commanded. "Put it on the booth between us… Good! In a few moments, get up to go to the bathroom and return in about 10 minutes. During that time, I will pick it up to read as if simply to pass time until your return. I will then put it back there for you to take before you leave. That will give me enough time to familiarize myself with the relevant portions of the report. Just so you know if we are to meet again, I am not to carry away any documents of yours to keep in my possession."

"Why? Is someone here watching us that we should worry about?" Judd reacted, nervously looking around.

"No, no one to worry about that I can see," Mike answered. His trained eyes had been surveying the place since he came. "Just precautions. You can say 'better to be safe than sorry,' or as cautioned by a similar type maxim emphasized during our training at the CIA 'you don't know what you don't know.'"

Following Mike's directions, Judd got up and asked the cashier where the bathroom was though he had used it on the way in, a deliberate move to draw attention away from the table. He was becoming a fast learner. When he returned a little over 10 minutes later, the Report was back at the same spot where he had left it.

"This is quite a thorough report," Mike greeted Judd upon his return. "The way this Martin Confidential Investigations detective agency went about gathering their information was of a quality that could match the work of any of our own intelligence agencies. I got what I needed from it. So how can I help?"

"Another favor," Judd spoke directly. "Given the nature of our relationship, I am sure I am asking for something that I have no right to ask. I promised Alan if he came aboard, I would have his back. But I can't have his back if I don't know what is behind all this. I need to know what the Dean is up to – what the P-7 Project is all about and whether Alan is being followed or otherwise in some danger. In short, I need you to see what you can find out and give me another weather forecast."

If he knew how much Mike liked and respected him, Judd would not need to be so humble in making his request. Though it was true that they only dated in Washington, off and on for a couple of months, with their mutually satisfying intimacies being somewhat intermittent, Michael enjoyed every minute he spent with Judd. He was mesmerized by Judd's historical knowledge, charmed by his wit and moved by his passion and genuine idealism. Mike was 12 years younger than Judd. He always felt that stood in the way of the relationship developing into more than a friendship that Mike would otherwise have preferred, but he also enjoyed just having Judd as a friend. He only wished that when he studied for his bachelor's and master's degrees in Criminal Justice in preparation to join the CIA, he would have had more dedicated and inspiring professors like Judd. He trusted Judd completely.

"I'll see what I can do," responded Mike. "But here is the deal...."

Judd interrupted before Mike went on. "Mike, I do want you to know just how much I appreciate it. I know I am asking you to do something very delicate."

"It's OK. Glad to be of help if I can. And you're right. If it isn't already, it will become very 'delicate', and from what I can see, that is putting it mildly. Besides the ones you mentioned, there are going to be other actors involved. Given your plan, you and this fellow Alan will be at the forefront of a well-publicized effort to stimulate a national antiwar protest movement. Trust me, if Alan is not being monitored now by those P-7 guys, or whoever is behind them, he and you will eventually be monitored by the FBI. You both will be added on to J. Edgar Hoover's Enemies List of anarchists or communists as soon as you begin, and who knows who else's list in and out of government, who will see you as unpatriotic."

"My God, you really think it is that serious? I will be careful," Judd responded and reached for his credit card to pay for the bill that had just been delivered.

"Put your Diners Club card away," Mike immediately reacted. "No really, Mike. I asked you here, my treat," Judd reacted.

"No worry, I'll let you pick up the tab, but with cash, not your credit card," explained Mike. "When I said you may be monitored, this is what I meant. If you had paid this bill by a credit card, recognize that the FBI, who will be on your trail as soon as you and Alan go into action, or maybe others, will have access to all your credit card accounts. They will know every place where you ate using that Diners card and therefore which city or place you were in on that day – and at what time – and perhaps how many people were there with you by the amount you paid. They would know all your traveling destinations from the purchasing of plane or train tickets, or the days and times you visited other locations from where and when you pumped gas or rented a car. If you used your credit card here in Washington at this restaurant, for instance, they could come here to get your check and see exactly what you ordered to determine how many people met you. They could show your picture to our friendly owner there and ask him if he could describe who was with you and whether he noticed any papers passed between us. Incidentally, that is why I ordered a Coke, which I never drink, rather than my favorite cocktail that is well known to my FBI and CIA friends. So, from here on in, load yourself up with a boatload of cash, for that is how you will pay bills at locations you do not want them to know where you were or with whom you met. Remember, they can match your credit card activity with someone else's card activity whom they suspect you are conspiring with. Welcome to my world, Professor."

A sudden gloom came over Judd. "My God, I never would have thought of that."

"Right, exactly. That is because 'you don't know what you don't know.' Now-more rules. We are not to talk on our phones going forward, even just to arrange a meeting. Next time we meet, which will be in two weeks when I will report what, if anything, I can find out, we will swap outside pay phone numbers. Make sure you look for one that is not close to your office or residence. If you need to initiate a call after that, have someone you can trust call me to solicit something, mentioning a price like 18 hundred dollars, which will mean 1800 or 6 pm. That will tell me the time for us to go to those pay phones. Got it?"

"Yes, I follow," Judd responded, still somewhat shaken but intrigued with Mike's ability and feeling somewhat secure because of it. He now had a greater appreciation for what it meant when Mike had told him that his job at the CIA was in 'clandestine services'.

"Now, I will be in New York exactly two weeks from today," continued Mike." I do not want you to fly there. Drive up with your car and do not use your credit card for gas, any garages, or anything else in the city. At 3 pm there is a ferry that takes you to see the Statue of Liberty. I will be on it. By the way, be particularly sure to buy that ticket with cash as well," added Mike, smiling at that obvious reminder.

They both left separately and met a block away to give themselves another goodbye hug and an additional thank you from Judd.

Judd made his 4 pm flight to Boston in plenty of time to board. Fate often arranges coincidences even if they are meaningless. As Judd passed through the first-class section to get to his seat in coach, he was heavy in thought about getting back to Boston to execute his plan to commence the antiwar movement. He had no reason to notice the gray-haired gentleman, impeccably dressed, buckling up his seat belt in those wider and more comfortable first-class seats, similarly thinking of getting back to Boston to execute his plan, but in this case to prevent any attempt at creating such a movement. A coincidence or was it just fate's way of enjoying a joke and getting a rush like the crowds at the Roman Colosseum observing two gladiators separately entering the arena at the same time about to fight to the death, readying themselves for the signal: "Let the games begin."

CHAPTER 23

SEVENA ARRIVED AT Judd's office for the meeting twenty minutes early just as he was finishing correcting a few of his students' papers.

"How did yesterday's meeting go with the meteorologist?" she asked, as she poured herself a coffee from Judd's ready-made pot. True to his word, Judd kept Mike's name in confidence even to Sevena.

"Quite good. He is willing to see what he can find out."

"Needle in a haystack again?" she asked.

"Maybe not. These intelligence agencies have their tentacles out everywhere even among their own sister agencies. What I learned from our guy is that while the CIA and the FBI do not share their information with complete transparency, they spy on each other and in that way get information gathered by the other agency. Would you believe they don't trust each other? More interestingly, the White House trusts neither of them, but chooses not to interfere with their clandestine operations."

"Why not? Why do they put up with it if they don't trust what they are doing?" Sevena asked incredulously. "The president appoints Hoover and the heads of these freaking agencies. He should be able to control them."

"A couple of reasons: I am told by my guy that Hoover spies not only on American citizens, but on all the presidents he serves, as well as under their cabinet members. Hoover was not reluctant to let Kennedy know what info he gathered about his sexual exploits and told him he would protect these from getting out to the public. Protection meant a form of blackmail to guarantee his reappointment and permit him to continue his operations as he saw fit. Also, if presidents have no knowledge of the illegalities employed by these agencies, they have complete deniability and can, without risk, benefit from all the ill-gotten intelligence of their political opponents. Not as Jefferson and our other founding fathers envisioned it, I admit."

"Any second thoughts about Alan now that you have seen him up close and personal?" Sevena asked, getting to the business at hand.

"No, quite the contrary. I am impressed with the methodical way he has gone about considering our proposal. What's even more impressive is how he has, without any trepidation, thrown himself into the final law school exams for an entire year's classes at the very last minute with little time to prepare or sleep. He displays a confidence and the ability to handle any crisis under pressure, and we are going to need that."

The last remark could have served as an introduction to Alan's entrance, though he was not privy to it as he opened the door exactly at 10.

"Ah, it smells like ready-made coffee," Alan commented as he came in and like Sevena went right over to the coffee pot and proceeded to pour himself a cup.

"You pull an all-nighter?" Sevena asked.

"No, when I can, I try to get at least a couple of hours of sleep to let what I learned be processed by my brain. But the coffee helps start the next morning." He looked at Judd. "So, shall we get to work?" Alan then pulled out the notebook from his handheld canvas briefcase containing the plan Judd had given him. "I looked over your plan and have a few questions, some comments and a couple of prayers I would like to offer."

"You don't need them. Judd is Jewish and so unlike us, he can reach the Big Guy with a local call."

"I already called him and he's not taking sides."

"As they say, not so important that *he* be on our side as long as we are on *his*," Alan remarked as he opened the copy of the plan. "Look, I buy Judd's premise. As crazy as it seemed to me at first, if the war is at all stoppable, and I am not sure it is, the energy will have to come from college students across the country. Though, to be frank, I think they are more interested in partying and smoking weed."

A small smile came over Sevena. Alan was complimenting Judd on that approach, but it was Sevena's idea to mobilize the students. In fact, Judd had ridiculed the idea when Sevena first suggested it. "Sevena, you got to be fucking kidding me. We would be relying on kids, barely out of high school, or should I say barely out of their diapers, whose only known hardship is to try to live on their dad's monthly allowances while at school."

Sevena had made a profound observation that not only gave credence to her proposal but pinpointed the undercurrent that was to define the upheaval of the 60s. "Sure, too many of my generation have lived prosaic lives till now. That's because their political libidos lay dormant, dulled by the conservative culture of the 50s. Many were spoiled by their parents wanting to give them things that they themselves could not afford. But it is precisely because of that dullness, the sons and daughters of what was probably the most courageous generation of Americans are now thirsting for their own relevance, for their own identity. I believe underneath they have a desire to create a counterculture of their own meaning and are bursting for rebellion if given a just cause to embrace."

Sevena had no interest in taking credit for the idea. More, importantly, both she and Judd were polished enough to know that Alan's opening kudos over the "premise" of the plan, was setting up a "but" and it came quickly and unapologetically.

"So, a good idea," Alan repeated as he turned the pages until finding the implementation section. He then riffled through one page after another that he had totally crossed out from top to bottom with Xs in red ink. Having displayed the redaction of just about the entire section, it was now almost redundant to say it, but he put it to them boldly: "This implementation approach simply can't work."

Judd had been prepared to welcome some helpful modifications, but was somewhat taken aback by the breadth of rejection. "Alan, you realize you just X'd-out the entire implementation section. 'Good idea' you say, but with no way to implement it, that makes it a 'bad idea' as I see it. So, I assume you would not come here tear apart most of our plan and freely partake of my coffee without having an alternative workable approach in mind?"

"That I do. I would never be that ungracious given the quality of the brew." Alan took another sip of coffee as if to punctuate the remark and continued in a way that indicated he had carefully considered their approach that he had now rejected. "I see it simply that without significant resources and student organizations already out there ready to join us, we wouldn't be able, nor have time, to build a national movement from scratch."

Sevena was all ears. Judd as well. The implementation section had been debated by Judd and Sevena many times over. They, too, saw the difficulties in developing a national organization but had not been able to come up with any alternative. Alan continued.

"The plan calls for organizing the students into a single national student movement led by a young charismatic leader, a young Martin Luther King, if you will, who would put a face on the movement. That is why you were searching so hard to find that leader. Even if such a national mobilization could be put together, which I seriously doubt, it could take a couple of years or more to do it. As you know, we simply don't have that time. Remember the Civil Rights Movement started with organizations dedicated to advancing racial equality already firmly in place. Martin Luther King's Southern Christian Leadership Conference, the Congress for Racial Equality and the NAACP were there from the get-go, long before I and others like me joined that fight. There are no such organized student antiwar organizations among the colleges to jump-start the movement."

Alan took another sip. "What's more, simply put, the students are just students, very independent and of all colors and sizes. We could never get them to agree to come under one umbrella or have them all discipline their behavior to prescribed conduct. We may be able to get many to join the effort, but if they do, it will grow out of organizations spontaneously and independently springing up at local campuses, not part of a national recruitment. In fact, as a bonus many more may join not out of idealism, but simply because demonstrations will present them with opportunities to get high and get laid."

"For that reason, not be unappealing to women either," Sevena remarked, thinking there was another revolution in the making. She was right. In fact, it would later be given a name: "The Sexual Revolution."

"So, Alan, how *do you* see us getting them organized?" she asked.

"That is exactly it, Sevena. I don't-we can't. We should not try to do so. Instead, we should consider their being undisciplined as strengths, not weaknesses."

Judd's wanting to hear more could not have been better demonstrated by his getting up while listening to freshen Alan's nearly empty cup of coffee. Sevena smiled as she observed the approving gesture.

Alan continued. "Here is what I suggest…a *blitz*!!"

"A blitz sounds shocking enough, but what's that?" Judd asked.

"We develop every type of protest against the war we can think of and then organize, deploy and concentrate all of them in a blitz of one single month of demonstrations on three campuses simultaneously. Perhaps here at BU, another at a college or university on the West Coast, and a third in middle-America, with the actions you outlined in your plan: day and night rallies, distributing antiwar pamphlets, teach-ins, sit-ins and acts of peaceful civil disobedience by occupying buildings-all to try to shut down classes and the operation of administrative offices. I would add that we attack the war effort directly by rupturing the relationship between the war establishment and universities. During the one-month blitz at the three universities, we should occupy ROTC buildings urging students to return their uniforms, protest the school's furnishing grades to draft boards and urging draft-eligible students to burn their draft cards in public."

Alan turned the page to see some other notes of his and continued at a more rapid speed reflecting his energy. "We plan a media blitz to go with the demonstration blitz. We light the match with a bursting flame fueled by every energy source and resource we can muster during that one month. It will either burn itself out and we lose, or if we are lucky, ignite the dormant dry brush on all the campuses, setting off a conflagration of wildfires popping up across the country that cannot be put out. During our blitz, we can demonstrate the models for effective types of protests that can work, as well as messages and chants others can adopt. I was thinking of a couple I saw on a poster, 'Make Love, Not War' and something like 'Hey, Hey, LBJ, How Many More Were Killed Today.' Hopefully, it will stimulate more antiwar signs and folk music that would create a powerful antiwar narrative that can appeal to both students and adults. We can create artwork with peace symbols. Then we see if our premise is correct that there is a volcanic rumbling under the stillness of the 50s ready to erupt if we heat it up. If it catches and momentum builds to a critical mass, then non-student sympathetic organizations and leaders like Martin Luther King may join in and lend their support to our growing independent movement."

True to his training, Judd was carefully evaluating Alan's remarks with the same rigid scrutiny that he judged the presentation of a graduate thesis. When Alan was done, he thought there would have been no mark high enough to score its compelling logic and imagination. Judd was even more astonished given that Alan had no more than hours, a day at most, to comprehend the entire undertaking and come up with such a feasible implementation plan. In contrast, he and Sevena had been wrestling to develop a practical approach for months on end and only because they were at wit's end, finally settled on their proposal, which in their heart of hearts felt like it had less of a chance of winning than a lottery ticket.

Sevena was just as awed by the soundness and appeal of the plan, but on a more visceral level.

She was mesmerized by Alan's energy and the excitement he generated in his animated articulation of the plan. To her, it had an exciting libertarian approach. As Alan put it, they would aim to fan the flames of whatever "brush fires" existed among the various diverse student bodies across the nation, leaving them to act on their own inspiration and imagination. That was what she had been trying to reach for in her prior argument to Judd. What's more, they had indeed found their leader. Another nice thing, she thought: if there were multiple movements and not a single national one, then there was no head at the top to cut off that would kill it.

However, with the elation came a solemn sense of responsibility and trepidation among all three of them. They recognized that if the 30-day blitz failed, their heavily publicized antiwar uprising could not only suffer a serious setback but perhaps sustain a fatal blow.

"So, which month?" Sevena asked. "What?" Alan responded.

"Which month do you suggest the blitz take place?"

"If we could be ready, and that is no small task, I would think September, during enrollment. The students are back from summer vacation. It's still warm, so conducive to holding rallies and demonstrations. The schools would be in the middle of organizing the enrollments and classes so it would be easier to disrupt their operations while the administration, faculty and security are busy getting things in place. Of course, we would need every day of the next 10 weeks, after I finish my exams, to recruit and organize a critical mass of students at each college without detection."

"How many students do you think we would need at each school to hit the ground running?" Sevena asked.

Alan thought for a moment. "I would think that we would need at least 100 committed and trained students in place at each school to both demonstrate and help recruit others during the first week of the blitz to join in as we expand the types of demonstrations during the rest of the month."

"We figured on similar numbers and have not been idle," Sevena moved the conversation forward. "Judd and I have been secretly recruiting students and some teachers here at BU and some other universities. They have been engaged in covertly recruiting students awaiting our word if or when we set the plan in motion."

"Alan, were you thinking of any particular universities for the other two sites?" Judd asked.

"No, just their geographical locations to get nationwide attention."

"Well, I think for the West Coast, I would suggest Baxter U in San Francisco," Judd added. "They have a reputation for conducting student protests in many areas over the years. Next, I would suggest America University in Oklahoma City. We are in contact with the leaders of their Students for Democratic Action and they are eager to conduct demonstrations against the war with our help. That normally conservative university would give us the credibility of being more than a liberal movement and access to both Midwestern and Southern media markets."

"I agree," added Sevena. "Also, I would think it best not to do it simultaneously from the get-go. We should begin with America U the first week by itself, Baxter breaking out in San Francisco the next week, and finally here at BU the week after, so that all three will be demonstrating together for the last two weeks. That way it will look like the demonstrations were contagiously breaking out independently. Hopefully, others will then follow."

"Good idea," said Alan, putting his cup of coffee down. "So, we have a plan. Now, on to my exams and I will see you in two weeks when I come out of my hibernation. By the way, I heard my Dean was promoted to president of the university. The nice thing about it is that he will be totally unprepared for our blitz as he will just be settling in. Do you know who we will be up against at Baxter in San Francisco?"

"The president of Baxter is a guy named Jack Wilson," Judd responded. "They affectionately call him by his nickname 'Speedy' carried over from his football days. All we know from researching him is that he has limited administrative experience and got the job because of his popularity with the alumni. So, I doubt if he will have a clue as to how to react to our blitz."

"And America U?" Alan asked.

"George Coburn is their president. He recently got some favorable publicity for securing a significant multi-year donation for the University from an anonymous donor. It looks like he sees his role as a fundraiser. We don't see anything special in his background to prepare him to deal with a crisis. Overall, I like the universities we selected."

Unknown to Judd, someone else would like the universities they selected as well, and that person at that very moment happened to be sitting on the top floor of his administrative office in the very next BU building.

CHAPTER 24

JUST AS MIKE directed, Judd caught the 3:00 pm ferry to the Statue of Liberty and as usual, in plenty of time. It was crowded, which was to be expected this time of year when the weather was turning warm. It was a top tourist attraction for parents wanting to give themselves and their kids a boat ride and a history lesson. In fact, on this day a group of French high school kids was visiting from abroad with a young female guide speaking to them in French, explaining that it was the French sculptor, Frédéric-Auguste Bartholdi, who designed and presented the statue as a gift to the United States from the people of France in October 1886. The guide was pointing to the statue, visible from the ferry that was still docked, and her voice revealed her pride as she shouted *La Liberté éclairant le monde.* Judd, slightly conversant in French, knew from his studies that was Bartholdi's dedicated name of the statue, translated: *"Liberty Enlightening the World."*

Later, when the ferry cruised close to the statue, the ferry's own tourist guide explained that the majestically robed female was meant to represent a Roman goddess of freedom holding her torch that bore the date of the Declaration of Independence, July 4, 1776, welcoming immigrants arriving at our shores.

Judd, as a professor, thought how history can meld events. Yes, it was a historic French gift, but not to be confused, the statue in its original form stood solely as a symbol for freedom, not a welcoming door for immigrants. It took the words of a young American New York-born poet, Emma Lazarus, written for the auction to raise funds for the statue in 1883, that made it a symbol for greeting immigrants. It was not until 1903 that a portion of her words was placed on a bronze plaque in the statue's pedestal that gave the Lady her welcoming to thousands upon thousands of immigrants fleeing their totalitarian nations.

"Give me your tired, your poor,

Your huddled masses yearning to breathe free,

The wretched refuse of your teeming shore.

Send these, the homeless, tempest-tost to me,

I lift my lamp beside the golden door!"

Filled with patriotic feelings inspired by the dedication and works of Bartholdi and the poetry of Lazarus, Judd wondered why there was so much trouble in the country. Given the suspicion of one another's ideologies and a runaway war machine, perhaps, as one writer put it, "we have listened too much to our politicians and too little to our poets."

The ferry was now on its return path back to the dock and, though Judd had observed every person on board, there was no Mike to be seen. He began to question whether he had mistaken the date and time, but he was quite sure he hadn't. He had been instructed not to call under any circumstances, since calls could be monitored, so upon disembarking, Judd decided to walk back to his car garaged three blocks away and drive back to Boston. There seemed to be no alternative.

He was halfway down a street when he observed a person in a hooded black jacket about 40 yards back walking behind him almost at the exact same pace. A few minutes later, Judd turned the corner to his right, looked back and noticed the person had turned on to that street as well and was continuing to walk at his pace, keeping the same distance behind. When Judd then deliberately increased his pace, that person appeared to do so as well. At this point, Judd felt he was being followed, but did not know for sure.

As Judd approached another intersection, he had a decision to make. Normally, he would go one more block to his car. However, if he were to make a third right heading back in the same direction he came from, and that person took the same turn, he would know for sure that someone was after him. However, taking that illogical turn would alert the person that he was on to him and that could be dangerous.

Judd decided to do it anyway. As soon as he turned the corner and was out of sight for a few moments, he started running to gain distance while continually looking back to see if the person took the turn as well. It was less than 20 seconds later when he saw the person turning the corner, coming at him on the run.

"What the fuck is going on?" he thought. His heart began to pound. The street was long with only apartment buildings on either side and devoid of other pedestrians. Would he be able to escape? Judd panicked, still trying to put some distance between him and his pursuer. He looked back again and saw the person wave down and jump into a cab now coming his way. As it slowed down upon reaching him, he saw the back window being lowered. Judd instinctively put his hands on his head, bending down as if to duck, when the cab came to a squeaking halt a few feet in front of him. He straightened up; sweat was pouring down from his forehead as he watched the rear door open. Then a voice rang out, "Judd, hop in." He looked up. It was Mike.

Judd entered the cab breathlessly, shouting, "Mike, what the fuck is going on?" Mike immediately put his fingers in front of his mouth giving him a shush sign.

"Glad I caught you, man. I heard it's going to rain." Mike spoke as if he was picking him up for a prearranged engagement. "Hungry? I know a nice out-of-the-way Lebanese restaurant not far from here with the richest hummus and baba ghanoush you ever tasted. Cabbie, 30 East 13th Street, please." Judd sat motionlessly and stunned, almost unable to decipher what Mike was saying.

The rest of the cab ride was relatively silent and remained so until they were seated at an Italian restaurant rather than a Lebanese one, 2 blocks from where the cabbie let them off. Orders were given to the waitress along with their drinks: Judd his coffee and Mike his Coke.

Judd, calmed down somewhat, could wait no longer. "So, what in the hell is it with the cloak and dagger stuff? You don't show up at the ferry and then proceed to scare the living shit out of me?"

"Truly sorry about that, professor, but given what I found out about what you asked me to look into, I needed to be extremely cautious."

"You found out something about the P-7 Project?"

"Yes and no," Mike responded.

"Yes and no?" Judd repeated the words. "That is all I need, Mike-a riddle added to a cloak and dagger mystery."

"Not to worry, my friend, you will have both answers by the time the tasty lasagna is served." As he spoke, Mike reached across the table grasping and softly squeezing Judd's arm as a reassuring gesture.

Mike then lowered his voice. "No luck so far in coming across any chatter about the P-7 Project in any of the CIA, FBI, or sister agencies' communications. But in the FBI files I accessed, I did run across the name of the so-called detective agency that did the investigation and report on Alan."

"Martin Confidential Investigations?" Judd asked, more like a reflex. "*So-called* you say?"

"Yes, it's a fictitious detective agency."

"But we looked them up and they have an office leased under their name right here in New York City," Judd responded.

"Yes, it was leased under that name and was even just recently renewed. Further, that agency has been incorporated here in New York as well. But they don't actually exist, and they did not do the investigation."

"Then, who did?" Judd unknowingly began to raise his voice.

"The FBI," Mike responded in almost a whisper, setting the volume level for Judd's further responses.

"The F-Fucking BI?" Judd repeated in a loud enough tone that Mike had to give him another shush sign.

"Yes, and not just Alan's, but many investigations commissioned by your Dean. The FBI funds the lease of the office and maintains the shell agency.

"What in the hell is going on?" Judd was looking for more of an explanation from Mike.

"I can't tell you. I don't know yet. That is all I could find out so far. But whatever the Dean's P-7 Project is about, Hoover is heavily involved in it. Maybe the Project is simply a way for the FBI to get first divvies in recruiting top law school graduates for special operations. Maybe that explains why Alan was rejected. He clearly doesn't fit into Hoover's right-wing policies. But what baffles me is that if that were so, it doesn't square with why the report indicated they would continue to monitor Alan's activities. That gets me to the cloak and dagger stuff I had to pull off today."

"How so?" Judd asked.

"Well, when I found out it was the FBI that would be doing the monitoring, that meant professional surveillance with significant manpower. At some point, if not already and for whatever their reasons, Alan may be closely watched, and all his communications monitored by the FBI. As a result, you and any others he communicates with would be monitored by them as well, depending on who they thought could be a threat to their Project or the Bureau's operations whatever that may be. So, when I learned it was the Bureau that was involved, I knew their surveillance would be carried on with a sophistication that private agencies can't duplicate.

There would be no way of my detecting if you were being followed and watched onboard the ferry. So, I decided I better follow you and not pick you up until I was sure no one else was on your tail. Speaking of which, do you have that number of the public telephone near you that I asked you to get me for our further telephone communications?"

"Yes, but I am learning your bad habits of not writing anything down and memorized it – 353- 5538. What's yours?"

"No more mine. If we send each other a coded message with the time for a call as we discussed, I will call your payphone from a pay booth wherever I may be at that time. 353 5538, I got it. Look, I will keep trying to find out what is behind all this and will let you know if I find anything. In the meantime, how is your antiwar effort going?"

Judd went on during the meal filling in Mike with each detail of the plan and its timing.

"Well, you weren't being followed today and hopefully any surveillance of Alan is still on the back burner. If it were not, they would already be making your adventure a bit more complicated. In the meantime, let's continue being cautious. Also, tell Alan and Sevena and the rest of your recruits that it's OK to talk to one another, but only about school or social items, nothing about your blitz, as you call it, unless in person or from a phone booth. OK, I'll get the check this time. You grab a cab back to your car and Judd…" Mike paused and squeezed his arm gently once again.

"What?"

"Be careful and I am not just talking about your ride back to Boston."

CHAPTER 25

"FIFTEEN MORE MINUTES," the Evidence Professor called out to the class of 76 students indicating that the two-hour exam was coming to an end. His voice woke up Alan who had dozed off holding on to his exam book. He had been staring at it with his eyes closed during the last 10 minutes attempting to review his finished answers before handing them in. This was Alan's fourth and last exam, all taken in the past two weeks. He had almost finished two prescriptions of Dexedrine pills to cheat on sleep to prepare for them.

When he again started a final review of his answers, he found his eyes involuntarily closing every 30 seconds or so interrupting his effort. But he did not call it quits. Instead, Alan left his book on the desk and went to the bathroom, splashed some water on his face and came back and spent the last eight minutes or so refining some points.

"Time's up. Drop your pencils and bring your exam books up front to this table, please," the professor called out to end the exam. Alan fell back on his chair, his arms falling to his thighs, letting most of the students move ahead of him before mustering enough energy to get up and deposit his exam book. He had indeed given the four exams everything he had and was thinking, "I have no fucking idea what marks I will get this time…". For some reason remembering two items they gave marks for in early grade school, he thought, "I certainly would have gotten an 'A' for Effort, but with all the notes, books and papers left scattered all around my apartment, an 'F' for Care of Property." He had no idea why his thoughts rambled like that, but someone else may have found his total deprivation of sleep and an overload of Dexedrine as the possible culprits.

Alan made it back to his apartment almost in a sleepwalk, fell into bed fully clothed, and slept without interruption for almost 18 hours before he was awakened by a phone call. It was Sevena.

"Did I get you up?" she asked. "No, I don't think I'm up yet."

"Well, maybe not, but you're alive and I would bet they will be promoting you to your senior year. Want some breakfast? My treat."

"Sure, just give me a week or so and I'll meet you at the BU Commons again."

Sevena laughed. "No, I want to get away from the school, and besides, as I recall, I seem to be too vulnerable to your charms there. Make it the Park Café near you in about an hour instead."

"All I can promise is that I'll try."

Once showered and with two nights' sleep wrapped into one, Alan felt surprisingly refreshed for the first time in weeks. He walked the few blocks to the Café warmed by the morning June sun.

"Alan, over here," Sevena called out to him as he began to pull up a seat at an indoor booth. "It's too beautiful this morning to sit inside, come out here." She waved him over to the outside patio table where she was sitting.

Sevena stood up to welcome him. She was in her running gear: shorts, sneakers, a slightly dampened V-neck T-shirt that had a patch with number 4 sewn onto the back, and a white cotton sweatshirt now rolled up and tied around her waist. She was slightly flushed, having just finished her morning run ending up at the Café. Alan had forgotten just how refreshingly beautiful she was. She greeted him with a respectable hug, though they both held on a bit longer than a greeting of hello.

"Staying in shape, I see." Alan was reaching for something to say to break up the slightly embarrassing intimacy of the moment.

"More than that, I want to be in condition to run the Boston

Marathon next Patriots Day."

"Really? But the Marathon is only open to men."

"Well, up to now that is," responded Sevena with half a smile.

As soon as Alan said it was only open to men, he realized that was precisely why she was planning to run. "Why practice?" he asked. "You may make your point by showing up, but they won't allow you to get to the starting line once you attempt to register."

"Don't intend to register. I am going to find a spot and slip in somewhere way back in the line just as they are ready to roll. Last month's Marathon, a gal named Roberta Louise "Bobbi" Gibb did exactly that. Without registering, she hid in the bushes near the starting line and then joined the middle of the pack as they got off the mark. She successfully passed herself off as a man most of the way by wearing a hooded shirt and finished ahead of most of the men, but since she was not permitted to register, her run as the first woman to enter and finish the race is not officially recognized. I want to run next year and encourage others to do the same."

No one believed that women had the stamina to successfully run marathons and so they were barred from participating. Sevena was hoping to prove that Gibb was not an exception and that women should become eligible to register and run with the Marathon's official sanction and with a designated official number.

"I see you are going to run with the makeshift number 4 on your shirt. Any significance in that?" asked Alan.

"Last time I looked at the Investigator's Report that was the date of your birth."

"Wow, I will be greatly honored." Alan bowed slightly as he spoke.

"Or greatly shamed," Sevena was quick to point out, "for when they spot me, still another intruder with a makeshift number, they may decide to drag me out of the race, and of course, they *will* have to drag me."

That turned out to be exactly what occurred the following year. Sevena was spotted by security guards less than 1000 yards from the official starting line with her makeshift number 4 and they dragged her out of the race. Sevena was not disappointed, she was playing another role, that of distracting security from another female runner.

Six months before the race, Sevena had contacted a 21-year-old female accomplished long-distance runner and suggested to her how she could register for the Marathon in an official capacity. Her name was Kathrine Switzer. Switzer agreed and trained by running over 80 miles a week before the race. When ready, she registered to run in the 1967 all men's Boston Marathon by sending in her application and signing her name as K.V. Switzer, so officials would assume she was a man, and she would enter the race with a short haircut.

Unlike Sevena who had been spotted by security immediately, it was a mile or two after the race began that Switzer was spotted by the co-director of the Marathon, Jock Semple. He immediately ran out, grabbed her and started to rip her official 261 number off her jersey while swearing at her profusely for entering. In what came to be called one of sport's most publicized moments, Kathrine's boyfriend, running by her side, with a thrust of his shoulder knocked Semple aside so she could continue to run with her ripped number and finish with the help of her boyfriend and other male runners by her side to protect her all the way. When crossing the finish line, she vowed to run again the following year. Photographs of the Marathon official being knocked aside went viral in the media. It made Time-Life's "100 Photos that Changed the World."

Switzer and women like Sevena and Bobbi Gibb, by running in succeeding marathons, eventually would be successful in changing the rules so women were finally admitted to officially register and run in the Boston Marathon five years later in 1972. Switzer would go on to run 32 marathons, winning the 1974 New York City Marathon and finishing the 1975 Boston Marathon in just two hours and fifty-one minutes, a time ranked sixth in the world.

Sevena would be there to celebrate as one who also ran and finished that race in well under four hours wearing an official number 428 and an unofficial number – 4 – sewn to the back of her T- shirt. Bobbi Gibb would later officially be recognized and recorded as the first woman to run the Boston Marathon in 1966.

At the Park Café, "How many causes are you engaged in?" Alan asked in a voice denoting admiration while breathing in the fresh air of the outside patio and thinking how good it was to have the exam pressure behind.

"Not many, only the ones that are worth fighting for." Sevena simply parried the question, being more interested in substituting it with a question of her own. "Alan, along those lines, I need to ask you about something that has been on my mind. You are aware that even with your improvements to our plan, the chances of our pulling off the blitz are, at best, doubtful. So, given the enormous commitment we are asking you to make, what was it that persuaded you to take on our cause?"

Alan remained silent in thought for a while and then responded. "Probably for the same reason you will spend almost every day of the next year getting in condition to try to finish the grueling 26 plus miles of the Boston Marathon next April when the odds of your even being allowed to run in it are less than our succeeding with our plan. I gather when a wrong comes your way that needs to be righted, the odds are never in your favor, but for some reason, you can't seem to walk away from it. In fact, to me, there is a rush in trying to see if I'm good enough to beat the odds." Alan hesitated and then resumed," And there is another important reason."

"What's that?" responded Sevena.

Alan leaned over with his elbows on the table, permitting him to rest his chin on his hands, and looking directly in her eyes, said, "You."

"Me?"

"Yes, you! I thought it would be nice to hang out with you for the summer."

"That long, huh?"

"Well, plus or minus a night or two?" Alan responded with equal playfulness.

"Well then, I owe it to you to make those nights interesting, don't I?"

"Coffee, folks?" interrupted the waiter coming to the table with a coffee pot and menus.

Alan and Sevena looked at each other and then broke out in a belly laugh simultaneously. Just as in the Vegas hotel, yet another waiter interrupts their moment of growing intimacy with coffee service.

"You know the fates are telling us that our getting together is just not to be." Alan smiled.

"Sure, but then you and I aren't afraid of bucking the odds, are we?" Sevena added, then quickly picked up the menu and said, "So, what are you going to have for breakfast?"

Throughout the meal that was to last well over two hours, each took turns waving off the waiter wanting to leave the check and instead ordering more and more coffee. They hardly noticed that people around them were now starting to order lunch rather than breakfast as they could not stop asking and learning about each other's lives.

Alan told her about his experience working for his dad selling newspapers in Boston as a kid. He even related to her how his dad took a beating to join the newspaper truckers' protest against unfair wages and poor working conditions when the fight was not his and he knew the likelihood of the consequences. Sevena thought his father's gift of idealism and courage to his son was another reason why Alan's awareness of the risks and likely harmful consequences in joining their cause did not prevent him from doing so.

Alan was fascinated to hear all about Sevena's encounters at St.

Mary's and laughed out loud when she told him about her suspension for insulting the basketball coach and the team. He then assured her he never prayed for God's help before shooting a foul shot, though maybe that would have been wise to do before he missed the game-winning shot at the State Tournament's champion basketball game. Time seemed to fly by quickly. Many couples who sat and ate together with hardly a word spoken, devoid of the spontaneity and joy they were witnessing, tried with envy to recall what had happened to the love they once shared, but could only muster, can you pass me the butter?

The last ten minutes turned to the business at hand as Sevena filled Alan in on what Judd learned from his intelligence source about the investigation and the need only to converse about the blitz in person.

"But, nothing about the P-7 Project itself?" Alan asked. "His source is still working on it."

"OK, I'm now free and at your command. What comes next?" asked Alan.

"Get some more rest this week. Next Monday evening, Judd reserved a conference room next to his office at the Liberal Arts School theoretically for a conference on Parliamentary Democracies. The only invited guests are our recruited student leaders here at BU and the other two schools in San Francisco and Oklahoma. We have been working with them for some time now. They are committed and can be trusted. We want to take that opportunity to introduce you to them as the overall leader and begin to map out our plans and frame the work we need to do over the summer."

"I will be there. Would you like me to walk you home?" Alan asked, getting up and finally calling on the anxious waiter for the check.

"Sure, if you wish, but not much to entertain you with when we get there. I'm feeling a little mucky from my run so all I will be doing is getting out of these wet things and taking a shower."

CHAPTER 26

AS SEVENA SUGGESTED, Alan took advantage of the rest of the week to tend to some personal needs, catch up on sleep and relax at the gym with some pickup basketball games. But that would be all the rest and leisure time he would get for the remainder of the summer. A twelve-hour day would turn out to be a light one during the next 10 weeks of preparation for the blitz.

He would spend a good deal of that time meeting with the student leaders from the three schools to develop, refine and coordinate the planned demonstrations in each of their campuses. The first such meeting at a contrived conference scheduled by Judd at BU's Liberal Arts School went exceptionally well. The Blitz Leaders, a name coined by Sevena for the five trusted leaders at each of the schools, got their first look-see at Alan.

At that first meeting, one could hear a pin drop. Alan was inspirational, but not with lofty rhetoric. The tone was metered and serious matching the gravity of the undertaking.

He related to them the recently declassified story of Alan Turing, the British mathematician and cryptanalyst, who was called upon by the British government to crack the intercepted German coded messages that could provide intelligence to defeat the Nazis in many of the upcoming crucial battles. Many of the other top scientists in Britain who were called upon had tried to decipher the German enigma code for years, but without success. When one was asked about the odds of doing so, he answered, "There are no odds, it is impossible." But Turing, working against the clock, was determined to break the code and shorten the war that was taking the lives of 50 soldiers and civilians every 10 minutes. That was on his mind whenever he took a 10-minute break to quench his thirst with a cup of tea. It was Winston

Churchill who said that Turing made the single biggest contribution to Allied victory in the war against Nazi Germany. It has been estimated that by breaking the code he shortened the war in Europe by as many as two to three years and saved millions of lives.

Alan drew the clear analogy. "In a sense, each of you is being asked to do the very same thing; to take on an impossible task to shorten the war to save lives. In the past 15 minutes that Judd took to introduce me, 16 soldiers and innocent civilians were killed, yes just now-like that (Alan snapped his fingers) and 16 more and 16 after that will be killed (he snapped them again and again) every 15 minutes that follows until we end this thing. You can play the key role in shortening this war by years and save hundreds and thousands of lives, not to mention all those additional tens of thousands of American soldiers who will return home needlessly crippled both mentally and physically. World War 2 was a moral war that had to be fought to protect freedom. This war, fraudulently started and needlessly prosecuted, is an immoral one that will not protect and enrich our way of life, but rather serve only to enrich the pockets of the suppliers of war."

Alan did not shrink from telling them about the risks and dangers. "Look, we are in uncharted waters here. I can't guarantee we will succeed and the risks and personal consequences to each of you, whether we succeed or not, can be very serious. You risk being jailed, seriously injured by overzealous cops or other law enforcement officers, and even the possibility of being expelled from school depending on whether we are treated fairly and granted our constitutional rights to peacefully protest. So, if anyone has second thoughts – if you want to back out – we will understand. We only ask that if you are considering it, please tell us now and keep our plans confidential."

Alan stopped speaking and for the next minute looked around the room for those who wished to signal that they wanted out. There were none. If there were any with second thoughts before Alan spoke, they had

none after. Alan had gained their complete trust. He continued to lay out
the mission in both words and manner that displayed a kind of idealism,
strength and confidence-in short, a capacity to lead that would have inspired
a regiment of soldiers to follow him into battle regardless of their chances
of survival.

Judd followed. "The element of surprise is vital to our undertaking.
So, your recruitment of 100 student protesters at your schools should mostly
take place off-campus during the summer, indicating that they will be
informed when they are back to school when a type of rally-I would use that
term-will take place. Do not share the nature, time and place of any planned
occupations of buildings or other such planned ventures in advance. As I
said, we need to take the administrations by total surprise. For that reason,
after this meeting, we will meet separately with the 5 Blitz Leaders of each
of the three schools to plan their demonstrations. That way, only the five of
you at each school will know your specific dates and plans for your demonstrations". Judd looked around. "Yes, Eddie, you have a question?

Eddie Carpenter, a tall 6'3" blonde, curly-haired senior at America
University was the leader of the Oklahoma blitz group. He had been president of the Students for Democratic Society for the past two years and
before meeting Judd had previously organized a small demonstration of
25 people in protest of the draft. "Alan, of course, we will be vigilant in
keeping the element of surprise, but I am confident we can avoid any unexpected pushbacks. President Coburn is not the type to do much to prevent
student protests. He did not interfere with the one I previously organized
to recruit more women in the faculty, nor the few admittedly small civil
rights rallies that took place a year ago, so I expect we pretty much have a
safe harbor at this university to get most of our protests executed without
major interference."

"Good to know, Eddie, but we can't be too cautious," replied Judd.

After the meeting, in private Judd was to inform Eddie, "Our very first blitz week, the most important one, will start where you are, at America University. Our current plans are to commence the very first demonstration there on Wednesday, September 5, two days after Labor Day, when enrollment is in its second day. We hope that the administration will have enough on its mind trying to get things set up for the opening semester, without the time or resources to deal with us."

OVER THE SUMMER, things were extremely hectic but went smoothly; five more meetings took place separately with the Blitz Leaders at each school. Plans were further refined at the meetings, slogans were settled upon, signs were designed, various pamphlets and circulars were developed and printed up, liberal media contacts were rollerdexed in anticipation of the events to follow.

Alan even flew to Vegas, compliments of Nick Manning of the Stardust Hotel, in an overnight junket and won an additional $6,000 at blackjack to pay some of the bills. The summer break was coming to an end and Luck was still being a Lady on all counts so far.

IT WAS HOTTER than usual even for late August when Alan landed at the airport in Oklahoma City the Friday before Labor Day for a final meeting with Eddie Carpenter and the Blitz Leaders at America University to go over the final plans for the initial demonstrations. He would await Judd's and Sevena's flight arranged to land an hour later to take precautions against any possible surveillance of their combined travels. August 31 was Judd's birthday and Alan and Sevena had planned to surprise him with a private birthday dinner that night after the meeting with Eddie Carpenter and the rest of the five Blitz Leaders.

Though few would be paying attention to school activities during the Labor Day weekend, their meeting at the SDS office that afternoon was arranged under the guise of an invited panel to discuss "Voting Rights for Minorities."

The meeting was all business. Refreshments were limited to a choice between a bottle of Coke or a bottle of Coke. The room was air-conditioned, which helped circulate the smoke that never ceased to flow throughout the room. Everyone smoked cigarettes except for Alan, who lit up an occasional cigarillo the size of a tall cigarette, and Sevena, who quit when she started to train for the marathon.

Eddie Carpenter took them through the planned opening day of demonstrations step by step. "Over the summer, we have recruited around 110 students mostly off-campus. With various degrees of commitment, we were able to determine their ant-war feelings. We held one general training session on how to conduct demonstrations in which 72 of them showed up. As Judd requested, to protect the surprise of our initial demonstrations, we did not discuss the specific plans or any dates but said we would be in touch with them when enrollment came around. I think the administration has noticed a little of our activity, and to the extent they have, they see it as SDS's usual activities to organize and ready itself for future rallies should one liberal cause or another arise. As Alan suggested, we have spread some disinformation that SDS was organizing to conduct a rally during the first semester calling for the university to appoint a minority member to its Board of Trustees. There appear to be no signs of any administration jitters over our activities."

Eddie lit up another cigarette as soon as he doused the one he just finished, though he ordinarily was not a chain smoker, and continued. "It will be a three-fold demonstration. On Wednesday, the ROTC is conducting a recruitment session at their building for students who wish to enroll. Many will consider joining to keep them out of the draft for a while. It is a great place to make our point."

Eddie moved next to Clifford's chair and placed his hands on his shoulders. "Under Clifford's direction, twenty of the trained group will enter and occupy the ROTC building's recruitment room. The group will remain sitting on the floor in silence, refusing to leave. We will then post the anti-war signs such as 'Occupy the ROTC Building, not Vietnam' all around the area to recruit the other students there to enroll, to join the sit-in instead."

Eddie then moved over to another member of his group. "Almost simultaneously with the occupation of the ROTC building, the second demonstration will take place at the Liberal Arts Administration Building where the largest number of students will be going to register. Roger here will lead twenty more of our trained volunteers to enter, occupy and conduct a similar sit-in inside its enrollment hall, singing and chanting the various 'end-the-war' mantras you provided us. Others of our volunteers will then be stationed outside the building urging the students entering to not register and instead join the sit-in. A third demonstration of 20 trained all-female student volunteers led by Betty here (Betty nodded in acknowledgment) will at the same time be staging a similar sit-in at the School of Nursing Administration where their enrollment is to be conducted. The next day, after we have marshaled hundreds of more student volunteers, we will together march to and then occupy the building on campus just a few blocks from here that was leased to the military for their recruitment of students to enlist into the armed forces upon graduation."

Alan then asked, "Were you able to get the podiums and speakers we need?"

"Yes, we have obtained three moveable podiums with loudspeakers that will be rolled out at each of the demonstration sites as soon as we occupy them. Thousands of circulars will be distributed to the large number of students coming onto campus to enroll and throughout all the dorm lobbies early that morning urging them to join the occupation at these sites and to attend a gala rally that evening to be held directly in front of the new Executive Administration Building that houses the president's office. At the rally, we hope to recruit even more volunteers for the movement to show momentum and acquire the needed manpower to carry out further creditable protests throughout the 30-day blitz."

"Perfect, that's great, Eddie, the ongoing recruitment is vital," Alan emphasized. "Getting those podiums out there at each site and distributing those thousands of circulars to students as soon as the occupations begin, urging them to join the sit-ins, are what will make the difference between success and failure. For the police, when called in, can easily arrest and remove the original groups of 20 students staging the sit-ins at the three sites without our making an impact. Also, it will appear as if only a handful of ineffective students are protesting the war. We are gambling on surprise so that before the university's response is organized, we will have recruited hundreds upon hundreds of students to join the sit-in at each site That would make a wholesale arrest by the university of so many of its own students politically impossible. And even if they did, the publicity of so many students protesting and willing to be arrested for the cause will only fuel greater numbers of student protests at the university and would gain national attention."

Alan was impressed with the thorough preparedness and very moved by the personal risks these five were willing to take on what everyone knew to be a gamble. He allowed his emotions to demonstrate his appreciation by walking up to Eddie and simply giving him a warm hug and continuing to give similar hugs to Clifford, Roger, Betty and to Harry, the other Blitz Leader who Eddie assigned to oversee the on-campus activities and distribution of the circulars. Similar rounds of hugs were followed by both Judd and Sevena. They then ended the meeting and said their goodbyes.

After the meeting, Alan, Judd and Sevena were to celebrate Judd's birthday by sharing a slice of the birthday cake and a bottle of Chianti that Sevena brought to Judd's motel room. It would not be hard to guess his wish as Judd blew out the candles. They again took separate flights home the next morning. To ensure the demonstrations would appear to be locally inspired, they stayed in Boston and not anywhere near Oklahoma. For better or worse, the show was about to begin.

CHAPTER 27

THAT WEDNESDAY MORNING following Labor Day started out like every September enrollment at America University. As in previous years, doors were to open at 9 am for registration at the Liberal Arts School and the School of Nursing. Their large assembly halls were set up with tables manned by staff that held signs with letters such as A-G and H-M and N-Z. The signs directed students with last names beginning with those letters to go to those tables to register.

At 8 am that morning, 77 student volunteers showed up to meet Eddie and the four other Blitz Leaders inside the crowded SDS offices, as requested. It was only then they were told of their assignments. At 8:45 sharp they proceeded out in three separate groups headed to the enrollment centers of the Liberal Arts School, School of Nursing and to the ROTC building to occupy the buildings and engage in a sit-in. A fourth smaller group headed to the baseball field parking lot where the evening before a U-Haul truck had been parked. The truck contained the three movable podiums, and all the signs and pamphlets to be distributed on campus and at each of the dorm lobbies housing live-in students.

The few University Security Police cars were patrolling the campus, none near the parking lot or stationed at the various enrollment buildings. The three Blitz Leaders going to the sit-in sites had walkie-talkies to communicate their progress to each other and to Eddie, who stationed himself at the SDS office. He was to give overall direction and, in turn, report the progress by phone to Alan, Judd and Sevena throughout the day. They were stationed at an out-of-the-way telephone booth far from BU and their apartments as a precaution in case their own phones were being tapped, though they had no reason to believe so. They parked their car with sandwiches and drinks next to the booth.

The first group to reach their destination arrived at the ROTC building exactly on time, 8:55 am. As planned, they were the first students to enter. The processing room for those who wished to explore joining ROTC was relatively small, about half the size of a basketball court, and was immediately to the right of the entry. Four desks were set up for the Army, Navy, Marine and Air Force ROTC recruiters. Each desk was staffed by a regular military officer and a student ROTC member, both in uniforms. There were no visible security police or other personnel there or in the vicinity, all of which was reported by Clifford to Eddie by walkie- talkie. "OK, then," Eddie replied. "It's a go. Continue to move in and occupy. We will set up the podium with speakers, signs and distributing circulars and antiwar T-shirts outside urging students to join you there shortly." Eddie gave similar approval to Betty at the School of Nursing and Roger at the Liberal Arts School and then contacted Alan. "Operation 30-day Blitz is now officially underway."

There was no real comparison, Alan knew, but he wondered whether General Eisenhower had the same lumps in his throat and ever-increasing heartbeats as he did, when after all the preparation and hope for surprise, he gave the order for the invasion of Normandy and could only stand by the phone, helpless as to what more he could do, anxiously awaiting the first reports.

Clifford and the other student volunteers marched into the ROTC processing room en masse and began to pull out thin white T-shirts from their pockets, with lettering on the back, "Let's Sit This War Out." They put them on in front of the Military and ROTC officers in the room and in unison sat down on the floor without a sound. Oddly, none of the ROTC personnel made any attempt to stop them. After the students sat down, the officers simply got up and left the room altogether without a word of protest.

Clifford immediately reported this bewildering phenomenon to Eddie. In moments, Roger and Betty reported the exact same phenomenon occurring at the Liberal Arts School and the School of Nursing. In all three buildings, the groups were allowed to enter and sit without any attempt to stop them in any way, with the weird reaction of staff leaving the buildings immediately upon their arrival.

Eddie then received an even more puzzling call from Harry at the ballpark parking lot. "Eddie, the truck is still there, but when we opened the door, it was fucking empty – no podiums, no signs, no pamphlets, no circulars, no antiwar T-shirts-all of it gone!"

"You got to be kidding me," Eddie exclaimed. "Did you lock it last night?"

"Tight as a drum, and it's fucking weird, it was also locked when we got here this morning, but there is nothing in the truck-nothing."

Eddie immediately reported the perplexing happenings to Alan.

Alan's face grew grim. He had the same feelings in his gut as when he realized his last- second-shot to try to win the State's Class A high school basketball tournament was going to fall short and the game would be over..

"Eddie," he yelled into the phone, "they know all our fucking plans. Somehow, they were ready for us. Tell all our people to get up and leave quickly before the cops come to arrest them.

Get them the hell out fast!" Alan knew arresting trouble-makers attempting to disrupt student enrollment would be a coup for them.

Eddie was quickly on the walkie-talkie contacting Clifford, Roger and Betty with the message to "get out fast." In less than one minute, all three leaders reported the same thing. "The doors are locked. We can't get out."

Immediately after, all three reported that 20-30 university security and local police stationed in each of their buildings on the floors above them were descending into the processing areas where they were gathered. They were in full gear, armed with billy clubs, shouting repeatedly as they entered, "Police, you are all under arrest, do not move," and began to cuff each of them.

Except for the females at the School of Nursing, they began to needlessly club some non- resistant students calling them Communists and Vietcong lovers. In less than 30 minutes, 55 of the 63 students, a few bleeding, were in paddy wagons on the way to be booked at the local police station, eight of them injured enough to be taken under guard to be treated at the Angel Hospital before being booked at the same station later that day. Eddie reported it to all to Alan, play by play as he received it until all the walkie-talkies at the sites were confiscated by the police.

"Fuck!" Alan exclaimed to himself. Then he looked at Judd and Sevena, "Nothing could be worse." It took less than 30 minutes to prove that thought wrong when Eddie was back on the phone.

"Alan, it's even crazier."

"What's happening?"

"An explosion went off a little while ago. Looks like in that military building, a couple of blocks away from the ROTC. You may recall we planned to occupy it tomorrow. I can see a lot of smoke rising into the air. Police and fire trucks are rushing in that direction. Sirens are blasting. I can see people, students and faculty some running toward it, some running away from it. Pandemonium has broken loose here on campus. Let me get back to you as soon as I can find out more."

"What the fuck do you think is going on there?" Judd asked, looking at Alan.

"I don't know, but you can bet it is not a coincidence and I am afraid we are going to learn what that is, sooner than we like. Meanwhile, let's call those Oklahoma volunteer attorneys we lined up to get down to the station to see about representing those arrested and arranging bail. Also, let's have them take pictures of those injured."

Alan was right; things were collapsing like a house of cards. It was

Eddie again on the phone in less than an hour. "Alan, the word is floating around that it was a fire-bomb that went off destroying a portion of the first floor. Luckily, no one was injured, but there was a lot of property damage. There are a ton of fire trucks out there trying to control the fire and we got word that the school is now closing down enrollment and other activities for fear that there could be bombs planted in other buildings. They say that bomb squads are going through those buildings to make sure they are safe before they reopen. What a fucking mess. I'd better get down to the police station and assess what is going on there. Wait, some people are coming in."

Alan held on waiting for Eddie to return to the phone. He was getting anxious, waiting for over 10 minutes, hearing some noise and exchanges of voices in the background. Finally, Eddie was back on the line. "You will not believe this shit. It gets worse and worse. There are over a dozen state troopers and a guy identifying himself as an FBI agent here. A state trooper handed me a copy of a search warrant and they are now emptying drawers, throwing papers around, tipping things over recklessly and gathering up files and other records. Any advice?"

"Yes, do not answer any questions. If asked, tell them you want to talk to your lawyer first.

Call me when they leave or…"

"Or what," Eddie interrupted.

"Or if something else happens before they leave," Alan replied, having a pretty good idea of what that might be.

The search took over an hour. The troopers even ripped down a few non-supporting walls to see if anything was hidden behind them. When done, they carried out drawers of files concerning SDS's policies, programs and political activities over the past 10 years and a bag of other physical items. Before they left, the FBI agent showed Eddie some material that he said was recovered behind books in Eddie's cabinet and asked him if he had seen it before. Eddie, remembering Alan's advice, said he wanted to talk to his lawyer before answering any questions. The FBI agent told Eddie it was material that is used to make a fire-bomb and called over the state trooper in charge.

"Eddie Carpenter, my name is Captain Mark Springer of the Oklahoma State Troopers. I am placing you under arrest under Oklahoma Statute Title 21 Section 1403 for arson in the third degree by willfully and maliciously setting fire to a military building owned by American College by means of an explosive device or by aiding or counseling thereof. It carries a maximum sentence of fifteen years in the State Penitentiary."

Eddie was then asked to turn around and his wrists were cuffed behind his back.

The trooper continued: "You have the right to remain silent and refuse to answer questions.

Do you understand?" Eddie did not answer.

"Anything you do say may be used against you in a court of law. Do you understand? Eddie did not answer.

"You have the right to consult an attorney before speaking to the police and to have an attorney. Do you…"

The Miranda rights continued to be read, but Eddie stopped hearing them. He was now in another place, deep in thought wondering how Alfred Dreyfus, the French Military Jewish officer, and Sacco and Vanzetti, Italian immigrants, felt when they were charged and convicted. In the case of Sacco and Vanzetti, ultimately electrocuted for alleged crimes of a political nature of which many historians have come to believe they were all innocent.

Alan, Judd and Sevena walked back and forth next to the phone booth for almost an hour waiting for a further call from Eddie, with the kind of anxiety and little hope one has waiting to hear whether a close friend survived a reported commercial airplane crash in the mountains. But as expected, no call came. They finally decided to go to Sevena's apartment to catch any radio or TV coverage of the bombing. It was being headlined by all three major TV networks. CBS already had its crew on the scene and were covering it live. By that time, the fire had been contained, but smoke continued to cover the skies around the campus and hoses and water from them covered several blocks around the bombed building.

"I still see a lot of fire engines and a large area blocked off by police around the building. Tom, can you confirm that there were no injuries?" asked Walter Cronkite, the CBS news anchor to a reporter on the scene.

"That's right, Walter. And it's a miracle that there were none. From what we learned, normally at that time in the morning, that side of the first floor is occupied by military personnel. Thankfully, it just so happened there was a staff meeting in another part of the building.

However, there was quite a bit of damage, but fortunately not as much as there could have been if the fire department and bomb squad were not on the scene in what appears to be record time."

"Kudos to them. What else are you learning about the cause of the blast?" asked Cronkite.

"So, Walter, we have confirmation that it was a homemade bomb deliberately set off with a timer. I need to stress what is not confirmed but coming from sources alleged to be high up in the FBI, is that it was set off by a communist-inspired antiwar student group that wanted to prevent enlistments and that it may have been Moscow directed. Again, we have no confirmation of that yet, but we just received word that President George Coburn of the University will be holding a press conference soon."

"Thanks, Tom, and we will be there to cover it live. We pause for a commercial but stay tuned for more on this breaking news."

Sevena turned down the sound of the TV. No one had touched the sandwiches they brought from the car. It was 2 pm Boston time and except for morning coffee, no one had eaten. Sevena unwrapped the sandwiches and upon seeing her do so, Judd began to brew coffee. They all knew there was nothing more to talk about until they saw what Coburn had to say. So, the next half hour was spent having a quiet lunch and listening to repeated news about the bombing by flipping from one channel to the next and back again. Finally, the CBS TV news cameras went directly to the president's office to cover his press conference and Sevena turned the volume back up.

"Good afternoon, ladies and gentlemen." President Coburn looked up at the cameras for a moment and then turned his eyes down to his written remarks. He was sitting behind his desk which held a very visible framed picture of him shaking hands with former President Richard Nixon. About eight feet behind his left shoulder was a large, standing American flag.

Directly behind him, there was a row of officials. To his right was his special counsel; next to him, the FBI agent who was at the scene when Eddie was arrested; and a Captain Springer of the State Troopers in full uniform adorned by ribbons and medals. To his left were the captain of the University Security Police and the chief of the local city police force, all in full uniform as well.

President Coburn started to read his prepared statement. "We are, of course, stunned by the bombing and other events that disrupted our today's enrollment of the University's 1966 -67 class. While we suffered significant property damage, fortunately, no one was killed or seriously injured. To ensure student and faculty safety, except for the dormitories, which have been swept clean for explosives and are safe and under guard, we have closed all other buildings until they are considered safe. We have also suspended the enrollment and all other university activities until we can resume them with the assurance of complete safety. We owe that to our students, faculty and personnel."

Obviously scripted, the president turned to the row of law enforcement officials behind him. "On behalf of myself and a grateful university,

I want to extend our thanks and appreciation to our first responders, our security and city police, the state police and the FBI, without whom we would have suffered much greater damage and disruption. What's more, by their uncovering a plot against the university, the details of which my special counsel and others here standing by my side will provide you, they prevented further, more devastating damage and disruption that most likely would have resulted in the loss of life." He then addressed his special counsel, "Roy, would you please pull over that standing mike and detail what the FBI and state police investigations uncovered so far?"

"With pleasure, Mr. President."

A tall, impeccably dressed, confident young man stepped to the mike. Alan shouted out, "I know him. Roy Armstrong. He was a senior at BU Law School when I was a freshman. He graduated number one in his class. As I remember, he was hired by the Dean's old law firm. He must have quit after a year to take this job. Strange, with his credentials and ability, I would think he would be following a path to a partner at some other prestigious law firm. He now shows up here in our narrative. Carrying out our plan for a blitz seems to be chock-full of weird coincidences."

"My name is Roy Armstrong, special counsel to the president." He was standing and speaking without a paper in his hand. "Let me take you through the details chronologically and when done, I and those with me are here to answer any questions. Yesterday morning, the FBI got an anonymous tip that a small communist-inspired group of students were planning to disrupt enrollment today, aimed particularly to prevent students from exercising their right to join the ROTC and to join the military at the Military Building that was bombed. The tip was reported to President Coburn, who directed me to alert the various law enforcement agencies so they would be prepared if the tip proved to be creditable."

Armstrong paused to adjust the standing mike to his height and continued. "Later that evening, the FBI contacted us again. They said that they received another tip from that same anonymous source indicating that the Liberal Arts, School of Nursing and the ROTC buildings were being targeted for disruption this morning. That ROTC facility was just two blocks from the Military Building that was bombed. We were not sure of the creditability of the tips, so decided at that time *not* to call off the school's enrollment at these buildings. Instead, at 7 am, both the university security force and local police dispatched and stationed a crew of officers out of sight of the three targeted buildings. We also decided to watch for any possible disruption at the dormitories as a protective measure."

Alan was anxiously waiting for a further shoe to drop, but on a professional level could not help admiring Armstrong's simply constructed sentences and metered tone to add credibility to the facts he was unveiling. Armstrong also was able, without the possibility of contradiction, to taint the movement as communist-inspired without having any evidence of that fact, since it was alleged to come from an anonymous tip.

Armstrong then picked up a pile of pamphlets from the table and continued. "At 7:30 am, university police, while watching two of the dorms, spotted two unidentified students dropping off what we found to be packets of these pamphlets, who ran away as they were spotted. We confiscated the packets immediately and will now distribute some of them to you. As you can see, the pamphlets show a Vietcong flag and a Russian flag waving on high, and in contrast, a soiled American flag torn and dripping with blood, with the words 'Stop the Fascist War' and 'Stop Military Enlistments on Campus by Any Means.'"

Alan moved closer to the TV to see the image of the pamphlet being shown. "They not only stole our pamphlets, but substituted them with this made-up anti-American garbage to make the movement look like a bunch of communist sympathizers prone to commit violence," he said and explained. "It was their way of tying the occupation of the three buildings to the bombing. Fuck, they must have been planning these countermeasures for some time. But, how could they? Where was the leak? And who is really behind all this? Who could have such muscle with the university-and more incredibly, with all the federal, state and city law enforcement agencies to pull this off?"

Judd and Sevena had no more answers than Alan and remained quiet. All three continued to listen to Roy Armstrong's presentation of the facts, knowing there were no boundaries to the fictional events being presented to a media hungry for a meaty story and willing to buy into it all without question. It was deja vu for Judd, remembering how the media readily bought the lies about the Gulf of Tonkin attack as the justification to start the war.

After passing out the pamphlets to the media, Armstrong continued. "At 9 am, consistent with the anonymous tips we received, three separate groups of now identified students entered each of the targeted buildings with the intent to disrupt the enrollment process and perhaps more destructive purposes, which are now under investigation. When confronted by the police and requested to leave or be arrested for trespassing, they did not. When requested a second time and they refused, the police rightfully placed them under arrest and removed them from the buildings. Some students forcibly resisted arrest and the police responded with appropriate force to defend themselves and secure their removal."

"My God, there is no shame. Outright lies!" Judd exclaimed in anger. "They never asked them to leave or be arrested. They locked the doors on them so they couldn't leave."

Alan was not at all surprised. He explained, "To convict them for criminal trespass, one of the elements they need to prove is that they asked them to leave and they refused. Police often feel justified to fill in the blanks if an element is not there when they believe the people are doing wrong. That is what is going on here. What is even more unsettling, is they are saying that they not only arrested the students for trespass, but they were under investigation as to whether they conspired to commit some other destructive acts. I assume that means the bombing. By convicting them on the trespass charge and allegedly keeping that investigation open, none of those students we recruited and trained, and especially given their parents' reaction, will dare participate in any further legitimate protests. They were ready for us and thought out every detail."

Armstrong then introduced the FBI agent.

"My name is William Andrews, FBI Special Agent. We were called in when it appeared that the ROTC building was one of the targets for disruption. After the arrests took place in that building, we interrogated some of the students. We learned that the protests were organized by the Students for a Democratic Society. When the bomb went off in the Military Building, given the tip that the disruption of that building was also a part of their plans, and given the provocative nature of the pamphlets we procured, we appeared before a magistrate and sought and received a warrant to search the SDS offices. The search produced material generally used to make the type of firebomb set off in the Military Building, along with several incriminating documents, including a copy of a memo found in the SDS president's desk drawer containing plans to bomb the Military Building, implicating him and four other defendants. As a result, the president of SDS and four of its members have been arrested for the bombing by the state police and we are continuing to conduct our investigation with respect to federal charges that may also be lodged against them. The names of those five members will be released after their bookings are completed. With that, we will take questions. Yes, the lady with her hand up in the second row."

"Hold your hat," Judd remarked. "The person recognized for the first question in a press conference is usually one with a planted question." Judd had become familiar with this tactic during his time working in Senator Morse's office. He was right on point.

A young reporter who did not identify the news media she represented asked, "Sir, is there any evidence to support the rumor that the occupation and bombing were somehow instigated by the Russians?"

"Sorry, but I can't answer that, since the involvement of those in the planning of the crime is a matter of an ongoing investigation."

"Very cute," Judd remarked. "By refusing to answer the question, knowing there was no such evidence, the agent succeeded in giving the impression that a Russian connection was under a serious investigation, fostering speculation that would likely find its way in most media accounts tomorrow."

And so, it did. The Oklahoman, the city's most popular newspaper would tomorrow lead with the story: "A military building on the American College campus was bombed today to prevent students from enlisting in the military. Five students alleged to be communist sympathizers were arrested for the bombing in a plot that may have been directed by the Russians. That connection is under further investigation."

Sevena turned off the TV as soon as the press conference ended. There was silence for a minute and then Judd was first to say what was on everyone's mind. "They planted the bomb themselves. They planted the bomb themselves! Can you fucking believe it? They set off a bomb and were willing to destroy their own property and risk lives just to stop our demonstrations."

"What's more," Sevena added, "they planted the evidence in the SDS office to frame Eddie and I am sure have forged some document that they now say they retrieved in the search to implicate him and the four others."

"You know what that means?" Alan asked rhetorically as he got up and began to walk around the room as if to aid him in his thinking. "*They* knew. *They fucking knew* everything about today's plans, and well in advance. They may know everything about our plans for San Francisco and Boston, everything about us for all I know! And the "they' must be pretty powerful people to pull together the university's administration, the FBI and all the other law enforcement agencies to stage all this." Alan stopped walking and looked toward Judd and Sevena. "That also means we have no choice but to suspend the blitz in San Francisco and Boston as well until we can fully assess what has happened."

"Yeah, for sure," Judd agreed and Sevena nodded her approval and said, "I will get right on the phone to call them off."

Alan continued, "Nothing we can do now. Let's see what else develops in the next few days and regroup then. Anyway, we need to spend tomorrow and the next day acquiring a legal team to represent Eddie, the other four SDS leaders and any of the 60 arrested students that want us to obtain counsel for them. I will grab a flight to Oklahoma this evening."

"Do you think that's wise? You may be spotted," Sevena asked with concern.

"Someone needs to arrange things. I will stay in the background as much as possible. Besides, I wouldn't be surprised if they already know we are involved-whoever they are."

While they were taking leave of one another, a person who also had been watching the press conference on TV with the same intense interest, but with a look of glee rather than despair, picked up the phone. "Hi, Mr. President, it's the Dean. I watched your press conference. You did great. You handled it magnificently. Congratulate all the boys for me."

CHAPTER 28

THE ALARM CLOCK went off just as the phone rang. Without getting up or opening his eyes, Alan reached to pick up the phone on the table next to his bed. He felt nothing but air. So he instantly leaned over and looked. There was no phone and no table. It was then that he realized he was not in his own bed, but in the motel room in Oklahoma City that he had checked into late last night. He leaned over to the other side of the bed where there was a table, turned off the alarm clock and lifted the phone after fumbling it once or twice.

"Hello," Alan answered clearing his throat.

"Hi, Alan, it's Sevena. It appears that I am always waking you up in the morning."

"True, but regrettably not in person."

Sevena smiled and decided to leave it alone. "Called to let you know that yesterday's events are all over the morning news. It appears that the court arraignments today are being covered by every TV and radio station in the freaking country. Expect a media circus at the courthouse when you arrive there. Our little episode at the campus seems to have gotten national, if not international, publicity."

"Yeah, as we were hoping, but unfortunately it turned out *not quite* how we envisioned it.

Look, thanks for the heads up. I'll call you as soon as I get a grasp on things."

"OK, good luck, and Alan- be careful."

Alan was content to skip breakfast and settle for drinking his morning coffee out of a styrofoam cup while driving to the Oklahoma County

District Court. Sevena was right. As he approached the courthouse, there were cameras, TV trucks and a series of lights in front of the courthouse that one would normally expect to see at a film shooting of a Hollywood blockbuster. Alan circled the area until he found a small parking space that he could barely squeeze into almost four blocks away. All the parking spaces in the court parking lot and on the nearby streets were taken up by the media and some of the 60 plus defendants who had been bailed out the night before, now back for arraignment with some of their parents.

Alan knew his way around courts. He had spent most of his second year at the law school in BU's Student Prosecutors Program handling the prosecution of misdemeanor crimes under the supervision of the District Attorney's office and the Criminal Justice professor who ran the program. As he entered the court, he saw a long line of people waiting in front of the main elevator hoping that their place in line would permit them to gain entrance to the court proceedings of the main attraction. Alan needed to bypass the line if he were to get a seat in the courtroom.

Having appeared in a number of courts under the Prosecutors Program, he looked for and found an out-of-the-way side-elevator to the upper floors that housed the four courtrooms in the building, generally reserved for judges. Alan knew these elevators were also used by attorneys who knew their way around the building. He waited near the side-elevator and when he spotted a local attorney heading that way, he greeted him with a "good morning" and followed him into the elevator and up to the first session where the arraignments were to take place. Except for a few attorneys, court officers, a probation officer and the assistant clerk, Alan entered a relatively empty courtroom and was able to pick the seat he wanted in the third row on the right side of the courtroom behind the defense attorneys' table.

At about 8:45 am, 15 minutes before the session was to begin, the clerk called out to the Chief Court Officer, in some courts referred to as the bailiff, a tall person in a stiffly pressed uniform with the posture and physique of an ex-marine and who never seemed to smile; "Jerry, call in the defendants on the trespassing charges and hold off on bringing the five defendants into the dock on the arson case until after."

The 50 plus student defendants charged with the single offense of trespassing began to march into the courtroom. Rather than setting bail, they had been released at the police station the day before on their own personal recognizance, a personal promise to return to court the next day, or be subject to penalties. However, Eddie and the other four SDS defendants charged with the felonies were held overnight without bail in the county jail and brought to the courthouse by the Sheriff's Department.

Three attorneys were sitting at the defense table and five more in the row behind reserved for counsel. Alan spotted the one he believed he was looking for at the table and signaled him to come over. "Hi, you Mel Goodman?" Alan asked as the attorney approached.

"Yes, you must be Alan Roberts. Good to meet you. How did you pick me out?"

"You looked the right age compared to the others. Thanks again for taking this on in such short notice." Alan reached out to shake Goodman's hand.

Alan had done some quick research before flying out to Oklahoma, and called Goodman and retained him on a limited basis to handle the arraignments of Eddie, the four others charged with arson and any of the students charged with trespass that morning without counsel. Goodman had been in practice for 10 years in a three-person firm. He was the firm's criminal defense lawyer. He had a reputation for being very competent and one who knew his way around this district court since his firm's office was in a building housing mostly attorneys directly across the street.

"Mel, how were our guys taking it when you visited them at the jail last evening?" Alan asked ,very concerned.

"Not well, as you might expect. Notwithstanding their innocence from what you told me and what they vehemently proclaim, they are beginning to realize that things do not look good and between the state and possibly fed charges, they could spend a good deal of their lives in prison. Eddie did say that he and the others appreciated your assuring them that you would be acquiring a strong defense team to represent them. As I indicated, I am glad to handle today and assist in the defense. But, I'm sure you know that you're going to need a very experienced criminal trial lawyer if you are to have any chance of acquitting them based on the alleged evidence and an already rattled community given the publicity of this case." Though Alan was already aware of it, hearing it said deepened his anxiety and concern.

"What are our chances of getting them out on bail until the trial?" Alan asked.

"I will be arguing that none of them have any priors and have roots in the community, but given the seriousness of the offense and the public reaction to the crime, you can expect that the DA's office will be asking that they be held without bail or an extremely high amount. By the way, I will be representing only two other students charged with just trespassing," Goodman added.

"That's all from the three sit-in groups who wanted representation?" Alan asked, a bit surprised.

"Yes, a few have their own attorneys, but mainly because the DA has come up with a deal that has been offered to them, and except for the two I am representing, they are all taking it."

"What kind of a deal?" Alan asked.

Just then a loud voice came across the entire courtroom and interrupted their conversation. It was coming from the Chief Court Officer standing by an open door to the judge's lobby. "All rise please!"

"Alan, gotta go. The DA's deal will be presented in open court."

Goodman abruptly ended the conversation with Alan as he hurried back to his seat at the defense table.

The Chief Court Officer opened the proceedings as he and the other court officers did every day. "Hear ye, hear ye, all those having business before the District Court for the County of Oklahoma draw near and give your attention and ye shall be heard, the Honorable Justice Joseph Clark presiding.

He no sooner finished, when Judge Clark in his black robe, a man in his early 50s looking a bit younger, with curly black hair slightly greyed at the sideburns, spryly entered the courtroom and approached his seat on the bench.

"You may be seated," the Chief Court Officer concluded.

Judge Joe Clark had been elected to serve in the district court 10 years earlier. He was re-elected twice and was now serving in his third term. During World War II, he enlisted and served with distinction as an air force tail bomber having flown on 51 missions over Europe. After the war, he opened an office as a sole practitioner and quickly gained a reputation as a skillful and successful criminal defense lawyer. Before serving on the bench, he served two terms in the Oklahoma House of Representatives where he was credited with authoring key legislation in bringing about needed major reforms in the criminal justice system, which helped catapult him into the judgeship. He was known as a fair, no-nonsense, unbiased judge respected by both prosecution and defense, and one with whom you did not screw around when it came to arguing the law.

"Good morning, everybody," Judge Clark addressed all assembled as he picked up the docket indicating the cases before him. "Mr. Clerk, I see defense counsel present and I assume ready, but unless my eyes deceive me, I do not see anyone at the prosecutor's table."

"Good morning, Your Honor," came a loud out-of-breath voice. The

Assistant District Attorney having just entered the back of the courtroom, rushed down the aisle to the prosecutor's table with a briefcase in his right hand and balancing a large pile of papers in his other, while trying to keep some from slipping out and falling to the floor. He was followed by another person holding a few files. "I apologize, Judge, for being a few minutes late, but we were busy working out dispositions of most of the cases before you that we can dispose of today."

"If we can do that, Mr. Renfrew (Renfrew was well known to the judge, having been assigned to prosecute cases for the DA's Office for close to a year), I will not only excuse your slight tardiness but give you my parking space for the rest of the week." It drew some laughter, especially because it was Thursday and there was only one day left in the week. "Mr. Clerk, let's proceed."

The clerk held up a packet of criminal complaints. "Your Honor, before you in court are defendants who were charged under Title 21 Section 1835 with willfully entering and remaining upon the premises to wit: buildings on state property operated and controlled by America University, after being expressly forbidden to do so by requesting them to leave." The Section went on to state that any person convicted of violating the provisions of that section shall be guilty of trespass and shall be punished by a fine of not more than $250.00 or by confinement in the county jail for a period not exceeding 90 days.

The Clerk continued, "I am advised that the Assistant District Attorney desires to address you on this matter."

"Mr. Renfrew, you wish to be heard?"

"Yes, thank you, Your Honor. For the record, sitting beside me is Attorney Roy Armstrong, Special Counsel to the President of America University and representing the school at these proceedings. Working with him, we have come up with a disposition we believe is fair and agreed to by 52 of the unrepresented student defendants before you, and counsel retained by six others of them." The six attorneys stood up. Goodman and a female attorney sitting at the defense table remained seated.

"I am all ears, Mr. Renfrew," responded the judge in a voice suggesting the great relief that judges tend to feel when their heavy docket is eased somewhat as cases are disposed of without the burden and time of lengthy trials.

"The DA's Office is prepared to recommend that all 58 cases be continued without admission of guilt in each case until the student is no longer enrolled at the university to be dismissed at that time and the record sealed, on condition that the student during his or her enrollment is not convicted of any other offense and does not participate in any way in the planning of or otherwise engage in any further demonstrations or protests in or around the university during such enrollment. Mr. Armstrong impressed us with the fact that these are their students. Therefore, President Coburn desires not to let this unfortunate incident interrupt their academic pursuits or otherwise taint their professional opportunities, which a conviction might do."

"So that's the deal. How fucking clever," Alan thought to himself. "They just succeeded looking extremely generous and caring, while completely dismantling the entire core group we recruited at the school not just for now, but throughout the entire time they will be at the university."

"You know, Mr. Renfrew," the judge said, "you are not only asking them to waive their constitutional right to a trial and a right to appointed counsel if they can't afford one, but uniquely asking them to waive their First Amendment constitutional right to assembly and free speech. There is no legal impediment to that. They are rights that individuals can waive if they and/or counsel consent to it. However, I will need to go over those rights with them, which I can in a group, so I am convinced that they are knowingly waiving those rights."

Judge Clark first had the DA read the police report of the events into the record. Then the 55 students were asked to rise. The judge then meticulously went over the complaint and all their rights and explained that if they waived their rights and then violated the conditions of the dismissal, they immediately would be brought back to court for a trial. If convicted, under the university rules, a conviction of such a misdemeanor could be grounds for expulsion from the university at the discretion of the administration. All 55 students accepted the deal, signed waivers of their rights, and agreed to the conditions of the dismissal.

The Clerk then proceeded to call out the names of the remaining two students charged with trespass represented by Goodman, asking them to come forward, and was about to begin to read the complaints.

Goodman rose. "Your Honor, Mel Goodman, I represent two of the students standing before you. I waive the reading of the complaint and request that a plea of not guilty be entered for each of them and a date be set for trial, on the same personal recognizance."

"So entered, Mr. Goodman. According to my calendar, we can set this down for trial on October 3."

"May it please the court," Goodman followed up. "Your Honor may have observed that these two defendants have bandages for injuries they sustained last evening. You should have before you their applications for a hearing on whether complaints for Assault and Battery should be issued against the named officers in the application who arrested them on the trespass charges. We would like the applications continued to October 3 as well, so they may be heard along with the criminal charges against them."

Upon hearing that request, Roy Armstrong leaned toward Renfrew and began to whisper into his ear.

"If you have no objection, Mr. Renfrew, I will schedule both matters for October 3," commented the judge.

"May I please have a moment, Your Honor, to consult with Mr. Armstrong?" Armstrong continued to whisper into Renfrew's ear for almost a minute.

"Your Honor," Renfrew rose and addressed the court. "Of course, the scheduling is a matter of the court's discretion and so we have no objection. But as the police officers contend in their report, the student injuries were a result of appropriate force used by the police to defend themselves when the students engaged in violence to resist arrest. Mr. Armstrong, on behalf of the university, had convinced our office to use our discretion in not bringing Assault and Battery charges against their own students if they accepted our plea offer, but of course, if the students insist on moving forward with their frivolous Assault and Battery Complaints against the officers on that date, we wish to reserve our right to file A and B Complaints against them as well at that time."

Judge Clark responded, "Mr. Renfrew, while not your intent, it does seem to smack like an act of retaliation to prevent the defendants from exercising their rights to bring charges. However, that is your right. Mr. Clerk, release the two defendants on their personal recognizance advising them of the penalties if they fail to appear on the scheduled trial date. Let's take a 15-minute recess to bring up the five defendants to the dock to arraign them on the arson charges and three of them on their trespass charges as well."

During the recess, one would have had to have brought a gas mask to avoid being choked by the amount of cigarette smoke in the corridors where everyone filed out of the courtroom awaiting the arraignments on the serious bombing charges. Alan also left the courtroom before it emptied to avoid being noticed by Armstrong while he and Renfrew remained at the prosecutor's table. Goodman caught up with Alan in the corridor but had only a moment since he had to be back inside when Eddie and the others were to be brought up to the courtroom dock from the court jail cells.

"Who is the female attorney sitting next to you representing?" Alan asked,

"Her name is Lisa Kelly and she told me she is representing Betty, the one in nursing school.

Betty's uncle flew down to retain her as counsel. Off the record, she does not seem to be a heavyweight, but that's based on the very limited discussions I had with her. Better get back in."

Alan waited until the courtroom was almost full again before entering, having reserved his seat by leaving a briefcase on it. Eddie and the others were already in the dock that was directly to the left and below the judge's bench. They were all in handcuffs, including Betty, and with a court officer stationed both within and in front of the dock. They also were asked to rise with all the others when the Judge entered.

Assistant District Attorney Renfrew again informed the court that he was representing the people of Oklahoma. Attorney Lisa Kelly identified herself as representing Betty Nowicki and Melvin Goodman as representing the other four defendants of arson and the accompanying trespass complaints. Goodman's request that the defendants be un-cuffed during the hearing was allowed by Judge Clark over the objection of Renfrew, after the judge enquired and received the opinion of the Chief Court Officer that it presented no risk to do so.

Not guilty pleas were entered to the complaints and Renfrew then expressed his desire to be heard on bail. He cited the serious nature and the recklessness of the offense. He argued that the 15-year prison sentence that the defendants faced created a risk that they would flee, warranting significant bail to assure their appearance. He stated that it was only by happenstance that the military personnel, generally in the room where the bomb was detonated, were called away for a meeting at that time. Otherwise, there would likely have been serious injuries and even loss of life. He informed the judge that the state was still considering whether to bring additional charges of committing arson with the intent to injure or kill. "For those reasons, Your Honor, the state is requesting they all be held for trial without bail, or at minimum, a bail no less than $300,000 each."

"Mr. Goodman, you wish to be heard?" the judge asked, calling on him to make his argument.

"Thank you, Your Honor. Indeed, these are serious charges, but my clients have pleaded not guilty, and last I heard there have been no constitutional amendments repealing the presumption of innocence. Yes, whoever committed these crimes committed a serious offense, but we expect to show at trial that my clients were not those perpetrators. As Your Honor knows, bail is set only to assure that the defendants will appear in court. The seriousness of the offense is one factor, but none of my clients have any prior records, they all have roots in the community, and aspire to professional careers, all factors that indicate they will appear to defend themselves and should be released on their personal recognizance. However, given the notoriety of these charges I understand it may induce that some bail be set. If so, we would request that it be no more than $10,000 each. My clients will have difficulty even raising that. Anything more would mean they would be incarcerated up until trial."

"Attorney Kelly," the judge was recognizing her to make her bail argument on behalf of Betty Nowicki.

"No argument, Your Honor. We have nothing more to add to Mr. Goodman's argument."

Both Goodman and Alan were stunned. Just adding a further voice, even with the same arguments, could have an impact. Alan wondered if she were that incompetent, what that would mean when the trial took place.

"Mr. Goodman," Judge Clark addressed him in particular in making his ruling, "let me assure you that whatever publicity this case has or will receive has no effect on today's decision on bail and will have no influence on any rulings I make at trial. However, notwithstanding the clean records of the defendants and their roots in the community, I must consider the serious penalties they face that create a risk they may flee if released with limited bail. Also, they are aware that federal charges and further state charges may be lodged against them. These could result in sentences totaling 25 years or more. That adds further risk of their fleeing before trial. I agree that $300,000 bail could be a bit excessive. I do, however, set bail at $200,000 for each defendant."

"Your Honor," attorney Kelly finally stood to address the court, which partially explained her silence over bail. "The uncle of my client has property of a value of twice that amount. May he post that property as surety for the bail of Ms. Nowicki?"

"Yes, upon proof of its value to the clerk. If any of the other defendants were not to make bail and remain in jail, they are entitled to a speedy trial, so I am setting the date for trial in 60 days unless any defendant requests further time for discovery."

"That would be November 7, Your Honor," said the Clerk.

"Mr. Renfrew, I am setting appropriate time limits on discovery in case we move ahead with a speedy trial and would request that you give this a priority and abide by the schedule."

"I am sure we will, Judge. But it won't be me. Given the seriousness of the offenses, District Attorney Lewis will be retaining a special prosecutor to try these felonies."

"Please inform the special prosecutor then. The Court is adjourned."

Before the judge got through the courtroom door leading to his chambers, both Renfrew and Roy Armstrong were rushing out of the courtroom to get to the cameras that were taking up half a block of the sidewalk in front of the courthouse to spin their story. Meanwhile, Alan, remaining in the courtroom, gave a thumbs-up encouragement sign to Eddie, Betty and the others in the dock as they were being escorted back down to the cellar courthouse jail cells. He then went over to Goodman, who was by now alone at the defense table.

"My God, a special prosecutor, what's next?"

"Good question" responded Goodman. "As I said, while I am willing to assist in the defense, frankly you need to get a barracuda to head the defense team. The threat of new federal and state charges, a special prosecutor-who you can bet will be one of the biggie criminal litigators-a parade of FBI agents, state troopers, local police and respected university personnel all called as witnesses, coupled with an unlimited budget for experts while we have none, all against a background of an aroused, angry public that won't be satisfied short of a lynching in the public square..."

"Mel, no need to go on, I did not take my depression pills yet. Trust me, I am beginning to get the flavor of your message. We need a barracuda."

"That's not where I am going, Alan. Sit down a moment."

By this time the courtroom was completely empty. Mel remained standing as Alan sat down.

In a softer voice, Mel bent over slightly and asked, "Don't you think you should start considering coping a plea?"

"They're fucking innocent, Mel. They are being framed."

"And, if the DA and the Feds go ahead with additional charges, Judge Clark was not whistling Dixie when he suggested that each of these innocent guys can spend the best 15 or 20 years of their lives fighting off bad guys in prison."

That sobered Alan up. He hesitated and then asked, "What do you think is the best we could expect with a plea negotiation?"

Mel thought a moment. "Well, if indeed one of these law enforcement agencies planted the incriminating evidence as you allege, I suspect they just want a guilty plea. So, they might be satisfied with a plea that will be considered a public confession of guilt. Then they can indicate that their investigation revealed that there was no tie to Russia, and these were a few otherwise clean-cut students who ran away with their misguided passion, and maybe, just maybe, agree to a sentence of three or four years."

"Three or four years in prison, a felony record and living their lives having confessed to something they did not do. It would be hard to get them to agree to that."

"No need to make a decision here and now, but it is a choice we will have to talk to our guys about," Goodman said intending to take off some of the pressure as he wrapped up the discussion while finishing packing up his papers, except for one.

"Alan, here, this paper has the names of the three barracudas and the phone numbers and addresses of their firms. If we decide to litigate, these are the best criminal defense attorneys in town. Maybe the high-profile nature of the case will appeal to their egos and better angels, or their competitive juices, so the small fee we can offer won't totally discourage them."

"Barracudas, you say, not a term we use back east"

"Well, you are a city boy, Alan. It's an expression used around here on occasion by litigators to describe a voraciously fearsome, opportunistic competitor, who relying on surprising tactics, can kill and consume a larger prey."

"You know, you're right, sounds like a lawyer." It brought a smile to Goodman's face for the first time. "In any event, exactly what we will need. Thanks, Mel, I will get right on it and see if I can arrange to meet with any of them this very afternoon."

CHAPTER 29

ALAN DROVE DIRECTLY back to the motel from the court and picked up two messages from Sevena. She and Judd were waiting anxiously to get any details not covered by the radio and TV news. He called and filled them in and promised to get back to them about his efforts in securing a lead attorney.

Alan then spent the next hour on the phone getting by protective secretaries and convincing them to schedule appointments that afternoon for two of the attorneys on Mel's list, one at 3 pm and the other at 5. The 3 pm one was with Mark Pearlman, a senior partner at a firm that had six different last names in its title. Pearlman headed the firm's criminal law division. Alan did not have to spend much time explaining the facts of the case to him. It had been all over the news for two days and of special interest to criminal defense lawyers who tend to follow every detail in such cases.

"So, Alan, I understand the case in general and your need for a speedy answer as to whether I would agree to represent these four defendants. I am interested, but would have to discuss it with my partners first. Here is my card containing my private number and if you call me back before I finish my day at 8 pm tonight – an early day today," Pearlman smiled as he spoke those last few words, "I will let you know. But I am curious, what is your role in all this?"

"I would like to tell you, but I need to know whether you consider this conversation about rating you as counsel is protected by attorney-client privilege."

"You're covered," Pearlman assured him,

Alan went on to tell him of his role in planning the Oklahoma sit-ins and feeling of responsibility in helping to provide for an adequate defense of the participants, but did not elaborate concerning the 30-day blitz for the other two schools and the overall aim of stimulating an anti-war national movement.

The subsequent 5 pm meeting was extremely encouraging with what seemed to be an enthusiastic response by the attorney, George Whitcomb, a former public defender, now in a midsize law firm. Because of his run of successful not-guilty jury verdicts in criminal corruption cases involving corporate executives, the firm had begun to attract a growing corporate civil business. Whitcomb was also noted for having taken on pro bono criminal cases lodged against civil rights protesters.

"Alan, I have been following the news closely," said Whitcomb. "When you have been doing what I have been doing for so long, you have a nose that can sniff out something that does not smell right. Are you familiar with Shakespeare's Hamlet?"

Alan immediately thought of his encounter as a kid selling newspapers with an obnoxious customer in a Boston restaurant who was trying to impress the girl with whom he was dining by misquoting a passage from Hamlet and erroneously attributing it to the Bible.

"Hamlet, yes, a little," Alan responded.

"Well," continued Whitcomb, "I forgot who said it, Hamlet's friend I believe. Sensing that things he observed were not quite right, said to Hamlet, 'Something is rotten in Denmark.' Frankly, even before I talked to you, it was exactly how I felt about the prosecution's case.

Everything falls in place so conveniently for them, like the memo the police just happened to uncover during the search of the SDS office detailing the plans to hit the Military Building Implicating all the defendants. The facts supporting a conviction are just too conveniently knit together."

Alan was impressed with Whitcomb's observation and encouraged by his expressed interest in taking the case. So, this time he found it prudent to restrain from filling in the blanks as to the name of Hamlet's friend who made the remark. He not only knew it was Marcellus, but that he said it to Horatio, another friend of Hamlet, not to Hamlet. Alan wondered why he even thought of mentioning it. Whitcomb also indicated that given the high-profile nature of the case, he too would have to talk to his partners. "Alan, call me in the morning. I get in early, and I truly expect that I will have a positive answer for you. Leave me your hotel phone number as well, in case I get clearance early.

Alan was so encouraged that he put off a call to the third attorney. He headed back to his motel, ordered a scotch and a sandwich at the bar, and went to make the telephone call to Mark Pearlman, the first attorney he saw that day. He asked the bartender to protect his seat and not hold back on serving the order while he left to make a brief call. He then dialed the number on Mark's business card, thinking he may have an embarrassment of riches in having a couple of attorneys to choose from.

"Mark Pearlman here."

"Hi, Mark, Alan Roberts"

"Oh, hi Alan." After a slight hesitation, Pearlman continued, "I am afraid I don't have good news for you." Mark Pearlman was a very seasoned lawyer. He had learned early that when having to deliver disappointing news, get it right out there quickly and make it less painful for both parties.

Alan was taken aback by the unexpected answer, but then adjusted and in a conversational tone calmly asked, "You seemed to show some interest during our conversation. Did your partners object?"

"Yes, it was simply that they determined the case could get very complicated and time-consuming, particularly if the Feds brought additional charges. In fairness to the firm, and frankly, to you and the defendants, it comes at a very busy time for us so we would not have the time and resources to do it justice."

Whatever the true reasons, Alan knew their worrying about fairness to him or the defendants were not among their great concerns, but it was a firm "no" and there was no sense pushing it. Besides, given an opportunity to hire Pearlman or George Whitcomb, he was leaning toward Whitcomb anyway and felt optimistic that Whitcomb would take the case.

Alan politely thanked Pearlman for at least considering it and then followed it up with a call to Sevena and brought her up to speed. The scotch and turkey sandwich were waiting for him when he got back to the bar. There would be periodic newscasts with pictures of the defendants and Renfrew and Armstrong at the cameras outside the court after the hearing. There was also coverage of the DA's press conference announcing that he retained a special prosecutor to handle the felony case. His name was Maxwell Jenkins.

The anchor on this CBS report gave Jenkins' background. "Jenkins is a highly-respected attorney with 30 years of successful criminal litigation under his belt, mostly as a prosecutor. He was a former First Assistant District Attorney for Oklahoma County and the US Attorney for the Northern District of Oklahoma, and now in private practice. He has been called upon as a special prosecutor on many occasions for both state and federal high-profile cases. And frankly, no one can remember when he lost one."

"Man, I would not want to be those guys," Alan heard a young guy at the end of the bar responding to the news.

"Hey, I have no pity for these communist fuckers," an older white-haired man shouted as he lifted his empty glass into the air a couple of times, signaling to the bartender for another.

Alan had just paid his check when the bartender, holding a phone, called out, "Is there an Alan Roberts here?"

"That's me," Alan responded.

"There is a phone call for you from a George Whitcomb on the line at the front desk."

"Please ask the desk to hold the call for a couple of minutes and then put it through to my room, 212."

The phone rang as Alan entered his room. "This is Alan."

"Alan, George Whitcomb, no need to wait until tomorrow. I got hold of my partners. But as they say, 'good news travels fast, bad news even faster.'"

Alan's heart began to sink. "Not happy with your opening, counsel."

"Neither am I. I will be completely honest. I very much want to do this case. However, before I even talked to our managing partner, he had already received a call from one of our biggest corporate clients that if we were in any way asked to be connected with the defense of this case, we must decline, or they would terminate any ongoing or further legal business with the firm."

"Fuck! That is unbelievable. How would they know I would be contacting your firm?" Alan asked incredulously

"That's exactly it, Alan. It gets more mysterious. I have called around to a number of my colleagues who are in firms you likely would contact for this type of representation, including a good friend, Mark Pearlman, whom you had talked to today as well. The top-notch criminal lawyers here all know each other and, in fact, have appeared as co-counsel with one another in many cases. Mark is in the same boat as I am, as are the others. Mark, too, wanted to take the case. We have never seen anything like this. All the firms have been called by one of their most lucrative corporate clients threatening to withdraw if they touched your defense."

"My God," Alan put the phone down on the table for a moment, took a deep breath, and picked it up again. "Thanks, George, for being up-front with me. It at least saves me from running around hitting my head against the wall. May I ask who was the corporate client in your case?"

"You at least deserve to know that, but it has to be off the record. It was World Engines, a supplier of Global Aircraft."

CHAPTER 30

THE PHONE RANG in Judd's office during his 9:00 am meeting with Sevena and Alan. It was the third such meeting since Alan returned from Oklahoma a week before. It was clear the planned demonstrations in Boston and San Francisco had to be postponed indefinitely given the Oklahoma disaster and the infiltration that blew their surprise there. Also, difficulties continued unabatedly in Alan's effort to secure an adequate defense team for the SDS defendants. He had called two more law firms recommended by Goodman with the same negative results. Trying to recruit a respected litigator to join the defense team had the same chance as a blacklisted actor looking for a role in a Hollywood movie after being named as a communist sympathizer by the late Senator Joseph McCarthy, the then Chairman of the House on Un-American Activities Committee. Considering these rejections, Goodman suggested that he continue to represent Eddie and ask the court to appoint public defenders for the other three. At least with Lisa Kelly representing Betty, they would have a five-person legal team, though they knew if this were a boxing match, for their own safety, they would be disqualified from stepping into the same ring with a Maxwell Jenkins and the caliber of the team that he was assembling. For the moment, there was no other choice. They would need that legal manpower just to carry out discovery before the trial.

Judd got to the phone on the fourth ring, "Hello."

"Professor Lambert?"

"Yes, it's me."

"Professor, I am calling you from Federal Mutual Insurance Company in Washington regarding your request for a quote for a $100,000 term life insurance policy. It would be $1,300 a year."

Judd had no idea what he was talking about. "Sorry?" he responded.

"$1,300 sir, just $1,300," the person repeated pronouncing it slowly.

Suddenly Judd realized the 1300 amount was probably code for a time that Michael wanted to call him at the phone booth. Recovering, Judd continued by repeating the word "sorry," but not as a question. "Sorry, sir, seems to be some static on the phone, did you say $1,300?"

"Yes, and that is a very competitive price."

"Sounds good. I will consider it."

Judd hung up and explained to Alan and Sevena what the call was about and that he was to be at the phone booth at 1300-1 pm. He speculated that Mike may have uncovered some info about the P-7 project, though that seemed secondary to their more recent concerns.

JUDD PARKED HIS car with his windows open beside the telephone booth at 12:45 near enough to hear the phone ring. Michael's call was right on time. Judd got to the phone on the second ring. "Hi, this is Judd."

"Hi, Professor. Hope you are OK. I was a bit worried about you. Looks like your Oklahoma leg of the blitz you told me about did not go so well."

"A fucking total disaster," Judd responded.

"True, but even worse than you think."

"Can't imagine how it could be worse."

"Well, after I explain, you won't have to imagine it. But I need to ask you, how much can Sevena and Alan be trusted?"

"I would trust them with my life," Judd responded without any hesitation.

"I know *you* do, but can I trust them with my job is the question?"

"Don't know what you mean?"

"The things I have uncovered warrant a face-to-face meeting with all of you. I need to know if I can trust them in keeping the stuff strictly confidential under whatever pressures they may face to use it-the same confidential conditions under which I shared the Gulf of Tonkin intelligence with you?"

"Yes, I am sure, but I will ask them to give me their solemn word."

"OK, then. I am in Boston today on CIA business. I already rented a room at the Copley Plaza, a different hotel from where I am staying. It is room 406 and I want to meet all of you this evening at 5 pm. Do not write down the room number. It is easy to remember. It is one less than Ted Williams' 407 baseball batting average record that you used to throw up to me repeatedly when I argued that DiMaggio deserved his MVP award over Williams for his consecutive game-hitting streak. But here is the deal. I have reason now more than ever to caution you about the possibility of being tailed. So, when you three get there, make sure you enter the lobby elevator when it is empty. Get off on the second floor. Then quickly walk up two flights to the fourth floor. My room is eight doors down to the right from the stairway. If you are being followed, they will observe the floor you get off at and go there and you will have lost them by then."

"Thanks, Mike, see you then. Just sent you a hug over the phone."

"That's nice, Judd. I hope you don't mind if I take a rain check until we see each other in person."

––––––––––

A SLIGHT DRIZZLE was starting when Judd came out of the phone booth. It gradually turned into a steady rain that kept up into the evening, as Judd got out of his cab in front of the Copley Hotel 15 minutes before the appointed time for the meeting with Mike. Alan and Sevena were already awaiting him in the lobby. They did not notice any suspicious people observing them, but still followed Mike's directions. They waited for an empty elevator and then got off on floor two to climb the stairway to the fourth floor. Judd lead the way down the hall and stopped at Mike's room. "Here we are, one less than Ted Williams' greatest achievement," Judd whispering to himself.

"Did you say something?" Sevena asked.

"Forget it, just a private joke," Judd responded

"We are in much greater trouble than I imagined when we start mumbling private jokes to ourselves," Sevena mused.

Mike could not have been any more welcoming to Alan and Sevena than if he were greeting some family members he had heard nice things about, but never met. "I would have had room service set up some freshly brewed coffee and some goodies but didn't to want draw attention to having company. But, there is some cold bottled water I took out of the fridge and some glasses on the desk. I gather you are all somewhat shook-up and confused over last week's events."

"Well, I *am* smoking a lot more of these cigarillos lately confronted with the herculean task of defending the students we asked – I motivated – to join us. Because they responded unselfishly, they stand to be imprisoned for their entire youth, and then some, on these trumped-up charges," Alan said, expressing his frustration and taking some responsibility for the failed outcome.

"Well, I think I can lessen your confusion somewhat, but I am not sure how much I tell you will actually help you deal with the mess." Mike sounded very sympathetic for a CIA operative. "I am sure you figured out that whoever was behind the countermeasures knew every detail of your plans well ahead of time."

"For sure, but the who, the how and the why is a mystery. Everything is on hold because we don't know how much they know about us or our plans for other demonstrations," Alan replied.

It was very early in the discussion, but Mike already could sense why Judd liked and trusted Alan, and although Sevena had not said a word as yet, there was something about the manner in which she moved and her concentration that showed she, too, was very much in the moment. It reminded him of how a movie director uses reactive shots of someone's expression to define the person's character. He knew she was not third among equals.

"OK, Judd told both of you the rules. You are going to hear things uncovered by my agency or by me as an operative. Anything I tell you, of which you now have no knowledge, you must agree to keep confidential and not disclose it to anyone, regardless of the consequences, unless I have given you my express permission to disclose it. Also, we have never had this meeting. I assume you have already agreed to this or Judd would not have taken you here, but please confirm your assent to me by nodding your heads." The three instantly did so without hesitation.

"Thanks. So, let me begin to give you some facts chronologically as I uncovered them. When the bomb exploded, the CIA was immediately called in to investigate to see if it were some terrorist act directed or instigated by a foreign nation, like Russia. Operatives of our agency in Oklahoma were on the site within hours. They teamed up with FBI agents named Andrews and Backman who were also on the site looking into it since it was a federal military building."

Alan was familiar with their names since they were the ones who found the incriminating evidence during the search of the SDS office, according to the police report read in court.

"The FBI ran whatever remnants of the bomb they found on-site, and their lab reported that the origin of the bomb could not be matched with any manufacturer. Our agency did the same, but to our surprise, our lab was able to trace it to Majestic Chemical. Majestic is the government's major supplier of explosives and bombs for the war effort. What was strange about it was that this was an explosive particularly designed to make a major blast and set off a great deal of smoke, but with limited damage and was classified and still in its experimental stage. Majestic had produced only a small quantity for testing. It was to be used in heavily populated civilian areas where the Vietcong would center its small missile launches. The explosive would cause a great deal of havoc and disruption, but the destruction itself would be confined to a very limited area."

"Perfect for the military building if you wanted to cause major concern and minimal damage," Sevena commented.

"Precisely! Of course, with it being classified, our agency was now even more concerned about some form of foreign espionage. They wanted to know how someone got his hands on one of these experimental bombs. I knew the CIA operative in charge of that investigation. We joined the agency around the same time and trained together. He, like me, is an avid Yankee baseball fan and we bonded on those discussions. He was willing to share what was going on as one professional to another at a lunch where I just so happened to run into him, or at least so he thought. He told me that they ran through the usual procedure of checking out all the SDS defendants' phone calls, travels, and even the lobby sign-in sheets over the last month at Majestic headquarters as well as all its manufacturing facilities and labs, and none showed any contact or connection between any of the SDS defendants and anyone associated with Majestic. He did mention that FBI agents Backman and Andrews were on the lobby sign-in list of Majestic's corporate headquarters in Texas two weeks before the bombing, but it was clear he thought there was nothing unusual about their being there on FBI business. But that prompted me on my own to check all airline passenger lists for travelers coming into Oklahoma City during the week before the bombing, and I found what I was looking for. Backman and Andrews flew into Oklahoma City not the day of the bombing, but three days earlier."

"Those fuckers, I sort of felt it was them." Alan was first to respond. "So now there is no doubt. The FBI guys planted the bomb which they got from Majestic. They picked that type of explosive because they wanted a bomb that would create havoc, but limited damage to the building. They must have been the ones who arranged the meeting among the military personnel in the other end of the military building that morning so they would be away from the area of the intended explosion to make sure that no one would get hurt."

Judd joined in, "I am sure those same agents framed our guys by planting the bomb material and a fake memo they pretended to uncover during the search of the SDS office. They were on campus before that day and in a position to steal our pamphlets and replace them with their Vietcong commie piece. They were pretty busy guys, weren't they? But how did they know our plans ahead of time and did the Dean fit in some way?"

"It gets better", said Mike. "I asked myself the same questions, 'where did the Dean fit in?' So, I investigated his background. He spent most of his legal career as an equity partner at the firm Latham, Hogan & McLeish and he and the firm were registered lobbyists. I looked up their annual lobbying reports and lo and behold, they represented Majestic Chemical and four other of the biggest arms manufacturers in the world."

"Was one of the other four Global Aircraft or World Engines?" Alan asked.

"Yes, Global Aircraft was another of their clients. Why would you think to ask?" Mike had a look of curiosity.

"A law firm that was ready to represent the SDS five defendants changed its mind under the pressure of a major client, World Engines, a supplier of Global. A lot of coincidences showing up here, no?"

"A lot more to come. The CIA can access federal income tax filings without a subpoena or the parties knowing about it. I decided on my own to review Global's and the filings of the other four arms manufacturers to see the extent of legal fees they were paying out to the Dean's firm. They were exorbitant as anticipated, no surprise there. In doing so, however, I found something that did surprise me. Each of them had taken tax deductions for a significant amount of money they donated to the same, newly incorporated charitable foundation. I looked up the foundations incorporation documents and reports and you can guess who managed it: Latham, Hogan & McLeish, the Dean's firm. Still more coincidences, as Alan put it, the foundation made very large grants to seven universities, one of them the very same America U in Oklahoma. The others included BU and Baxter U in San Francisco, the two additional sites Judd told me you targeted for your 30-day blitz. Anybody care to connect the dots?"

Alan and Judd instantly looked in Sevena's direction as if anointing her as the responder, both knowing that when it came to her intuition and solving puzzles, she could complete the New York Times Sunday crossword in less time than it took either of them to peruse the obituary page.

Sevena, without hesitation, began to connect the dots in a simple logical cadence. "Majestic Chemical, Global Aircraft and the other arms dealers make gazillions of dollars during a war. The Vietnam War is their cash cow. They would want to milk it for as long as they can. It stands to reason that they are not enamored of any effort to shorten that duration. The Dean and his firm, Latham, Hogan & McLeish, make a ton of money in legal and lobbying fees based on the amount of government military contracts they win for Majestic and the rest. Those fees also diminish greatly when the Vietnam War ends. Therefore, the arms dealers, the Dean and his firm do not want to see demonstrations take hold and gain the kind of traction that could ultimately shorten the war.

"Universities also are unwelcoming to protests and demonstrations on their campuses. Long, sustained demonstrations can cause havoc to orderly administration. Lastly, the FBI under Hoover, as Judd informed me, sees civil rights and antiwar demonstrations as un-American, inspired by communists or anarchists. It is a well-known public secret that they have a group of special undercover operatives assigned to prevent or break up civil rights and I am sure antiwar demonstrations through covert means. So, we have four groups aligned by differing interests that could be united for the common purpose of thwarting our efforts to conduct antiwar protests on campuses."

Sevena walked over to the desk and poured herself a glass of water. She took a sip and continued. "As far as connecting the dots, so who was it that pulled all these groups together to counter our efforts, especially in Oklahoma? We need only ask who had contact or relationships with all of them. Only one person-our infamous Dean. He was the one who received all the investigative reports on the premier law school students from, as it turns out, the FBI. He, through his firm, represented all four armament manufacturers. He, through his firm, formed and managed the foundation that provided funds donated by these manufacturers to bribe the universities that were hot spots for student protests, and fortify them with effective countermeasures. Here is the irony. The Dean actually arrived at the same conclusions we did, that only a breakout of student protests on college campuses could bring on the kind of pressure needed to stop the war.

"And Alan," Sevena continued, "I think we now finally can answer the question that has been plaguing you all along. What is the P-7 Project? Mike said there were 7 universities involved. My guess is that the P-7 Project is connected to these universities, and the P-7 Project stands for the Presidents-7 Project. That would explain why they were recruiting the top conservative lawyers, with opposite political leaning than yours, to assign them to each of the presidents at the universities to assist in the countermeasures. That may suggest why Roy Armstrong, the highest-ranking student in his senior class at BU Law School, ended up in Oklahoma of all places as the America University's President's Special Counsel. It was no coincidence. Neither were all the others we have been talking about."

"Clearly a conspiracy," said Judd. "But here is what doesn't fit. These are presidents with distinguished careers. While I can understand how they can be tempted by large donations to take stronger measures than ordinarily needed to control or neuter demonstrations that they would want to control anyway, I can't believe they would be a party to the contrived bombings to frame the demonstrators."

"I am sure they weren't," Mike responded. "I am sure neither they nor any of the local police or other law enforcement agencies knew that the FBI planted it and the incriminating memo. I am sure they believe that the SDS defendants did it. No doubt that Backman and Andrews would have had to have gotten Hoover's prior approval. I don't know to what extent, if any, the Dean was involved in the planning of the bombing or had prior knowledge of it. But for sure, after the bombing, he knew it was not the students."

"So here is the 64 million-dollar question." Alan was to pose the most mystifying one. "How did they know our exact plans ahead of time? We only discussed the school's plans with that school's five blitz leaders. Judd and Sevena and I had checked them out thoroughly. All of them had been involved in prior civil rights demonstrations and other similar liberal activities since high school. I cannot believe any of them was a plant, and if so, who?"

Sevena took a stab at it. "I was trying to figure that out as well without any definite conclusion. But assuming it was one of them, who would stand out? What I know is all our SDS guys are in jail. I say, 'guys' because one of the group who is not in jail at this moment-is Betty. All the guys are being represented by attorneys we are supplying. Betty has her own.

However, what stops me there is that she, like the rest of them, is facing serious charges."

"Sevena, how the CIA would love to recruit you as one of their specialty analysts," Mike commented and was now to fill in the remaining blank. "You are absolutely right in identifying Betty Nowicki as the plant."

"My God, was she the plant?" Judd reacted in total surprise.

"Yes," responded Mike. "There is no way you could have known or could have flushed out anything to alert you of that while screening the blitz leaders. The fact is, you did get it right. Betty is as committed as you are in her antiwar activism. Armstrong, pursuing the Dean's planned countermeasures, had no way of knowing what, if any kind of demonstration would be planned to oppose the war. He then went to work with FBI guys to find someone they could plant as an informer. They knew you would have to be forming a very small planning group to prevent leakage of your plans and that you would carefully vet them. They reviewed the backgrounds of a lot of potential volunteers to find someone who was totally dedicated to your cause, could win your confidence to become a part of the inner circle, but had something in his or her background that made that person compromised to be blackmailed into becoming an informer. They found someone who was perfect – Betty Nowicki."

"What was it they found and how did they find it?" Alan asked.

"My check into her and her parents' background revealed that her parents, her younger one- year-old brother and she entered the country illegally when she was three-years-old. The parents forged green card papers and had been living undisturbed in the USA since then. I know this because when I checked on your five Oklahoma blitz leaders that were arrested, I found that our agency had at one time discovered the Nowicki illegal entry while looking into another matter. We did not pursue that violation since it was unrelated to our investigation. They had been living responsible lives and were not otherwise a threat to national security. However, our records showed that FBI agent Backman had requested information from our agency on several people living in Oklahoma and she was one of them. I am sure that the FBI threatened her and the entire family with deportation unless she cooperated and volunteered to be part of the blitz leadership group and report all plans. I would guess that she thought that she was reporting only on your planned sit-ins and had no idea that it would lead to the imprisonment of her colleagues. I also checked the property the uncle put up for bail. With the existing mortgage, it did not have the equity to cover the amount of bail. The mortgage was paid up the very day of the arraignment, so it had the necessary value to be put up for her $200,000 bail. You can guess where that money came from to pay up the mortgage, and that the house will be re-mortgaged back after the trial so the money can be returned to the FBI. They will then find a way to get her case dismissed."

The discussion was intense as evidenced by the fact that no one interrupted Mike.-and it was about to get even more intense.

Mike continued. "You know what Betty being an informer also means?"

Judd was quick to know where Mike was going with it. "*Yes*, that means that they know who we are – Alan, Sevena and me. All three of us met with the Oklahoma blitz leadership many times with Betty present."

Sevena followed. "And worse still, there may be a similarly compromised informer in both the five-person Baxter San Francisco blitz leadership team and in our leadership group here at BU. They could know all our plans for these two schools, as well."

Alan reacted. "*Wow*, given all this, we need to figure out our next step. Perhaps we should begin by getting this conspiracy before the judge."

Mike quickly responded. "Take another breath. I am not sure there is anything we talked about that would prove there is a conspiracy. As you know, connecting dots with speculation is not evidence. First, you can't cite the CIA stuff we uncovered. That would compromise me and our agency. Even if you can find your own way to show that the Dean and his firm got their clients to donate to a foundation that gave grants to seven universities, one of which was America U, what does that prove? What is so unusual for a law firm to encourage their clients to donate funds to universities that can be used for new science buildings or other endeavors that could produce qualified engineers and scientists for those industries? That is what they would say. Also, even if by some means you could prove that the funding was donated for the schools to counter – they would say 'manage' – demonstrations on campus, how would you be able to get that into evidence? The prosecution would object to it as irrelevant as to who set off the bomb."

"What about if I can independently get proof that the FBI agents visited Majestic Chemical two weeks before the bombing without referring to the CIA report that you mentioned? I could subpoena in Majestic's records," Alan pushed further

"The problem is that for you to subpoena in Majestic's records you would first need to show that you had reason to believe that the bomb was manufactured by Majestic. I don't know how you would explain why you were looking at Majestic in particular, without revealing you got the information from the CIA. Even if you could subpoena their records for some reason, they would object to producing any classified information and would state you were just on a fishing expedition. I have been involved in several cases like this in which classified information is sought and the scenario is always the same, and I am sorry to say it leads to a dead end."

Judd thanked Mike for his information and insights and assured him they would treat the information with strict confidentiality. He then stated the obvious. "There must be a smoking gun somewhere. Our only chance is to find it."

Alan agreed. "But it won't be an easy chore. We need to encourage Goodman and the defense to use the discovery process and the trial as a way to point to the involvement of the Dean, the foundation, Majestic, the FBI, and President Coburn. I need to get them started fishing for those leads right away…tomorrow even."

"How are you going to get them to focus on the Dean, Majestic and the rest when you can't tell them what you know? I think only you could do it, but unfortunately, we don't have a year until you pass the bar to join the team," Sevena remarked.

Alan considered what Sevena said. Then after remaining quiet for a few moments, a eureka look came over his face. "Maybe we don't have to wait that long for me to become directly involved, and perhaps there is a way to obtain some leads without awaiting discovery."

CHAPTER 31

ALAN GOT LITTLE sleep after returning to his apartment from the meeting with Mike. He tossed and turned all night, physically mimicking the swirling of his thoughts and his frustration over the obstacles to proving the conspiracy that thwarted their efforts. He would muster the energy to begin the difficult task when he awoke, but would have to wait until 9:30 am to make his first call.

"Hi, Evelyn, it's Alan, Alan Roberts. How are you?"

"Alan, what a pleasant surprise. I'm fine, thank you. Can't tell you how happy I was to learn that our prodigal son is not only back but remarkably turned-out grades somewhat comparable to your first year, despite all the time you lost."

"I surprised myself."

Alan, I'm sorry, but the president is not here today. He is off to a conference in Florida. Were you looking for an appointment to see him?"

"No, to see you actually."

"*Me?*"

"Yes, you said you would take a rain check on the drink I promised for telling me about the lost Investigator's Report. I need to ask you for another favor and am willing to add lunch to that drink whether you decide to do the favor or not. I could pick you up at the office at noon today if that works." Alan wanted to tell her about the favor up front so it would be clear he was not using the lunch invitation to spring it on her.

"I am free today and expect to be both hungry and thirsty by noon and would also be interested in finding out what you have been about, but I need to ask you about the favor...." Evelyn, having remembered Alan's disturbance over the then Dean investigating him, finished her sentence jokingly. "Will you be asking me to poison anyone?"

Alan laughed. "Well, not literally. Look, there is a great Indian restaurant in Kenmore Square, and they make a very potent traditional toddy drink made from the sap of coconut palms. We can walk there from your office and I promise to ask you to consider the favor before I get you high."

"If you are driving here to my office, there is a parking lot across the street from our building." This was Evelyn's way of accepting the invitation.

Alan had never been to the Castle, the building whose architecture resembled a European castle and housed the president's and other university executives' offices. He took the elevator to the top floor that stopped within the entry hall of the president's office. Evelyn and he greeted each other and after a minute of pleasant chatter, Alan came to the point.

"Evelyn, what I am about to ask of you is something I have no right to ask, for I can't even tell you the reason why I need you to do it. They say, 'where one stands on an issue depends on where one sits.' You sit here in President Lauder's office and so you owe him your loyalty. I can only tell you at this point that there is a higher loyalty that I am acting on and asking you to honor it based only on my say-so and nothing more."

Evelyn could hear the honesty and idealism in the way he spoke. She could tell from his tone that he was asking for something he deemed very important and likely adverse to her boss's interest, but to his credit, he was not selling.

"What is the favor you are asking of me?" she inquired.

"It is to go to the ladies' room or somewhere else in the building for 20 minutes and leave me here alone for that time. I can assure you that when you come back nothing will be taken, and everything here will be exactly as you left it. But we cannot speak of it again, nor can you tell anyone else."

Evelyn thought for a moment and then spoke. "Alan, you never asked me this."

"I understand," Alan immediately replied without showing his disappointment.

Without pausing, Evelyn continued, "I do, however, need to talk to someone in the Public Relations Office on the floor below. It won't take more than 25 minutes, so if you don't mind keeping busy with some magazines there on the table and then if you would be kind enough to lock the door with this key, we can meet in the front lobby and go to lunch." She then walked to the elevator without another word.

Alan did not have time to dwell on his appreciation for Evelyn's favorable response and the clever way she gave herself deniability. The door hardly closed when he immediately began to search Evelyn's room first and then the president's office, looking on top of the desks, into each of its drawers and some of the filing cabinets carefully so as not to disturb things. Within 15 minutes, he found the two items he was looking for and a third that was of interest. He made copies of some parts of the items on Evelyn's copy machine and put everything back exactly where he found them. The copies he put into his shoulder briefcase. He was done in 18 minutes, locked the door and called up the elevator to take him down to the front lobby.

Dinner was fun. There was no further mention of the favor. They talked for over two hours, laughing and sharing many of their interests and likes; she confessed an uneasiness working for her boss, whom she did not completely trust for many reasons. They genuinely liked each other.

"Alan, I gave my notice and will be retiring in June. I will be 50 and have 20 years with the state and am eligible for a small pension. I have some savings and I want to do some traveling. I got married at 22 and had a little girl to bring up by myself when my husband died during the invasion of Normandy. Thelma, that's my daughter, is now a teacher and married with a kid of her own, so for the first time, I can go and *explore the interesting world out there*. Alan, do those words ring a bell? It was your advice to me when you left the Dean that morning and it has been on my mind almost every day ever since."

"Good for you. I can only hope it turns out to be the right advice."

As they got up to go, Alan went over and gave her a caring hug. Though it was meant to be a friendly caress, Evelyn, without letting on, felt a sexual awakening as their bodies pressed together. She had not felt that way for a very long time. She wondered whether that stimulation would continue to play out in her travels, which would be another reason for her to be thankful to Alan.

CHAPTER 32

"WHAT A DIFFERENCE," Alan thought, as he drove into the court's empty parking lot exactly three weeks from the day of the arraignment session. This time, he went up to the second floor in the front elevator and entered the first session where the only people there were the Chief Court Officer, the Clerk, the Special Prosecutor Maxwell Jenkins with Assistant District Attorney Renfrew sitting at the prosecution table, and Goodman representing Eddie Carpenter, Lisa Kelly representing Betty and three public defenders representing the other 3 blitz leaders, all sitting at an extended defense table. Alan sat down on the empty seat reserved for him next to Goodman.

At exactly 1 pm, Judge Joe Clark entered after the Court Officer called the court into session. It was scheduled to hear motions on discovery. All parties introduced themselves and whom they represented for the record. Goodman then rose and addressed the court. "Your Honor, sitting next to me," Alan stood up, "is Alan Roberts. He completed two years of the three-year curriculum at Boston University Law School. He is a member of their law review and completed their one-year Student Prosecutors Program having tried misdemeanor cases under supervision. He has joined our office to work as an apprentice for one year, which would, in some states, make him eligible to take the bar next year without having to graduate law school."

"I am familiar with it," Judge Clark interrupted. "Apprenticeship is an approach available, but not pursued by many, though a good number of our distinguished attorneys in the past obtained their certificate to practice in this manner without graduating law school-Daniel Webster, Patrick Henry, Clarence Darrow, John Jay, the first Chief Justice of the Supreme Court and another gentleman you may have heard of, Abraham Lincoln. So, Mr. Roberts, if you succeed you will be in good company. Mr. Goodman, I will allow Mr. Roberts to sit in court at your table as an apprentice to assist you in your preparations."

"Thanks, Your Honor, but we will be asking the court to allow Mr. Roberts to fully participate in the defense of my client, including presenting and cross-examining witnesses."

Maxwell Jenkins stood up with a smile on his face. "You certainly will get no objection from the prosecution, but maybe the court should instruct Mr. Goodman that if he is giving up from the start, and I can understand why he probably should let his client know." Even the rest of the defense team laughed along with the others.

"My client is the one who asked me to make this request," responded Goodman.

"Mr. Goodman," the judge followed up. "While I am not sure of the appropriateness of Mr. Jenkins's attempt at humor, he does have a point. I will take into consideration the desire of your client to have Mr. Roberts participate in the trial proceedings if that is his wish, but this is a high-profile case and I cannot turn this into an amateur hour, or a chance of an appeal of a conviction based on incompetent counsel. The ability to litigate requires a sophisticated knowledge of evidence that I would sincerely doubt Mr. Roberts could possess given his limited experience."

"We believe Mr. Roberts is qualified and would submit to any method by which the court wishes to test him," responded Goodman.

"You're serious?"

"Very much so Your Honor. It is my client's express wish that Mr. Roberts be permitted to fully participate on his behalf," responded Goodman

"Mr. Goodman, for the record, am I to understand that your client gave you specific instructions to request the Court to allow a second-year law student to examine and cross-examine witnesses on his behalf in such a serious matter that could result in his imprisonment for the better part of his youthful years?" Judge Clark posed the question in disbelief.

Goodman took out a signed affidavit from Carpenter containing the request and handed it to the Judge, stating, "I know it is highly unusual Your Honor, but as you can see it is my client's fervent wish, and as you know, even a request from a defendant to represent himself though he has no legal education or acumen of any kind, must be granted."

"Well, it is quite different than a defendant seeking to represent himself though I get the point of your analogy." The Judge thought for a moment. "Well, if there are no objections by any of the parties, there is a way to test the extent of Mr. Roberts' qualifications. I conduct a class on evidence for the members of the American Trial Lawyers Association in their continuing education courses. I have a film of a court trial we play that requires them to raise an objection and state the basis for it when legally impermissible questions are asked. We score how many of them they spot and the correctness of the stated grounds for their objection. It is as good a test that exists anywhere. Of course, I won't hold Mr. Roberts to the average grades of those in the Association since that organization contains the premier trial lawyers in the country, but he would have to attain a grade sufficient to indicate a trial lawyer's competence for me to entertain your client's request.

"Any objections?"

None of the lawyers raised any. "There being none, the Court will be in recess for 45 minutes while the clerk sets up the projector and screen."

Alan took the time to make a call to Sevena and asked her to call him back from a pay-phone. "Look, I got to get back to the courtroom. I will explain later, but I got hold of the Dean's appointment book and some of his telephone bills showing his long-distance calls during the last six months. I made copies of some of the things that looked interesting. He had a notation about a May 24 meeting with university presidents at the Harvard Club. I need you to find out if any of the P-7 presidents had rooms there. Pretend you're from the Dean's office checking on whatever. Also, two days later on

May 26, there is a notation 'Meeting Washington Office.' Have Judd get in touch with Mike to check commercial airline passenger lists to see if any of the five arms dealers that contributed to the foundation flew in that day or the evening before. Oh, with these guys, he better check airport logs for private jet landings as well. Adios."

The Court Officer dimmed the lights, and the sound of the projector tape rolling was soon replaced with the sounds of a prosecutor examining a witness on the stand in a simulated courtroom trial. Alan was to object to any impermissible questions. After two questions, the prosecutor asked, "Isn't it a fact that it was so dark you could not see anything when you arrived?"

"Objection, leading the witness," Alan called out.

The prosecutor continued to question the witness and after another minute asked, "So what did the gas station attendant tell you about the make of the car that pulled away after the shot?

"Objection, hearsay," Alan said.

As the prosecutor and defense attorney continued to examine witnesses over the next 60 minutes, Alan would stand and raise objections to a number of questions:

"Objection, irrelevant."

"Objection, the document is inadmissible. It is not an original copy."

"Objection, the gun cannot be introduced without proving a chain of custody from the time of finding it to its introduction here in court."

"Objection, the question assumes a fact not yet in evidence."

"Objection, the witness is giving an opinion and has not been properly qualified as an expert."

In all, Alan made 39 objections which Judge Clark noted as they were being made. The lights were turned back on and the screen lowered and removed from the courtroom along with the projector. Judge Clark looked up from his notes. "Frankly, I don't know what to say. There are 40 objectionable-questions and you raised the proper objections, stating the correct reasons for 39 of them. The average among our country's premier trial attorneys is 32. The highest score ever recorded in the four years we have given this test to literally hundreds of trial lawyers was

38. You hold the record. I will approve your full participation under attorney Goodman's supervision, though I somehow get the feeling he may be performing under yours."

"Thank you, Your Honor," responded Allen. "But I hope I do not seem presumptuous in asking you to point out the one question to which I failed to object."

"Sure. The 19th question asked of witness two. You should have objected to it on the grounds of hearsay. Let me read it to you."

"No need, Your Honor. I remember it. It was a question posed during cross-examination by the defense lawyer, 'Wasn't there a taxi driver at the scene who told you that the color of the hair of the person running from the robbery was blonde and not brown like the defendant?'"

"Precisely," responded the Judge. "He was asking for hearsay, which of course is objectionable because you don't have the taxi driver there on the stand to cross-examine as to matters such as how close he was, or the lighting conditions when he made the observations, so it is unreliable to admit into evidence that the person's hair was blonde."

"That was my first thought too, Your Honor," Alan replied. "But the question could be interpreted as not being asked to prove the truth of what the taxi driver at the scene said to the witness regarding the defendant's hair color, but only to show that the witness saw and heard a taxi driver at the scene. It would prove that the police officer who just testified there were no witnesses to the robbery was wrong. The rule, as you know, is that hearsay is not admissible to prove the truth of a fact stated by someone not available for cross-examination, but is admissible to impeach a witness's creditability, in this case, the cop's observation. We don't know from this case the reason for the question, but if it is admissible for any reason, my objection would be overruled so I did not raise it."

All the attorneys in the courtroom were dead quiet witnessing this extraordinary exchange between Alan, still a law school student, and the well-respected judge, feeling like they were the students in the room, not Alan.

"Well…you could be right. I am going to take it up with my colleagues at the Trial Association." Judge Clark was admittedly stunned by the scholarly performance by Alan. "Mr. Roberts, let me ask you something if it is not too personal. What were your grades in Evidence?"

"I did pretty good, a 99."

"Well, from what I have seen, I can't believe they were able to come up with a question that kept you from getting a 100."

"Like the debatable objection we just discussed in your test, I am not sure they did." Alan smiled indicating that he may have been joking. The judge and the attorneys all roared in laughter, including the prosecution, though the laughter from the prosecution's table was less vocal than the others.

The rest of the session dealt with discovery and pre-trial issues. Goodman and Alan asked for the production of copies of any lab tests on the bomb material, the right to inspect the original copy of the incriminating memo and any other material found at the SDS office. They also requested copies of the application and affidavits filed for the search warrant, copies of any documents, manuals, written policies, or other such written material reviewed by the law enforcement agents or anyone at the university prior to the sit-ins, all of which were granted.

Anything else?" asked the Judge.

Goodman stood up. "One last thing, Your Honor, except for Betty Nowicki, I represent the two remaining defendants charged with the trespass matters. They are due to be heard in nine days. We move that they be continued to be heard at the same time as the trial on the arson charges."

"No objections? Motion granted, and we will see you all at the trial in a little over five weeks from now. I suggest you wear your Sunday suits. There will be more cameras and media around than Oklahoma University Sooner fans at opening games. And I give you a polite warning, this court will not tolerate anyone playing up to the cameras or the press both in and outside of the courtroom. This will not be a sequestered jury and I don't want them considering anything from any of you other than the evidence they hear in the courtroom."

As soon as Alan said his goodbyes to Goodman, he went directly to visit Eddie and the others in confinement. They were anxious and he could see a look of despair on their faces. In his heart, he carried a heavy burden and felt singularly responsible for their misfortune. He brought them up to speed and to give them some semblance of hope, he renewed his commitment to work day and night to free them.

Alan flew out of the city knowing that his next trip back would be for the Big Show. He knew he was not ready for it. He tried to think of a saying from the ancient scholars or prophets of all faiths, or from the philosophers he revered, that would give him more hope. None came to mind.

CHAPTER 33

FIVE WEEKS SEEMED to go by like five days as Alan and Goodman did all they could to prepare for a trial stacked against them in every conceivable way. Normally, they would waive their right to a speedy trial to give them more time to prepare the case. But more time was not going to help them prepare to any greater degree while giving the prosecution more time to do so. Mainly, they did not want Eddie and the others lingering in a jail cell for many more months, so the day of trial was upon them.

All three, Alan, Sevena and Judd, flew from Boston to Oklahoma together the night before.

The cat was out of the bag, so their traveling together did not have to be kept secret. Sevena had to park the rented car a great distance past the courthouse to get a space. The sidewalks and curbs were overrun with nationwide radio and TV personnel and their equipment. The coverage by the press and broadcast media even exceeded the heavy coverage of the arraignment. Security was tight. Alan was by now well-known to the court personnel, so he was waved in ahead of the long line that had begun to form 5 am that morning by people hoping to get into the courtroom to watch the trial. Media attention to the bombing had slowed a bit over the 90-day period since the arraignment, but had picked up considerably as the trial drew near. Even psychiatrists were being interviewed on TV for their opinions as to what was happening in society that would produce such depravity in college kids who grew up wanting for little. Dr. James Schmitt of Loyola University offered his theory that these sons of World War II soldiers were simply showing empathy for their dads by creating a situation to relive the bombing and violence their fathers had experienced. Talk shows could not let it go either, with some callers suggesting that it was time to return severe corporal punishment in elementary and high schools to discipline an unruly generation. The question being discussed was only why they did it, not whether they did it.

Alan knew that the publicity was not good for defendants being tried by a non- sequestered jury. The judge could instruct them that they were not to listen to or read the news, but jurors are always tempted to do so. In most cases, they already have, despite stating at the jury impaneling that what they heard would not affect their impartiality. Goodman and Alan had considered filing a motion for a change of venue due to the pretrial publicity, but decided against it. They knew it most likely would be denied on the basis that such publicity could be cured by carefully choosing jurors during empaneling and by the judge's instructions to the jurors to only consider evidence heard in court. More importantly, Alan did not want to change judges, since he believed that Judge Clark, more than any other judge, would likely allow him greater flexibility in his cross-examination of witnesses, which he needed to fish for leads to find a smoking gun. The circus atmosphere reminded Alan of the famous Scopes trial with Clarence Darrow defending a teacher being prosecuted for the crime of teaching evolution to high school students. In addition to selling bibles, vendors were even peddling hot dogs and drinks to the crowd directly outside of the court.

Alan got out of the car reminding himself to give Sevena a business card identifying her as a legal assistant in Goodman's law office so she would be able to gain admittance to the courtroom. Alan expected to utilize her as a runner and information gatherer as needed during the trial. Judd had obtained a press pass from a friend, an editor at the Boston Globe, that would get him into the press section corded off in the courtroom.

Except for going to Boston on last-minute errands the previous weekend and returning with Judd and Sevena yesterday, Alan had spent the last month in Oklahoma working with Goodman to prepare the defense. Not unexpectedly, formal discovery provided little helpful evidence.

Though Alan obtained some further information from Sevena's

follow-up on the Dean's meetings, none of it provided any exculpatory evidence that by itself would aid in the defense of Eddie and the others. Alan was coming in on a wing and a prayer, with the hope that somehow, in some way, something would reveal itself at trial that could lead to a smoking gun-if, of course, one existed.

It was agreed that with discovery over, Alan would ask the three defendants to dismiss their public defenders so Goodman and he could then represent them along with Eddie. That way, except for Betty's attorney, they would have complete control of the defense tactics at trial. Alan and Goodman had met with Eddie and the others several times to prepare their testimony, and, just before his last Boston trip, Alan discussed the option of a plea. He told them that the best the prosecution was offering as a plea negotiation was a 40-month sentence for each with credit for time served awaiting trial, along with a subsequent five-year probation term and an agreement by the Justice Department that if they accepted the plea, no federal charges would be brought. That meant another three years of confinement in state prison and a blow to their professional careers for some time thereafter, and perhaps permanently.

"What are the chances of winning? And if we reject the offer and go to trial, and lose, what kind of jail time can we expect?" asked a very concerned Clifford looking for bottom-line answers to weigh in making his decision.

Alan told them candidly that the only thing they could rely on as a defense at this time was putting them on the stand and proclaiming their innocence. He told them that would be tricky, given the very experienced prosecutor to cross-examine them and that, in general, such testimony is generally dismissed as self-serving. Otherwise, they needed to catch a real break at trial that might reveal who planted the bomb. "At the moment, things are not at all in your favor," Alan said, not holding back from giving them a sober account.

As to what the sentence could be upon a conviction, Alan told them the charge carried a 15- year maximum. However, given that they all had no previous criminal records, were young and relying that Judge Clark would not be influenced by the public outcry for a figurative lynching, a 5 to 7-year sentence would not be out of line, but no one could assure them it won't be more.

The defendants huddled, and then all told Alan the plea negotiation offer was not enough for them to plead guilty for something they did not do. So, despite their sober awareness of the heavy odds against their being acquitted and the anticipated significant penalties if found guilty, they would take their chances and gamble on a second-year law student, who for some unexplainable reason gave them hope.

Alan had no sooner joined Goodman at counsels' table when Special Prosecutor Jenkins, accompanied by attorney Lisa Kelly, approached them. "I have requested a lobby conference with the judge, something has come up," said Jenkins. Before they could ask why, the court officer approached. "The Judge said he can see you all in his chambers now."

Judge Clark had already donned his robe. "Gentlemen, come on in, please. Did I hit the lottery? Have you all come in to bless me with a plea and a joint-sentencing recommendation so I can go golfing this afternoon?" He knew from their faces that he was not going to be so lucky.

Jenkins responded, "If only, but I am afraid not. I was just informed by attorney Kelly that her client flew the coop, so to speak. She is not here, and attorney Kelly has reason to believe she skipped town."

"Flew the coop – skipped town – I hope Mr. Jenkins will bless us with fewer clichés at trial , if, , in fact, we get one, given what I am hearing. Ms. Kelly, please, where is your client?"

"Judge, I have tried unsuccessfully to contact her to finish preparing for trial for over a week now. So yesterday I went to her home where I had been before. She was living with her parents and when no one answered, I rang the bell of the landlord who lived above them. He informed me that they all moved out five days before and left no forwarding address. I called her uncle, who made bail for her. He said that he was unaware they left. I was hoping that she would still show up today, but that now seems very unlikely."

"Not an unreasonable assumption, I'd say. Well, that's a fine kettle of fish," Judge Clark said, looking at all of them.

Alan thought to himself, "An interesting expression for a judge who just a moment ago did not seem to welcome clichés."

The Judge continued. "Well, Ms. Kelly, I will default Ms. Nowicki, revoke her bail and issue a default warrant for her arrest. Now, I hope none of you are thinking of making a motion to continue the case until we find her. That could take a week, a month, but it could also take a year or two or never. So, I will sever her case from the rest and would deny any request for a continuance if you were to make such a motion. It does not prejudice any of you to go forward today since as a defendant she was not available to you for testimony or cross-examination anyway unless she voluntarily took the stand and waived her 5th Amendment rights to remain silent and not incriminate herself. Are we in agreement?"

Al knew it would be futile to attempt to persuade the judge to reconsider even if they wanted the delay, so he and Goodman, along with the prosecution, gave their approval.

"Thanks, gentleman," acknowledged the judge. "I will excuse Ms. Kelly and have the Court Officer bring up the defendants to the dock and call the session to order in 20 minutes. We will then impanel the jury and get this thing finally started."

Goodman then addressed the judge on one matter. "Your Honor, as to bringing the handcuffed defendants into the dock for trial, that would create great prejudice in the minds of the jurors no matter how you instruct them that the defendants are presumed to be innocent until proven guilty.

I would request that they be un-cuffed and allowed to sit in the courtroom directly behind counsels' table, which would be the case if they had made bail. There is enough security at this trial to guard the president of the United States, so there is certainly no danger of them fleeing while the court is in session."

The prosecution objected but was overruled by Judge Clark and the request was granted.

By the time all parties returned to the courtroom from the judge's chamber, the courtroom was packed, with the large section reserved for the media completely filled. Alan spotted Judd in that section and Sevena was already sitting in a row behind the defense counsel's table, giving Alan a smile and wink of support as he took his seat. Eddie and the rest of the defendants were then brought up and released into the courtroom to sit at a table directly behind defense counsels' table. They were conservatively dressed in suits and ties purchased and brought to them by Goodman the evening before.

"All rise," the court officer commanded in a loud voice and one could hear the sound of everyone standing with all the chatter coming to a silence. Judge Clark entered the courtroom from his chamber door, walked up two stairs onto his bench and sat down as the court officer again instructed," You all may be seated."

With that, Alan's heart began to beat a little faster with anticipation, excitement and some nervousness. It was the same feeling that came over him when the dealer began to deal the first hand of blackjack when he was to test his skills and strategy against all odds to beat the casino. He also remembered his high school basketball coach telling him that this rush of adrenaline and nervous excitement at the start of a contest was a good thing. It was how all champions reacted. It put them on edge, so that it heightened their determination to perform at their highest level. But in the last analysis, championship contests were won on preparation, skill, intense focus and, all too often, luck. As much as possible, Alan left as little as possible to chance. He had spent the last five weeks with little sleep, utilizing his ability to read, concentrate and digest the materials gained by discovery, Oklahoma law related to the case and volumes of books and treatises on cross-examination of witnesses, legal strategy, as well as local politics and customs.

In that regard, he felt as ready as he could be, but clearly understood that they were up against a veteran professional prosecutor with all the facts and resources in his favor.

After two hours of selecting a jury and a short recess, a jury of 12, seven of whom were women, were led into the jury box. Goodman and Alan had succeeded in stacking more women on the jury. They felt that they might look more favorably on young students as a matter of instinct. They did not have the resources to hire a jury expert to investigate the entire pool and make more refined strategic decisions about which ones to try to impanel, as did the prosecution.

However, that was the least of their concerns. Without some forced error on the part of witnesses that could lead to a smoking gun revealing the truth, the evidence of guilt would be overwhelming and sure to lead to a conviction, regardless of the makeup of the jury.

"Mr. Jenkins," began the judge, "you may open to the jury."

"Thank you, Your Honor.

In trials, unlike football, there is no coin toss as to who gets the ball to take the offense. It is the prosecution since they have the burden to prove guilt beyond a reasonable doubt. Jenkins was a seasoned attorney with tons of experience before juries and he knew the best way to open was to keep it short, simple and to the point.

"Ladies and gentlemen of the jury, good morning. This is not a complex case. Yes, a serious one, but not a complex one. Serious, because an explosive-let's call it what it is-a bomb was set off on campus where thousands of young students go to learn and where they, their parents and loved ones can expect them to do so safely. Instead, one sunny morning, that otherwise serene environment was shattered by an explosion in one of its buildings on campus, causing serious damage, but worse still, except for the grace of God, many would have been killed or crippled. Luckily, a meeting was called in another part of the building and the bombed area was free of the personnel that normally occupy it. Well, you do not have to consider what could or could not have happened in terms of injuries or death if that meeting had not occurred, which will be considered by the judge in sentencing if, and I can confidently say when, you find the defendants guilty."

Jenkins then walked over to his table to pour himself a glass of water, which he drank slowly, letting the impact of the potentially serious injuries or death from the bomb sink in, though no one was actually injured.

He then walked back in front of the jury box. "So, what is it you have to consider? Simply whether a bomb was placed in the military building that exploded causing a fire and damage to the building, and who put it, or plotted to put it there. We will introduce an apparatus found at the scene that was used to set the time in which the bomb was to ignite, and residue material found at the scene that an FBI laboratory report will show was the material used to create a bomb. Second, we will introduce the same type of material found hidden at the SDS office where the planned bombing took place, along with a memo describing these SDS defendants' plans to set off the bomb, all uncovered during a search of that office based on a search warrant. That memo describes how all four of these defendants induced over a hundred innocent students to occupy three other buildings on campus supposedly to peacefully protest the war, but instead intended to stage those demonstrations as a decoy so they could go about the real business of their planned criminal escapade. The pamphlets they were distributing, which we will introduce, stated clearly the reason for the bombing. It read 'Stop Military Enlistments on Campus by Any Means.' We now know the means. There is nothing complicated here. When all our evidence is submitted, I am confident that you will find that we will not only have met our burden that these four defendants are guilty of the heinous crime for which they are charged beyond a reasonable doubt, but beyond any doubt whatsoever. Thank you for your attention."

When Jenkins mentioned "these four defendants" he walked right up to them, looking them in the eye, and pointed at them one at a time as if counting with his finger. He knew from his experience that if you are asking a jury to be able to stand up in front of the defendants and the court and render a guilty verdict, you needed to show them there should be no reluctance or compunction in standing before them in doing so. Alan knew they were up against the very best.

Alan and Goodman decided that Alan would do their opening and summation at the end of the trial. Alan would also be doing the entire cross-examination of the government's witnesses and Goodman the examination of all four defendants in giving their testimony, since it was likely they would need each of them to take the stand. Alan's opening statement was to be short and general, since at this point there was no evidence of innocence to point to.

Alan, in comparison to Jenkins, had curly black hair and though he combed it neatly, it did not disguise his youthful look. Jenkins, on the other hand, presented a more mature look with his salt-and-pepper hair and almost fully grayish sideburns. In one way, the look of maturity was probably to be more trusted, but both Goodman's and Alan's youthful looks gave them an appearance of being the underdog. That could evoke feelings in others to root for them, provided they could prove to be legitimate contenders.

"Good morning, ladies and gentlemen." Alan chose to greet them as he was getting up from his chair. Then, while walking toward the jury box in a calm voice, he said, "I totally agree with Mr. Jenkins. He is absolutely right. This case is not at all complex." Alan was now in front of the jury box facing them directly.

"We all agree there was a bombing. Indeed, a serious crime was committed. There is no issue here. Yet, I am sure the prosecution will still needlessly pile on a lot of evidence about the fact there was a bombing and that it caused serious damages and could have caused serious injuries, though it did not, even though no one contests any of those facts. Nonetheless, they will do so to try to appeal to your emotions and legitimate repulsion over such an atrocious act, so that you will not want to go home without convicting someone for doing something so horrendous. So if you are angry enough over these horrific events, as you should be, and want to convict someone..." Alan then paused and for about 15 silent seconds walked in one direction and then another as if looking around the courtroom for someone, before continuing, "Yes, if you want to convict someone- I don't see any others here you can or be allowed to convict before you go home, except these four kids sitting here." Alan placed his hands gently on a couple of their shoulders. Well, here they are. Forget the presumption of innocence. After all, there are people on the airways and outside this very courtroom carrying signs calling for their convictions before you go home."

In a conversational tone, he continued. "To convict these innocent kids on the insufficient evidence that you are about to hear, so you don't have to walk away with at least someone paying the price for this terrible crime, means not only convicting them for crimes they did not commit, but almost as bad, letting the real guilty perpetrators who committed these horrendous acts forever go free. And that, my good people, would be a double tragedy." Alan let the words hang just as Jenkins did by walking over to his table and also pouring a glass of water, but not just for that effect.

"You just saw me pour a glass of water. Earlier, you saw Mr. Jenkins do the same. Testimony by you or any witness who saw us would be very convincing evidence that we did so. But in this case, you will be presented with no such convincing testimony-for no one, I repeat no one saw any of these defendants ignite the bomb or place the bomb or the device to set off the bomb in the building or saw any of them even enter the building, or even *near* the building at any time. They didn't' see them because they weren't there. They were never there. The prosecution wants to convict them on what is called circumstantial evidence based on the convenient finding-I repeat a convenient finding-of similar bomb material and an *unsigned* memo at the SDS site, without a thread of evidence of who put that material there or who drafted the unsigned memo.

They just want you to make what they will say are logical inferences, more fancy words for 'assumptions', assumptions that these defendants were the ones. But ladies and gentlemen, assumptions are just that... assumptions. They are not proof beyond a reasonable doubt to convict these young men. For as we will show, they never saw that material or that memo before. All we ask you to do is what the law requires you to do. Wait until *all* the evidence is in, and there will be no doubt of their innocence."

Alan sat down and did not see the looks of approval on the faces of Sevena, Judd and Goodman. They were not only impressed with the cleverly constructed opening with very little to work with, but with the tone and sincerity in which it was presented. The attentiveness of the jury confirmed what they had experienced.

"We will adjourn for a brief morning recess and hear the first witness for the prosecution upon our return," Judge Clark instructed as he got up to leave the courtroom.

In hearing Jenkins's opening, Alan had realized that they had caught a small break. What allowed Alan to claim that the government was relying solely on circumstantial evidence was that the FBI had intended to fortify the prosecution's claim of conspiracy by having Betty confess and falsely testify that she was in a meeting where all the defendants discussed the plot to bomb the military building. That would also provide the grounds to dismiss her case by informing the court that she was given immunity for her cooperation in incriminating the others. He speculated that was probably the reason she and her family fled, for she did not want to perjure herself to put people she otherwise admired in prison and feared deportation of her and her family if she simply refused to so testify. Her fleeing was a break. But Alan knew even without her false testimony, the prosecution had an airtight case and a very formidable litigator who would never fumble the ball crossing the goal line.

Alan walked over to the side of the courtroom and looked out the window waiting for the session to reconvene. He saw a line of people outside the courthouse holding the signs he referred to in his opening: "Convict the Commie Terrorists," "Give Them Their Day in Court – Then Sentence the Traitors to Life in Prison." He wondered if they were plants or just angry citizens when his thoughts were interrupted with the call back into session.

"The prosecution calls its first witness, State Police Captain Mark Springer." Assistant District Attorney Renfrew would examine him. Springer testified to the basics-the anonymous tips received by the FBI about the intended occupation of the three buildings, the state, local, and university police dispatched to the sites, the arrests when the student protesters would not leave and then the explosion at the military building.

"And Captain, did you personally go to that site after the explosion?" Renfrew asked.

"Well, after the fire department declared it was safe, I entered the building," said Springer as he went on to describe the damage.

"Who else entered with you?" Renfrew asked.

"Two FBI agents." He then gave their names.

"Then what happened?"

"The inspection of the premises indicated that it was a bomb that caused the explosion. Upon questioning a couple of students arrested for trespassing, they revealed that they were dispatched from the Students for a Democratic Society's office. I then immediately obtained a search warrant and I and William Andrews, one of the FBI agents I mentioned, conducted a search of the SDS office."

"And did you find anything of interest?" Renfrew asked in a louder voice, looking at the jury instead of the witness.

"Yes, we found material hidden behind books in a cabinet that later proved to be the same material as the bomb, and a memo incriminating the defendants in the top drawer of the one office desk in the room."

Alan rose. "Objection, Your Honor, we ask that you instruct the jury to disregard the conclusion 'that the material was the same as the bomb' unless, and until, a lab report is introduced with that finding."

"Objection sustained," ruled the judge. "The jury will disregard that portion of the testimony."

Alan, still standing, requested, "We also ask that the conclusion that the memo was incriminating also be struck. The memo when introduced will speak for itself."

"Also sustained. The jury will strike that conclusion as well."

"Captain, were both the materials that were found at the explosion site and the SDS office submitted to a lab for testing?" Renfrew asked, without appearing distracted in any way by the objections.

"Yes, sir, they were both submitted by Agent Andrews to the FBI Lab."

"And when you found the material and after you read the memo, what did you do then?"

"I placed Edward Carpenter, the president of SDS, who was at the office, under arrest for arson and filed similar charges against the other three defendants who were already under arrest for trespassing."

"Thank you, Captain Springer. Your witness, counselor." Renfrew spoke in a triumphant voice, turning and walking away with his back toward the witness like a bullfighter turning his back on a bull after making a successful pass.

Alan waited a moment and then slowly got up without a note or a pad in his hand and walked in front of the counsel's table. "Good morning, Captain."

"Good morning, sir."

"Captain, can you tell us who it was that told you that the FBI received a tip that there were going to be these three sit-ins at these buildings?"

"I believe our dispatcher contacted me about the FBI tip that there would be the planned sit-ins."

"Did the dispatcher tell you who called him to tell him about the FBI's tip?"

"I believe he said that the call came from President Coburn's office."

"So, it was President Coburn's office that got the tip from the FBI and relayed it to the state police. Is that your testimony, Captain?"

"Yes, sir."

"Well, as a matter of fact, after you received the dispatcher's message, it was Roy Armstrong, President Coburn's Special Counsel, that contacted you about how you all were to be dispatched to those three buildings, isn't that correct?" Alan suspected this, but had no idea if that occurred. Here was his first attempt to fish for information, but put it in a form as if he knew.

"Yes."

Bingo Alan thought there was probably a meeting and would now fish deeper, but without having to guess. "Tell the jury when that occurred and the circumstances surrounding that communication."

"At the request of the president's office, we all gathered that morning around 8 am inside the ROTC building and met with Mr. Armstrong. We were told that what was to occur could disrupt the school's enrollment and he went over the way we would deal with the planned sit-ins."

"It was Mr. Armstrong, was it not, who told you and all the officers of the various law enforcement agencies, how you should be deployed and how to confront the planned student occupation of the buildings?"

"Well, we made some suggestions, too."

"You made some suggestions to Mr. Armstrong, a civilian, as to how all of you should do your police work, is that what you are saying?"

"Objection," Mr. Jenkins shouted out as he rose to his feet. "The court should remind my brother counsel that we are trying the arson case, not the trespass cases. The question is entirely irrelevant to the arson charges that occurred in a totally different building. I would ask Your Honor to instruct my brother to refrain from continuing with this line of questioning until he tries the trespassing cases and get on with the issues of the case at hand."

Alan expected the objection at some point and quickly reacted. "Your Honor, may we approach the bench?"

So here it was – the crucial decision in the case. Alan needed as much flexibility as possible to fish for leads examining all aspects of the activity relating to the countermeasures taken to dismantle the protests related to the trespassing charges. This was vital if he were to have a chance to fish and hopefully find a smoking gun to prove that someone else set off the bomb. On strictly legal grounds, a judge could partially sustain Jenkins' objection by allowing only a brief cross-examination of the trespassing incidents in the other buildings, but not to dwell on it.

Alan's gamble in not moving to change the venue was based on the assumption that Judge Clark might give him much more leeway here. Without that ability to fish to find out things, the case would be over. Judges' rulings on close questions of whether evidence is relevant, is a matter of their sole discretion. It was a lot like baseball umpires calling strikes when pitches are thrown to the corner of the plate. Some were known to have a bit wider strike zone than others. Alan was hoping Judge Clark had that wider zone based on the pitch he was about to serve up.

Alan began his plea in a low voice at the bench, since the jury was not allowed to hear these arguments. "Your Honor, according to Rule 401 of the Rules of Evidence, and I quote," Alan continued without a note, "*evidence is relevant if it has the tendency to make the existence of any fact that is of consequence more probable.* We will be introducing important facts later and the evidence we now seek to elicit will help in providing a complete picture of that evidence. So, we need wide latitude in exploring these trespass issues and the way it was handled."

Jenkins was quick to respond. "If that is the case, then Mr. Roberts should provide us with an offer of proof right now as to what are the facts he intends to introduce that make this line of inquiry relevant."

A reasonable request, and, of course, Alan at this stage had no such facts. It was the smoking -gun he was hoping to uncover during the trial by means of a fishing expedition.

"Sounds reasonable, wouldn't you say, Mr. Roberts?" Judge Clark responded. "I could call the stenographer up here to put it on record."

Alan searched for the best answer he could provide. "Judge, if I were to do that, I would be giving the prosecution my entire defense strategy and that would place us at an unfair disadvantage." Alan remembered that Judge Clark made mention of the Oklahoma Sooners, so he was obviously a college football fan. He decided to appeal to him with a football analogy.

"That would be like asking Coach Mackenzie of the Sooners to turn over his game plan to Missouri State before their big game here at Memorial Stadium next Saturday." Alan had done his homework familiarizing himself with every aspect of local happenings and culture.

He continued, "I would suggest a compromise. You take the evidence *de bene esse*," It was a legal term allowing it in evidence conditionally, to be struck at a later time if it is not tied to relevant facts that are later introduced.

Jenkins objected strenuously. Probably it was partly because of the eloquence of the argument, but maybe stimulated by a feeling of wanting to even the playing field for an underdog, Judge Clark overruled the objection, stating, "I will allow the evidence of the trespass and the countermeasures to the protests *de bene esse* and give Mr. Roberts the leeway to examine witnesses in this area, but I must warn you, Mr. Roberts, that if you fail to tie all of this evidence about the trespass into the bombing by the conclusion of your case, I will favorably rule on Mr. Jenkins' motion to strike all of this type of evidence and instruct the jury to totally disregard it." Alan took a deep breath of relief.

"Well, Captain Springer, sorry for the delay," Alan resumed his cross-examination. "Let me rephrase the question. How were the state police and the other officers deployed inside the three buildings that were temporarily occupied?"

"We stationed ourselves in the building at around 8:30 am before the doors were to open."

"Yes, but not on the first floor, but hidden out of sight on the second floor in all three buildings, is that not correct?"

"Yes."

"Yes, you say. Why didn't you station yourselves outside the building and simply not allow them to enter? That way you would protect the building and not have to arrest over 20 students just trying to engage in a peaceful protest."

"That would have been an option, I suppose," answered Springer.

"A better one, I think you would agree. But wasn't the reason you all chose to hide on the second floor was so that a trespass would occur subjecting these students to an arrest? And wasn't that so that these students, once arrested, in order to avoid punishment, would then agree to refrain from conducting further protests for the rest of their enrollment at the university? And wasn't that because the President's Special Counsel, Roy

Armstrong, instructed you to do so, right?"

"Objection! Objection! Objection!" shouted Jenkins three times while the question was being asked and while the judge banged his gavel several times, unable to interrupt Alan's determination to complete it.

Alan knew it was objectionable, but wanted to get it all in. "I withdraw the question and will simply rephrase it. Captain, is it not true that Roy Armstrong directed that the troops be employed in that manner – yes or no?"

"Yes."

"Thank you. No more questions."

Jenkins, keeping focused, chose not to redirect on the deployment of the police to the occupation sites. He felt nothing damaging had been elicited during Alan's cross-examination related to the bombing charges. He merely asked one question: "Captain, let's get back to the case at hand, did you tell us everything you know about the defendants' involvement in the bombing?" It elicited a "Yes" and Jenkins then proceeded to call FBI Agent William Andrews to the stand.

Andrews went through all his testimony in the language generally used by trained agents and law enforcement officers that makes everything sound official and unchallengeable. He testified that he and his colleague, Fred Backman, were assigned to go on campus a couple of days before the incidents after the FBI received an anonymous tip that an ROTC building might be targeted by students for an illegal sit-in to prevent student enrollment into the ROTC. He had reported the tip to President Coburn. They were kept informed as to the university's preventive countermeasures that were to be taken. He testified that being on-site, he and his colleague immediately went to the military building after it was bombed, obtained whatever evidence they could, including a powdered material they sent to the FBI lab, and found and retrieved the incriminating evidence at the SDS office during the search. After Andrews' direct examination was concluded, Jenkins introduced, without objection, the FBI lab reports indicating that the bomb material found in the SDS office matched the material found at the bomb site, but the lab was unable to determine the manufacturer of the bomb.

"I believe this is as good a time as any to break for lunch," Judge Clark declared. "We will resume at 2 pm for the defendants' cross-examination." Alan was pleased with the break, but not because he was hungry.

CHAPTER 34

A COURT LUNCH break means different things to different people. To jurors and prisoners, it means time to get something to eat-jurors being served generous thick sandwiches in a comfortable room or nearby restaurant compliments of the state, prisoners served much thinner sandwiches in dark jail cells reflecting the sheriff's limited food budget. To other people observing the proceedings, it means scrambling to get something at the court cafeteria or finding a nearby café to grab a bite to eat and hurry back to the courtroom. In this case, however, many did not leave the courtroom for fear they might lose the opportunity to gain re-admittance to one of the more publicized cases in the decade, at least in that part of the country. To the prosecution and the defense legal teams, it meant a chance to regroup in preparations for the afternoon session in the upstairs conference rooms. But to Roy Armstrong, it meant the opportunity to call Dean Lauder from the pay phone outside the courthouse for advice and instructions.

"Hi, Dean, it looks like Alan Roberts will be carrying the load for the defense and enquiring about my instructions to the police in dealing with the protests. I am to take the stand after he finishes cross-examining FBI agent Andrews, and I am sure Roberts will be pressing me on that point."

"Alan Roberts, who would have guessed my dithering second-year law student, would be out there taking on this task. Roy, nothing to worry about. He is smart, but wet behind the ears and knows nothing about the elaborate plans we formulated to put these countermeasures in place. He is just fishing. Volunteer nothing. He will try to pose questions in a way to make you think he knows something. I know you will not fall for it. It is OK to say that President Coburn wanted you to handle the situation for him to ensure that everyone carried out the countermeasures in a legal manner. Just don't let him take you down a path where he can unravel our more elaborate set-up since that could lead to my doorstep and prove to be somewhat embarrassing. Though even that won't help him, for it has nothing to do with the bombing that his clients perpetrated."

"I will, but I am not going to get caught committing perjury either."

"Come on, Roy. You graduated number one in your class at law school. It is why I picked you. You can dance around any of his probes. He's no match for you."

———————————

WHILE ARMSTRONG WAS on the phone, Sevena rushed to beat the line to the court's food concession to get some coffee and sandwiches for Alan, Goodman, Judd and herself. Sorry, guys, all they had left was ham and cheese," said Sevena as she laid down two court cafeteria cardboard trays with four wrapped sandwiches and indented pockets holding the four cups of coffee.

She could have said filet mignons in a red wine reduction prepared by a famous French chef, and she would have gotten the same reaction, or more accurately, the same non-reaction. Food was not on their minds. Alan had done as well as he could with Captain Springer to try to suggest something was – in his dad's words – not kosher. He had exposed the highly unusual tactics in dealing with the student sit-ins. He also succeeded in drawing Roy Armstrong into the picture so he could be called as a witness. He was the only possible link to the Dean, but Alan also knew that without some unexpected revelation in that testimony, it would lead to a dead end.

Alan was painfully aware that he had only two more witnesses to cross-examine if he had any hope of discovering something that could lead to what really happened. One was FBI agent Andrews, whom he would be cross-examining after lunch. He had no direct leads to connect Andrews or the FBI with the bombing, though he was certain that it was Andrews who planted the material and incriminating evidence at the SDS office, most likely at the very time he said he uncovered it. The other witness was Roy Armstrong, whom Alan knew would be formidable in any attempt to unnerve him.

Goodman made a suggestion or two. Alan then requested that he visit with Eddie and the others to bolster their spirits a bit, but mainly to be left alone with Judd and Sevena so he could review what Sevena was able to find out about the Dean's scheduled meetings at the Harvard Club in May and the meeting two days later at the Dean's Washington law firm office. None of what she uncovered revealed any contact between the FBI and the Dean. Alan finished his coffee, but took only one bite of his ham and cheese sandwich before heading back to the courtroom.

"Good afternoon agent Andrews," Alan began his cross-examination when the court convened for the afternoon session. He took Andrews through the various parts of his testimony elicited by Jenkins. "And after you had the bombing device and material properly preserved to be able to send it to the FBI lab, what was the very next thing you did?" Alan asked.

"I accompanied Captain Springer to a magistrate to obtain a search warrant of the SDS office," answered Andrews.

"You determined the explosion was caused by a bomb and immediately assumed that the SDS members must have done it?"

"Well, two and two make four," Andrews responded.

"And by two and two, you mean the bomb and a sit-in that was SDS directed?" Alan followed up.

"Enough for probable cause to get a search warrant and go see," Andrews answered.

"Well, speaking of 'go see' before you left to go see the SDS office, you did *go see* the officer in charge of the military building who told you that he, himself, secured the building with its high-security door lock the night before and it was he who found it still locked when he came to open it the next morning. You knew that. Is that not true?"

"Objection, Your Honor, hearsay," Jenkins exclaimed.

Alan addressed it immediately. "I am not introducing it as to its truth. We will introduce that the doors were locked on both occasions when we call the officer in charge of the building to the stand during the presentation of our case. I am only introducing it now to show the agent's state of mind, which, I am sure as Mr. Jenkins is quite aware, is an exception to the hearsay rule."

"For that purpose only, I will withdraw the objection,"

"So again, agent Andrews you knew that the doors were locked all evening, did you not?' "Yes."

"From your questioning of the employees, you also knew that no one saw any of the defendants enter the building, in it, or leave it, is that also true?" asked Alan.

"Yes, but there was a time when all the employees were out of that room. It could have been placed there then."

"Did you determine when the employees were called out of that room for the meeting?"

"At 9:05 and the bomb went off at 9:30; plenty of time for the bomb and the incendiary device to be placed there," Andrews answered in a confident tone as if he fortified his position.

"But three of the defendants, including Betty Nowicki, a person also charged with this offense were part of the sit-in at other buildings at 9:05 and arrested and in custody during that period."

"Yes, but Eddie Carpenter was not, and the memo said he was central to planning it." Andrews countered.

"Well, let's get to the memo now that you brought it up." It was a nice segue for Alan to leave doubt and not have to deal directly with the last answer.

Alan walked over to the table near the stenographer and picked up a document. "I show you the memo already introduced as Prosecution's Exhibit 7. Is Mr. Carpenter's signature on it?"

"No, but his name appears after the word 'From."

"I did not ask you about what comes after the word 'From,' but it was kind of you to bring it to my and the jury's attention. The word 'From', which you have focused us on, as well as all the words on this memo, are not written in handwriting, are they? All of them have been typed. Is that not so?"

"Yes, it is a typewritten memo."

"So, unfortunately, there are no signatures on the memo to compare with Eddie Carpenter's signature, correct?" Alan, like a crafty chess player, had just moved a piece that looked harmless, but he was looking five moves down the board.

"You nodded your head, agent Andrews, so I take it that was a *yes?*"

"Yes," Andrews confirmed.

"But we can indeed compare something," Alan followed up. "You confiscated not just the material as you say hidden behind some books in a cabinet and the memo in the top drawer of Eddie Carpenter's desk, but also the typewriter on that desk as well, is that not so?"

Andrews answered "yes".

"Did you or someone in your agency conduct a test by typing out an exact copy of the words on the memo with the SDS typewriter you confiscated and compare whether SDS font matched the memo?"

"We may have, but I have no such report," Andrews answered.

"Well, the SDS typewriter has already been marked as Defendant's Exhibit 4. I would ask the court to allow Mr. Goodman to type an exact copy of the memo on a sheet of clean paper so I can show it to agent Andrews for the jury's observation as to the comparison of the font."

The Judge overruled Jenkins's objection and Goodman typed out a copy. No surprise to Alan, it greatly differed from the font of the memo. Alan first showed the newly typed copy to the prosecution and had it marked as Defense Exhibit 9. He then held it up alongside the memo and walked slowly across the jury box showing it to the jury. Jurors were standing up to see it more clearly. It was dramatic and Alan would end the testimony there, knowing that Jenkins would reexamine to rehabilitate the font differential and he would be ready with his 3-dimensional chess move.

As he envisioned, Jenkins was quick to jump up and began questioning Andrews while doing so.

"Agent Andrews, Mr. Roberts went to some theatrics to demonstrate to the jury that the memo was not typed on the SDS typewriter. Did that fact surprise you?"

"No, sir," Andrews answered firmly.

"As we established in my examination of your background, you have worked on a good number of cases involving documents where the identification of the writer was in question?"

"Yes, including many kidnapping ransom cases."

"Did you ever find them to be typed on that person's own typewriter?"

"No, never, not one time. Obviously, the perpetrator knew if his typewriter were to be found, it would, as you say, incriminate him."

"Your witness, Mr. Roberts, if you care to re-cross," Jenkins' voice was loud and sounded victorious.

Alan was ready to move toward a checkmate at least on this issue. "So, in this case, you indicate that Eddie Carpenter would have used a typewriter not associated with him to hide proof of his identity on this unsigned memo in case it was found?"

"Exactly," answered Andrews.

"Just like, as you claim, Eddie Carpenter tried to hide the bomb out of sight behind books in a cabinet in case there were to be a search?"

"Yes, I could not have put it better," Andrews responded, feeling his oats.

"So if your theory were to have any credibility, can you explain to the jury why any rational person who would go to lengths to hide bomb material that he did not want discovered in case of a search, and would leave this terribly incriminating memo that he went out of his way to type elsewhere, in the very top drawer of his desk that would be the first place one conducting a search would look?'

Andrews was caught off guard and allowed more than a couple of embarrassing silent moments to go by, as he attempted to come up with an answer. Just before he was about to respond, Alan beat him to it. "I take your silence as the answer and withdraw the question. Let me ask you just one or two more questions, then I am done. You…"

Jenkins rose to object. "I ask the court to strike counsel's remark 'I take your silence as the answer.' That is not a question."

Judge Clark sustained the objection. "The court will instruct the jury to disregard counsel's remark." Jenkins did what he could, but both he and Alan knew that no matter the instruction, jurors, like anyone else, can't inflict self-amnesia on themselves. They would still remember what they heard, or more to the point, what in this instance they did not hear from the witness when asked Alan's last question.

Alan continued. "I understand that Roy Armstrong, President Coburn's Special Counsel, asked and received reports from all the law enforcement agencies involved to keep the president informed. I take it you met with him and gave him a report of what occurred?" Alan was not asking the question expecting to learn anything. It was only to set up the next few questions.

"I did meet with Armstrong but gave him a verbal report along the lines of my testimony."

"For identification sake, the person you met, is he the one sitting in the third row over there in a nice neat blue business suit? Sir, would you stand please."

Armstrong rose. a little embarrassed by the introduction. Alan looked him straight in the eye with a staged confident glare like a boxer looking to gain a psychological advantage by intimidating his opponent at the weigh-in before a fight. Alan would be calling him as his next witness right after the prosecution rested its case with Andrews. But intimidating Armstrong was not the only reason for the question. It was also to set up a more important question.

"Sir, thank you. You may sit down," Alan said in a commanding voice to Armstrong after Andrews identified him. "Just for transparency, Your Honor, since I will be calling Mr. Armstrong to the stand, we both attended Boston University Law School at the same time. He was a senior and I a freshman, so for the record, we never met or knew each other, though I believe I had heard his name mentioned by our then Dean, William Lauder, now the university's president."

Here it came, the real reason for this unnecessary disclosure. Alan wanted this to come out of the blue and take Andrews by surprise for he still had not released him from the stand. "By the way, Mr. Andrews, have you ever met or communicated with my very celebrated Dean at any time?" The attempt was to learn if there was some relationship between the Dean and the FBI.

Alan observed him closely. Andrews hesitated for just a moment and concluded that it was more of a fishing question and that Alan knew nothing of his and Backman's meetings or discussions with the Dean, nor could he have known. "No sir, I have never had the pleasure of meeting with the Dean."

Alan could tell from his hesitation and manner that he was lying, which was reassuring, but of no help without evidence. As the Judge adjourned the proceedings until the next day, Alan could feel the mounting pressure, realizing that he was now down to Roy Armstrong as a witness to find some way to prove the FBI and perhaps the Dean were involved in the bombing. "Roy Armstrong," he thought, "the number one student in the class that preceded him by 2 years, Editor in Chief of the law review and winner of the prestigious Philip C. Jessup International Law Moot Court Competition with participants from over 550 law schools in more than 80 countries". Roy Armstrong, the thought brought on a few shivers.

THE TRIAL OF the SDS Four was the lead story dominating all the national news that evening and the next morning. The astonishing court-room performance by this 23-year-old second-year law student, who was yet to take the bar exam, competed with the hard news of the case itself. Alan's picture was on the front page of almost every national and local newspaper and leading all the TV broadcasts. He had refused any interviews, but the media hungered to get stories about him. They even went back to his home-town of Chelsea to dig up some of his feats as a star basketball player and his last-minute substitution and stellar performance at the high school debating championship finals, all proudly portrayed on TV through interviews with his coaches, teachers and players. On her way into her office at BU, Evelyn smiled as she read the Boston Globe coverage. At the Stardust Casino in Las Vegas, the Pit Boss, Nick Manning, spotting a picture of Alan on TV while at one of the casino bars, turned to the dealer he was with, "Hey, that's the guy I was telling you about a few months ago that bet everything during a hand and beat us for several grand. "

Alan was not uplifted by the coverage. While the coverage on his handling of the case was reassuring, the coverage on the facts of the case was a reminder of how grim the prospects were of gaining an acquittal. There was general agreement among the columnists that while the defense had done a good job in highlighting some conflicts and disparities in the prosecution's case, there was nothing elicited to shake the solid evidence that pointed to the SDS four defendants as conspiring to set off the bomb. Added to the finding of the bomb material and incriminating memo in the SDS office was the introduction in evidence of the pamphlets that the FBI claimed were being distributed just before the bombing, "Stop Military Enlistments on Campus by Any Means." The pamphlets were flashed in the TV coverage.

Alan, Judd and Sevena went through the same ritual on day two of the trial. They dropped Alan off at the court, parked the rented car, and used their respective passes to gain entrance into the crowded courtroom. The prosecution had rested. The usual motions were filed by the defense alleging that the prosecution failed to present a case that should go to the jury that they knew would be denied. They were to call their first witness.

"The defense calls Roy Armstrong as its opening witness," Alan informed the clerk. "Mano a mano" is a term in Spanish most people know that means "hand to hand" combat. Here was to be a duel between two prize students from the same Boston law school oddly playing out in distant Oklahoma courtroom-one of them a graduate who finished at the very top of his class, now an attorney with multiple awards for his legal acumen; the other among the top of his class, but with only two years of law school under his belt and technically having to try the case under the supervision of another attorney.

"Good morning, Mr. Armstrong, kind of interesting to see you here in Oklahoma," Alan began.

"I could say the same about you, Mr. Roberts. A pleasant surprise to see you here as well." Armstrong was up for the battle.

"Yes, but I did not leave one of the most prestigious law firms in the country to be here. Can you tell us what prompted you to do so to take on the position of Special Counsel to President Coburn, a good distance from where you were?" Alan did not waste any time with any further formalities.

"Well, it would be a bit more accurate if you added a couple more words to the word 'leave'. I took a leave *of absence* for just a year to come here. And here, because I thought this was a unique opportunity to get the experience of a corporate in-house lawyer, given the varied issues that could arise at universities," Armstrong answered in a calm, professional tone.

"And those issues as came up very quickly involve dealing with protests, did they not?" Alan did not wait for an answer to continue. "For you met with Captain Springer and the other heads of law enforcement early that morning before the incidents took place to advise them on how President Coburn wanted them to handle the expected protests that the FBI warned him were coming based on an anonymous tip they received, isn't that so?"

"Yes." A short straight answer, for Armstrong knew that the defense had in its discovery asked for and received all documents relating to the countermeasure plans, including the written instructions he gave to them.

"I show you Defense Exhibit 10, do you recognize it?"

"Yes, it is a written copy of the instructions I gave to the assembled officers that morning as to how the president wished them deployed in the buildings." Armstrong gave more than a "yes." intending to sound forthcoming.

"Allow me to read a few lines from page 2 of those instructions." Alan turned the page of the document. "You are not to place your men outside the building. You are to position them on the floor above the entrance out of sight until all protesters are in the building and then after asking them to leave, arrest all that remain. Did you compose that?"

"Yes, I hope you are not about to criticize my writing style," Armstrong answered intentionally trying to make the questioning appear frivolous.

"No, sir, I am not about to criticize your writing style, but I am about to criticize your originality."

Alan then walked over to the counsel table and took out a manual from his briefcase. It was one of the three items he had retrieved from the Dean's office, compliments of Evelyn. "I ask the court to mark this as Defense Exhibit 16 for identification. Now, Mr. Armstrong, I hand you this document entitled 'Manual for Dealing with Protests and Demonstrations' and ask you to examine it carefully and further ask you if you have ever seen it before?"

Jenkins stood up several times to raise a series of objections that the line of questioning was irrelevant. Each objection was overruled by Judge Clark on the basis that the evidence, as was previously ruled, would be admitted de bene esse and subject to all of it being disregarded if the defense failed to tie it into the arson charges when its case was completed. In the meantime, Armstrong had been examining the front and back cover of the manual and quickly rifled through its 28 pages.

Alan picked up on the questioning. "Before Mr. Jenkins gets up to raise yet another unsuccessful objection to stop you from answering, let's try to hurriedly slip in your answer to my question: have you ever seen this manual before?"

Jenkins started to get up once again to object to Alan's characterization of his objections when Judge Clark simply motioned him to sit back down with a downward wave of his hand, causing laughter in the courtroom. Then the judge took command. "The jury will disregard Mr. Robert's remarks and the witness will answer the question."

"I have examined it and I am fairly sure that I have not seen this before," answered Armstrong. "It does not have an author or the name of a party or an organization that purports to have written it. I am not familiar with any of it." Armstrong reached out to give it back to Alan, but Alan did not return the reach to receive it.

"You may find that you are indeed familiar with some of it. If you would kindly turn to page 19 and read the second paragraph out loud so the jury can hear you, please."

Armstrong turned to the page and a genuine look of surprise, bordering on shock, came over his face. He looked up at Alan. "I want you to know that I have never seen this before."

"I believe you," Alan responded, "but please read the paragraph out loud."

"You are not to place your men outside the building. You are to position them on the floor above the entrance out of sight until all protesters are in the building and then after asking them to leave, arrest all that remain." Armstrong fumbled through it, recognizing they were the exact words in the written instructions he distributed to the law enforcement officers.

"Sound familiar?" Alan asked in a polite but victorious tone. He again did not wait for an answer, so his question registered as a statement. "Counselor," Alan switched to his title for the first time. "I accept your statement that you had no idea that the sentences on your written instructions came from this manual. I will go further, and I can assure the court that no objection will be forthcoming from Mr. Jenkins this time. Mr. Armstrong, you are one of the most celebrated learned graduates of our law school in both ability and integrity, and so I will ask the jury in summation to find all your testimony you are about to give as creditable as we move forward."

Alan had just thrown Armstrong a lifeline after tripping him up. He was signaling his commitment not to ask him any more hidden or tricky questions that could set him up and render him vulnerable for a possible perjury charge, but rather pose straightforward ones in exchange for honest, straightforward answers. Alan was gambling that Armstrong knew nothing about the bombing. He also thought that Armstrong was now beginning to believe that he was more than a match for him, especially being the one empowered to ask the questions and looking like he knew much more than Armstrong did. What's more, he felt sure that Armstrong was not about to throw away an extraordinarily promising career by perjuring himself out of any allegiance he might owe the Dean.

"Attorney Armstrong, to put this matter to rest, may I ask who typed out the instruction sheet?"

"I did. It came from a note from President Coburn asking me to instruct the law enforcement officers and I saw no basis to consider it an improper instruction." Alan would let that last remark go. He knew he had to allow Armstrong to save face, if, in what he hoped was now an unspoken agreement, he could elicit some other important facts, such as that the instructions to the police were crafted by President Coburn.

"I gather you believe that it was a proper instruction because it was a way to contain the possible disturbances."

"Exactly!" Armstrong knew Alan was again letting him off the hook here and would soon be asking for something in return and here it came.

"But what if the reason for not lining up the police outside the building to turn the protesters away as is customary, was solely motivated to enable the trespass and the subsequent mass arrests of these 100 students attempting to wage a peaceful demonstration? And by effecting such arrests, being able to craft a plea negotiation whereby, as a condition of not prosecuting them, the students would be required to forfeit their constitutional rights to conduct any further protests while at the school. That would be improper, would you not agree?"

"Certainly, if that were the sole motive, it would be improper." It was easy for Armstrong to give him this one.

"Getting back to your leave of absence to take this job, who at your firm brought this job to your attention, and asked you if you would like to consider it?"

Armstrong was now concerned. The question was asked in a non-accusatory way. It looked like Alan already knew everything but was willing to get what he wanted on record through him without embarrassing him if he would be forthcoming. However, he remembered the Dean saying something like "He will make you believe that he has something, but don't fall for it, give him nothing."

Alan was witnessing the hesitation and guessed what Armstrong was thinking: "How much did Alan know? Is he just fishing? Can I deny things and not get caught?" Alan decided to send him another fact suggesting he knew more than he did. A fact he was gambling was correct based on the usual accuracy of Sevena's analysis when she was connecting the dots after hearing Mike's intelligence reports at the meeting in the Copley Plaza.

"Let me rephrase the question slightly," Alan walked up closer to Armstrong as if to say, Hey, pay attention to this one; it will give you the answer to what you are agonizing over. "I believe these types of in-house counsel jobs were created to assist seven presidents of key universities, not just America U, so I ask you who at your firm asked you to consider one of these positions."

That was it. Armstrong now thought Alan knew everything. Armstrong would now give Alan whatever he asked for. He believed Alan was being more than generous in throwing him a lifeline. "It was my law school Dean, William Lauder, now president of BU who was an equity partner at my firm. He asked me to consider this job."

The rest of the testimony was straightforward and took less than an hour. Alan elicited from Armstrong that he was recruited by Latham, Hogan &McLeish directly out of law school with the recommendation of Dean Lauder. Armstrong testified that the salary and potential bonuses were extraordinarily lucrative and the prospect of climbing up in the firm was exceptionally promising, so he had decided to turn down a Federal Appellate Judge Clerkship to take the job. He spent the past year at the firm as an associate to the firm's senior partner who headed their constitutional law department. He and others were specifically trained in a new specialty dealing with civil rights as they pertain to demonstrations and protests. It was the Dean who encouraged him to specialize in this interesting niche practice.

"And how was it that you chose this university?" asked Alan.

"Dean Lauder stated that there were temporary in-house legal positions created in several universities that could offer a unique experience in this specialty, given both the flare-up caused by the civil rights movement and the emerging protests over the war that were likely to find their way onto university campuses. I chose this school over the others because that would give me a chance to spend time with my older brother, who is a professor at Oklahoma State."

"So, to sum it up in a nutshell, your job description was to give legal and strategic advice to President Coburn in dealing with protests and demonstrations?"

"Yes."

"Were you consulted on the recommendation to have the trespass charges dismissed provided the students agreed not to engage in future demonstrations?"

"Yes."

"How so?" Alan asked.

"I was asked to give a formal opinion on the legality of the recommendation. I informed them that it was legally permissible to require an individual to waive his or her constitutional first amendment rights to engage in a protest or demonstration in consideration of dismissing the case as long as the individual freely and knowingly waived such rights."

"And who asked you for your opinion and to whom did you give it?" The jurors and those in the courtroom were focused on this answer more than any other so far.

After a pause, "President Coburn."

Alan then informed the court that he already had President Coburn under subpoena as a witness and that after cross-examination by Jenkins and the morning break, he would be calling him as his next witness.

CHAPTER 35

THE MORNING BREAK allowed Alan to huddle with Judd and Sevena for 30 minutes. "I certainly can't complain about Judge Clark," Alan began. "He has been extremely lenient in allowing me to examine the witnesses on matters related to the sit-ins. If we were trying the trespass cases, I might even be able to convince him to charge the jury to consider entrapment as a defense, given the way they hid the police in those buildings. But I haven't been able to link the improper conduct to the bombing. Unless I can find some way to get some exculpatory evidence about the bombing real soon, I fear that his patience may soon run out. He could direct the jury to disregard all of this stuff as being irrelevant in the arson case and that would be the end."

"Alan, I believe you got more time than you think," Sevena said, giving him some encouragement. "The masterful way you have conducted the trial so far has caught everyone's attention. What's more, the jurors- and I watched them closely, especially the women-are really drawn to you. You've been successful in making them and the judge suspicious as to whether, as Sherlock Holmes would put it, 'foul play is afoot.' I know you got to make something happen soon. I may be wrong, but I believe they are willing to grant you more time to develop whatever they think you are trying to establish."

Alan was a little encouraged because when it came to Sevena's instinct, she was rarely wrong. "Maybe so, but it is imperative that I get the Dean on the stand if I am to have any chance of squeezing out any leads he may have about the bombing. And I will need to get Coburn to make the Dean relevant to this case."

Goodman began to approach them signaling that the court was being called back into session.

"Call your next witness, Mr. Roberts," said the judge.

The courtroom got quiet as an impeccably dressed, white-haired, tall, very distinguished- looking gentleman in about his mid-60s walked erect as he came down the aisle to be sworn in by the clerk. This time it was the judge who welcomed him to the courtroom. "Good afternoon, President Coburn," the judge greeted him with noticeable respect just as he was about to take his seat on the witness stand.

"Good afternoon, Judge Clark," Coburn replied in a tone that displayed he felt he was entitled to the respect.

This exchange told Alan that to avoid Judge Clark's ire, he would have to tread very carefully in his examination. In any event, Coburn was a small fish. This was all about getting the Dean relevant so he could be called to the stand to testify.

"Good afternoon, President Coburn," Alan also greeted him in a respectful tone. "I understand that you have prior commitments for this afternoon, and for my part, I will be short and try to make sure that we do not keep you a minute longer than need be."

"Thank you, Mr. Roberts," Coburn responded looking down at his left hand while moving up his sleeve revealing a gold shiny watch, as if concerned with the time. He clearly did not want to be subject to any more questions than necessary.

Alan surmised that given the morning break, one of Coburn's flunkies monitoring the court proceedings would have already briefed him on Armstrong's testimony and he would be prepared. So, Alan went right to the basics by showing him Armstrong's written instructions to the police. Coburn confirmed that he had provided the language to Armstrong. When asked where he got the language from, Coburn was ready for the question. He readily admitted it was copied from a manual. When shown the manual that was marked as an exhibit, Coburn said that was a copy of the manual that was his source. Alan expected he would admit it. What else could he say, given Armstrong's testimony?

When asked why he used that strategy of deployment when it could be interpreted as a form of entrapment to secure arrests, Coburn said that was not the intent. He believed that this type of deployment allowing the students to enter the building seemed to make sense in order to confine any confrontation to a controlled area and keep it from spilling over and disrupting enrollments going on in adjoining areas of the campus.

Alan picked up the manual. "President Coburn, if you would, sir, I would like you to read to yourself the following pages from this manual, all of pages 3, 4 and 5 and 6 that I have marked for your attention. Please let me know when you are done." Alan provided Jenkins with a copy. After a few minutes, Coburn put the manual down.

"I quote from the bottom of page 4 that you just read. 'At the first sign of what you can rationalize as potential violence, establish curfews. It is an effective means to keep the protesters from assembling and waging further protests.' And I read where it continues from the top of page 5, 'Expel from the school the first protesters that are arrested for violating the curfew as an example to deter the others from further demonstrations.' Sir, would you not agree that these instructions you just read and others in this manual of similar nature are designed to discourage on-going protests and as so, are totally inappropriate and contrary to the tenets of our Bill of Rights, specifically the right of free speech and assembly?"

"I would agree and would never employ such tactics." Coburn was not about to marry these instructions that clearly would be offensive.

"Good to hear, sir. May I then ask whose idea it was to offer a plea negotiation to dismiss the trespass cases in exchange for the students waiving their constitutional rights and to agree to not engage in any further protests or demonstrations while attending the university?"

"The idea, I believe, arose out of several discussions I had with my staff and law enforcement people and obtaining an opinion as to its legality." Coburn was being fuzzy, trying to make it seem like a consensus decision.

Alan again picked up the manual and handed it back to Coburn. "Sir, if you would now turn to page 6 and this time read out loud the first paragraph that I marked for your attention."

Coburn read it quickly to himself and then asked for a drink of water before reading it.

"I know this is ..." Coburn began to try to give some explanation about what he was asked to read out loud, as Alan interrupted him politely and asked him to first read the paragraph.

Coburn began reading in a soft voice and was asked by the judge to speak a bit louder so the jury could hear. "Another method to quash demonstrations is to find a way to secure an arrest of a large number of the protesters and offer a plea negotiation to drop the charges if they agree not to engage in any further protests."

"Is that what was done in this case, President Coburn?" Alan asked.

"Yes, but not for that reason. We did not want to be harsh with our own students and fully prosecute them. Also, at the same time, we were worried that future such activities by them would risk their being arrested for another similar offense, making them vulnerable to expulsion. We did not want to lose our students." Coburn had been well briefed and prepared,

Alan kept on him. "Maybe so. But the very approaches you requested be employed, your very directive, word for word, came directly out of this manual. Do you not agree from just the pages you read, and from this manual overall, that these words advocate despicable tactics to prevent peaceful protests? Is that not so, sir?"

Coburn hesitated and took another sip from his glass of water, preparing his answer. "Look, as administrators of institutions of higher learning, we receive lots of pamphlets, articles, yes even manuals, and other materials at conferences, meetings and in the mail relating to the administration of our colleges and universities. Some of them are even more inflammatory than this one. If I choose to read any of them, and I only glanced at a small portion of this manual before this morning, I take from them only those suggestions that seem proper and helpful. In this case, I thought the deployment to contain any larger outbreak made sense, so I adopted that. As to the rest, I agree it goes way overboard in its reach to maintain order."

"So, we both agree this manual went 'way overboard', as you put it, to prevent peaceful protests. Then can you tell us how you obtained it?" Alan now closed in to get to the real purpose of the examination.

More objections were raised as to relevance by Jenkins and overruled by Judge Clark, stating again, "Let's see where this goes." He, like everyone else in the courtroom, was interested in this narrative that was playing out.

"I believe it was distributed at a meeting with other college presidents?" Coburn answered. He felt Alan knew too much, so he would not dare lie, but would reveal only as much as the question demanded. But Alan did "know too much" and wanted Coburn to know it to keep his answers honest.

"Six others to be exact. Seven university presidents, including you, met at that meeting, isn't that so?"

"I believe so," Coburn answered, now squirming a little in his chair.

"At the Harvard Club in Boston, early May, is that not also so?"

"Yes," he replied simply and directly for the first time.

"In fact, there was a discussion about the handling of student demonstrations, correct?"

"Among other things." Coburn was trying to minimize the subject somewhat.

"Who hosted the meeting?" Finally, the question that Alan had been building to ask all along.

"The newly appointed President of Boston University, William Lauder, still dean of the law school at that time."

"And who produced and distributed the manual to all the presidents at the meeting?"

"I believe he did." Alan had Coburn in a position that short and truthful answers now seemed to be his only option

"By the way, congratulations are in order to your development office. It was reported in the media with fanfare that America University received a series of grants in the millions of dollars from the American Way Foundation. May I ask who signs those checks?"

No sense in Coburn hiding it. It was clear Alan knew the answer. "The law firm of Latham, Hogan & McLeish. I believe they manage the Foundation."

"President Lauder's firm."

"I believe so."

"And in fact, some of the Foundation funds you received financed the new legal position that attorney Armstrong now holds as your special counsel."

"I can check on that."

"And Armstrong is a constitutional lawyer on leave from President Lauder's law firm, specially trained in civil disobedience law, is that not so?"

"If you say so,"

"Do I take that for a 'yes'?"

"I don't know how he was trained at that firm."

"I have no further questions for President Coburn and he should be able to make his flight this afternoon if Mr. Jenkins is not too long in his cross-examination."

"I only have a few," Jenkins replied as he stood up. "President Coburn, was there any mention of bombing or setting off explosives, or how to deal with it in that manual?"

"Not that I read so far."

"Nor in any of it, as a reading of the entire manual will show. Was there any mention of bombings at the meeting at the Harvard Club?"

"Of course not. Not a word of any violence. I would never be associated with such a thing."

"As to these charges, did you receive any prior warning about a potential bombing?"

"None whatsoever."

"And how did it come to your attention?"

"I was in my office when I heard a loud noise like an explosion. I then looked out my window and saw heavy smoke coming from the direction of the military building and later received a call that it had been bombed."

"So, my last question. Everything you testified to this morning had nothing to do with the bombing?"

Alan immediately jumped to his feet and raised his objection that the question called for a conclusion. The objection was sustained by Judge Clark. Of course, that question was relevant if Alan were somehow to be able to tie it all into the bombing charges, which led to a bench conference.

Alan informed the court, which came as no surprise to anyone, that given Coburn's testimony, he would be issuing a subpoena for the Dean, now president, to testify. Jenkins objected, stating that this was just a continuation of this lavish fishing expedition, and if allowed, the defense will have taken up the time of two important university presidents who have nothing whatsoever to do with the arson/bombing/case.

Judge Clark then admonished Alan. "I know the charges are serious and carry significant penalties upon conviction. So, the court has given you wide latitude to present any exculpatory evidence on behalf of your clients and therefore will not stand in the way of allowing you to subpoena President Lauder. However, if after his testimony, you have not shown a likelihood of tying all this in with the bombing, I will entertain and seriously consider attorney Jenkins motion that I direct the jury to disregard all or a good deal of the trespassing and its countermeasures testimony as evidence not relevant in this arson case."

Although not requested, Alan nodded in approval and then asked the court to recess until the day after tomorrow to give the necessary time to arrange for the president's s travel requirements. The court dismissed the jurors until the day after with the usual admonition not to discuss the case among themselves, their families or with anyone else, or pay attention to any accounts of the proceedings carried in the media. One wonders to what extent all twelve jurors would totally abide by such restrictions in a case that carried so much interest and media attention.

CHAPTER 36

ALAN WAS HAPPY to have a full free day before the next session to assess where everything was at the moment and prepare for the Dean's testimony the next day. Goodman was at the county jail preparing the defendants for their testimony and Judd and Sevena were to meet Alan in the morning at Goodman's office where they had set up a small cubicle for Alan to work out of.

Judd brought the morning papers with him. The case continued to dominate the news with lead story coverage of Alan's adeptness in dampening the credibility of the law enforcement agencies and the university. Many in the media suggested that he was attacking the "sleazy" way in which the school and the police conducted the countermeasures to the sit-ins to make them look like bad guys to give the upcoming self-serving testimony of the defendants some believability. Judd showed Alan the column in the New York Times by a Pulitzer Prize winner who covered their criminal justice stories. He wrote, "By this imaginative strategy and astute performance of making the school and law enforcement officials look bad, this brilliant young, still to-be-lawyer was likely not looking to win the impossible 'not guilty,' but rather to gain some sympathy for the SDS four to win more lenient sentences."

Sevena pointed to the column she liked the most in the local paper. This columnist had earned quite a readership, gaining a reputation as Oklahoma's own Jimmy Breslin, Breslin being the New York City no-nonsense reporter who gained national prominence telling the news from a common-man point of view.

She turned to the page for Alan to read. "This kid Roberts, an undrafted rookie, facing the three most important witnesses, hit all three balls out of the park and over the railroad tracks and the balls are still sailing. However, it is the last of the ninth, and his three home runs at as many times at bat, as spectacular as they were, still leave his team behind by a dozen runs. To win, you need a pitcher as well as a hitter, and in this case, there just aren't any facts favoring the defendants to pitch. Hey, Roberts, as they say when a good team loses the pennant, and you are good, wait till the next case."

Alan smiled at the style, but one thing was obvious; he and the other columnists were right.

The game was coming to an end and he needed to come up with some facts to pitch or the game was over. "Do we have anything else connecting the Dean to the FBI other than Mike's discovering that the Dean's Investigator's Reports were done by the FBI and even that has to remain confidential?"

"Nada," Sevena answered.

"Then, from what we know about Hoover's hatred for 'commie' demonstrators, the FBI could have planted the bomb without the Dean's knowledge and that would leave me with nothing I can learn from him," Alan voiced his concern.

"From what we know about our Dean, his dirty prints are everywhere. He had to be in on it," Judd reacted.

Sevena agreed. "We can't use Mike's stuff, but we know he is connected in many ways with the FBI. He got the FBI to do the investigator's reports to recruit the special counsels for the P-7 group of university presidents. We know the bomb was manufactured by one of the arms dealers his firm represents, an unlikely coincidence. Not just his finger, but I believe his whole hand has to be in this pie."

"Well, he is all we got left in any event, but examining him won't be easy," Alan responded. "Remember, I am calling him to the stand, so I am *not* allowed to cross-examine and try to impeach the creditability of my own witness unless I can get him declared a hostile witness. In law, I have to first show he is averse to what we are trying to prove to have him so declared."

"If you can't connect him to the bombing, at least take him down so he's a really bad guy. Maybe then, we stand a chance of acquittals based on our defendants' testimony declaring their innocence." Judd offered some hope.

"If that is all we got, I'd say it's about as good a chance as winning the national lottery with one ticket," Alan declared, not holding back. "If they testify, they will have to admit they planned the protests to end the war. Jenkins will also get them to admit they oppose the draft and recruitments into the military, which takes place at the very bombed building. Also, I bet that Jenkins has already been informed by the FBI what they learned from Betty, that I was coordinating the planned sit-ins. If we must put them on the stand-and it looks like we have no choice-Jenkins will have an opportunity to elicit that from them, shooting down any creditability I may have won with the jury, especially when I give the summation. No, getting something about the bomb out of the Dean is crucial and as of this moment, I don't know where that will come from."

"So, what's to be done?" Judd asked.

"Do you own a prayer book? Look, I am going to visit the defendants at the jail this morning, spend a little time with Goodman about their testimony and then spend the rest of the day and evening preparing for tomorrow. Judd, could you reach out to Mike to see if he has anything else that can help? Sevena, if you could find a library, I would like you to go through the national newspapers over the last year or so and see if there are any stories of any kind about the Dean's firm, about him or anything else that may be of any help to me tomorrow."

"Another needle in a haystack if one even exists," she whispered to Judd.

Alan overheard. "The grasping at straws cliché is more like it," he retorted as he began to pick up some notes and put them in his briefcase. "Tomorrow's session is not scheduled to begin until 11 am to accommodate the Dean's travels. Let's meet at my room at the motel tomorrow at 9 am to go over what we got."

Alan went directly to the county jail to visit with the defendants, trying to give them some hope, without diminishing the uphill battle they faced. He tried not to reveal his feelings of personal responsibility for inspiring them to take on such a risky endeavor. He looked at each one of them, all as young as he, about to be crucified on a cross of political expediency, much like the young soldiers sent off to war to be similarly sacrificed that Alan, Judd and Sevena hoped to save, and he was in danger of failing all of them as well. As hard as it was, he knew that he needed to bury those feelings and concentrate solely on the Dean's upcoming testimony,

———————————————

ALAN SPENT THE rest of the day and well into the evening at his makeshift office at Goodman's firm reviewing transcripts of the trial over the previous two days, the exhibits and other documents, making notes preparing for the Dean's examination. He finally arrived back at his motel room at 11 pm. He was tired and uneasy over the fact he had not yet found a path of inquiry that could trip up the Dean to reveal something that would open the can of worms that they were gambling existed. As when he went sleepless cramming for final exams, but always made sure to get some sleep the night before the exam, he decided he needed to go right to bed to let things soak in. Yet, as he lay in bed for over an hour, dozing but unable to fall completely asleep, tossing and turning, he was unable to get his mind to stop thinking about how to find that path and the devastating consequences that awaited Eddie and the others if there were none. Suddenly, he heard the judge's gavel bang overruling his objection and it banged louder and louder until he completely awoke and realized that the banging of the gavel was a dream, and someone was knocking at his door.

"Who in the hell could that be?" Alan muttered to himself as he got up to unlock the door. "Sevena? Hey, what time is it?" he asked with his eyes half-open.

"A little past midnight. I got the feeling you would be tossing and turning and thought if you had someone to toss and turn with you for just a bit, it might relax you so you could get some needed sleep."

CHAPTER 37

ALAN AWOKE THE next morning a bit more rested and revived with his arms around a pillow that Sevena had substituted for herself earlier. She had left a note pinned to the pillow. "I trust you got a more restful sleep… and thanks to you, so did I." It was 7:30. He showered, dressed, glanced at his latest notes and had just finished making a pot of coffee when Judd and Sevena arrived for the meeting sporting some cheese Danish and the usual morning papers.

"All the columnists are speculating about what the Dean has to do with it all," Sevena said as she laid down a few newspapers.

"TV also got a picture of him boarding the early flight at Logan this morning," Judd added.

"The way they are covering this thing, I probably should have brought fewer law books and more ties." Alan pooh-poohed the celebrity nature of the coverage that had taken hold, including the universally favorable portrayal of his legal acumen.

"Find out anything?" Alan asked of Judd.

"I reached Mike. He has nothing new but is standing by if we find something that he may be able to follow up on," Judd responded.

Sevena shook her head as if to answer Alan's anticipated next question in advance, so he did not bother to ask it.

"So OK, that's it. It is what it is. I am as ready as I am going to be. Let's enjoy the Danish before we go into the ring." With that, he reached for one and winked at Sevena, as if to say thanks for the pleasurable sleeping pill.

———————————

THE DEAN WAS already sitting in court next to Armstrong directly behind the prosecutor's table when Alan arrived 15 minutes before the session was to begin. As he passed the Dean walking down to counsel's table, he greeted him in a friendly tone. "Good morning, sir."

The Dean, forcing a little smile to cover the sarcasm of his remark, replied, "Thanks for the invitation." It had already begun.

"Sir, do you swear to tell the truth, the whole truth and nothing but the truth, so help you God?" asked the clerk.

"I do," responded the Dean in a loud clear voice with his hand raised high as he was administered the oath as a witness.

Alan had tried enough cases as a student prosecutor to know that defendants and witnesses with skin in the game don't hesitate to stretch the truth even to the point of outright lying. He had mused to himself that maybe witnesses could be kept more honest if instead of having them swear on a bible to tell the truth, they were asked to swear on a copy of Dante's Inferno to illustrate what happens to sinners that bear false witness.

"You may now examine the witness," Judge Clark said, looking at Alan

"Thank you, Your Honor. Good morning again, President Lauder," Alan said in a slightly loud voice as he got up and walked a few steps toward the Dean.

"And a good morning to you, Sir," responded the Dean, trying to sound both respectful and even friendly to show no hostility. Being a seasoned lawyer, he was aware that having been called as a witness by the defense, he could not be cross-examined with leading questions unless he were to be considered a hostile witness.

Alan asked the Dean to provide his educational and professional background and was surprised when he highlighted the fact that his firm, of which he was still an equity partner, represented the major armament

manufacturers. Alan asked him whether he had met with six other presidents at the Harvard Club in Boston in early May. Again, to Alan's surprise,
he confirmed not only that there was a meeting, but volunteered that he,
himself, had organized the meeting.

"What was the purpose of the meeting?" Alan asked.

Once again, to Alan's surprise, the Dean took advantage of the question to admit to things Alan thought he would have to extract. "I had
formed a non-profit foundation, called the American Way Foundation, to
be managed by my firm in which I asked the major arms manufacturers
that we represented to make significant donations. The purpose was to fund
the universities to expand their facilities to serve the national interest. We
met to discuss the grants and methods by which they could prepare to deal
appropriately with issues of civil disobedience on campus that could arise
out of the war."

The Dean had come fully prepared. He knew that Alan would attempt
to elicit this information in a way that would make it look sleazy and he was
going to give the opposite impression by appearing completely forthcoming
about something that was proper and above board.

"How many millions of dollars were distributed to the universities?"

"I don't have those exact figures at my disposal at this moment, but
I would gather between $8 and $9 million to each of the seven universities
annually."

"You said annually. Since these were multi-year grants, about how
much would that be in total to each university?"

"About $45 million to each," the Dean answered without hesitation.

"That would be over $300 million in contributions to this project.
That is huge, is it not? What was the incentive for these four arms dealers
to donate this kind of money?"

The Dean took advantage of this open-ended question that he was required to receive as a non- hostile witness to score some points. "Well, these four armaments manufacturers produce the major weapons to properly equip our men and women in the armed forces who are fighting to protect our freedom and way of life, including yours and mine and everyone in this courtroom. In my opinion, they are patriots. They, like President Johnson and the American people, oppose the war, but when necessary are willing to do what they can to help our nation be victorious They know that there will be elements both foreign and domestic that will try to sabotage our war effort and that these subversives prey on young people to do their bidding. These patriotic companies are willing to give back a substantial amount of their profits to further support our war effort on the home front as well as on the battlefield."

It was now clear to Alan that the Dean, being fully briefed as to the court proceedings, had decided not to try to distance himself from the P-7 Project that was beginning to look sleazy. There were too many of his fingerprints on it for him to do so. So instead, he would defend it and make it a virtue to have formed and organized it. They say the best defense is a good offense and

Alan realized that the Dean had smartly adopted the tactic. He concluded he could wait no longer to take off the gloves.

"Well, President Lauder, when you say that the real motive of these arms dealers is to prevent the sabotaging of the war effort on the home front, you really mean to prevent peaceful demonstrations and protests against the war, don't you?"

Jenkins objected and Alan asked for a bench conference before Jenkins stated the reason. Both the judge and Alan already knew the basis of his objection.

"The defense is asking leading questions of the witness. This is his own witness. He can't cross-examine him to impeach his testimony. That is where he is going. I already let some lesser important ones go by, but not these."

Alan responded, "As you can determine, Your Honor, this is a hostile witness. He is clearly adverse to the defendants' interests. It is vital to our defense that we be permitted to cross- examine him on that basis." Alan could figuratively throw in the towel if he lost this one.

"Frankly, Mr. Roberts, it's a reach to call him a hostile witness at this early stage in the testimony," explained the judge. Alan gasped. "But, I will allow you to proceed in that manner since the court has the discretion and I believe at some point President Lauder will indeed be ruled so, and I don't want to have this trial delayed by you then going back and raising these same leading questions at that time. So, for efficiency reasons, you may proceed on that basis." Alan began to breathe a little easier. He had gotten over his biggest procedural hurdle and could now open up with whatever his fishing rod could catch.

The judge asked the court stenographer to reread the previous question.

Mr. Roberts: "Well, President Lauder, when you say that the real motive of these arms dealers is to prevent the sabotaging of the war effort on the home front, you really mean the preventing of peaceful demonstrations and protest against the war, don't you?"

"No, that is not so," the Dean answered forcefully. "I meant preventing unlawful, not peaceful, disruptions."

"Well then, let's examine that contention. Let's get back to your meeting at the Harvard Club when you all got done eating the New England baked-stuffed Maine lobsters and the aged filet mignons wrapped in double-smoked hickory bacon, the Crepe Suzettes or banana fritters, and finishing with those outlawed Cuban Montecristo cigars along with the brandy and cordials..." Little snickers among those in the courtroom mounted into uncontrollable laughter by the time Alan got to the cigars, causing the judge to bang his gavel several times for order, and he warned Alan to get to the question he wished to ask. "I know those were the goodies," Alan continued, "because I got the menu you devised from the Harvard Club, so to complete my question, after that food orgy"-laughter broke out in the courtroom, including the jurors- "you then distributed this manual, which is designed, not to prevent unlawful disruptions, but to prevent legal demonstrations against the war, is that not so?"

"Objection, objection, objection!" shouted Jenkins several times while the question continued to be asked over his objections and the laughter.

"I'll rephrase the question," Alan responded before the objections were sustained and he would be called to the bench to be chastised. "So, after you consumed the tidbits I mentioned" – more laughter – "you distributed this manual, correct?"

"Yes." The Dean could do nothing but simply answer.

"You are familiar with its contents, correct?"

"Yes."

"Well, sir, in testimony given by President Coburn, he agreed that the instructions in the manual were designed to discourage on-going protests and were totally inappropriate and contrary to the tenets of our Bill of Rights, specifically the rights of free speech and assembly, and that he would never employ such tactics. Would you also agree with his assessment?"

"I agree that on its face it appears to be, but let me explain. It was not my..."

"Thank you, sir. You already answered my question when you said *it appears to be that*. I will give you a chance to expand on it soon."

Alan continued, "So when you say the arms dealers are motivated in helping us fight a war to protect our way of life, do you not consider our Constitution, the Bill of Rights, its first amendment guaranteeing the right of free speech and the right to freely assemble to express dissent openly for public debate, central to our way of life?"

The Dean, caught by the question, was slow to answer allowing Alan to quickly follow up by adding to it. "And do you not find that this manual"-Alan picked up a copy waiving it a bit-"that your patriotic arms dealers financed, and you, sir, distributed to be employed by seven of America's finest universities, is in direct conflict to what you have said were their motives-protecting the constitution and our way of life?"

The courtroom gasped at the elegance and the cutting nature of the questions.

"Look. That was not our intent. I agree that I should have more carefully reviewed the manual produced by our young associates in our law firm before distributing it. But the intent was not to prevent legitimate dissent," the Dean answered, in what appeared to be an apologetic, less confident tone with some loss of poise.

Sensing he had him on the defense, Alan followed up quickly. "Well, let's examine that intent. It is true, is it not, if demonstrations expressing opposition to the war were to gain public support, that could bring pressure to bear to end the war earlier than it might otherwise?"

"Possibly, hard to know."

"And that would be extremely detrimental to the bottom line of your four patriotic arms dealers, would it not?"

"In wars, as in all things, there are winners and losers economically, but that does not mean that any of them would act in any manner to extend an unnecessary war," the Dean responded, trying to regain some high ground.

"True and there are winners and-there are big winners. For instance, how much were these four patriotic arms dealers awarded in military contracts this year alone?"

"I would have to review our records to give you that answer." The Dean was trying to avoid giving the figures that he knew better than his own Social Security number.

Alan already knew the answer having done the research in preparing the questions. "You need not trouble yourself for I will be introducing government documents indicating that it was $39.5 billion, yes you heard me right – 39.5 billion dollars – and that is estimated to grow many more millions each year as the war intensifies. That is a lot for your clients to lose, is it not, if these demonstrations were to catch hold and bring the war to an earlier end?"

"Indeed, a lot for the government to spend, but as we all know, war and defending our nation's security are not inexpensive." The Dean was attempting to be somewhat philosophical.

"Yes, and legal and lobbying fees paid by these arms dealers are expensive as well, and your firm helping them win military contracts would lose quite a bit of those fees if the war came to an earlier end, is that not also true?"

"Look, young man, I suppose, like every law firm we do charge for our services if that is what you mean," responded the Dean, losing it just a bit, sounding a bit angry at the question.

"True. But *not* every law firm makes *hundreds of millions* of dollars more if there is a war going on, is that not also so?"

Jurors and attendees alike sat forward, eyes squinted as they either glared at Lauder or admired Alan's tactics.

"Objection, it's argumentative. Don't answer that." Jenkins looked up at the judge as if to say, you can't help but sustain this one.

"I will withdraw the question." Alan had gotten out of it what he wanted. "And instead I ask you, President Lauder, if it is true that two days after you met at the Harvard Club in early May with the six other presidents, including President Coburn, you arranged a meeting at your Washington office to meet with the CEOs of all four of the arms dealers that were contributing all that money to the foundation?"

The Dean was taken by surprise-in fact, somewhat shocked. He had no idea how Alan could possibly know that. He would have to stay close to the truth as much as he could for fear of being caught with a perjury charge. "Yes, that's true."

"What was that day, date and time?" Alan asked.

"I believe it was a Thursday at 10 am. I am not sure of the date."

"Would it refresh your recollection if I suggested it was May 26?" Alan was trying to suggest he knew more than he had found out from the Dean's scheduling diary, which he was able to copy thanks to Evelyn.

"Could be. Now come to think of it, it was the 26th. The Harvard Club meeting was on the 24th. I remember because it was the day after I was promoted to president of BU; and the Washington meeting was two days after that." The Dean was deliberately trying to sound both important and honest by trying to figure it out right there in court.

"The meeting started at 10. What time did it end?" asked Alan.

"It was not a long one. I would say about an hour or so, maybe ended around 11:30 am."

It was crunch time. Alan was about to fish for leads in finding a smoking gun in either the answers or in the body language to questions that he expected the Dean to deny.

"The main purpose of those meetings was to inform these arms dealers that student protests could start a national movement to end the war and jeopardize their significant profits and something had to be done to stop them. Isn't that so?" Alan walked close to the Dean looking him in the eye as he asked the question.

"Ab-so-lute-ly *not!*" The Dean responded loudly pronouncing every syllable separately for emphasis.

Alan picked up papers suggesting they contained the figures of government-awarded military contracts and asked as he lifted them up, "Did you not go over all the figures about how much they stood to make or lose if the war would continue or come to an end earlier because of protests?" Alan was guessing as to what took place.

"No, we did not. We did talk about their continuing to help universities appropriately deal with disruptive behavior on campuses, but not at all linked in any way with their potential loss due to a shortening of the war."

Assistant District Attorney Renfrew bent toward Jenkins and whispered, "Even with the president's denials, I think Roberts is scoring some points here. The jury could believe there was an effort supported by these arms dealers to quash legitimate protests, to protect their financial interests."

Jenkins, the more seasoned of the two, who had learned at the circus to keep his eye on the ball and not on the magician's distracting movements, responded, "First, these are only conjectural questions about the project that have been denied and so there is no admissible concrete evidence of any impropriety. Secondly, and most importantly, even if improprieties in quashing protests were to be proven somehow, we are trying a bomb case not a trespass case. It is all irrelevant. The issue at hand is who set off the bomb and so the judge will instruct the jury to disregard all of this if it cannot be linked to the bomb, and so far, I don't see how it can be."

Alan continued. "You say there were no discussions whatsoever about the potential effect of an antiwar student protest movement on these companies' bottom line. Are there any written minutes, notes, or transcripts of the meeting to verify your answers?"

"No, we do not record these types of meetings."

Hearing this, Sevena gasped and quickly opened a file she was carrying with her and pulled out a torn piece of a newspaper that contained a couple of paragraphs that she re-read very quickly. She then hurried over to Goodman and whispered something in his ear while Alan continued his questioning.

"President Lauder, do the names William Andrews and Freddie Backman mean anything to you?"

"Can't say they do," the Dean answered, looking down as if to wish away any further questions about the subject.

"Well, they are FBI agents of particular interest in this case. They are here and I will ask them to stand up." Alan looked around the courtroom and when he spotted them, motioned to them to stand up. "Have you ever seen or communicated with these gentlemen?" Alan asked.

Knowing what he knew, there was no way the Dean was about to open that can of worms; besides, Alan could know nothing about his relationship with them. The Dean was confident he was fishing. "No, never have."

It was over. Not a single lead about the bombing, No more arrows in his quiver. Alan had no more witnesses to call, except the defendants. He looked away from the jurors to hide his disappointment. He looked at Jenkins, "Your witness," and then turned to walk back to the defense table when he saw Goodman franticly waving his hands signaling him to hurry over. "One moment, Your Honor, I need to consult with co-counsel."

Sevena gave Alan the torn-out piece of a newspaper to read. "I saw this while searching at the local library looking for leads about the bomb, I thought nothing of it," Sevena said. "However, because it mentioned Latham, Hogan & McLeish, I cut it out and saved it, not realizing until now that it might prove important."

Alan read it and gasped, and then read it again. He then whispered to Sevena in an excited voice, "The cat may get one more life." Alan then

approached the Dean. "I just have one more question or two and I will let
you go. The meeting with the four arms dealers was held in the Executive
Conference Room at your Washington office, was it not?"

The Dean was stunned that Allan would know this detail. Actually,
he didn't, but worded it as if he did as calmly as he could, not to let on that
his heart was beating even faster than the Dean's.

"Yes, I think it was," The Dean responded.

You could see Godman and Sevena jump up from their seats clutching their fists silently mouthing their own "yeses."

A look of relief came over Alan, as he then handed the Dean a torn-
out piece of a newspaper and asked him to read it to himself. "Sir, you will
note this is a copy of an article appearing in this year's March 17th edition
of the Wall Street Journal written by a reporter covering a lawsuit brought
against your firm by a company called the Dawson Engineering Group. They
sued for work they alleged they performed for your firm under an oral contract they claimed was agreed to at a meeting that took place in the Executive
Conference Room at your Washington law office. In this article, it says that
counsel for *your* law firm indicated that there was a video device that was
installed in the Executive Conference Room that automatically records all
discussions and meetings that take place there. In fact, the article states that
the same counsel for your firm produced the videotape of the meeting in
question in court to prove that no such oral contract had been agreed to by
the parties. Are you aware of such a video device that automatically records
meetings conducted in the Executive Conference Room?"

"I heard some mention of it, but I can't confirm if it were operational
at that time." The Dean was crafting an answer to avoid getting caught in a
lie, but not wanting to confirm the existence of the recording.

"Your Honor, I ask that we recess until Monday so I can subpoena
any video or other recordings of meetings that took place in the Executive

Conference Room on May 26, 1966, at the Washington Office of Latham, Hogan & McLeish."

Jenkins strenuously objected several times but was overruled and the judge addressed the Dean directly. "Sir, I am going to allow the issuance of the subpoena so if any such recordings exist, we will obtain them. But today is Thursday and I would rather not lose a day of trial time by delaying the session until Monday. So, if you would agree to accept service of the subpoena on behalf of your law firm today, you could call your firm and ask the appropriate person to fly here tomorrow and appear with any such recordings if they so exist, at the expense of the defense."

The Dean, wanting to appear as if he were anxious to deliver the recording as soon as possible to confirm his testimony, responded, "I would be more than happy to accommodate the court, and without waiting for the subpoena to be drafted, I will phone my office as soon as the clerk makes one of the court's phones available to me."

"Thanks, that would be most helpful," said the judge. "The court stands in recess until 10 am tomorrow."

No sooner had the Dean left the stand when he was approached by Jenkins. "All I want to know is whether explosives or bombs were in any way mentioned at the meeting with the arms dealers?"

"No," answered the Dean.

"Good, I have no concerns then no matter what else was discussed," a reassured Jenkins responded. An experienced trial lawyer, he was always keeping his attention narrowly focused on the arson charges that were being prosecuted.

However, the Dean, on the other hand, had a lot of concerns as evidenced in his call to his colleague Walter Myers, who conveniently was in the Washington office that week. The Dean explained to Walter what had occurred in court and in a somewhat panicky voice demanded, "Destroy it!

Walter, you were there. No way can we let them see that tape."

"Not that simple, Bill," Walter replied. "I first need to get the tape from the company that installed the system. They keep it protected in storage for us. Once they give it to me, I can't say it didn't exist. Don't worry, though, I agree they cannot be allowed to view it and trust me, no matter what, they won't. I will think of something and I personally will be there tomorrow to represent the firm regarding the production of the tape."

CHAPTER 38

FRIDAY MORNING WHEN Alan arrived in court, he and Goodman were informed that Attorney Walter Myers, a senior partner of the Dean's firm, had arrived and the judge asked the parties to meet in his chambers at 10 before he would be calling the session into order. Walter Myers was already sitting in the chambers with a videotape recorder and some video-tapes on the table in front of him when Alan and Goodman were escorted into the room by the Chief Court Officer. Jenkins and Renfrew, who arrived a moment earlier, were just beginning to sit down next to Myers.

The night before, Alan had met with Eddie Carpenter and the other defendants at the county jail once again. Looking for some encouragement, Eddie asked him, "What are you hoping for when you view the videotape of the meeting?"

Alan knew the truthful answer: "A miracle." But he knew that they needed some hope, not despair, so he kept that to himself. Besides, the video recording represented the first possibility to uncover something that could suggest possible conspiracy. Alan answered simply, "Hoping the tape will reveal them for who they really are."

As Alan was about to leave, Eddie said to him, "Everyone here wants me to tell you that we appreciate how all of you are standing by us. And Alan, we know if anyone can free us from these trumped-up charges – it's *you*." Alan blocked his emotions, for they would reveal his fears as to the outcome and could only think of responding by saying, "from your mouth to God's ears."

"Good morning, gentlemen," the judge addressed the group as he entered the chambers in an open shirt, carrying his robe in his hand. "I thought we ought to see what is in store for us with the showing of the video.

Mr. Myers, welcome to Oklahoma. What do we have here?"

"Well, judge, we were subpoenaed to produce the video recordings of the entire day in question. It is true our firm had installed a recently developed modern device, called a videotape recorder, designed to record video and audio material on individual reels of two-inch-wide magnetic tape. I have eight videotapes of 60 minutes each. Each one is marked by the hours they cover beginning at 9 am until 5 pm. We ran the tape. It appears that the meeting with the CEOs of our arms manufacturing clients took place between 10 am and 11:15 am, so that would be tapes marked 2 and 3."

"OK," said the judge beginning to have the chief court officer assist him in putting on his robe, "let's get the show on the road and show those two tapes in open court."

"We do have a problem, Your Honor, and it is embarrassing," Myers said, standing up and addressing the judge. "Tape 2 begins with each one of the four CEOs, President Lauder and I greeting one another. That took up about two minutes or so of the tape and then the remaining portions of tapes 2 and 3 are completely blank."

"What do you mean?" asked the judge immediately stopping the court officer from helping him on with his robe.

"Well, we were given the tapes for that day from the company that operates the system and stores the tapes and we asked an associate to copy tapes 2 and 3. In that way, our attorneys could review them after transporting the originals here. In the process of trying to copy them, the tapes were accidentally erased. This type of videotape is a relatively new technology and apparently the wrong method was used to make copies."

"That is absolute fucking bullshit," Alan shouted furiously.

"Counsel, I can appreciate your anger and frustration, but remember my chambers are an extension of the court and that outburst is inappropriate. Mr. Myers, this is most upsetting to me as well, to say the least. I will want to put you and the associate under oath and interrogate both of you under the pains and penalties of perjury after we decide what to do with this disturbing revelation."

"I anticipated that, and the associate involved is here waiting in the courtroom. All I can do is apologize for this very embarrassing error." Myers acted humbled as he began to sit down.

Sometime later, a similar embarrassment would take place over an erased tape involving the United States president, eventually forcing him to resign because of what other of his tapes revealed.

Over 30 minutes of discussions and arguments took place with Alan insisting on playing the erased tapes to the jury to show consciousness of guilt on the part of the law firm. Jenkins argued to do so would create undue prejudice that would cause the jury to wildly speculate on what was on those tapes, including bombing discussions that never took place. The judge finally ruled on it.

"As astonishing as this development may be, I cannot permit evidence to go to the jury that the tapes were erased for the reasons mentioned by Mr. Jenkins. It's of relevance for sure, and I have grave suspicions as to what really happened, but on balance to allow it would be too prejudicial.

I will merely inform the jury that tapes containing the recording of the meeting are not available and no inferences may be drawn from their unavailability, and under the penalties of contempt, you all are all directed to withhold any public statements about the tapes until the trial is over.

You may only repeat what I will inform the jury in open court."

Alan vigorously objected and took exception to the ruling for the record. He then asked that after informing the jury about the tapes, the case be in recess for the rest of the day and resume on Monday. He argued that given this surprising and shocking event, the defense legal team needed the weekend to determine how to proceed with the remainder of its affirmative defense. The request was granted. Alan left the room still fuming over what he knew to be foul play.

Reporters were seeking interviews from the attorneys, who merely regurgitated the Judge's statement. Alan thought of leaking it but felt it would be clear that he would be the only one with a motive to do so, and that would only backfire with the judge. Alan, Judd and Sevena, the triumvirate as Goodman would call them, picked an out-of-the-way restaurant to try to figure out what had just happened and the next steps, if any, to deal with it. They were to meet at the restaurant in an hour at 1 pm after Alan and Goodman met with the defendants to bring them up to speed. In the meantime, Judd called Mike and related the bad news to him.

———————————

WHEN ALAN ARRIVED at the restaurant, having just talked to a very discouraged and dismayed group of defendants, Judd was waiting outside. He informed him that the restaurant lunch was called off. They had to get to Goodman's office in a hurry. Sevena was getting some take-out sandwiches for them to eat in an awaiting cab with its meter running that Judd had already readied.

"Shit, I've had enough surprises for the day to last me a month, what's this all about?" asked Alan in no mood for one more.

"Tell you in the cab on the way. Get in." Sevena came running out of the restaurant with the sandwiches and some cokes and got in front, giving the cabbie the address with a loud "Step on it, please". By the time the cabbie pulled up at Goodman's law office, Alan was fully briefed of the circumstances leading to this dash to Goodman's office.

"OK, given what you told me," Alan was saying to Judd while stepping out of the cab, "we will need to serve a subpoena to an officer in that company's corporate office in Washington. Let's see, it's almost 1:30. That office is bound to close by 5 pm. That means we have a little over three hours to retain Washington counsel acting on our behalf to get it done. I will grab Mel and get to work."

CHAPTER 39

THAT MONDAY, THE courthouse as usual was jammed with the media and people trying to gain seats to the session. The Dean and Walter were in the row behind the prosecution table talking and at times laughing. They and the courtroom suddenly went quiet to the court officer's "Hear Yees" announcing Judge Clark's entrance. After the jury was let in, the judge asked Alan whether he wished to proceed with the examination of President Lauder. Alan said he would be resuming that examination, but with the court's permission, he would interrupt that examination to call another witness first.

A gray-haired gentleman looking like he was in his late 50s took the stand and was administered the oath. Alan began with a conventional first question. "Would you please tell the court your name, the company you work for and your position in that company?"

"My name is Harris Feldman. I am the owner of Audio-Video Recordings, with offices in New York and Washington, DC."

Both the Dean and Walter Myers suddenly looked at each other in astonishment. "You know this guy?" whispered the Dean to Myers in a bit of panic.

"It's our video company, but no, never met him. Shit! What is Roberts up to?"

"What is the nature of your business?" asked Alan

"We specialize in installing audio or video recording devices for businesses to electronically record meetings or discussions that take place at their offices."

"And did you so accommodate the law offices of Latham, Hogan

& McLeish by setting up such a video recording device in the Executive Conference Room of their Washington Office?" asked Alan.

"Yes," answered Feldman, who went on to explain how the device he invented was activated by human sound and recorded onto video magnetic tapes that they keep in safe storage for their clients until called upon to produce any of them.

"You have been informed by me, were you not, that without my going into the reason, the original May 26, 1966, magnetic tape recording of that Executive Conference Room's activities was not available to the court?"

"Yes, sir, that's true."

Now came the question of epic proportions to the case. "Would you, sir, now tell the jury whether your company as a matter of protocol makes copies of all original recorded tapes and whether you did so with respect to the original May 26 tapes?"

Jenkins immediately called for a bench conference and demanded to know whether such tapes were going to be introduced and if so, the prosecution desired to review them first outside of the jury to determine whether all or a portion of it warranted an objection. Alan indicated that the witness and the tapes were in court in response to his subpoena and given that the original tapes were unavailable, the Rules of Evidence permit a copy to be introduced, and Mr. Feldman had brought a copy with him.

"Mr. Roberts, have you or anyone on your team reviewed this copy of the tape?" asked the judge.

"No, Your Honor. Mr. Feldman came to this court directly from the airport."

Judge Clark, still very upset over the so-called accidental erasing of the original tape, which to him, did not pass the smell test, denied the prosecution's request, stating, "We have already lost significant trial time over these tapes because of no fault of the defense and I don't want to dismiss the jury for another half a day today while the tapes are reviewed by counsel. Neither party has had the advantage of knowing what's on them. If these tapes can be authenticated as true copies by the witness, who I will make available to you to cross-examine for that purpose only before they are introduced, then I don't see how the conversations involving President Lauder and the CEOs of the arms manufacturers are subject to objection. If any portion appears to be inadmissible while the tapes are viewed in open court, then, Mr. Jenkins, you can register your objections at that time and I will stop the recording to rule on it then. We are going to get this case tried without further delay. So, let's go to work."

Feldman resumed his testimony and indicated that copies of each original were made as a matter of best practice so if any one of the original tapes were lost or damaged, there would be a duplicate available should a transcript be needed.

When Judd called Mike to tell him the bad news that the original tapes were erased, it was Mike who told Judd to have Alan subpoena the company for a duplicate. Mike told Judd that the CIA was involved when that same company originally installed their audio device in the president's Oval Office in the West Wing of the White House. Those tapes were to be kept by the President. When the company informed the CIA that they generally make copies as a matter of best practice, a joint opinion was rendered by the CIA and FBI that for security reasons, duplicates should not be made in the case of the president's discussions at the White House.

However, they were made for all other customers, including the Dean's firm. Mike had come through again when it counted.

"So, do you have those copies of the May 26 original tapes with you?" asked Alan.

"I do," answered Feldman and produced them. Feldman went on to testify as the chain of custody to show that the duplicate tapes were never out of the company's control along with other evidence to authenticate that the tapes represented a true recording of what took place, particularly during the hours between 10 am and 12 noon that day. Jenkins chose not to cross-examine Feldman as to the authenticity of the tapes for it would have been a futile exercise given his testimony, and he did not want to appear to be worried about them, especially having been assured by the Dean that there were no discussions about the bombing.

The court recessed for 20 minutes to set up a screen behind the Judge's bench. The court lights over the bench were turned off to view the tape recording of the meeting between 10 to 11:15 am, which was the total duration of the meeting among the Dean, Walter Myers, and the CEOs of the four arms manufacturers.

Although not quite loud enough to make out most of the words, there appeared to be an argument of sorts breaking out at the prosecution's table. It was the Dean scolding Jenkins. "You cannot allow them to show this tape," demanded the Dean. "Renew your objections, please. The company is bound by a confidentiality agreement,"

"As you well know as an attorney," Jenkins responded as quietly as he could, "a confidentiality agreement is no defense to a subpoena. The company had to produce it and the judge is adamant in allowing the jury to view it. Besides, there was no mention of a bomb, right?"

The Dean was trying to remember what was said and before he could speak, again the court officer asked the two of them to be quiet since Judge Clark was now coming off the bench to sit in the clerk's chair directly in front of the screen. You could not hear a pin drop in the courtroom or among the area reserved for the press.

CHAPTER 40

"GENTLEMEN, THANKS FOR coming." The jury and those in the courtroom viewing the video recording heard the voice of the Dean beginning the meeting at the Executive Conference Room at the Washington law office of Latham, Hogan & McLeish. They also saw on the screen four elderly gentlemen dressed in expensive suits shaking hands with the Dean and with his colleague, Walter.

Alan gave Sevena and Judd a look as if to say, "For better or worse, here we go."

Those watching could not help noticing the exceedingly long, shiny mahogany conference table that went the full length of the plush conference room, as they all sat down dwarfed in one corner. At that point, Alan asked the judge to interrupt the recording for a moment so he could request the Dean, while still under oath, to identify for the jury the four gentlemen they were about to see as the CEOs of some of the largest arms manufacturing companies in the world, including Max Schmitt, the founding Director of Majestic Chemical. The recording was turned back on.

"Sorry for not meeting in a more intimate setting," explained the Dean, "but, we will be talking about some very delicate matters and would not want any uninvited eavesdroppers listening in."

The Dean's comment brought heavy laughter from the courtroom, given that every word would now be splashed all over the newspapers, on radio and TV throughout the United States and other parts of the world. There was that much interest in the case, especially in this recording.

"I know how busy you all are," the Dean said, still welcoming the group, "and I will try to have you back on your private jets before lunch, though our chef stands ready to prepare anything you would like at any time during or after our meeting."

To a jury whose average family income was no more than $5,400 a year, and most of them lucky if they owned a used car, never mind a private jet, what they saw were people not of their world, so there was a level of mistrust from the very beginning.

The jury saw the Dean casually pouring himself a glass of water from one of the Waterford lead crystal pitchers on the table and set the tone for the meeting. "In about an hour, Walter and I and some of our firm's specially trained attorneys will be meeting with a couple of Hoover's special agents that he assigned to help us in a matter we are about to discuss, so l want to get our end of the business completed before their arrival."

The mentioning of the FBI caused a buzz among the regulars in the courtroom who had been following the case closely, knowing that the FBI had been involved in the events that took place. Alan took note that the Dean had denied meeting the agents Andrews and Backman. Were they the same agents at that meeting? Had he perjured himself? The jury watched with great interest as they saw the Dean press a button on the table that pulled down a large screen with the first slide entitled, *"Percentage of US Expenditures on Defense."* The videotape had it clearly in focus. It revealed a graph of the percentage of federal expenditures on defense for the past five years and projections for the current and future years.

"This year you collectively will be awarded over $39 billion in military contracts," the Dean said proudly, explaining it was 13% of the entire defense budget of $301 billion.

"It is why we pay you the big bucks without blinking an eye," responded Brian Nowinski, the CEO of Military Armaments and Systems Limited. "An annual retainer to your firm of $500 million from our four companies."

The astronomical amounts of the military contract awards and legal fees by themselves added more unsettling feelings among the jurors, evidenced by their looks of astonishment. It was as if their collective unconscious recognized a time-proven reality, that such out-of-the-orbit profits could not be in play without ominous happenings around it. And indeed, that was about to be revealed in spades.

The jury then saw the Dean at the meeting bend forward and lower his voice to almost a whisper, but the law firm had paid well for a good video recording for it picked up his remarks.

"Let's be candid, guys. We are all grownups here. From a business standpoint, we have a significant amount to gain if the war does not, shall we say, end prematurely. Dissent will build as deaths and casualties of our soldiers mount and are flashed on news reports each evening, but unless some critical mass of protest grows from the grassroots against the president and our government, we believe this will be one of our country's longest wars,"

The Dean continued with comments such as, "If we add your resources to well-designed countermeasures to prevent the evolvement of a grassroots movement to end the war prematurely, the benefit is enormous," and "the profits to each of your companies during those years will be staggering, and, of course, our firm's fees as well. To be brutally frank, from a business standpoint, we both benefit from a protracted war."

The jury was hearing pure unadulterated greed at its most base level. Alan also took note that the Dean perjured himself in answering his question whether they had talked about how much they stood to make or lose if the war continued or ended.

The tape continued to roll on as the jury, the judge, the media and others in the courtroom, even Jenkins and ADA Renfrew, viewed with total disgust as the Dean went on to tell the arms dealers how their donations through the foundation to the universities would help degrade any student demonstrations to shorten the war. He named the colleges where he expected the initial protests to break out, one of them America University.

Their cold, calculating discussion of how to keep the war going so they could get richer and richer at the expense of thousands of dead American boys coming home in caskets shocked everyone in the courtroom. It was even shocking to juror number six, a woman Alan had unsuccessfully challenged for cause to keep her off the jury because she had a cousin in the Marines who recently died in battle in Vietnam. As she heard about this "secret pact" to keep the killing going so they could make money, she buried her head into her two open hands covering her face, whispering to herself, but overheard by her fellow jurors, "murderers…murderers."

The recording of the end of the meeting could not have displayed more the utter greed and the disrespect of these profiteers for the very nation and its brave soldiers they were contracted to defend. The Dean, displaying his desire for the wars to go on, ended by offering a toast mocking one of America's hallowed salutes, "Long live the battle for freedom!" joined by the others repeating the toast with some laughter.

All the court lights were then turned on. Not a sound could be heard, but everyone turned to look at the Dean and Walter with utter disgust and curiosity as to how they would react to their disgrace. Both looked straight ahead with their eyes slightly turned down as if trying to cut out the world around them. There was nothing else they could do. They and the FBI agents, Andrews and Backman, had been instructed by the clerk not to leave the courtroom since they were still under subpoena in case they were to be recalled as witnesses. They hoped the session would be suspended for the morning recess so they could get some relief, but no such luck.

The judge called Alan and the prosecution to the clerk's lower bench where he had been sitting during the showing of the video. "Mr. Jenkins, I am sure you are as shocked at what we heard as I am. But, that aside, I wanted to hear from both of you as to the relevance of all this to the charges at hand, that of arson by means of explosives."

"Precisely, Your Honor." Jenkins was first to respond. "None of us can condone what we heard, and it may have some relevance to the trespass cases we are to try right after the jury verdict in this case. However, it has no relevance whatsoever regarding the bombing. There is no relevant evidence here as to who set off the bomb than the indisputable evidence that we presented incriminating these defendants. What we heard is indeed atrocious behavior on the part of President Lauder and his partner, attorney Myers, and those in attendance at that repulsive meeting, but unless Mr. Roberts can present a witness to connect all this to the bombing charges, we now ask that you instruct the jury to disregard not only the video recording evidence we just saw and heard, but all the other evidence related to the actions taken by the university and the law enforcement agencies dealing with the sit-ins. They simply have no relevance to the bombing charges at hand."

Judge Clark looked at Alan for his response. Alan went to the heart of the argument. "What we heard at that meeting was not only atrocious, as Mr. Jenkins described, but conduct that demonstrates a strong motive to demonize all organizers of antiwar demonstrations. They are a group of men so consumed by greed, they would not rule out any devious means, including the setting off a bomb, if need be, to frame and stop these organizers from protesting the continuation of the war. The defendants are entitled to have the jury consider whether their possible involvement in this matter raises a reasonable doubt as to my clients' guilt."

"There was no talk of a bomb whatsoever throughout that entire meeting," Jenkins immediately responded in a raised voice. "It would be impermissible for the jury to draw such a prejudicial inference from what they heard. It would be pure speculation and wild conjecture- an impermissible reach. Again, all that evidence is irrelevant to this case and the jury must be instructed to disregard it."

Alan knew that Jenkins had raised the more formidable argument. With all that had been exposed, he still had not produced the smoking gun needed to link all the greed and deceit to the bombing. He had one more play, perhaps better described as a hope and a prayer, so he quickly addressed the judge. "Your Honor, I would ask you to delay your ruling until the defense rests. We are not done producing evidence to tie it all in. I suggest we take the morning break and then proceed."

"I am not sure what else you have to produce, but it is time for the morning break, particularly for the jury, so let's take it," said the judge, taking it more for himself to consider a ruling that could decide the outcome of the entire case.

CHAPTER 41

"YOUR HONOR," ALAN addressed the judge without the jury in place after the break. "As you know, the Lauder and Myers meeting with the arms dealers ended at 11:15 am." Alan had intentionally dropped their titles as if they no longer deserved respect. "There was mention in that meeting that a subsequent meeting was to take place between the Dean, Walter and the FBI agents after the arms dealers left the Executive Conference Room. The defense intends to recall Mr. Feldman to the stand to continue to play Tape 2 and see if that meeting took place in the Executive Conference Room and was similarly recorded."

Addressing both the defense and prosecution, the judge asked if any of them reviewed the portion of the tape after 11:15 am or knew what was on it, to which both parties answered "no".

"Then, we will proceed to hear it in open court under the same conditions I established regarding objections. Mr. Court Officer, please recall the jury," instructed the judge.

As Alan watched the jury enter and take their seats, a chill went down his spine. What if the meeting were in a different room and not recorded? What were the chances that a bomb was mentioned, even if it were? It could all fall flat on its face, but there was no other play to be made.

The court went quiet and the videotape began to roll. The jurors saw Walter alone with the Dean in the Executive Conference Room. After a couple of minutes, Walter picked up the phone calling down to a secretary. He asked her to bring up the two FBI agents waiting in a room next to her office and 20 minutes after that to bring up the seven lawyers waiting in another smaller conference room on a lower floor. "And Joyce," Walter gave further directions, "Max Schmitt of Majestic Chemical and Brian Nowinski of Military Armaments and Systems are going to be having lunch here. Tell the chef to prepare something special for them."

Alan gave a big sigh of relief. The meeting was taking place in the Executive Conference Room and for better or worse, being taped for all to hear.

Just as the Dean hung up, the two FBI agents arrived. The Dean was waiting for them at the door. "Hi, I am Bill Lauder and that gentleman is my partner, Walter Myers," said the Dean, extending his hand.

"Bill Andrews, glad to meet you both, and this is my partner, agent Freddie Backman." They all shook hands.

When Jenkins heard the agents' names, he looked back in the courtroom at the Dean displaying some trepidation. The Dean had falsely testified that he never met these agents. Jenkins then looked at Alan, whose head was bent over making a note as soon as he saw Andrews and Backman enter the room.

"Would you fellers like some coffee?" asked the Dean.

"No thanks, we had some in the waiting area. That's quite a conference table, ever fill it up?" asked Backman.

The Dean smiled. "Actually, we need to move in some extra chairs behind the ones here when we have our general partners meeting. It is an international law firm, so many of the partners fly in from many other countries."

"Impressive," responded Andrews and then began the discussion for which they came. "As you know, the director assigned us to be of service to you in any way we can. We had been fully briefed at headquarters as to your plans to quash any student demonstrations on the campuses of the seven most likely universities where they could first breakout. We have read the investigative reports done by our agency on each of the seven attorneys we are to meet today. We understand they will be assigned to each of those schools as special counsel to each of their presidents. It is good that you arranged for us to meet with them today since we will be working with them closely on an ongoing basis from here on."

"Good, in a few minutes they will be brought in," responded the Dean. "Is there anything, in particular, you want to discuss with them at this time?"

"No, just meet them and get acquainted at this time," answered Andrews.

"We just got the assignment and a packet of info about your plan a couple of hours ago, so while we are familiar with it, we will need some time to come up with some ideas," Backman added.

Jenkins felt greatly relieved, for it now appeared that no substantive plans would be discussed. On the other hand, Alan looked at Sevena with that desperate expression seen on the faces of the hometown fans whose team is 3 runs behind, with 2 outs and no one on base in the ninth inning and just having watched the remaining batter swing and miss for strike 2.

Those in the courtroom then saw a group of seven young males impeccably dressed in blue suits, white shirts and conservative ties escorted into the conference room and greeted by the Dean.

"Come in, please. Thanks for flying down for the meeting. I would like to introduce you to FBI Agents William Andrews and Freddie Backman who will be working with you on our project."

One by one, they came up to shake hands and introduce themselves to Andrews and Backman telling them at which university they were to assume their new positions. That included Roy Armstrong. They discussed logistics, but reserved talking about specific plans in employing counter-measures to any demonstrations until they were to meet again during the month.

"One thing before we end the meeting," Andrews addressed them in a slightly more serious tone. "Freddie and I were chosen to assist in this project because we have had a good deal of experience in preventing and disrupting agitators from causing trouble. We learned that we mustn't be taken by surprise. So, when you start your jobs on campus, important you tell us anything you hear about volunteers being recruited to demonstrate."

Walter again called down to Joyce to have someone escort the seven attorneys to the dining cafeteria. Andrews and Backman were then seen following them out of the conference room.

The tape continued to run, but there were no voices or sound except for the rustling of papers being picked up by the Dean and Walter getting ready to leave the conference room. After 5 more minutes of the same, the judge signaled to the court officer to turn the lights on and the recording off. It was called strike 3.

Just as Feldman reached to turn off the recordings, Andrews and Backman are seen on the screen re-entering the conference room and closing the conference room door behind them.

Alan was the first to jump up to call it to the attention of the judge and ask that the recordings be turned back on. "So, there appears to be more, why am I not surprised?" Judge Clark responded in a voice suggesting the unusual twists and turns in the case were now commonplace. He signaled to Feldman to restart the recording.

Some of the press who started to leave the courtroom hurried back, anxious to join a spellbound courtroom not knowing what to anticipate. While others were coming back in, the Dean, Andrews and Backman were heading toward the door, when they were stopped by the other court officers at the entrance reminding them that the case was still on and they could be recalled to the stand.

"Now that the attorneys have left, we want to suggest something for you to seriously consider," Andrews spoke a little above a whisper, but loud enough for those watching the tape to hear every word. "No matter what your particular motives are – we assume it is to keep campuses peaceful – the agency believes that these type demonstrations are inspired by communists or communist sympathizers. Therefore, we believe that we have to fight fire with fire."

Andrews came closer. "We found from our experience with civil rights demonstrators that law enforcement countermeasures such as the ones you are planning do not by themselves stop, but only delay the continuation of organized protests. You need to demonize the organizers at their very first effort to gain support for their movement and do it in such a way that they can't recover. The public must see their actions for what they are-unlawful, horrific and devoid of any sympathy."

"For sure, but how can we achieve that outcome?" asked the Dean.

"Well, first we need to know their plans for their very first demonstration. I am confident we can infiltrate their planning group to gain that intelligence. Then we have to create an incident that will outrage the public with indisputable evidence that they planned it." Andrews laid it out in a calm, matter-of-fact, professional manner and looked to the Dean and Walter to see if there was any shock over what he was implying.

On the contrary, the Dean was intrigued and simply asked, "What kind of an incident?" A question that gave Andrews full license to feel free to reveal the plan they had in mind.

"Please hear me out with an open mind and remember the importance of our effort to stop these communist sympathizers." Fighting "fire with fire," normally a figure of speech, was to turn out to be literal in what Andrews was about to propose. "We would set off a bomb in a nearby building where they were demonstrating, causing a blast and a fire that would bring the fire department and first responders to the site with their sirens blasting causing great alarm. But we would make sure no one was in the area when it went off and that the damage would be relatively limited. We would plant evidence incriminating the organizers of the demonstrations."

The courtroom burst out in anger and sounds of disbelief. "Oh my God!" from the jury box. "The fuckers," from the back of the courtroom. "Thank God," from one of the defendants.

"Order, order," exclaimed the judge banging his gavel several times on the clerk's bench. Feldman, who was operating the video player, had placed it on pause until the noise subsided.

"There will be silence in the courtroom or we will empty the court-room to obtain it. Mr. Feldman, continue playing the tape," ordered the judge having obtained silence.

The next voice was that of Walter. "Who would have to be in on it?"

"Just us. Freddie Backman and I would handle the entire operation ourselves. It's foolproof.

We just need to find the right type of explosive that causes a big fuss, but with damages confined to a limited area."

"Wait," responded the Dean to Andrews. "Give me a moment. I may be able to solve that problem with someone we can take into our confidence."

The Dean called down to the executive dining room. "Is Max Schmitt of Majestic Chemical still there? Good, ask him if he would please come back here on the double." In less than five minutes, Max entered the room.

"Max, better I don't tell you why, but do you have a bomb you are manufacturing for the military that can make a significant blast covering a very small area with limited physical damage?"

"It just so happens we do, but it is classified."

"These are FBI agents assigned to us by J. Edgar. Certainly, it would not be violating any confidential policy to cooperate with the FBI's request for that bomb material?"

"Not if you say it doesn't. You're my attorney," Max responded, smiling. The tape ended showing everyone leaving the executive conference room.

There was some small chatter in the courtroom as the lights were turned back on, but as the judge got up from his seat at the clerk's table and resumed his place on the bench, there was not a sound. Everyone was shocked and stunned by what they heard and anxious to see what came next.

The judge asked that the jury be taken to the jury room, stating that they would be returned soon after some legal matters were disposed of. As soon as they were out of hearing distance, he ordered the court officers to lock the doors and addressed Jenkins and Assistant District Attorney Renfrew. "Based on what I have heard, I am issuing warrants for the arrest of President William Lauder, attorney Walter Myers, FBI agents William Andrews and Edward Backman on charges of arson by means of explosives, conspiracy to commit arson by means of explosives, perjury and I would expect the District Attorney's office to add additional charges that are warranted. I will also request the District Attorney's office and the Justice Department to formally conduct criminal investigations related to these matters to determine if any other crimes or wrongdoings have been committed by the presidents and attorneys of the seven universities, as well as Majestic Chemical and the other three arms manufacturers mentioned in this case. I shall also forward transcripts of this case to the Department of Defense and appropriate congressional committees dealing with the awarding of military contracts."

The judge then paused to take a sip of water. "I will now call the jury back into session and unless I hear an objection from the prosecution, which I assume I will not, I will entertain and grant a motion from Mr. Roberts that I order a directed verdict of not guilty on the arson charges for each defendant."

Wild applause broke out in the courtroom. Alan looked toward Goodman, Judd and Sevena. Goodman looked back at Alan, smiling with two thumbs up. Judd cupped his hands and raised them high above his right shoulder and shook them back and forth as a victory sign, while Sevena simply placed her two hands below her mouth and blew him a kiss. Alan then turned to the defendants and saw Eddie, with tears in his eyes, mouthed him a "thank you" and the others tearing and smiling and hugging each other.

Court officers instinctively approached and surrounded the Dean, Walter Myers and the two FBI Agents who were now sitting close to one another mainly for protection should some of the angered crowd attempt to attack them.

The press busted out of the courtroom to file their stories. The jury was officially dismissed with praise from the judge for faithfully executing their duty throughout the trial. The electronic media were pushing Alan to come outside for interviews. He indicated that he would, but only after the trespass cases were heard and disposed of, stating, "There is a major issue involved that is yet to be addressed in the trespass cases in court and what comes next, could turn out to be as important as anything you heard so far." With that, the media all scrambled to get back into the courtroom.

CHAPTER 42

THE JUDGE TOOK no more than a 15-minute recess before asking whether the prosecution and Alan were prepared to try the jury-waived cases of trespass immediately. Both Jenkins and Alan responded affirmatively and to avoid recalling witnesses, agreed to stipulate that all the testimony already heard in the arson case was to be admitted as evidence in the trespass case, permitting them to move directly into summation. The one exception would be that Goodman would call one defendant to briefly testify that no warnings were given to the defendants to leave before being arrested for trespass, and when they tried to leave, the doors were locked so they couldn't.

The two defendants, Clifford and Roger, just acquitted of the arson charges, and the two other recruited volunteers injured during the sit-ins were now standing trial on the lesser trespass charges. Also, Eddie Carpenter and Harry Lee joined them as defendants, having been charged with aiding and abetting the defendants in the commitment of their crimes of trespass. The courtroom went completely silent again as Alan got up to give his argument.

"Your Honor, there are three defenses to the charges of trespass. First, if you were to believe the defendants instead of the arresting officers, they were not given a prior verbal warning to leave before being arrested. Given that there was not a single no-trespassing sign posted in the area, the element of 'prior warning' has not been proven and as a matter of law, they would have to be acquitted. Second, even if you were to find they were given a warning, I believe the facts indicate that this was a setup to get them inside the building so they would be arrested and that constitutes entrapment. Lastly, and the most important defense upon which I wish to elaborate in some detail is that they have a common-law defense, the defense of 'Competing Harms-that the limited harm of their civil disobedience was conducted to prevent the greater harm of continuing the war with its horrific bloodshed."

Alan moved a little closer to the bench. "Your Honor, as you may know, the commission of a 'crime' of lesser harm to avert the occurrence of an even greater harm has long been considered a defense to prosecution. One can find these defenses of 'Competing Harms' or 'Necessity' dating back to over a century ago. For example, the 1834 case of United States v. Ashton, in Massachusetts, where a crew was acquitted of committing the crime of mutiny, having reason to believe that a takeover of the unseaworthy command was necessary to save their lives. Or in a more recent case, Baender v. Barnett, where to prevent an unjust punishment, the court held that the crime against escaping from prison does not extend to a prisoner who breaks out when the prison is on fire. Similarly, the courts have held that a person lost in the woods and starving, could steal food from a cabin to survive without being punished for theft. The cases throughout the century are replete with this principle of 'Necessity' or 'Competing Harms' as a defense to conviction. An act normally considered criminal is justified and is not to be considered criminal if in the minds of the alleged violators there is a reasonable belief that their so-called 'unlawful' actions are necessary to avoid a greater harm and they could reasonably succeed in preventing that harm by such an action."

The courtroom and the judge were intrigued by the defense being raised. Alan then walked behind the chairs where the defendants were sitting and when directly behind Eddie, placed his hand on his right shoulder and spoke.

"So, what is that greater harm these defendants were trying to prevent by the crime of trespass? Simply put, they intended to start a movement to end a needless war costing our country dearly in untold American lives, a war in a far-off land that by any stretch of the imagination could not pose any kind of threat to our national security to warrant the horrendous sacrifices that our young soldiers are being called upon to make."

Alan then began to put some meat on the bones. "It is not just a needless war, but a costly one. If it goes on and escalates on its current course, economists tell us it will cost our nation more than 100 billion dollars – an enormous expenditure that would serve only to fatten the coffers of arms dealers like the ones we heard this morning whose greed is unbounded. Yes, a staggering 100 billion dollars wasted on fueling a senseless war abroad, while weakening the War on Poverty to help those in need here at home. But much more important, these *dedicated and caring* students standing before you as defendants-and all their other committed classmates- were calling on their own generation of Americans to join them in stopping no less than half a million American soldiers being sent into battle to kill, or be killed, in battles where tens of thousands of them, many just out of high school, would needlessly be cut down in the flower of their youth and shipped back home in caskets. The only consolation for their grieving parents and loved ones would be that the caskets delivering their sons, brothers, husbands, or fathers back to them, were draped with an American flag."

Alan paused for a moment to let the solemnity of that statement sink in. "These 60 students were trying to prevent their classmates being recruited on campus to wear American uniforms from being wounded and crippled, many of whom never to be able to walk again, too many who would permanently lose the ability to move any of their limbs again, and almost all emotionally crippled and scarred by the stress and nightmarish horrors they would be forced to endure, witnessing the killing of their brothers in battle, and forced to kill thousands of Vietnamese, Laotians and Cambodians, including innocent women and children that the fog of war would serve up as victims of battle, in the steamy-hot rice fields of those desolate countries. These were the harms these students in front of me, and those they recruited to their cause, sought to prevent with the only tools they had, their bodies, their voices and the courage to face the consequences of being condemned, arrested, or injured during their peaceful civil disobedience of trespass so their message might be heard."

Alan paused again with his head bent down a bit thinking about how to end the plea. He then looked up. "These courageous students were protesting to bring about an earlier end to the war, so when it did end, we would avoid once again having to sing those sorrowful lyrics, 'Where have all the flowers gone?'

Alan then began to slowly move down the row of seats in which the six defendants were sitting, placing his right hand on each of their shoulders as he passed. "These men, these heroes, each of these heroes, Your Honor." Alan paused for a moment and then raising his voice in a most laudatory, appealing tone continued, "Yes, each and every one of these heroes... deserves not to be punished...but to be praised."

The eloquence of Alan's plea froze the courtroom with a deafening silence for almost 15 seconds, and then, as before, the silence was broken by thunderous applause. But this time the entire courtroom was now standing, and as they did, it took many multiple sounds of the gavel and requests for order to resume decorum. Those in the courtroom knew this was an historic moment and they were given the privilege of bearing witness to a moving presentation sanctifying the antiwar cause by this charismatic young attorney-to-be.

Judge Clark was experienced enough to know that such moments cannot be cut short, so he waited until everything subsided to ask a key question. "With respect to your 'competing harms' defense, Mr. Roberts, it is in its appeal most convincing, but you correctly indicated that one of the key elements to prove a competing harms defense, is that the defendants must reasonably expect that their unlawful action will be effective as the direct cause of abating the danger of the greater harm. Are you contending that with just 60 students staging a day's sit-in in a building of a university in Oklahoma, they might succeed in bringing about an end to a war that the full force of our government and its military support are deeply invested in pursuing? Am I to be convinced that is possible?"

Alan thought for a moment and then began to walk from behind the row of the defendants back toward the defense counsel's table giving him time to consider his response. He then stood in front of the defense counsel's table so there was no barrier between him and the judge and in a moderate voice responded, "In a few weeks on December 1, it will be the 11th anniversary when a 42-year-old black woman got on a bus on her way home from a hard day's work in Montgomery, Alabama. The bus was full and a white man boarded. As usual, she was asked to give up her seat to him and ride the rest of the way standing in the back. She refused to do so and was arrested for violating the laws of segregation, the 'Jim Crow laws' as they were coined. She refused to pay the fine and appealed the case all the way to the Supreme Court challenging the constitutionality of segregation. Motivated by her refusal to obey an unjust law, a young Baptist minister organized a boycott against the Montgomery bus operation that lasted for over a year. The following December, when the Supreme Court found the segregation law to violate the Constitution, black men, women and their children for the first time could ride in a non-segregated Montgomery bus. The Montgomery Bus Boycott, sparked by a single black woman refusing to obey an unjust law, along with the passionate and unrelenting determination of a Baptist minister, started a movement and a decade of monumental non-violent protests that led to the passage of the landmark civil rights legislation that was enacted two years ago outlawing discrimination and segregation that existed here in the United States since the Civil War."

Alan paused for a moment and concluded, "Of course, the two people were Rosa Parks and Martin Luther King, Jr. In answer to your question, Your Honor, *yes*, given these examples, I believe that what these few students were attempting to do, could reasonably start a wave and a movement of protests to stop this unjust war. In fact, I believe what the late President Kennedy said: *ONE PERSON can make a difference...and everyone should try.*"

The media, which already showered Alan with praise for his legal acumen and eloquence, had now seen an idealism and spiritual verse in his presentation that would have some of them comparing this law student to Clarence Darrow, one of the most celebrated attorneys and civil libertarians in recent history.

For all intents and purposes, the trial was over. The defendants who were facing prison and disgrace knew that regardless of the judge's decision on the trespass charges, Alan had already exonerated them and ennobled their actions and the cause for which they acted. Goodman knew that the criticism and degradation he had to experience daily for being the only law firm in Oklahoma willing to defend these arsonists and communists, as they were perceived before the trial, would now turn to praise. Alan had done what made the public in awe of Perry Mason in that popular weekly TV show. Not only did he free the innocent, but at the same time exposed the guilty, and most important of all, he might have accomplished what Judd and Sevena recruited him to do all at the same time. With the favorable national publicity of his defense of the SDS antiwar protesters and the merit of their actions, he had set the tone for the launching of their cause that could go hand-in-hand with the ongoing momentum launched by the civil rights movement. Together, they could shake the tranquility and test the morality of the nation regarding two of the most important issues of the decade, racial equality and the ending of a costly, unjust war. But the next several weeks would tell.

As Alan started to go back to the defense counsel's table to await the judge's decision, all those in the courtroom witnessed something unusual. As he approached the defense table, first Mel Goodman, then each of the other six defendants sitting behind him, and Sevena and Judd behind them, all together rose to their feet in unison and remained standing at attention until Alan took his seat, a sign of great respect generally reserved only for someone held in the highest esteem.

When Alan observed this, he was overcome. He had to call upon whatever reserve he had left to hold back shedding the tears that began to well in his eyes. There was not much reserve left. He was totally exhausted. He had needed to keep strong and encourage others to do so all through the past three months and almost the entire trial when there appeared to be very little hope. He had called on every strength he had to be able to cope with the heavy burden and responsibility he carried for the lives of those he had persuaded to join the cause and for the cause itself.

Some of the tears were just a release of the inner tension and pressure he would not permit himself to succumb to during the long ordeal, but other, more uncontrollable tears, began to flow from a strange feeling that came over him when they all rose to honor his effort. The last time he had cried was when he rushed from a class at law school to the Mass General Hospital to be with his father at his death bed. Sammy, his dad, had just suffered a massive heart attack and Alan again was trying to hold back his tears at his side. "Dad, I don't want to lose you. Tell me what to do?" pleaded Alan, who adored this kind man who had helped shape his life and whom he could not bear to lose. Sammy, who always thought of the woe of others and never himself, gave his blessing to his son by gathering the last energy he had utter two last words to Alan's question of 'Tell me what to do'. He answered in a loving whisper, "Do good." The emotion that came over Alan in the courtroom as they all stood to salute him was a feeling that his dad had been standing with them, for he had honored his dad's final command.

When the judge began to speak, Alan swiped his sleeve across his brow pretending to wipe away some sweat but was wiping away the tears he could not hold back, so no one would notice. But there was at least one person who was emotionally connected, aware of his tears without having to look, for at the same time she, too, was wiping away tears of empathy, joy and love.

"Mr. Roberts," the judge was to render his decision, "I am sure there is no precedent to guide the court as to whether your proposed defense of 'Competing Harms' would apply to well- intentioned civil disobedience as a means to prevent the alleged greater harm of a war that is sanctified by the United States government. I am also sure since you have raised that defense in this very high profiled case, regardless of my decision, many protesters against this war or any other government activity they deem harmful, will now be advancing it in a variety of such cases in other forums. We then may learn whether, or under what circumstances, such a defense can be legally raised. However, I need not ponder the complexity of that question in this case to make my decision, for I find the testimony of the defendant Mr. Goodman put on the stand to be creditable that no warning to leave was given prior to the arrest and that the manner of the arrest also constituted entrapment. Given the validity of both defenses that you raised, I therefore, find each defendant not guilty of the crime of trespass or aiding or abetting that crime."

Though almost anticlimactic, more applause broke out in the courtroom and the defendants again hugged each other and shook both Alan's and Goodman's hands as an expression of thanks.

Alan was not done and rose to address the judge. "Your Honor, as you recall, another 58 students were placed on pretrial probation to have their cases dismissed upon condition they do not engage in protests during their attendance at the university. Since they accepted those conditions to avoid a conviction that you have found legally unjustified, I request that you dismiss their cases as of this moment, thereby removing such inappropriate conditions."

Judge Clark asked Jenkins whether he had any objection. At this point, Jenkins, disgusted with having been drawn into prosecuting this fraudulent case and its possible effect on his reputation, was now anxious to join the good guys in any way he could. "We would not only refrain from opposing it, but we join Mr. Roberts in his request." The judge proceeded to dismiss the case of the 58 other defendants.

"Anything else the court can do for you, Mr. Roberts?" asked the judge somewhat satirically given that Alan had gotten everything he could possibly want.

"Yes, one more thing, Your Honor, but it is only a suggestion since it is regarding a defendant we do not represent."

The judge was intrigued. "Yes, I will listen to your request if you promise it is indeed your last one," the judge responded with intended humor.

"Betty Nowicki is the defendant charged with both arson and trespass, and in default for non- appearance. I would suggest that her attorney be notified to find a means to communicate with her client and bring her before the court to have her charges dismissed. When you take up her default for non-appearance, I believe that you will find some extenuating circumstances."

"The clerk is instructed to do so, and this court stands adjourned," announced the judge. He then called Alan to the bench. "When you submit recommendations to whichever state bar you apply to practice, I would feel very disappointed if you did not request one from me and *I will* be correcting that one mistake in our evidence test." Alan laughed while shaking his hand with both of his, and thinking to himself, "Without you having a wide strike zone, none of my pitches would have kept us in the game.

The media was gathered outside the door of the courthouse waiting anxiously to interview Alan. He met briefly with Mel Goodman, Judd and Sevena to prepare for them. Judd then stepped outside to inform the media that Alan would be coming out shortly with Mel Goodman and all the defendants to make a statement and answer their questions.

Alan was swamped with reporters and blinded by the flashing lights as the still cameras clicked away without stopping upon his stepping out onto the courthouse steps along with Goodman, Eddie and the three other defendants, all smiling and waving. A huge crowd of people that had been following the radio and TV reporting that day had gathered there and all the way across and down the street. A local TV station had managed to get the video recording of the Dean's meetings and make a copy, and with its national TV affiliate, play it repeatedly throughout the week. There was sure to be an investigation as to who in the courthouse got the tape to the TV station so quickly, but the station would, of course, not release the anonymous source and whether they paid to obtain it. The trial already had its effect. Alan looked out and saw signs popping up all over the place: "Bring Our Boys Home." "Make Love – Not War." "Don't Send Them to Bleed for Greed."

"I have a statement to make," he said as he stood behind a makeshift podium that Judd had set up in a hurry, "and then we will answer any questions."

The TV cameras were rolling and dozens of radio station microphones in place as Alan gave his statement. "We call upon the student body here at America University to join these patriots standing by my side when tomorrow and during the next 30 days they engage in teach-ins, sit-ins and an array of demonstrations on campus to bring an end to the war and bring our heroic soldiers back home to their families. We call on the student bodies at Boston University and at Baxter University in San Francisco to join in on a 30-day blitz of protests and demonstrations that will begin tomorrow on their campuses to end the war, and we call on student bodies on every campus, in every city of every state, tomorrow-and until we bring the war to an end-to join this movement to end this unjust, unnecessary war and bring our boys home."

Eddie and the other three defendants thanked and praised Alan and Mel Goodman for winning their freedom and similarly called upon their fellow students to join them on campus for the demonstrations. As Alan, Mel and the defendants were answering follow-up questions, Judd and

Sevena were already busy finding phones to call the blitz leaders at BU and Baxter to give them the go-ahead to start their planned demonstrations the very next day.

The blitz leader at Baxter responded to Sevena's call with the same message as the blitz leader at BU.

"No need, in the last few minutes, students have already been rushing out of their dorms onto the campus grounds on their own and have already begun demonstrations here, and TV stations have begun reporting similar protests breaking out on other campuses all across the country."

EPILOGUE

THE VIETNAM ANT-WAR movement was termed "the most successful antiwar movement in U.S. history". Begun and fueled by a spattering of
student demonstrations, it grew like wildfire. The independent outbreaks
of student sit-ins and rallies on a few campuses, with time, became daily
occurrences on mostly all of them. It moved on to the public streets with
marches and moratorium protests that grew across the country in increasing numbers, with widening support from groups and participants of all
ages and walks of life, all drawn into the movement by its vitality and the
righteousness of its cause.

Protest music, a creation of the counterculture, was to provide the
spiritual verse for the movement. Musicians like Joan Baez, Bob Dylan,
Pete Seeger, Phil Ochs, Barry McGuire, Judy Collins, Country Joe and
the Fish and John Lennon composed, recorded and sang protest songs at
rallies like "Blowin' in the Wind," "The Times They Are a-Changin'," "Eve
of Destruction," "Give Peace a Chance," and "I Ain't Marching Anymore"
and what many called the anthem of the protest movement, "I Feel-Like-
I'm-Fixin'-to-Die Rag," songs that were to become the drumbeat for the
antiwar effort.

It would all be needed to go up against an unyielding commitment
of two presidents and the most powerful government in the world, intent
on using as much modern-day deadly force and armaments necessary to
achieve an ultimate victory abroad and using the full force of federal and
state law enforcement agencies, including the national guard, to quell any
resistance at home. The arrests, jailing and beating of student protesters
in peaceful demonstrations were also daily events. In what was to become
one of the most dramatic incidents of the antiwar confrontations, Ohio
National Guardsmen fired live bullets indiscriminately into a crowd of

student demonstrators at the Kent State University campus, killing four young students and injuring nine others.

However, the arrests, intimidation and indiscriminate beatings did not slow down the anti-war protests. Day and night rallies, tearing up of draft cards, teach-ins, sit-ins and acts of peaceful civil disobedience to occupy and shut down the operation of administrative offices related to the war effort, including a march on the Pentagon, were all being conducted in every part of the country over the weeks, months and years that the war was being waged, putting enormous pressure on the administration,

As the movement took hold, Martin Luther King, like so many leaders of civil rights and other more traditional groups, was to give his formal support on both moral and racial grounds.

Muhammed Ali was willing to see his heavyweight crown taken away from him and fight to appeal a conviction for draft evasion rather than be inducted into the armed services, stating, "Why should they ask me to put on a uniform and go 10,000 miles from home and drop bombs and bullets on brown people while so-called Negro people in Louisville are treated like dogs".

Over 25,000 returning veterans from the war joined the movement by becoming members of the organization Vietnam Veterans Against the War, with 1000 of them going to Washington to protest the war, throwing their medals and uniforms on the Capitol steps. They gave testimony: *We went to defend the Vietnamese people and our testimony will show that we are committing genocide against them.* They had in mind the My Lai Massacre. Frustrated by the turn of events of the war, American soldiers entered the two hamlets My Lai and My Khe of Son My village, and without provocation, killed as many as 500 unarmed civilian men, women, children and infant babies, found among the dead. Many more horrors of the war were unfolding and were being brought to the attention of the public by the movement.

President Lyndon Johnson, who could not go anywhere without hearing the loud and repeated shouts, "Hey, Hey, LBJ, how many kids have you killed today?" was forced to announce that he would not run for re-election. His approval rating dropped from 80% in 1964 to 35% in 1968. Bob Kennedy and other Democrats were to run for president on the platform "bring the war to an end. "On Nov. 15, 1969, the Vietnam Moratorium Committee staged what is believed to be the largest antiwar protest in United States history when as many as half a million people (predominantly youth) attended a mostly peaceful demonstration in Washington DC, with millions more demonstrating across the nation during that same Moratorium month.

Then came the coup de grace. Daniel Ellsberg, influenced by the antiwar movement that the war was unjust, worked on a highly-classified study commissioned by the Defense Department reviewing the US political and military conduct leading up to and during the Vietnam War, which would gain notoriety as the Pentagon Papers. He leaked copies of the study to the New York Times and Washington Post. It showed that the government lied on how it was conducting the war, casting the worse possible aspersions on its motives for continuing to do so.

Finally came the announcement on January 27, 1973, that the Paris Peace Accords were signed formally ending the war, and as one person put it "in response to a mandate unequaled in modern times."

However, the Pentagon would slowly withdraw its troops until it had to rush to evacuate the last of them from South Vietnam's capital of Saigon on April 29, 1975, when the North Vietnamese, who continued to fight after the Peace Accords, entered and occupied it the next day. The extensive TV coverage of US soldiers being chased out of the capital under fire, and the need to airlift them by helicopter at the very last minute to bring them to safety, proved to be an embarrassing ending to this protracted war. The so-called purpose of the war, to ensure a free and independent Vietnam and keep it out of Communist control, as was secretly predicted by intelligence all along, failed. The Vietnam Civil War in which America intervened ended with South Vietnam being unified into one nation under the control of the North Vietnamese.

The Anti-war Movement is credited with shortening the war that had already cost the lives of 58,282 American soldiers, with 303,644 more wounded. Tens of thousands would suffer Post Traumatic Stress and Traumatic Brain Injuries for the rest of their lives from the horrors they experienced. Four million Vietnamese, Laotians and Cambodians lives were lost while their countries were being devastated, creating 11 million refugees. The spending of 173 billion dollars to support the war before it was stopped, triggered double-digit inflation and mounting debt that crippled the US economy for a decade, as well as a decade of a divided and traumatized nation.

No one can estimate exactly how many more years this ten-year war would have gone on, or how many tens of thousands more American soldiers would have died as a result, or how many hundreds of thousands more of our soldiers would have been wounded or crippled during those additional years, or how many more millions of Vietnamese, Cambodians and Laotians would have been killed in addition to the already four million if the student-inspired anti-war movement didn't bring it to an earlier end. But Alan probably would not look to calculate the number of lives saved by assessing the movement's contribution to shortening the war. Instead, he would likely turn to Rabbinical sages of the Talmud for that answer, where it is written "Whoever saves *one* life, it is considered as if he saved the entire world."